THE RASPUTIN RELIC

Also by William M. Valtos

WILLIAM M. VALTOS

THE RASPUTIN RELIC

A MYSTERY

HAMPTON ROADS
PUBLISHING COMPANY, INC.

Cover design by Grace Pedalino
Cover art © 2003 Digital Vision/Getty Images.
© 2003 Stockbyte/Punchstock

Hampton Roads Publishing Company, Inc.
1125 Stoney Ridge Road
Charlottesville, VA 22902

434-296-2772
fax: 434-296-5096
e-mail: hrpc@hrpub.com
www.hrpub.com

If you are unable to order this book from your local
bookseller, you may order directly from the publisher.
Call 1-800-766-8009, toll-free.

Library of Congress Cataloging-in-Publication Data

Valtos, William M.
  The Rasputin relic : a novel / William M. Valtos.
    p. cm.
  ISBN 1-57174-279-4 (alk. paper)
  1. Rasputin, Grigori Efimovich, ca. 1870-1916--Relics--Fiction. 2.
Hemorrhagic diseases--Fiction. 3. Police chiefs--Fiction. I. Title.
  PS3572.A4135R37 2004
  813'.6--dc22

                        2003027725

ISBN 1-57174-279-4
10 9 8 7 6 5 4 3 2 1
Printed on acid-free paper in Canada

For Michael Waltosz,
who followed the old ways

THE FOOLS DON'T UNDERSTAND WHO I AM.
A SORCERER, PERHAPS, A SORCERER MAYBE.
THEY BURN SORCERERS, SO LET THEM BURN ME.

—Grigorii Effimovich Rasputin

I HAVE NOT THE SLIGHTEST DOUBT THAT SOONER OR LATER
THE MEMORY OF RASPUTIN WILL GIVE RISE TO LEGENDS
AND HIS TOMB WILL BE PRODIGAL WITH MIRACLES.

—Maurice Paleologue,
the last French Ambassador to the Russian court

Prelude

Once again, as he had done so often before, the old man took the boy up to a high rock ledge in Pennsylvania's eastern mountains. There, following an ancient Russian tradition, the old man had been passing along the oral histories of his people.

"It was in the eighth decade of the nineteenth century," the old man said, beginning the day's lesson. "Word spread through western Siberia about a child who had been born with strange powers. The first stories were carried down the Taurus River by boatmen who had stopped at Pokrovskoe, a poor farming village located on a hillside overlooking a bend of the river."

A teacher in his youth, the old man sounded more like a tutor than a grandfather.

"It was a land and time in which the borders between religion and superstition were difficult to define. Our most fundamental Orthodox beliefs were being challenged by schismatics, sectarians, and bizarre religious cults, some of whom were said to practice human sacrifice in their ceremonies. Shamans and frauds roamed the steppes."

The rock outcropping where they sat offered a magnificent view of the Lackawanna River Valley. From this height, the towns below were almost indistinguishable from each other. The one exception was the Borough of Middle Valley, identifiable by the golden domes of its three Russian Orthodox churches. It was where they lived.

"What are shamans?" the boy asked. There were other words he didn't understand, but this one, in particular, caught his fancy.

"Ah, yes, shamans." The old man didn't mind being interrupted with questions, because his goal was to pass along knowledge of a culture and way of life the boy would never know. "Shaman is a Russian word, from the Tungus region of Siberia. It means a sorcerer, one who claims to cure the sick with mystical powers, one who can divine that which is hidden, and control events that others can only watch."

"Like a wizard?"

"Yes, but a religious wizard. In those days, the shamans competed with monks and holy men for the hearts of the people." The old man spoke to the boy as if he were an adult. Knowing his own days were numbered, he had little time to waste on childish language. "Our people were mostly peasants, muzhiks living in unspeakable poverty in the most isolated region of a primitive land. Like peasants everywhere, they were always searching for a new prophet, someone who would lead them to a better life. And it was upon these muzhiks that the stories of the Taurus River boatmen had the greatest initial impact."

The old man closed his eyes in what seemed to be an effort to see those days more clearly.

"The boatmen told of a small boy in Pokrovskoe who could foretell the future, a mere child who could read the thoughts of grown men, who was able to cure fevers and heal the sick and cure the lame through the laying on of his hands. They told of local farmers who claimed the mysterious child could communicate with animals, and worked his remarkable cures on their livestock as easily as he did on humans."

"Was he a shaman?" the boy asked.

The old man smiled.

"They called him many things during his lifetime," he said. "Some called him a drunkard and a womanizer; others called him a miracle worker and a holy man. Politicians dismissed him as a filthy peasant who ate with his fingers and seldom bathed; yet the most elegant women allowed him to fondle their breasts in public." The old man was not embarrassed to say such things to the boy. The boy was, after all, the old man's grandson, whom he had raised in his own image after the boy was orphaned.

"The head of the Russian Parliament called him an evil creature who lurked in the shadows of history," the old man continued. "Yet he kept Mother Russia out of the Balkan war, fought for the rights of the muzhiks and Jews, and almost succeeded in keeping our Motherland out of the First World War."

"He must have been a very important man."

"Yes, he was," the old man said. "His name was Grigorii Effimovich Rasputin, and he became, for a time, the most powerful man in Russia. He appointed ministers and cabinet officials. He banished his enemies, and *named a friend to be the head of the Russian Church. The Emperor and Empress did his bidding. His powers were so great that even the Angel of Death hesitated to confront him."*

The boy shivered with delight as his grandfather lowered his voice to a whisper. These were always the best parts of the old man's stories, when he spoke of mysteries that even he didn't seem to understand.

"How could that be?" the boy asked, remembering the awful finality of the deaths of his own parents. "I thought no one could defy the Angel of Death."

"There are witnesses who saw him rise from the dead, not once, but twice. There are also witnesses who testified how his prayers restored life to others."

"Was he a saint?"

"Those whose lives he saved considered him a saint. Others still consider him a sinner. But remember this: Only those upon whom God's favor shines have the ability to cure others."

One

The young widow couldn't believe her husband had anything valuable enough to keep locked in a bank vault.

Yet shortly after dawn, less than seven hours after her husband's death, the key to the safe-deposit box decided to make its presence known.

She found the key in a small yellow envelope beneath the bedroom dresser, where it had apparently fallen from its hiding place. The envelope was faded and brittle with age, but curiously free of dust. The tape which had held it in place broke apart when she touched it.

The key was made of flattened brass, characterless except for the number "52" stamped into its shank. A penciled notation on the envelope, not in her husband's handwriting, identified the bank where the box was located. Closer examination of the bottom of the dresser revealed a hidden ledge, from which the envelope must somehow have become dislodged after years of concealment.

Why, she wondered, had the tape chosen to release its grip on this particular morning?

Nicole knew it wasn't an accident. She had been taught by her mother that nothing happened by accident, that all natural events were determined in advance by an unseen hand, and that once set in motion, nothing could alter the course of Fate.

Those early beliefs in predestination had been reinforced by the Ukrainian psychic she occasionally consulted in Brooklyn.

But her mother was dead and buried in an unknown cemetery, the psychic had ominously refused any further readings, and the young widow was left alone and heartbroken to consider the significance of her discovery.

1

The more she tried to reason it out, the more confused she became. If Fate intended her to possess whatever hidden wealth might be in the safe-deposit box, then had that same Fate long ago planned the death of her husband? And before that, the still-unexplained circumstance of their brief marriage? And even before that, the shadowy procession of men who took control of her destiny? If life was decided by the whims of Fate, as her mother believed, how far back would she have to go to trace the sequence of events that brought her to this small bedroom in this strange little Pennsylvania town?

And what awful destiny yet awaited her?

Two

She would never forget the faces of the men who had come to her bedroom the night before.

They were strangers to her, these men who surrounded the bed where she and her husband had been making love, but she would never forget their faces. She remembered them speaking in low voices, too low for her to understand what they were saying.

All attempts at resuscitation having failed, they prepared Paul's body for removal. When they were finished, one of them pulled a wrinkled bed-sheet over his naked form. Another opened the window to remove the embarrassing smell of sexual activity from the room. They were the bureaucrats of death, going about the grim rituals of their professions.

Nicole watched from the doorway, standing as far away from Paul's corpse as she could bear to be. She wanted to scream, to beg them to understand her pain, but no sounds came from her throat. She wanted to cry, but no tears came from her eyes. The enormity of what had taken place in that bed had momentarily overwhelmed her mind's ability to cope. She felt paralyzed, drained of all emotion. Her eyes didn't want to focus. Her ears barely heard what was going on in the room.

The young policeman, who had been the first to arrive, moved away from the others to make a call on a small folding cell phone.

The last one to arrive, the one they called the coroner, stood at the foot of the bed, slowly unwrapping a stick of Juicy Fruit gum as he listened to a paramedic describe the circumstances of Paul Danilovitch's death. The other paramedic was packing up the emergency medical equipment, which had proven useless in the end. The coroner listened patiently, carefully folding the stick of gum in half before placing it in his mouth.

After the paramedic finished his account, the coroner lifted the bed-sheet and bent over to examine the body more closely. When he appeared satisfied that the paramedic's explanation conformed to the condition of the body, he replaced the sheet and turned away. The paramedic brushed past Nicole to summon the two white-coated morgue attendants from downstairs.

Using the top of his briefcase as a desk, the coroner filled out some preprinted forms. He tore off one carbon for the paramedics and another for the morgue attendants.

After finishing the paperwork, he came over to talk to Nicole. He walked stiffly across the room, dragging the weight of a heavy steel brace that encased his right leg. The bottom of the brace was cut through the heel of his shoe and ran up the inside of his trouser leg to his hip, where the top joint of the brace had worn a shiny spot in the dark blue fabric.

"You're the wife?" he asked.

He gave her what she assumed was his official smile. He was a fleshy middle-aged man, pale-skinned except for hypertensive reddening of his cheeks and spider veins on his nose. His thinning hair was a freshly dyed black with razor-cut sideburns. He smelled of talcum powder and floral hair tonic. The room was too hot for his three-piece blue suit, and a thin sheen of perspiration showed on his forehead.

His puffy mouth worked the Juicy Fruit gum while he waited for an answer.

When Nicole didn't respond, he led her from the doorway into the hall at the top of the stairs, where the air was a little cooler. The metal brace creaked as he walked.

"My name is Thomas O'Malley," he explained in a gentle voice. "I'm the Lackawanna County coroner. I'm sorry about your husband, but I hope you understand that I have to ask you a few questions."

Nicole leaned against the wall and averted her face. She pulled the smooth silk robe tighter around her. She was naked under the robe.

"Were there any warning signs?" O'Malley asked. "Anything unusual you noticed?"

She shook her head without looking at him, but sensed him admiring her figure, the way men always did.

Nicole was a twenty-two-year-old woman who sometimes regarded her beauty as a curse, inflicted upon her by a God determined to make her suffer.

Her flesh had ripened at an early age, too early for her to understand the dangerous passions a little girl's first innocent swellings can arouse in men. Her loss of innocence, when it came, was as brutal as it was unwelcome. Her eyes gave no hint of all she had endured since then. Yet those innocent-seeming eyes warily studied all men who approached her. And those voluptuous lips, too often brutalized, rarely smiled.

"Was your husband on any medication?" O'Malley asked. "Or seeing a doctor for any reason?"

"No."

"Was he taking Viagra?"

Nicole slowly shook her head.

"I don't mean to get personal," O'Malley explained. "But a man of his age . . ."

"My husband was a lot older than I," she said in a flat voice, "but we never had that kind of problem."

"What about herbal medicines or nutritional supplements?"

"I think so. Yes. He was taking some sort of supplement. They said it would help prevent Alzheimer's." After a pause she added, "His father had Alzheimer's, and he was worried he might get it, too."

"Most of those supplements don't work," O'Malley said. "Some of them can even be dangerous. Where did he get it?"

"Some friend of his gave him a bottle in Las Vegas, right after we were married."

"I'll check the medicine cabinet," O'Malley said. "Do you remember your husband saying anything at the end? Any last words?"

Nicole closed her eyes, trying to recall those awful, final moments.

"No," she murmured.

"Was there anything bothering him? Any special worries, tensions, or stress?"

"Not that I know of."

O'Malley seemed to be dancing around the subject, as if he were trying to extract information without coming right out and asking her exactly what happened during those last sweaty moments in bed. Would he understand if she told him the tangled story that led to the death of a man who was innocent of anything except falling in love with her? Would anyone understand how she could curse the physical charms that aroused such hunger in men's eyes? For in the end, she knew that was what had killed Paul. A lonely older man had rescued a lovely young woman from the nightmare her life had become, only to fall victim to the erotic passions her body aroused in him. He was destroyed by the very thing that attracted him to her.

"Did you get the feeling that he might have been hiding something?" O'Malley asked.

Nicole's eyes flew open. Such an odd question.

"What do you mean?" she asked.

She was suddenly suspicious of this man standing so close to her. Too close, she thought. She could smell the sweetness of the gum on his breath, see the spidery tracings of red in his florid Irish cheeks.

"Sometimes men have problems . . ." O'Malley quickly elaborated. "Things they don't want to worry their wives about. They keep it quiet. Bottle it up inside. That's not healthy."

"Paul wasn't like that," she responded. "He didn't keep any secrets from me."

Paul Danilovitch wasn't a sophisticated man, not like most of the men she had encountered. Not handsome either. But he was thrilled to have Nicole as his wife, and she would catch him at odd moments staring at her with those puppy-dog eyes, as if he couldn't believe she belonged to him. Until death do us part, she thought. She looked over O'Malley's shoulder through the bedroom doorway and saw the attendants lifting Paul's limp corpse from the bed. Tears welled in her eyes. She bit at her lower lip to keep her jaw from trembling.

She could tell what the attendants were thinking by the way they kept glancing at her, like little boys hoping to see a sudden flash of breast or thigh. Probably wondering what wild sexual tricks she must have been performing on her husband in that bed. The man was old enough to be her father, and he dies between her legs just four weeks after the wedding. She could imagine the pornographic pictures that must be running through their minds.

The hell with them, she thought.

"It was probably his heart," O'Malley said, his approach turning more sympathetic. "I'll try to keep it low-key. There's no need for the whole town to know the details."

"I'd appreciate that," Nicole said.

But she knew there was no way to keep the details from getting out. Not in the tightly knit ethnic enclave of Middle Valley, where a story like this would be cheerfully passed from neighbor to neighbor, and embellished with each retelling.

Although, as with most American towns, a number of nationalities were represented in Middle Valley, the soul of this small town in the hill country of northeastern Pennsylvania was distinctly Russian. Its major population growth had come from the great wave of panicky White Russians fleeing the 1917 Revolution. The wealthier exiles—the Romanovs, the Obolenskys, and the others—had gone with what treasures they could carry to Paris, London, and the Riviera, while the less affluent had joined the stream of European immigrants who were offered free passage to America in return for contracts that obligated them to work in the coal mines of towns like Middle Valley. They were followed over the years by a trickle of Russian Jews, political exiles, and asylum seekers, with the latest surge of immigrants coming after the breakup of the Soviet Union. The customs, superstitions, and suspicious natures they brought from the old country were passed along intact to their children and grandchildren, along with the great Russian passion for gossip. As a result, the circumstances of death were always of interest to the people of Middle Valley, particularly when a newcomer like Nicole was involved.

"Cases like this, there's no need for an autopsy," O'Malley went on. "My people will transport the body to the local funeral parlor if you like, save you the cost of the undertaker doing it."

"Thank you."

"You want to stay with some friends tonight, I can drop you off."

"I don't have any friends here," she sighed.

"Not even your neighbors?"

"No. It's hard to make friends in this town."

"I know what you mean," O'Malley said. "They're too damn suspicious of outsiders around here."

He touched her arm to move her out of the way as the morgue attendants wheeled Paul's shrouded body from the room, wheeled it right in front of her, wheeled it so close she could have touched it, and maneuvered it around the corner so they could get it down the stairs.

O'Malley leaned forward and lowered his voice, as if he wanted to be sure no one overheard him.

"Did your husband ever tell you . . ." He paused, apparently choosing his words carefully. "Did your husband ever tell you about anything he might be hiding?"

"Like what?" she asked warily. The words were different, but it was the second time he had asked the same question.

"I don't know," he said. "Something he might have wanted to keep secret." As if sensing her distrust of him, he quickly tried to explain himself. "If there was something bothering him, and he didn't want to tell you about it, it could have been a source of stress. Maybe just enough to be a contributing factor in his death."

It was a reasonable explanation, but his nervous manner did nothing to lessen her uneasiness.

"I already told you," she said, "Paul never hid anything from me."

O'Malley studied her for a long moment, apparently trying to decide whether she was being completely honest with him.

"I guess you're right," he finally said. "A beautiful woman like you, I wouldn't hide anything from you either."

He pressed a business card into her hand.

"Give me a call after the funeral," he said. "Maybe we can help each other."

Nothing ever changed, she thought. Even with a dead husband downstairs, she was still considered fair game by the nearest male.

She was accustomed to ignoring such clumsy solicitations.

What was harder to ignore was the coroner's strange insistence that her husband might have been hiding something from her.

Three

That same night, in another part of town, Viktor Rhostok pretended not to hear the man who had slipped into the police station and was creeping up behind him. His face illuminated by the pale glow of his computer screen, the acting police chief of Middle Valley knew he made a tempting target. He had two patrolmen on duty that night. One was out on a 911 response, assisting paramedics. The other hadn't called in. As a result, Rhostok was alone in the police station. It was the perfect opportunity for the intruder to make his move.

As acting police chief of Middle Valley, Rhostok was temporarily in charge of five other full-time policemen and four part-timers. They worked out of four rooms in a freestanding brick building that had once housed a tavern. The beer cooler in the back had been remodeled to serve as a holding cell. The four rooms on the other side of the building housed the borough offices.

During the boom years, dozens of similar taverns had prospered in the town, whose population at one point exceeded fifteen thousand. That was when the anthracite veins buried beneath the region were so vast and so profitable, and available workers so few, that mining companies advertised throughout Europe for workers. Passenger liners were chartered to bring the immigrants to New York and Baltimore, where they were loaded onto special trains that brought them to northeastern Pennsylvania. The boom lasted a half-century. When the deep veins were exhausted, the mine owners retreated to their mansions in Newport and New York, leaving behind scarred valleys, polluted rivers, and impoverished towns.

Yet for many of the eastern European immigrants, particularly those from Russia, life in these depressed communities was still far better than life in the poverty-stricken *shtetls* and villages of their homeland. They had electricity, running water, and free schools for their children, and although many left for other industrial centers, enough remained to keep small towns like Middle Valley alive, if barely. It was this environment in which Viktor Rhostok had been raised.

"I could cut your throat right now," the intruder suddenly growled. He was a giant of a man who had an uncanny ability to move almost silently.

Rhostok didn't even turn around.

"With what?" he asked. "A six-pack of Mountain Dew?"

"Oh, hell," the huge man grumbled. "You saw my reflection in the computer screen."

"That and heard your breathing." Rhostok turned slowly to look up at the enormous policeman towering above him. "You always forget about your breathing."

It was a game they played to relieve the boredom of being policemen in a town where no felony arrests had been made in two years. Otto Bruckner was a Special Forces veteran, well-practiced in the art of taking unwary adversaries by surprise. He was amazingly agile and light on his feet for a man of such enormous proportions. He kept his cranium bald and highly polished, and his upper lip decorated with an enormous handlebar mustache. Bruckner took a wicked pleasure in his appearance, which most people found overpowering.

"How many nights are you going to stare at that file?" Bruckner asked.

Rhostok responded with a shrug. Although a foot shorter and a hundred pounds lighter than the big patrolman, he wasn't intimidated by Bruckner's size. He enjoyed playing the big man's war games, a competition he seldom lost. Although Rhostok had never been in the military himself, he understood the warrior mentality. It was a trait he inherited from his Tartar ancestors. He had the powerful chest and shoulders of those forebears, whose bodies were shaped by struggling against the gray clay soil of the potato fields of the Don River valley, and whose fighting ability was forged in defending that land. Barely diluted by two generations in America, their genes were still evident in his broad, solid face. It was a face that didn't smile easily.

"I guess I lost track of time," Rhostok said. He yawned and stretched, although he didn't feel all that tired.

"You should be home sleeping," Bruckner said. He offered Rhostok a can of Mountain Dew from the six-pack he brought in with him. "You're back on the clock in another seven hours."

When Rhostok declined the offer, Bruckner split the six-pack of soda in half. He put three cans in the refrigerator and brought the other three back across the room, where he popped the top of the first one. Because coffee upset his stomach, Bruckner used the high-caffeine beverage to stay awake on the night shift.

"Give it up already," Bruckner said. "That old man's case was closed two months ago. When the coroner says a man commits suicide, you can't turn it into a murder."

He settled himself into a swivel chair that creaked under the weight of his huge frame.

The Scranton sportswriters had labeled Bruckner "The Incredible Bulk" when he played high-school football. He had grown even larger and more muscular since those days, and the nickname stuck with him, although it was now used more in awe than in jest.

"O'Malley doesn't see things the way I do," Rhostok responded.

"You're kind of, like, obsessed with that case, aren't you?"

The green can of Mountain Dew disappeared into the brush of his mustache. He drank what seemed like half the can in a single swallow.

"I'm not obsessed," Rhostok said. "Just curious. I think it's a death that needs further investigation."

"There's nobody, except for you, who thinks old Vanya was murdered," Bruckner argued. "O'Malley recorded it as a suicide. He said the guy killed himself by jumping off the roof of the Lackawanna Mental Health Facility."

"A man who's going to commit suicide doesn't break all the fingers on his right hand before he jumps off the roof. It doesn't make any sense."

"The guy was in a mental institution," Bruckner pointed out. "He was there because he had a violent psychotic breakdown. Why would you expect anything he did to make sense?"

"He was only there for two weeks," Rhostok said. "Before the break-down, he was living a perfectly normal life, not a hint of anything wrong."

"Except he had Alzheimer's. The guy was eighty years old, Rhostok. You really think somebody's going to break into a maximum-security ward to kill an eighty-year-old man who was suffering from Alzheimer's? I mean, what's the point? Why kill a man who doesn't remember anything?"

"His memory wasn't totally gone," Rhostok said. "He was only in the early stages. He was still pretty lucid most of the time."

"But what's the motive? Even if he knew some awful secret, the Alzheimer's probably wiped it out. What I think is maybe during what you call his lucid time, he got scared of what was happening to him and decided he didn't want to live like a vegetable. That's why he jumped."

Bruckner finished his first Mountain Dew, crushed the empty can in one hand, and tossed it into the recycling bin. The noise woke up the two canaries in their hooded cage, who chirped softly and fluttered their wings before going back to sleep.

"Anyway," Bruckner went on in a quieter voice as he opened the second can, "O'Malley said he must have busted the fingers when he hit the sidewalk, probably had his hands out in front of him, trying to break his fall. He says he's seen it happen before with jumpers."

"If he had his hands in front of him, there'd be more damage to the wrist and elbow bones," Rhostok muttered.

"So what are you now, a medical expert?"

"I'm just reading what's in the autopsy."

"Get real, Rhostok. After all, what have you got?" He nodded towards the folder Rhostok had been studying. "A file on an eighty-year-old mental patient who took a dive off the roof. You ever consider how many times that must happen around the country?"

"Vanya Danilovitch didn't take a dive," Rhostok insisted. "He was pushed. And I think it had something to do with the break-in at his house."

"Here we go again." Bruckner rolled his eyes. "That break-in was just vandals. Teenagers, probably, looking for stuff to steal."

"Nothing was stolen, according to the son."

"How would Paul know if anything was missing? He was living out in Las Vegas. He never came home to see Vanya until the old man was dead."

"It didn't look like vandalism to me," Rhostok said.

"The mattresses were cut open, the drawers were emptied, and even the cushions on the old man's Barcalounger were slit. That sure looked like vandalism to me."

"Vandals would have smashed things. But the old Victrola was taken apart with a screwdriver, the back of the TV was removed, but it still worked. Everything from the drawers was neatly piled in the corners. Even the bedding and cushions were sliced along the seams. You'd expect vandals to just slash away. And the photographs—none of the frames were broken. They were all carefully removed from the frames and arranged in a stack on the dining table, as if somebody wanted to make sure they weren't damaged."

"So they were neat," Bruckner said. "Maybe they were obsessive-compulsive vandals."

"Get serious. If it was teenagers, they wouldn't have been so neat upstairs and then dug all those holes in the cellar floor. And druggies would have stripped the house of anything that could be sold. No, Otto, I think it was a very careful search. Somebody spent a lot of time in that house looking for something. And whatever it was, I think it might be the motive for killing Vanya."

Four

"You already tried that goofy theory on the old man's son and he threw you out of the house. What'd he call you—incompetent, wasn't it?"

"Paul doesn't want to believe his father was murdered."

"And neither does anybody else, except you. You'll excuse my saying so, Rhostok, but you're pissing in the wind if you think you can prove the old guy was murdered."

"I will. Eventually."

"And you think this is some big unsolved murder case that's going to get you appointed permanent chief of police if you solve it? Don't kid yourself. The chief's job is all politics. The trustees will appoint the cop that can deliver the most votes for them on election day. And that's not you. With all due respect, Rhostok, you're a loner. For God's sake, nobody even calls you by your first name. The only vote you control is your own."

Bruckner wrapped his massive fingers around the second can of Mountain Dew. It went down in three swallows before the crushed aluminum shell was dispatched to its environmentally correct resting place.

Rhostok frowned at the noise, but this time the canaries didn't wake up. "Anyway," Bruckner said, "if you take Vanya's file to the D.A. and try to convince him it was murder, he'll laugh you out of his office."

"I'm not ready for the D.A., yet," Rhostok said, returning his attention to the computer screen. "But I know the answer is in this file. I'm just not seeing it. At least, not yet."

"Maybe because there's nothing to see," Bruckner said. "What I think is that you're being Russian again. With all due respect, Rhostok, maybe O'Malley is right. You *Russkies,* you're always looking for conspiracies."

"It's our way," Rhostok said with a shrug. "We're a naturally suspicious people."

"Especially you," Bruckner said. "You're ready to suspect everybody of almost anything."

"That's how I was brought up," Rhostok said. It was a criticism to which he had long ago grown accustomed. Although Bruckner's comments were made in a friendly spirit, Rhostok felt a need to explain. "My bedtime stories weren't about Peter Pan escaping Captain Hook. They were about real people, little children and their parents, being betrayed by their neighbors, burned out of their houses, and hunted down by the Bolsheviks and the Communists. The ones who survived were always the heroes of the stories. And you know how they survived? By not trusting anyone."

"The Cold War is long over," Bruckner said. "All that Communist stuff is ancient history."

"Not to anyone who lived through it," Rhostok persisted. "There are people in this town who survived the slave labor camps, people who were tortured in Lubyanka prison, who had run-ins with the *nomenklatura* and the secret police. We have old-timers here who survived Stalin's deliberate starvation of two million Ukrainians, and the secret biological and chemical warfare experiments that killed hundreds of thousands in the northern Urals in the 1950s. People who survive situations like that learn not to trust anyone. And they teach their children to be suspicious, too."

Five

Trust no one. Expect betrayal.
It was a lesson Rhostok learned all too well from his grandfather,

Aleksander Voyonovich Rhostok. His grandfather was an educated man, a schoolteacher who fought alongside the Don Cossacks as they battled the Bolsheviks on the Southern Front. Wounded during the slaughter at Voronezh, he was captured by the Red Army and spent two years in one of the earliest slave-labor camps before escaping and making his way through the winter snow to the Crimea, where a sympathetic freighter captain allowed him to stow away. He followed the first wave of Russian emigres to Middle Valley, where the only work open to him was in the coal mines. Late in life, he married a Russian woman and had one son.

The good times in the new land lasted until Aleksander's beloved wife, Elisaveta, passed away. The old superstitions said that death always comes in threes, and so Aleksander could only wait for destiny's cycle to be completed. Within the year, his son, Viktor Rhostok's father, died in a methane-gas explosion in Middle Valley's last operating coal mine. It was a tragedy Aleksander claimed would never have happened if the old tradition of taking canaries down into the mines had been followed. The next to go, eight months later, was little Viktor Rhostok's mother, Irina. Before taking her life, cancer of the cervix put her through agonies no child should ever be condemned to watch. By the time death had walked through the family, seventy-two-year-old Aleksander Rhostok and his five-year-old grandson were the only survivors.

The old man raised the little boy in his own image. It was at his side that Rhostok learned Russian history and the ancient legends, the Cyrillic alphabet, and the Old World values that would have been ridiculed anywhere except in similar immigrant communities. To help the boy survive in a land that he considered as treacherous as the one he left, Aleksander taught Rhostok to be secretive, suspect everyone, trust no one, and expect betrayal. It was, after all, the way he himself learned to survive.

The boy was fourteen when the old man's stubborn heart finally gave out. Rhostok lived alone in the empty house until he was eighteen years old, helped by neighbors whose mistrust of authority shielded him from the custody of Children's Services.

"Come on, Rhostok, lighten up," Bruckner said, snapping Rhostok out of his reverie. "You can't spend the rest of your life living in the past."

Rhostok dismissed the comment with a shrug. He didn't expect Bruckner to understand. The big man had grown up in Scranton, where his German ancestors had so thoroughly assimilated themselves that he seemed to have forgotten his heritage.

"Okay," Bruckner said. "Just for argument's sake, let's suppose Vanya really was murdered. You still haven't come up with a motive. Why would anybody sneak into a mental institution to kill an eighty-year-old patient? That's a hell of a lot of trouble to go through just to get rid of someone who probably didn't have much longer to live anyway."

Before Rhostok could answer, his cell phone emitted a series of electronic beeps. The caller ID indicated it was from Walter Zanko, the patrolman out on the 911 paramedic call.

Rhostok's face hardened as he listened to the message. He gave a terse command on the phone as he rose and headed for the door.

"That was Zanko," he called over his shoulder. "The coroner is trying to move a corpse out of the Danilovitch house."

"What the hell's the county coroner doing in Middle Valley without notifying us?" Bruckner asked as he hurried to catch up.

"I don't know," Rhostok said. "But the dead man is Paul Danilovitch. Vanya's son."

Six

O'Malley was retrieving his briefcase from Nicole's bedroom when an argument erupted downstairs.

Two uniformed officers had arrived. One of them was the biggest policeman Nicole had ever seen, a menacing giant with a shaved head and a heavy brown mustache. He took a position just inside the front door, blocking the morgue attendants from leaving the house with her husband's body. The other policeman was Viktor Rhostok, whom Nicole recognized from an earlier visit, when he and Paul had had an argument about the vandalism that left the house a shambles. The investigation had gone nowhere. No suspects had been identified. And finally, when Rhostok seemed to be trying to tie the vandalism to the death of Paul's father, Paul had had enough and ordered Rhostok out of the house. It was the only time she had seen Paul lose his temper.

Now Rhostok was back on the premises, and the expression on his face suggested he wasn't here to offer his sympathy. He seemed a small man when compared with his huge partner, but he was powerfully built and, although he spoke softly, had a way of dominating any space he occupied. Right now, he was insisting on examining Paul's body, and no one downstairs was arguing with him.

O'Malley swore softly when he came out of the bedroom and saw what was happening. He gave a halfhearted wave to the policemen, acknowledging their presence.

"Looks like the local police are upset," he sighed. "I hope they're not going to make things difficult."

Rhostok was apparently waiting for O'Malley to come downstairs, but the coroner didn't seem to be in any hurry.

He moved closer to Nicole.

"There's no need to tell anyone what we talked about," he whispered to her. "Especially the police."

She pulled away from him.

"They're waiting for you down there," she said.

O'Malley nodded and again waved to Rhostok, indicating he'd be right down.

"It's in your own best interest not to stir things up," O'Malley warned her.

She made no attempt to respond.

"I'm trying to be nice to you," he said, his voice taking on a harder edge. "I told you I'd keep this thing quiet, but you've got to cooperate, too. All I ask is that you call me if you come across anything your husband was hiding."

She was tired of this man, the flowery odor of his hair tonic, and his strangely insistent manner.

"I have no idea what you're talking about," she said.

He stared at her for a long moment, as if trying to decide whether she knew more than she was admitting.

"You've got my card," he finally said.

Nicole watched O'Malley stiff-leg his way down the stairs to where the policemen were waiting.

She could clearly hear the conversation that followed.

"What are you doing here?" Rhostok demanded.

"Obviously, I'm doing my job," O'Malley replied. "A man died. It's my responsibility to check it out."

"Since when does the county coroner show up before the local police call him in?"

"You're the one who's late," O'Malley said. "I happened to be driving through the area when my scanner picked up the call. Now why are you blocking the doorway?"

"The body doesn't leave here until I find out exactly what's going on."

Rhostok didn't seem like the kind of man who could be moved once he planted his feet. His muscular physique gave him the appearance of being stolid and slow-witted. But Nicole knew from her first encounter with him just how deceptive such a judgment could be.

"The guy died of a heart attack, Rhostok. Your man upstairs already interviewed the widow."

Nicole couldn't hear the rest of O'Malley's whispered explanation of the specific circumstances, but she knew what he must be saying about Paul's final moments.

"I don't want the body removed before I can examine the scene," Rhostok protested.

"I'm doing it out of courtesy to the widow," O'Malley said. "Did you know the deceased?"

"He grew up in Middle Valley. Everybody knew him."

"Then I'm sure you don't want to put his widow through any more pain," O'Malley said. "I told her my people will take the body to the nearest funeral home."

Rhostok's expression, when he glanced up at Nicole, was impassive, with none of the sexual curiosity the others had exhibited. There was no way to tell from his face whether he felt any sorrow at Paul's death. Part of it was Russian stoicism, Nicole knew. She had seen the same trait in many of her friends and relatives, an inherited ability to accept misfortune without complaint. But with Rhostok, it went much deeper. She remembered how cold and completely devoid of emotion he had appeared during their first encounter. He was an attractive, even handsome man, yet he showed an unusually suspicious attitude towards others and seemed wary of any attempt to befriend him. In that way, he reminded her of herself.

"You're making a mistake sending the body to a funeral home," she heard Rhostok say in a flat voice. "I think you should do an autopsy."

"The man died of a heart attack," O'Malley responded. "I don't have to open him up to tell you that."

"He was in good physical condition," Rhostok said. "I saw him out jogging every day."

"Jesus, Rhostok, he was fifty-six years old. Guys his age die in the saddle all the time. There's no reason for an autopsy here. There's absolutely nothing unusual or suspicious about the man's death."

"What about his father? Are you forgetting what happened to his father? That was just two months ago."

"You mean Vanya Danilovitch? I didn't know that was his father." O'Malley sounded surprised, as if he hadn't made the connection. Nicole knew enough about men to know he was lying. "Sure, I remember him. But that case has absolutely nothing to do with this one. Vanya Danilovitch died under entirely different circumstances."

"He was murdered," Rhostok said.

"Don't start that again. He was a mentally disturbed old man who jumped off a rooftop. It was an obvious case of suicide."

"It wasn't suicide," Rhostok insisted. "Someone pushed him off that roof."

"You have no way of proving that."

"I'm working on it."

"For God's sake, Rhostok, what are you trying to do, pin it on one of the homicidals up there? There are at least eight of them in that institution. That's why they're there, because they kill people. But that doesn't automatically mean one of them killed the old man."

"A father and son die two months apart. How often does that happen?"

"More often than you think. Besides, there's no similarity in their deaths. The father died of massive trauma sustained in a fall. This guy died happy. You looked at the body. Not a bruise or a scratch on it. Let it go, Rhostok. Why look for trouble where it doesn't exist?"

Nicole stared down at them as they talked.

There must be some mistake, she thought.

Paul had never mentioned anything about his father dying a violent death.

All Paul had ever said was that his father died in a nursing home.

"You could pull some blood," Rhostok persisted. "At least run some blood tests."

"And look for what? The trouble with you Russians, you think everything is some kind of goddamned plot. It's the same story every time I come up to Middle Valley. You people have been here for generations. But you still think you're in the Old Country. You always think someone's out to get you."

"All I'm asking for is a blood test."

Rhostok glanced up at Nicole.

"Okay, okay," O'Malley finally gave in. "I'll tell the guys to draw a sample. But we're not going to find anything out of the ordinary. I've got twenty-two years in the coroner's office, and I can tell a heart attack when I see one."

Nicole withdrew from the railing, uneasy about the way Rhostok kept glancing at her. What troubled her about his expression was its resemblance to something she had seen on the faces of other police officers when she was picked up in Las Vegas and New York.

It was the deceptively blank stare that policemen normally reserve for suspects.

Seven

"What was that all about?" Bruckner asked as they headed back to the car.

"What?"

"That business with the coroner, insisting on a blood test?"

"Just trying to get him to do his job," Rhostok said.

"He already told you how the guy died. Don't you believe him?"

"Do you?"

"Yes, I do. He says the guy died making love, and I believe him. I mean, did you get a good look at the wife? They say she was a showgirl in Las Vegas, and I believe it. Man, she's absolutely spectacular, even without makeup. Real *Playboy* material."

"Come on, Otto, show a little respect. They just carried her husband out feet first."

Bruckner grinned as he unlocked the patrol car. "With a woman like that, I'd probably have a heart attack myself. But what a way to go."

"Drop me off at the station," Rhostok said, as he slipped into the front seat.

"It's after one in the morning. Shouldn't you be getting some sleep?"

"I've still got some work to do."

The big man stared at him before starting the car.

"What?" Rhostok asked. "Is something bothering you?"

"Promise me you're not going to try to turn this one into a murder, too," Bruckner said. "The coroner already ruled it a heart attack."

When Rhostok didn't respond, Bruckner shook his head.

"You don't trust anybody, do you?" And after a moment, he added, "You probably don't even trust me."

But Rhostok barely heard the wounded pride in his friend's voice. He was thinking about the word Bruckner had used to describe the widow: spectacular. That was certainly true. She was a spectacular beauty. As beautiful last night as the first time he had met her. It had been all he could do to keep from glancing up at her. She was young and blonde and sensual. The kind of woman most men dream about.

And that was exactly what was bothering him.

Women like her have their pick of men. They become trophy wives. Las Vegas showgirls don't suddenly marry underemployed construction workers in their fifties, pack up their fancy clothes, and go to live in run-down houses in small towns.

And if they do, Rhostock was certain, their husbands don't usually die within one month of the marriage ceremony.

Eight

All Rhostok knew for certain about Nicole Danilovitch was the information Officer Zanko had for some reason copied down from her Nevada driver's license. Everything else was hearsay. Paul had occasionally bragged that his wife had once been a Las Vegas showgirl who performed at the Mirage and Caesar's. The word around town, however, was that her stage career had been short and she was working for an escort service when she met Paul. Although everyone could guess how they met, even why Paul fell for her, no one could figure out what attracted her to him. A woman like that, young and beautiful enough to command top dollar from her clients, doesn't usually marry a man whose main income is a union pension check, and then follow him from the glitz and glamour of Las Vegas to a place like Middle Valley.

What he needed was to find out more about the young widow with the *Playboy* physique. And the best way to do that was to run a background check through the FBI's National Crime Information Center, which would list any contacts she might have had with law-enforcement agencies. He logged on to his computer and entered her maiden name and Social Security number.

Fifteen seconds later, the NCIC database revealed that twenty-two-year-old Nikoleta Baronovich also used the names of Nikki Baron and Nicole Barone, had three solicitation-for-prostitution arrests, one in New York City and the other two in Las Vegas, one arrest and conviction for passing bad checks, and one charge of possession of a controlled substance, which was later dismissed.

Not exactly major crimes, Rhostok thought. But the NCIC summaries were limited to offenses for which formal charges had been brought. To get a better idea of the kind of woman the late Paul Danilovitch had married,

Rhostok called the Las Vegas Police Department. After a half-hour of switching his calls from precinct to precinct, he finally found a bored female vice cop who knew something about Nicole.

"I'm looking for some information on a hooker who used to work in Vegas," Rhostok said. "Her name is Nicole or Nikoleta Baronovich, also known as Nicole Barone and Nikki Baron."

"Nicole Barone?" the cop thought about it for a moment. "I knew her, but she wasn't a hooker, not the Nicole Barone I knew. She worked for an escort service."

"Isn't that the same thing?"

"Not always. The service she worked for was mostly legitimate, as far we could tell. They advertised in the local papers and the Yellow Pages, and they were registered with the Better Business Bureau. They hired showgirls who were out of work, really good-looking women, the kind of women a man would be happy just to have dinner with, or have on his arm at a party. Of course, that doesn't mean some of the girls didn't have consensual sex if they went out with a man they liked, but as long as there isn't a direct financial quid pro quo, that isn't any more illegal than what any other woman does after a date."

"But going out on dates with strangers for money?" Rhostok persisted. "That isn't a normal occupation."

"These days, what's normal?"

"She's got a record, though. The NCIC shows arrests for forgery, prostitution, drugs."

"I never said she was a saint. Let me look her up on my computer."

Rhostok heard the vice cop's fingers working her keyboard.

"Here she is. Nicole Barone. She also went by the professional name of Champagne. That was because of the color of her hair, I guess. Let's see, born in Brooklyn, ran away from home at sixteen, lived on the streets, arrested for prostitution when she was eighteen. That's not unusual for young female runaways. There's always somebody ready to take advantage of them. The judge gave her six months probation and a lecture. She came to Las Vegas with a male friend who promised he could get her a high-paying job in one of the shows at the Mirage. He got her the job, all right, but it only lasted three months. She had the look they wanted, but she didn't have dance training."

"You've got all that in the computer?"

"Standard procedure. These days we put all our notes and interviews on the computer. That way, the information is available to every officer. You want me to continue?"

"Please."

"She lived in the old part of town with the male friend until their money ran out and he forged her name on a check at a liquor store. Or at least that was the story she told the judge. I met that boyfriend once. What a beautiful woman like her saw in a lowlife like him is beyond me. Anyway, when she was released on bond, the only legitimate work she could find was at the escort service. They put her on the books under the name of Champagne and charged her out at two hundred dollars an hour. Her first arrest for prostitution was thrown out on a technicality. Six months later, our guys picked her up in a drug raid on a French tourist's hotel room. The D.A. charged her with prostitution and possession. But guess what? The Frenchman got three years, and Nicole got a dismissal."

"She had a good lawyer."

"The escort services always have good lawyers. Anyway, the Frenchie was a confirmed doper."

"And Nicole?"

"No trace of drugs in the hair analysis. We got a subpoena for her apartment and checked it out with a drug-sniffing dog. The place was clean. No surprise. I don't think she was the type to do drugs." After a pause, she added, "You want my opinion, she's a good person who got caught up in a bad situation."

"Three arrests in Las Vegas, and you say she's a good person?"

"No convictions, though," the vice cop reminded him. "She's doing better than a lot of the girls we see coming through here. They get trapped in bad situations for a variety of reasons: drugs, divorce, money problems, abuse, or just falling in love with the wrong man. They make bad decisions, but that doesn't always mean they're bad people."

"It's always somebody else's fault, isn't it?"

"Sometimes it's true. Anyway, what's your interest in her? Is she in some kind of trouble?"

"No, not yet. You know she got married and left Vegas."

"I heard about it. It happened last month. An older guy from out of state."

"Thirty-four years older than her, to be exact," Rhostok said. "Old enough to be her father. Didn't that strike you as peculiar, a woman as beautiful as her marrying a tired old man on a pension?"

"Yes, it did. She was well known on the Strip, and it made for some prime gossip. You want the why or the how?"

"Let's start with the how."

"Well, part of it is simple. She was hired by this guy one evening, it was supposed to be for dinner and a show at Caesar's. Next morning she wakes up in a room at the Flamingo with a wedding ring on her finger, and the guy is showing her a marriage certificate and two Polaroid photos taken at the Little Chapel Around the Corner. She doesn't remember marrying him, or anything that happened after dinner, but the wedding was legal, witnessed by people she knew."

"Maybe the guy drugged her."

"Not according to the witnesses. They said she acted normal all night. Now the interesting thing is that the escort service is rumored to be owned by the local Russian mafia."

"The *Organizatsya?*"

"That's what they call themselves. And both of the witnesses were Russian."

"So was the man she married," Rhostok said. "He was second-generation."

"I didn't know that," the vice cop said. "That certainly makes it more interesting. There were rumors that the man she married won her in a poker game, but that was doubtful, because the Russian mafia poker games are all fixed. There were other rumors that it was some sort of an arranged marriage, some sort of old Russian tradition, but that didn't sound right either, because she was in demand as an escort and producing too much income for the Russians to let her go. Yet they honored the marriage and released her. Strange, isn't it?"

"What's strange to me is the why. If she only knew the guy one night and didn't even remember getting married, why did she leave town with him?"

"Well that's simple," the vice cop said. "You talk to these girls like I do, and you hear them tell you over and over how they hope to turn their lives around. Even the druggies, in their rational moments, all still dream about the little house with the white picket fence, the loving husband, and the kids in the backyard. It's the eternal dream. Maybe Nicole saw her chance and took it. Maybe she bought her way out. The last I heard, she was happily married and living in some small town and was trying to put the old life behind her. She was one of the lucky ones."

"Not anymore," Rhostok said, as he explained how Nicole's husband had died.

When he hung up, Rhostok wondered if Nicole was really the innocent victim the vice cop so sympathetically described. It wouldn't be the first time a young woman had fallen in with the wrong kind of people.

Or was she a clever woman who used her beauty to manipulate everyone she encountered? There was plenty of precedent for that, too.

He was sure there were other cases of a former showgirl marrying a man old enough to be her father. But those were cases where the older man was wealthy.

It would take a while to learn the truth about her, Rhostok thought.

With a tired sigh, he turned his attention once again, as he had earlier that evening, to the Danilovitch file. He was still looking for something he could take to the D.A. to prove that Vanya was murdered.

Because if the father had been murdered, then no matter what O'Malley said, Rhostok was certain that the son had been murdered, too.

Nine

The funeral mass for Paul Danilovitch was held three days after his death, in accordance with local custom, at the Old Ritual Russian Orthodox Church of Saint Sofia.

It was one of three Russian churches in Middle Valley. The cluster of golden onion-shaped domes in the middle of the Lackawanna River Valley had delighted Nicole when she first saw them. The Byzantine domes stood out in gleaming contrast to the scars left on the hillsides by the valley's long-abandoned anthracite mines. As a young woman hoping to put her past behind her, she thought she saw a promising omen in those golden domes: Her marriage to Paul would be a golden time, helping her forget the suffering and despair of a life forced upon her by others.

But the brief golden time was over, and now here she was, standing in the center of Saint Sofia, with her new husband lying dead in the coffin before her. It was the first time she had been inside the church, and it was obvious that the building she had admired from afar was showing the signs of its own approaching demise, the victim of an enormous environmental crime.

Paul had told her about the vast network of abandoned mine tunnels beneath the valley, left behind when the coal companies went out of business. The Pennsylvania Department of Mines had spent hundreds of millions of dollars trying to fill and seal them, but the project was too complex to guarantee that every underground passage had been filled. Some of the remaining tunnels were benign, but others leached sulphur into the groundwater supply; occasional tunnel collapses caused surface subsidences and damaged buildings; and toxic, even explosive gases such as methane regularly seeped upwards into basements. The tunnels below

Middle Valley were particularly unstable and were slowly damaging Saint Sofia Church.

The altar was located behind ornate gated doors cut into the *ikonostasis,* a screening wall of gilded wood covered with elaborate icons. But the icons were faded, the gold paint was peeling in places, and one end of the screening wall was beginning to buckle, possibly due to underground settling. The stained-glass windows were badly warped by their shifting casings. Two of them had been replaced with plywood. A once-magnificent Renaissance-style fresco of the Assumption of the Blessed Virgin Mary was spread across the vaulted ceiling. But it was badly damaged by dark water stains. Huge structural cracks shot up the walls like ragged lightning bolts, warning of impending collapse. Chattering sparrows lived in nests beneath the dome, their droppings painting white streaks along the ancient wooden beams. The damp smell of mildew filled the air. As a precaution against the dangers of seeping mine gas, all the real candles so beloved by the Russian faithful had long ago been replaced by cheap plastic imitations topped with small electric bulbs.

It was a miserable place for Paul's funeral. Nicole wished she had had the strength to resist the priest's demands.

The priest, who identified himself as *Episkop* Sergius, had appeared at Nicole's front door the morning after her husband's death. He was a strange and somber figure who seemed to belong to another era. Unkempt and smelly, he wore a black floor-length cassock and filled her doorway with his bulk.

"Mother of God," he murmured, admiring her figure unashamedly.

He seemed to be a throwback to an earlier, earthier form of the priesthood. His cassock was woven of rough woolen cloth. An ornate Orthodox crucifix was tucked into the purple sash that encircled his waist. Graying hair was unevenly combed, hanging in long, loose strings below his shoulders. His gray beard ended in two ragged tails.

But the most unnerving aspect of his appearance was his eyes.

They were cold eyes: cold and gray and cruel.

Too cruel for a priest, she thought.

They sat shrouded in deep sockets under thick-boned eyebrows, two menacing gray demons that seemed ready to leap from their dens and attack her if she dared turn away from him. She felt locked into place by the intensity of his gaze.

He introduced himself to Nicole in a cavernous, heavily accented voice, informing her that he would personally conduct a solemn funeral mass for the immortal repose of the soul of Pavel Pobodovnestov

Danilovitch, such mass to be celebrated according to the old rituals. It was the first time she had heard anyone use the full Russian version of Paul's name.

"I can't afford a fancy funeral," Nicole said.

"You have no choice in this matter," the *Episkop* said. "Arrangements have already been made. Your husband was baptized into the Church of Saint Sofia when he was born, and his remains will be consecrated at the Church of Saint Sofia now that he is dead."

Nicole didn't know how to respond. She had never faced a Russian *Episkop* before. This towering figure in black was the personification of the dogmatic church that had excommunicated her mother for having dared to give birth outside the sanctity of matrimony. She wanted to slam the door in his face. But she was too intimidated by his manner.

There was also the question of Paul's wishes. Would he have wanted an Orthodox funeral? She realized she knew nothing of his religious beliefs. Their Las Vegas marriage had been sealed at a civil ceremony, not in a religious rite.

"Paul never mentioned your church." She hesitated before adding, "We never talked about religion." In fact, they never talked much about their backgrounds. She was too ashamed of hers, and he, thankfully, avoided any conversation that might open that subject.

"Your husband long ago turned his back on the faith of his ancestors," the *Episkop* explained. "But that does not mean we can deprive his soul of the eternal blessings that flow from a traditional Orthodox funeral."

"I'm not sure . . ." Nicole hesitated, feeling herself weakening under the *Episkop*'s gaze. "I want to do what's right, but I'm not sure what he would have wanted."

"I understand, *malyutchka*. This is a very difficult time for you. But there are many factors to consider. A Mass for the Dead must be celebrated for your husband before he can be buried in our cemetery. It is a requirement of the Old Ritual Russian Orthodox Church. Your agreement is merely a formality, because a grave has already been opened and awaits him."

"I didn't know Paul owned a cemetery lot."

"The purchase was made in anticipation of his inevitable death," the *Episkop* said. "The same arrangement has been made in anticipation of your death. There is a place waiting for you in the cemetery beside your husband's grave."

Ten

Nicole was unable to find her voice.

"Don't be frightened, *malyutchka*," the *Episkop* went on, reading her thoughts as clearly as if she had spoken them aloud. "The grave sites were purchased long before you were married, in the hope that Paul would take a wife and that his wife would rest beside him when her time came. We have only a small cemetery, and it is a normal practice to purchase graves long before they are needed."

"Who made the . . . arrangements?"

"The graves were purchased by Vanya Danilovitch," the *Episkop* said.

"Paul's father," she murmured.

"Vanya selected the grave sites, including his own, many years ago. He wanted to be surrounded in death by those he loved in life. He was a true believer, faithful to the old ways. His death was a loss to all of us, but particularly the Church, which he loved so deeply. May the dear Lord embrace his immortal soul." The *Episkop* slowly blessed himself.

"If that's all settled, then why are you here?" She was getting irritated with this priest, who kept looking into the house, as if he expected to be invited inside.

"I am here for the remembrance," he said.

"I'm sorry, but I don't have any money for you."

"You misunderstand. I am not here for money. I am here for any object of remembrance you might wish to place in the coffin." Apparently seeing the confusion in her face, he quickly elaborated. "It is one of our traditions to place something the deceased held dear inside the coffin."

"I can't think of anything," she said, just wanting him to leave.

"Perhaps a rosary . . . an icon . . . a sacred object . . . ?"

His eyes were boring into hers again. She tried to turn away, but found she couldn't.

"I . . . I don't think so," she murmured.

"Perhaps some object his father might have left him?"

"He left Paul the house and the furniture . . ."

"I mean something of a more religious nature. Perhaps something Paul might not have wanted you to know about."

The oddly precise query caused her to remember the coroner's similar line of questioning.

"Has someone else inquired about such an object?" The *Episkop* suddenly asked, as if reading her mind.

She shook her head, but knew it was useless to lie to him.

"It was that spy, the coroner!" the *Episkop* exclaimed. "The fool! But you did not find it yet, did you? You must keep looking. Vanya would have wanted you to keep looking."

Later, after the *Episkop* left, she would remember the safe-deposit key and wonder if that was what he came here looking for. Fortunately, she had forgotten about it at the time of his inquiries. Apparently, whatever telepathic powers he possessed couldn't penetrate a memory lapse.

Eleven

A few dozen mourners showed up for the funeral, mostly older people who were probably friends of Paul's father. The policeman, Rhostok, was also there. He stood in the back of the church, far enough away to be removed from the service, but close enough to watch Nicole.

The *Episkop* celebrated the entire Mass for the Dead in Russian, a language incomprehensible to her. She seethed at his oration in front of Paul's coffin. As majestic as the *Episkop*'s voice was, the choice of language excluded and therefore affronted the young widow. She felt as if the *Episkop* were signaling his possession of Paul's soul, welcoming it back into the embrace of an ancient religion to which Nicole could never truly belong.

Later, at the cemetery, the *Episkop* continued in the alien tongue. The only acknowledgment he proffered to the young widow was an occasional wave of his hand, indicating where she should stand at various times during the graveside ritual. She avoided his direct gaze, fearful of his ability to read her thoughts and somehow discover information she would prefer to keep hidden.

Just as the *Episkop* had said, there was an unused plot next to the open hole that received Paul's coffin. It was the one reserved for her, courtesy of an old man who apparently planned for other deaths as carefully as his own.

After the funeral, Nicole returned to the old two-story house that Paul had inherited from his father and which now, through Paul's will, belonged to her.

It was a shabby structure, badly in need of paint, but apparently worth a great deal of money. The day after Vanya's death, a local lawyer informed Paul that a buyer who wished to remain anonymous was offering three hundred thousand dollars for the house. In what Nicole was convinced could only be the workings of Fate, Paul had rejected the offer, gone back to Vegas to wrap up his affairs, and on the night before he was to return to Middle Valley, met and married Nicole. But why had Fate thrown them together, she wondered? Why had it brought her here, taunted her with a taste of a normal married lifestyle and then, when she had finally fallen in love with the stranger she married, snatched it all away, leaving her lonelier and sadder than she had ever been before?

Her steps echoed on the wooden floors that Paul had so lovingly restored to their original luster. Life had been happy here, but for so short a time.

It was in this house that she felt, for the first time, a connection to a family. She had never known her biological father, much less any of her grandparents. The parade of men entertained by her mother remained strangers in her life, creatures of lust whom she worked hard to erase from her memory.

In four short weeks in Middle Valley, however, she had not only fallen in love with Paul, but also developed an almost daughterly affection for Vanya, the man who, had he lived, would have been her father-in-law. There were times, as she helped Paul clean up the house and repair the damage done by the vandals, when she thought she felt Vanya's presence. It was never a menacing presence. She imagined him as a friendly, patriarchal figure, saddened by what the unknown intruders had done to his possessions. The worn leather Barcalounger, which Paul identified as his father's favorite, was beyond salvation. The vandals had dismantled it and removed the stuffing by carefully slicing along the seams. The stuffing was inexplicably stored in plastic bags, as if for some strange reason, they thought the chair could be rebuilt. Few of the other items were damaged, however.

What was most remarkable was the way the photographs had been treated. They were all removed from their frames and albums, and arranged in a loose pile on the dining-room table, as if the intruders had made a careful effort to preserve them. It was these photographs that were the real treasure, Nicole thought, and she was convinced Vanya Danilovitch was watching over her shoulder as she studied them.

The photographs traced the family back through the years. There were faded silvery images of *kulaks* standing stiffly outside log huts in Siberia. These ancestral photographs were taken, Paul explained, by itinerant photographers who were paid in cabbages and potatoes. There was a sepia print of a little boy, no more than three years old, in a dark woolen suit standing by a fence made of sticks. It was the only childhood photograph of Vanya before the family emigrated to America, according to Paul. There were the obligatory First Communion and confirmation photographs of the growing Vanya, a high school graduation picture, and a series of U.S. Army photographs, including one of Vanya in some small town in Germany during World War II. That would explain the medals, she thought. After the war, a wedding photograph with Zenaida, and then the pictorial life story of Paul: the baby with a bottle in his mouth, the smiling little boy who wore short white pants, the school years, sitting on a wooden sleigh in winter, playing with his dog. Her favorite was a hand-tinted photograph of baby Paul lying in a crib, a blanket covering everything but his little round face and baby fingers.

The photographs were a visual history of a normal immigrant family growing up in a small town, and were a terrible reminder of what she had lost. Any hope for a normal life and a new future died with Paul and were buried forever by the foreign rituals of a bearded Russian priest.

Was there anything left to keep her here? she wondered.

She went upstairs to the small guest bedroom, her refuge for the previous two nights. It had been Paul's bedroom when he was growing up, and it was still filled with the treasures of his life. It was the one room in the house where she could still feel his presence, as if some part of him still adhered to the things he loved best, the way a shadow adheres to a photographic negative.

She remembered the tears in his eyes when he spoke of the mess the vandals had made of his room, and how it had taken days to put everything back in its proper place. Incredibly, he told her, nothing seemed to have been stolen.

The room now remained exactly as he had restored it. Luminous stars were pasted on the ceiling. Built-in shelves with wonderful cubbyholes and drawers were stuffed with stacks of old baseball cards, a deflated football signed by some little-known professional player, a pair of rusty ice skates, a Boy Scout uniform, tattered comic books that he claimed were collector's items, and even one drawer that was filled with his baby toys. It was the Russian way, he once said. Never throw anything away, because you might need it someday.

These items were the history of his life. And every individual piece evoked a response from her. She found it comforting to touch the things he had loved. It was a ritual she had begun the morning after his death. She had worked backwards, from the newest items to the oldest, just as an archeologist would do, tracing Paul's life back to his youngest days. Late last night, she had reached the last drawer, the very earliest items connected with her husband. It contained baby toys, a rattle and teething ring, and even an artfully folded and boxed baptismal gown.

Nowhere did she find any clue, any scrap of paper that hinted at the existence of the safe-deposit box or its contents.

At last there was nothing left to examine, no more unopened drawers or hidden boxes to reveal more of her husband's past.

It was time, she decided, to learn what secrets were locked away inside the bank vault.

Twelve

The investigation into Vanya's death led Rhostok to a worn vinyl booth in the nonsmoking section of the local American Legion hall. It was midafternoon, and the rest of the barroom was empty, except for a few men watching the ball game on TV. Sitting across from Rhostok was Roman Kerensky, the official historian of the Middle Valley American Legion. An oxygen tube ran from the old man's nose to a portable tank at his side. Emphysema had destroyed Roman's lungs, and the daily struggle for breath had reduced him to a fragile shell of the powerful man he once was.

With one hand wrapped protectively around a bottle of beer, Kerensky was calmly describing the murder of two other eighty-year-old men who had once lived in Middle Valley.

"I got the story from Florian Ulyanov's wife," Kerensky said. "They were living in a mobile home in Kingman, Arizona. Florian was a retired railroad engineer. He and Irene were what you call 'snowbirds.' They spent their summers in the mountains of Arizona and their winters in Mexico." Kerensky spoke with a wheeze, pausing regularly to catch his breath. "The wife came home from Wal-Mart one day and found Florian dead. His skull was crushed and all five fingers of his right hand cut off. The autopsy says the fingers were amputated before he died. That was three weeks before Vanya's so-called suicide."

Rhostok waited while Kerensky took a long drink of beer and licked the foam from his lips. "I had to give up smoking with the emphysema, but at least I can still enjoy a good beer."

After adjusting the oxygen connection at his nose, he continued. "Now, you could say that was a coincidence, Florian and Vanya dying just three weeks apart. But fifteen days before Florian was killed, Boris Cherevenko was found drowned in his basement in Ocala, Florida. Boris lived alone. There was a garden hose stuck down his throat and the hose was still running when a neighbor found the body. By that time, Boris was floating in three feet of water. The fingers on his right hand were crushed, every bone smashed, like the killer used a hammer on them." Kerensky described the scene with the dispassionate voice of an old veteran who had seen death on a far larger scale than any policeman ever would.

"And you think their deaths are somehow connected to Vanya's?" Rhostok asked. He had already jumped to that conclusion himself, but he wanted to hear what else Kerensky knew.

"Damn right," Kerensky said. "The thing is, they all grew up together. Right here in Middle Valley. They were buddies. They kept in touch. And Florian knew about Boris's murder. He told his wife about it, and the wife swears she heard him on the phone discussing it with Vanya."

"I can check the phone records," Rhostok said, "see when the call was made. But I'll have to go through the Kingman police for that. Do you know if either of those two police departments came up with any suspects?"

"Nobody specific, according to Florian's wife." Kerensky gave a sour smile. "The police down in Florida thought Boris might have been killed by a Haitian refugee. Or maybe a Dominican. There're a lot of refugees in the area, and supposedly they have a reputation for really brutal crimes."

"Sounds to me like the police don't have any idea who did it. What about the mutilation of the fingers on his right hand?"

"The cops say he probably had money hidden somewhere, and the killers tortured him to find out where it was."

"Sounds like they're just guessing," Rhostok said. "What about Florian? Any suspects in his murder?"

"You're not going to believe this one," Kerensky sneered. "The widow said the cops got a search warrant and went through the place looking for a drug stash. All those trips back and forth to Mexico, they figured maybe he was a drug courier."

"Oh, come on," Rhostok groaned, "an eighty-year-old man running drugs?"

"That's what the widow said, too. The cops told her they get a lot of those kinds of cases in the Southwest. They said old people make the best couriers. Senior citizens look law-abiding and respectable, so nobody suspects them. And a guy living on a railroad pension could always use some extra money."

"What about the missing fingers?"

"That's what made them suspect it was a drug deal gone sour. Apparently, when a courier steals from the Mexican cartels, the punishment is either cutting off a few fingers or the whole hand, depending on the amount stolen. Like in Saudi Arabia."

"So we've got three dead men, all the same age, all with mutilated right hands," Rhostok murmured.

"And they all grew up and went to school right here in Middle Valley," Kerensky added.

"Plus the phone call to Vanya, before Florian was killed," Rhostok backtracked. "Did Florian's wife hear much of that conversation?"

"Only the part about Boris's murder. But she said Florian acted scared after that, like he was worried he might be next."

"Unfortunately for him, he was right," Rhostok said. "But still, if the Ulyanov and Cherevenko families used to live here, I'm surprised I never heard their names before."

"You wouldn't have known about them," Kerensky said. "That was long before your time, Rhostok. Over fifty years ago. And the families didn't stay here long. They came over from Russia sometime in the early nineteen-thirties."

"During the famine," Rhostok said.

"Famine over there, the Great Depression over here." Brittle lungs added a whistling sound to Kerensky's words. "There were still a few jobs in the coal mines in those days. Not much pay, but steady work, and at least they had food on the table."

Although talking appeared difficult for Kerensky, years of being on oxygen had apparently taught him how to pace himself.

"It wasn't until after the Second World War that the mines started to close, and a lot of people drifted away. Especially the veterans and their families. The Ulyanovs went to Detroit, to work in the car factories. The Cherevenko family moved to Levittown, out on Long Island. But that was a long time ago. That's why it was so hard for me to trace Florian and Boris. The reason I was calling them was to tell them about Vanya."

"So they were all friends of yours? Not just Vanya, but all three of them?"

"I didn't know them well in high school," Kerensky recalled. "They were a couple of years ahead of me. The three of them enlisted the day after they graduated. I didn't get into the service myself until the summer of '44, just in time to finish basic training and get shipped to the Ardennes. But I got to know them better after the war. We were drinking buddies, before they went their separate ways."

"It said in his obituary that Vanya was a paratrooper." Rhostok spoke slowly, giving Kerensky time to catch his breath.

"All three of them were," Kerensky said. "They served in the 101st Airborne Division, which was known in those days as the Screaming Eagles." He adjusted the oxygen tube again before continuing. "It was one of the most heavily decorated units in the war, you know. And those three guys got their share of individual medals, too."

"Wait a minute." Rhostok wanted to be sure he heard it right. "You're saying they went through the war together? In the same division?"

"Same division?" Kerensky forced a chuckle. "Hell, they were in the same platoon. The Special Reconnaissance Platoon of the 506th Parachute Infantry Regiment."

Rhostok took a slow sip of ice water while he considered the significance of what the veteran was telling him.

"Isn't that unusual?" he asked. "I mean three men from the same town ending up in the same platoon?"

"Well, they did enlist on the same day, and they volunteered together for the paratroops, so that's not unheard of, not in those days, when there were block assignments. But when you consider that the original airborne training was so tough that two out of every three volunteers washed out, I'd have to say, yes, it was very unusual. But they were unusual men."

"Were there any other men from Middle Valley in the same outfit?" Rhostok asked. "Or from other nearby towns?"

"Oh, sure, about a dozen more local boys made it into the 506th," Kerensky replied. "But none of them survived the war." He ticked off the casualties with the certainty befitting his role as Post historian. "Six were killed in the first week of combat in Normandy, four of them were killed in Holland, two at Bastogne, and one died in a noncombat accident in England."

The veteran paused again, but this time it wasn't to catch his breath.

"And now the last three are dead," he said. "God rest their souls."

Kerensky adjusted a valve, and the oxygen tank responded with a hiss. The beer stood neglected on the table while he drifted off into silent thought, his eyes focused some place thousands of miles in the distance. Was he thinking about the carnage of a long-ago war? Or about the more recent deaths of three old warriors?

"Why didn't you come to me with this information earlier, Roman?" Rhostok asked. "Why wait until now?"

"Like I said on the phone, I only found out about it last week, when I finally tracked down Florian's widow. And frankly, I was a little scared."

"Scared?" Rhostok asked. "Why would you be scared?"

"Well, all three of those guys were buddies of mine. Whoever killed Florian and Boris must have killed Vanya. Which means the killer might still be in the area right now, maybe right here in Middle Valley. How do I know he's not going to come after me next?"

Rhostok could come up with no words to reassure him.

"It's not right," Kerensky wheezed. "Those guys were all around eighty years old. Older than me. Anybody wanted them dead, all they had to do was wait a couple more years and let nature take its course."

Kerensky shook his head slowly from side to side. For a moment, Rhostok thought the hardened veteran was going to cry.

"It doesn't make any sense," Kerensky said, his eyes suddenly narrowing, his voice turning harder. "Random killings, crimes of passion, maybe muggings, I could understand. But one killer takes down all three of them? I don't believe it."

"Why not?" Rhostok asked.

Kerensky let out a low, menacing chuckle.

"Because these guys weren't your ordinary senior citizens." The chuckle turned into an evil smile. "They were killers themselves."

Thirteen

The Middle Valley State Bank was a relic of a bygone era in banking. It was built in the concrete-fortress style popular with bankers at the turn of the twentieth century. Heavy steel doors guarded the narrow entrance. Inside, the teller windows were still adorned with the elaborate wrought iron grills that were designed to protect the original tellers from their customers.

The bank guard directed Nicole to a fragile, powdered woman who seemed well past the age of retirement. The heavy layer of makeup on the woman's face couldn't hide the hollowness of her cheeks nor still the tremors that shook her head. The hand she extended in greeting was as desiccated as the rest of her body and felt so delicate that Nicole was afraid she might break a bone if she squeezed it too hard. In spite of all that, the woman was alert and quick of movement.

She introduced herself as Sonya Yarosh and explained that she was in charge of customer relations. She quickly acknowledged that the brass key Nicole presented was indeed issued by the Middle Valley State Bank. She examined the single-page notarized will Nicole gave her, the one Vassily had insisted Paul sign after the wedding. Everything seemed in order. But after consulting a large green clothbound ledger, the old woman seemed puzzled. She led Nicole to the desk of Harold Zeeman, placing the ledger, key, and will in front of him.

Zeeman was a thin man with a narrow face, sharp nose, and pointed chin, all of which identified him as a descendant of the bank's founder, whose huge portrait hung prominently on the wall behind him. He sat dwarfed behind an enormous antique rosewood desk that was also replicated in the founder's portrait.

"I'm sorry about your husband," Zeeman said, rising to greet her with a weak handshake. "Please accept my condolences." His voice had a pinched nasal quality that perfectly suited his appearance.

Zeeman motioned Nicole to one of the chairs in front of his desk. Sonya Yarosh quickly brought him another ledger, a much older one, which he examined with even greater interest. He pursed his lips and shook his head in apparent bewilderment.

"I'm afraid we'll have to notify the authorities," Zeeman said. Sonya Yarosh quickly scurried back to her desk to place the necessary telephone call.

"Is there a problem?" Nicole asked in a wary voice.

"There are certain procedures we have to follow when a vault customer passes away," Zeeman explained. He paused to listen while Sonya whispered some urgent instructions into the telephone. "I hope this won't take too long, Mrs. Danilovitch," he said. "I know how you must be feeling. I understand your husband suffered a heart attack while he was watching TV. A terrible tragedy. Especially so soon after you were married. I'm truly sorry."

That was the story released by the coroner. It had been repeated with sympathy by the mourners who came to pay their respects at the funeral, but Nicole knew that none of them believed it.

"What sort of procedures are you talking about?" she asked.

"We'll need a witness to the opening," he said. "We'll need an official inventory of the contents for tax purposes. The government wants to be certain it gets its share. My secretary is calling the Pennsylvania Department of Revenue as we speak."

"Maybe I should come back another time," she said, nervously.

"It's really no problem, Mrs. Danilovitch. It's strictly a formality. Even if your name were on the signature card, we'd have to go through the same procedure. When any individual signator on a vault box dies, the box is sealed to prevent the removal of valuables such as cash, gold coins, jewelry, bonds, or any other items that would be subject to state and federal taxes. It has nothing to do with your rightful claim to the property. It's simply a legal requirement that the contents be inventoried, so there won't be any future dispute over taxes. As Paul's sole heir, you'll be free to walk out of here with whatever was kept in the vault, as long as you sign for it."

The vault was at the far end of the corridor. Whoever went into it had to pass Harold Zeeman's desk after signing the appropriate form.

"So you automatically sealed the box when you heard of Paul's death?" she asked.

Zeeman gave her a nervous smile, a tight little grin that revealed the perfectly aligned rows of his neatly capped teeth.

"The truth is," he said, "the box was already sealed before your husband died. It was sealed two months ago."

"I don't understand."

"The box was originally rented by Vanya Danilovitch, Paul's father. When he died, the box was sealed in accordance with our policy. We were expecting Paul to come in with his father's key, at which time we'd do the official inventory."

"He never came in?" she asked.

"No."

"Maybe he didn't know about it."

"Perhaps. And if that's the case, I personally apologize for not contacting him."

"So the box hasn't been opened since Paul's father died?"

"Longer than that," Zeeman said, shaking his head. "As Miss Yarosh just pointed out to me, that box hasn't been opened by anyone since the day Vanya Danilovitch first rented it."

"How long ago was that?"

Zeeman glanced down at the open ledger on his desk.

"That particular box was rented in 1946. October 16, according to these records. Vanya Danilovitch rented the box and had the annual fee automatically deducted from his checking account until 1985, when he became eligible for our Golden Years Club. We offer our senior citizens free checking and free safe-deposit boxes." Zeeman looked up from the ledger and smiled. "Which turned out to be a very good deal for Vanya. He had a free safe-deposit box for, what is it now, 18 years."

"And he never opened it in all that time?" she asked. "Never put anything in or took anything out?"

"Not according to our records. You'll be the first person to open that safe-deposit box in over half a century. It'll be like opening a time capsule."

Fourteen

Roman Kerensky rose unsteadily to his feet. He adjusted the oxygen tube at his nose, carefully tilted the portable tank back on its wheels, and motioned for Rhostok to follow him.

"Come on," he said. "I'll show you the kind of men we're talking about."

He led the way down a narrow corridor to a locked door in the back that led to what he called the Trophy Room. In all the times Rhostok had been inside the Legion building, whether for the regular Friday night fish fries, or meeting friends, or responding to 911 calls to break up fights among drunken members, he had never suspected the Trophy Room existed. It was apparently open only to authorized members.

The air in the room was warm and stale. Kerensky switched on the overhead fluorescent lights, revealing walls that were covered with a haphazard collection of memorabilia from two world wars, the Korean War, the Vietnam War, Operation Desert Storm, and the United Nations Peacekeeping Operations in Somalia and Bosnia. Each item was carefully labeled with the name of the veteran who donated it. The collection included a German swastika armband punctured by what appeared to be a bullet hole, a Japanese samurai sword, a padded Chinese Communist winter uniform, a spike-topped German ceremonial helmet, various battle flags, knapsacks, canteens, and other gear from the world's armies.

Locked glass cases displayed a German Luger, a Colt Model 1911 .45 automatic, a Russian Kalashnikov, a British Enfield, a Japanese Mitsui machine pistol, an Israeli Sten gun, an M-1, a Thompson submachine gun, a German Krag, a BAR, a grenade launcher, various bayonets, and an assortment of deactivated grenades, all neatly labeled.

At the far end of the room were wooden racks containing rows of huge, leather-bound scrapbooks. These were the archives maintained by Roman Kerensky and the Post historians who preceded him.

Roman wheeled his oxygen tank to the back of the room. He tapped his finger against one of the thickest scrapbooks. It was part of a three-volume set covering the year 1944.

Rhostok pulled out the volume for him and carried it to the reading table, where Kerensky quickly leafed through the oversized pages. The book was filled with yellowed newspaper clippings, official military orders and citations, V-mail, telegrams, and photographs ranging from small black-and-white snapshots to large hand-colored portraits.

Kerensky pointed to a glossy photograph of about two dozen young men in combat gear posing in front of what he identified as a C-47 troop carrier. A half-century ago, someone had inked in the names of each of the soldiers above their heads.

"That's the Special Reconnaissance Platoon," Kerensky said. "The picture was taken at Maidenfern, England, about a month before D-Day. That's Vanya and Boris and Florian on the left."

Boris Cherevenko had the biggest wide-cheeked grin of any of the group. Florian Ulyanov's eyes were closed during the long-ago moment when the picture was taken. The man Kerensky identified as Vanya was the smallest of the group, and the most serious. He was square-faced, with his jaw thrust defiantly forward. He looked familiar, but the name inked in over his head wasn't the one Rhostok knew him by.

"If that's Vanya, they got his name wrong," Rhostok said.

"No, that's the name he used in those days." Kerensky smiled. "Vince Daniels. He Americanized his name when he was in high school, like a lot of immigrants did. Vanya Danilovitch became Vincent Daniels. That was the name he enlisted under, and that's how his military records list him. After the war, he changed it back to the original Russian version. That picture was taken five days before D-Day, just before they got their haircuts."

"Haircuts before D-Day?" Rhostok asked.

"It was a gung-ho thing," Kerensky smiled. "They cut off all their hair except for a long strip down the center of the head, so they'd look like Mohawk Indian braves when they went on the warpath."

He turned the page to a photograph of a group of paratroopers with Mohawk haircuts and camouflage-blackened faces talking to Eisenhower.

"These guys were the toughest of the tough. They volunteered to be Pathfinders, the ones who go in ahead of the main body of paratroopers to light up the drop zones. They landed near Sainte Mere-Eglise at 0015 on D-Day," Kerensky said. "That's military time for fifteen minutes after midnight. They were the first American troops in France. Those three men were on the ground, fighting Germans, six hours before the first Allied troops landed on the beaches."

"They made a movie about that," Rhostok murmured.

"A couple of movies," Kerensky said. "But they never got it right."

"The real thing was worse."

"A lot worse," Kerensky said. "Put yourself in their place for a moment. Eight months after you graduate from high school, you get on an airplane in England with a dozen other kids. Two hours later, just after midnight, you jump out of the plane over Normandy. Waiting for you in the darkness down below is what seems like the whole damn German army. They start shooting at you, machine guns, antiaircraft, eighty-eights, everything they've got. You see a lot of your buddies get killed before they even hit the ground. A few of your friends explode in midair when bullets hit their grenade pouches."

The terror of that long-ago night was reflected in Kerensky's voice. The words began to pour out more rapidly. Apparently energized by the drama of the events he was describing, he seemed to forget about the oxygen tank at his side.

"By some miracle, you manage to land safely. The first problem is that you're lost because the pilots dropped you in the wrong place. It's the middle of the night, there's only a few dozen surviving Pathfinders scattered over the countryside, and you're surrounded by thousands of German soldiers, which by now are all out looking for you. Somehow, you're supposed to find and light up the drop zones for the main body of paratroopers and glider units. Eight hundred forty-two planes and gliders are already taking off from England, each one loaded with troops and equipment, and if you don't set up the radio beacons for them, the air drop will be a disaster.

"You hear gunfire, and you know more of your buddies are getting killed, but you manage to set up your beacons, and around two in the morning, the main body of paratroopers starts jumping. But that's just the beginning. When the rest of your division comes in, you're supposed to link up and attack the German army so they can't reinforce the Normandy beaches, where the main invasion force is supposed to land at dawn."

"They were just eighteen years old?" Rhostok shook his head. "Christ, they were just teenagers. Kids that age today are playing video games and going to rock concerts."

"You've got that right," Kerensky agreed. "But somehow these young kids, just out of high school and never having been in combat before, somehow they managed to clear and hold their objectives until the invasion forces broke out of the beach areas."

Kerensky was growing more excited now, thoroughly caught up in the history of these events. He turned the pages to more clippings, more photographs of the Screaming Eagles.

"Two months later, they're on another plane. This time, they're dropped behind enemy lines in Holland. It's Operation Market Garden. The stupidest plan in the whole damn war. Another of Montgomery's dumb ideas. It turned out the Germans had some of their most battle-hardened troops and Panzer tanks waiting for them. The whole operation was a disaster. But out of fifty thousand American and British troops, the 101st was one of the few units that managed to achieve all its objectives and hold them until Eisenhower wised up and ordered Monty to pull the plug."

"Tough guys," Rhostok said, making no effort to hide the admiration in his voice.

"That's a hell of an understatement," Kerensky said.

He turned the pages until he reached news clippings from the middle of December 1944. The headlines described the Battle of the Bulge.

"Now Vanya and his buddies are in western France, just before Christmas," Kerensky went on. "They're getting their wounds patched up and most of their weapons are in for repair. On December 17, Hitler launches the biggest counteroffensive of the war. He sends two hundred fifty thousand infantry troops, two Panzer divisions, and three artillery divisions into Belgium. They catch the American 17th Division totally by surprise. It's a disaster. The American troops panic. They're throwing down their weapons and running, actually running, to the rear. Eisenhower sends the 101st to Belgium on what seems like a suicide mission.

"The objective is to hold a major crossroads in a small town called Bastogne. Supplies are so short, the paratroopers have to beg the retreating soldiers for weapons and ammunition. Within hours after they set up in Bastogne, the Germans have them surrounded. It's snowing, the ground is frozen, and our boys didn't even have blankets or winter uniforms, thanks to Headquarters' screwups. They're running low on ammunition, and the cloud cover makes it impossible for the air corps to drop supplies.

"They're fighting Panzer tanks with rifles and Molotov cocktails. Things are so bad that the local women are giving them bedsheets to use as camouflage in the snow. Somehow they hold out against everything the Germans throw at them. Outnumbered, outgunned, and surrounded, those guys stopped the cream of the German Army in its tracks. And then they went on the attack for the next month, helping drive the Nazis back into Germany."

Kerensky paused finally, although it seemed more of a pause to gather his thoughts than to catch his breath. He turned the scrapbook pages to a photograph of medals being pinned on the three men by a general named MacAuliffe.

"You see what I'm saying?" Kerensky asked. "Those three guys were war heroes. Genuine war heroes. They went through some of the bloodiest combat in the war. Between them, they earned two Silver Stars, one Distinguished Service Medal, three Bronze Stars, two Purple Hearts, and nine Battle Stars. And those were just the individual medals. As a division, the 101st was the most highly decorated unit in the war, getting the Presidential Unit Citation and the highest medals awarded by the French, British, Dutch, and Belgian governments."

"I see what you mean," Rhostok said, "about them not being your average senior citizens."

"That's why it doesn't make sense," Kerensky said. "The Nazis couldn't kill those guys. They faced Panzer tanks, rocket attacks, machine guns, land mines, booby traps, snipers, mortars, and heavy artillery. They fought all their battles behind enemy lines. They were always surrounded, always outnumbered, always outgunned. But they survived. And you know why? Maybe it's not nice to say, but they were very good at killing people. If you read their citations for valor, you'll see they accounted for one hell of a lot of dead Germans. Of course, what they were doing was killing people who were trying to kill them. But that's not something anybody ever forgets how to do. They weren't the kind of men who'd ever let a killer sneak up on them."

"But they were old men," Rhostok countered, "in their eighties. Their war was over a long time ago."

"What you learn in combat stays with you forever. You learn to smell danger. It becomes instinctive."

"Even the best of us get careless sometimes," Rhostok said.

"One guy gets picked off, okay, I can see how that could happen," Kerensky said. "Maybe even two of them. But all three? Especially when they knew someone was after them? I don't think so."

"But it happened," Rhostok reminded him. "Somebody managed to get to all three of them."

Kerensky thought carefully before answering.

"Then it would have to be somebody who was better at killing than they were," he finally said. "And there aren't many of those people around."

"A professional?"

"A very good one," Kerensky said.

It was hard to disagree with the Post historian's logic. But that left another question unanswered.

"They were old men," Rhostok said, still trying to puzzle it out. "They didn't have any money to speak of. Why would a professional killer go after them?"

"Like I said, that's the part that doesn't make any sense."

Kerensky took another sip of beer, licked his lips, and finally got around to one last question that was troubling him.

"Do you think maybe Vanya wasn't really crazy?" he asked. "I mean, except for the Alzheimer's, of course."

"They had him locked in a padded cell," Rhostok pointed out. "They don't usually do that with normal people."

"Exactly," Roman said. "The guy manages to get himself placed in a high-security area, protected by guards and barred doors."

"I'm not following you."

"Well, I checked the dates of Florian's phone call and Vanya's admission to the mental hospital. He had his so-called violent mental breakdown two days after the telephone call. I'm thinking that's not necessarily a coincidence."

"It could be a triggering factor. Maybe what they call a panic attack."

"I'm thinking it was something he might have thought out very carefully," Roman said. "Remember, you're dealing with a man who spent a lot of time under enemy attack. When I was in the army, there was a tactic called 'strategic retreat.' When you're caught in an exposed position, and you can't respond with accurate fire because you don't know where the enemy is, you retreat to a more defensible position."

"You're saying Vanya faked his breakdown, that he wanted to be committed to Lackawanna?"

"Think about it, Rhostok. An eighty-year-old man finds out a killer might be after him. He figures he's too old to fight back. What could be safer than being locked up in a maximum-security cell with guards watching over him twenty-four hours a day? I'd say it was a pretty smart tactic on his part."

"Except it didn't work," Rhostok said.

Fifteen

The agent from the Pennsylvania Department of Revenue didn't arrive until twenty minutes after five. The bank was closed for the day. All the employees were gone except for Zeeman, Sonya Yarosh, and the bank guard. The air conditioning automatically went off at five. The bank soon began to grow uncomfortably warm, as the concrete walls released the heat they had been collecting all day from the late summer sun.

"It's on a timer," Zeeman explained. "There's no need for air conditioning when the bank is closed. It might seem like a little thing, but it saves us about four thousand dollars a year, probably even more now that the summers seem to be getting warmer."

The tax agent was already perspiring when he entered the bank. Wendell Franklin was a short man, with a stomach that had outgrown his suit jacket years ago. A soft layer of neck fat rolled over the top button of his shirt. He had the face of a frog, with thick lips, heavy cheeks, and bulging eyes magnified by thick-lensed glasses.

At first he apologized for taking so long to drive up from the Scranton regional office. He blamed it on construction on Route 81, and northbound traffic being reduced to one lane near the university.

"But you didn't give me enough notice," he quickly added, as if he didn't like the idea of apologizing to people. "You call me at three-thirty and expect me to come rushing up here, like I've got nothing else to do."

Franklin raised his glasses and wiped the perspiration from around his eyes with a neatly folded handkerchief, then refolded it so that the sweat-stained portion was on the inside.

"You didn't have to come yourself," Zeeman countered. "You could have authorized me to conduct the inventory. There's nothing in the regulation that says an agent has to be physically present, as long as your office is notified that an opening will take place."

The tax agent turned to examine Nicole, his eyes shamelessly appraising her figure.

"This is the woman who wants to open the box?" he asked.

Nicole forced a smile. She already disliked the man.

"This is Mrs. Danilovitch," Zeeman said. "Her husband passed away, leaving her in possession of the key."

"Do you have a death certificate?" Franklin asked.

"I can vouch for the fact that her husband is dead," Zeeman said. "The funeral was held this morning."

"Your secretary said something on the phone about a different name on the box."

"That would be the original renter, Mrs. Danilovitch's late husband's father. He passed away two months ago. We sealed the box at that time. Technically, of course, the contents of the box are now part of her husband's estate, but Mrs. Danilovitch has produced a will naming her as sole heir and is entitled to exercise her rights to those contents."

"The will hasn't been through probate yet," Franklin said. "What about other possible heirs of the original owner who might contest the will? Children? Maybe a divorced wife somewhere? The mother?"

"There are no surviving blood relatives," Zeeman said. "The person who originally rented the box was Vanya Danilovitch. He was the only son of Peter and Galina Danilovitch. The three of them came here from Russia in 1918, one year after the revolution. Vanya Danilovitch's wife died in 1955. Paul was their only child. As far as I know, he had no cousins, aunts, uncles, half-brothers, or half-sisters. Mrs. Danilovitch has the key and the notarized will and is the only person who appears to have a claim to the estate.

"You know all about these people, it sounds like," said Franklin.

Harold Zeeman raised his chin and narrowed his eyes, apparently resentful of anyone questioning his integrity.

"The Middle Valley State Bank has been a Zeeman family bank for one hundred and two years," he said. "My family did business here before the Irish arrived, before the Polish arrived, before the Russians arrived. There is very little that goes on in this town that I don't know."

"Okay, okay," Franklin raised a hand. "I'll take your word for it." He removed a document from his briefcase and passed it to Nicole. "I'll need your signature before the opening," he said. "The full signature, including your maiden name and Social Security number."

The paper was a cheaply printed form with a short paragraph of legal language and lines for her signature and those of two witnesses.

Nicole hesitated.

"It's just a formality," Zeeman explained. "They want you to acknowledge that you haven't removed anything from your husband's safe-deposit box in contemplation of his death, and that you won't dispose of any assets you remove from the box without notifying the IRS or the probate court."

"But I didn't even know he had this box," Nicole protested.

"You're his wife and he didn't tell you?" Franklin's curiosity was aroused.

"I don't think my husband knew about it," she said.

"You mean this was a secret depository of some kind?" Franklin asked.

"Whether she knew of it or not is quite irrelevant," Zeeman pointed out. "As the surviving spouse, Mrs. Danilovitch is legally entitled to open the box."

"Yes, well, now that we have your word on it, I guess it's settled," Franklin said in a sarcastic tone. "Ah, what the hell, sign the paper and let's get on with it."

"And if I don't sign?" Nicole asked. She glared angrily at the bulging eyeballs behind Franklin's thick lenses.

He didn't blink. He was apparently accustomed to dealing with angry people. "Then I'll get a court order and open it myself," he said. "We'll confiscate the contents, sell them at auction, deduct any estate taxes that are due, and give you the remainder. Assuming you're legally entitled to it, of course. That's the normal procedure when people try to stop us from doing our job."

"I'm sorry you have to go through all this," Zeeman apologized to Nicole. He seemed eager to stop the arguing, hurry things along, get them out of his bank, and close up. "It'll be best if you sign the paper."

"Maybe she has a reason for stalling," Franklin taunted. "Maybe she doesn't want to sign because she already knows what's in the box. Or what isn't in it. Maybe she already removed the contents."

"Impossible," Zeeman retorted. "Mrs. Danilovitch has never been in this bank before today. And I can assure you, that box was sealed months ago."

Zeeman offered Nicole a pen. She quickly scrawled her signature in the proper space. Zeeman smiled and signed his own name as witness before handing the document back to the tax agent.

"Let's get on with it," Franklin said.

"I believe you're supposed to sign your name also," Zeeman reminded him.

Impatient now, Franklin hastily scribbled his name on the bottom line. His sweaty fingers left smudges on the cheap government paper.

The bank was getting uncomfortably hot and stuffy. With the air conditioning off and the windows permanently sealed, there was no way to expel the heat.

Sonya Yarosh waited at her desk, and the bank guard watched with bored disinterest as Nicole followed the two men into the vault. Inside the massive circular steel door, the interior was divided into two separate areas. The larger area, the one on the right, was lined with dozens of metal doors in a variety of sizes, some resembling small safes with black handles and combination locks.

The area on the left, where Zeeman led them, was a narrow space between two walls that were subdivided into hundreds of identical small steel doors. Each was about the size of a three-by-five index card. On the front of each door were two round brass inserts containing narrow key slots. There was barely enough room for the three of them to squeeze into the narrow passageway at the same time.

Nicole frowned at the smell of Wendell Franklin's body odor, which was beginning to overpower the deodorant he wore.

The two keyholes of safe-deposit box number fifty-two were sealed with red plastic plugs. Zeeman used a special tool to remove them. He inserted the bank's key in the left slot and instructed Nicole to insert Paul's key in the other. At first the keys didn't work. Zeeman had to spray some WD-40 into the keyholes before he could turn both keys simultaneously.

"Probably corrosion," he explained as he tugged at the small door, which was also stuck. "We have a dehumidifying system in the vault, but after being closed for over fifty years, I guess a little corrosion is inevitable."

The half-inch thick steel door finally popped open, revealing the wire handle of a gray metal box inside.

Nicole held her breath in nervous anticipation.

Zeeman slowly pulled the box halfway out of the metal slot and raised its lid.

He let out a gasp and recoiled from the contents.

"What the hell is this?" he hissed.

Instinctively, he wiped his hands against his jacket, as if trying to clean them.

Nicole stared at the contents of the box in disbelief. She felt the sour taste of bile rise in her throat.

She wanted to turn away from the box, but the shock of what she saw transfixed her.

Jammed inside the metal box was a massive human hand, larger than any she had ever seen. It was a man's hand, partially wrapped in a thick, wax-impregnated brown paper. It was lying with its palm upraised, the fingers curling towards her, as if begging for help.

The hand was severed at the wrist, in the middle of the joint where the bones of hand and forearm were once connected. The cut was clean and slightly angled away from the thumb. The flesh was still pink and healthy looking. A thickening ooze of uncongealed blood formed at the severed end, where the round bone of the wrist joint was barely visible. The little finger, she noticed, was slightly deformed. The fingernails curled inward.

A dry, wheaty odor crept out of the box, slowly pervading the vault. Nicole put a hand over her nose, too late to prevent the musty smell from entering her lungs.

Sixteen

Nicole wanted to scream. She wanted to run. She wanted to be anywhere except in this overheated metal chamber staring at the awful thing in the safe-deposit box. But she was hemmed in by Franklin and Zeeman, and like them, she found herself strangely fascinated by the grotesque discovery.

"What the hell is this?" Franklin repeated Zeeman's question.

"It . . . it looks like a man's hand," Zeeman said in a frightened voice. "A man's right hand."

"Don't be a comedian," Franklin said. "You know what I mean. How did that goddamned thing get locked up in here?"

He reached over to pull out the box, but quickly recoiled, as if stung by his contact with the metal.

"Damn door is sharp," he muttered, shaking his finger in pain. A small red drop quickly formed at the tip. It grew larger and fell, only to be replaced immediately by another drop of blood. "You should keep the edges filed down," he told Zeeman. "You could get sued for that."

"The police . . ." Zeeman said in a shaky voice, "I'll have to call the police."

"Damn right, call the police," an angry Franklin said. "Looks like we've got a problem here. I don't know what the hell is going on, but my guess is something of major value was removed before we showed up. Probably cash or jewelry, maybe even gold bars. That . . . thing . . . must have been put in there to confuse us." He gave Nicole an accusing glare. "You sure you didn't empty out this box right around the time your husband died?"

"That would have been impossible," Zeeman interrupted, in an icy tone. "I can assure you Mrs. Danilovitch was never in the vault. We're very careful about such matters."

"Yeah, well, you're so careful that somebody came in here and left a human hand behind, that's how careful you are."

Nicole continued to stare at the hand.

The fingernails were neatly manicured, but a thin edging of dirt was trapped under the tips of two nails. The rest of the hand looked as if it had been carefully washed. A few drops of blood glistened on the wrapping in which the hand rested.

"You don't look all that surprised," the tax agent accused Nicole. "This is maybe what you expected us to find? Maybe you knew about the hand before you came here?"

"No. I never . . ." Confused and frightened, she struggled to find the right words to answer him. "I just . . . I really don't know . . ."

"Is that your husband's hand?"

"Of course not!"

"There's no need to be rude," Zeeman interrupted. "Mrs. Danilovitch just lost her husband. Show some respect for her feelings."

"It's all right," Nicole said in a weak voice.

"No, it's not," Zeeman angrily went on. "He represents the Pennsylvania Department of Revenue. There are standards of behavior for employees of public agencies. If he doesn't conduct himself properly, I'll report him to his superiors."

"Okay, okay, I'm sorry," Franklin muttered. "It's just the way she was looking at the damn thing, I thought she recognized it."

Nicole leaned against the metal wall, her knees weak.

"I'll call the police," Zeeman said.

When the bank president left the vault, Wendell Franklin grinned and winked at Nicole.

"Come on, honey. You sure you don't know anything about this?"

She closed her eyes and wished he'd go away. All she wanted was to be left alone, to close her eyes and open them and find that this was all an awful dream.

Seventeen

The first policeman who arrived was the bald-headed behemoth who had shown up at the house the night Paul died. Thankfully, the oversized cop made no attempt to enter the crowded vault.

Right behind him came Viktor Rhostok, and this time Nicole was glad to see him. Somehow, having a familiar face around, even someone in a police uniform, made the situation seem less threatening. She tried to greet Rhostok with a friendly smile, but if her lips worked properly, it seemed to have no effect on him.

Nicole had to draw herself up against the metal wall to allow Rhostok to reach the open box. As he squeezed past her, the hard muscle of his right bicep brushed against her left breast. Her nipple tingled in response, and she blushed as she felt it stiffen and grow erect.

Fortunately, he didn't seem to notice. He appeared to be interested solely in the contents of the safe-deposit box.

"Doesn't look like it's been here very long," he said. "At room temperature, especially with no air conditioning after hours, it wouldn't take long for the flesh to start changing color and swelling up. If it was here overnight, there'd already be a pretty strong odor. It must have been placed here sometime during the day."

He poked at the hand with the tip of a mechanical pencil, pushing the point into the soft flesh at the base of the palm. The skin rebounded when he pulled the pencil away.

"That's impossible," Zeeman said. "The box was sealed. No one could have gotten in here and opened the box without my knowledge. Anyone entering the vault has to pass my desk, and when the vault is open, I can see inside from where I sit. I was at my desk all day today, and all day yesterday. I didn't see anything unusual."

"What about overnight?" Rhostok asked. "Or before the bank opened for business today?"

"We have motion detectors and infrared sensors, as well as special alarms built into the vault door. As you know, the alarm system is wired directly to the police station. If anyone had come in here during the night, you would have been alerted."

Rhostok poked at the bloody end of the wrist. A drop of dark red fluid stuck to the tip of his pencil. "Look at that," he murmured. "The blood is still uncoagulated. The flesh is still pink. There's no way it could have been here very long. I'd say a couple of hours, maximum. Who was in the vault this morning?"

"I opened the vault door myself at eight A.M," Zeeman explained. "It's on a time lock, and we can't gain access before then. I personally brought out the teller cash, which I do every morning. Nobody else entered the vault all day. Except for Mrs. Danilovitch, of course. I should point out that even the bank employees don't have access to this side of the vault. As you can see, it has its own gate, which we keep locked separately, so we can maintain better records of everyone who enters." He nodded towards the barred steel door behind them. "We open the gate only when there's a customer, and lock it as soon as they leave."

"Well, that hand didn't get in here by itself," Rhostok snapped. "When was the last time Paul was here?"

"To open the box? Never."

"But I thought . . ." he turned to look at Nicole. "Wasn't this your husband's safe-deposit box?"

"Perhaps I didn't explain it properly on the phone," Zeeman said. "Mrs. Danilovitch had the key, but the box was originally rented by Paul's father."

"Old Vanya?" Rhostok frowned.

"Yes. He rented this particular box in 1946."

"1946?" Rhostok repeated the date with disbelief. "That's more than fifty years ago."

"Exactly. I rechecked the records while we were waiting for you. This particular safe-deposit box was originally rented on October 16, 1946, and it hasn't been opened since that day. Not once."

A sweaty silence descended on the crowded vault.

Wendell Franklin's body odor became almost overpowering to Nicole. It seemed to her that everyone was sweating now, as much from tension as from the heat. She could feel a rivulet of her own perspiration trailing down inside her bra, into the hollow between her breasts. She desperately wanted to get out of there, out into the evening air, which even though it was hot, was at least dry and devoid of the mixture of man-sweat and the peculiar musty odor emanating from the hand. It reminded her of . . . what? Straw? Dried mushrooms? Nuts?

It was Franklin who broke the silence.

"Well, somebody must have put the damn thing in there."

"And it couldn't have been Vanya," Rhostok said. "He's been dead for two months now."

"I assure you, no one could have entered that vault without my knowledge," Zeeman insisted.

"Well, what about you, Zeeman?" The accusation came from Franklin, who was mopping his brow with the same handkerchief he had been using to staunch the flow of blood from his fingertip. "You own the bank. You have all the keys. You're the guy who turns the alarm system on and off. Maybe you emptied the box when nobody was around, and stuck the hand in there to distract attention from yourself."

"How dare you!" Zeeman shouted. For a moment, Nicole thought Zeeman was going to physically attack the tax agent. Just as quickly, he seemed to gain control of himself and lowered his voice. "The only asset a bank really has is the integrity of its ownership," he said. "The money in this bank is here because the people of Middle Valley trust me, the same way they trusted my father and his father before him. I would never do anything to compromise that trust. Never. I demand an apology."

"What about your employees?" Franklin continued to badger him. "Your secretary? She's the one who maintains those records, isn't she?"

Rhostok quickly squeezed in between the two, separating them with his broad shoulders.

"Let's not get upset," he said. "It doesn't help anything for the two of you to be arguing."

"He has no right to come into my bank and make such accusations," Zeeman insisted. "There has never been the slightest discrepancy in any of our accounts. The employees of my bank are all above reproach. I know them all. I know their families. I know their backgrounds. Each of them was personally hired by me, or in the case of Miss Yarosh, by my father. None of them, I can assure you, would ever take part in anything as horrible as this."

Glancing at Sonya Yarosh, Nicole had to agree. It was inconceivable that at this advanced stage of her life, the fragile old creature who watched from her desk would ever do anything to disrupt the bank's routine.

"I agree with you," Rhostok told the bank president. Turning to Franklin, he added, "It wouldn't make any sense for a bank employee to do this. If it was an inside job, they would have just cleaned out the box and left it empty, and nobody would be the wiser."

"In addition, it takes two keys to unlock the box," Zeeman added. "The bank only had one key. Mrs. Danilovitch had the other."

"Maybe you're right," Franklin grudgingly admitted. "What the hell, the only two men who would have known what was originally in that box were probably the two Danilovitches. And they're both dead, so proving any theft occurred would probably be impossible. But that still doesn't answer how a human hand got into a locked box inside a locked bank vault."

The tension temporarily defused, Rhostok returned his attention to the metal box.

"Be careful you don't cut yourself on that," Franklin warned him. The tax agent was pressing the handkerchief against the tip of his finger, still trying to stem the flow of blood that oozed from the tiny wound. There were already a dozen drops of his blood on the floor, some of them smeared by his shoes.

Something on the heavy wrapping paper seemed to catch Rhostok's attention. With the tip of his pencil, he folded the paper back.

"But that can't be . . ." he started to say, and then suddenly stopped, staring in silence at the wrapper.

The policeman's shoulders blocked the view of Franklin and Zeeman, but Nicole could see what had drawn his startled comment. There were heavy penciled markings on the side of the wrapping paper. It looked like three words, but they were written in a script and a language she didn't know.

"What did you say?" asked Franklin.

Rhostok recovered quickly.

"I was just thinking out loud."

"No. You said, 'That can't be.' I heard you. What did you mean by that?"

Rhostok pushed the paper back, hiding the markings from view. "It means I can't figure out how the hand got in there. It seems impossible, given the time frame and the condition of the flesh."

Nicole knew he was lying. She was certain it had something to do with the strange markings, but she decided to remain quiet for the time being.

She watched as Rhostok made a show of inspecting the edges of the small door.

"Looks like a little rust around the sides," he murmured. "Did you have a hard time opening it?"

"Yes, it was stuck, and the locks were hard to work, too," Zeeman replied. "But after all, it's been over half a century since the box was last opened."

"You keep saying that," Franklin muttered. "But the blood on that hand is still fresh. Even this cop says it couldn't have been in there more than a few hours."

Rhostok leaned in closer, examining the contents of the box more carefully. Nicole wondered how he could bear to get so close to the gruesome object.

"Will this have to be reported to the press?" Zeeman asked. "It would be terrible publicity for the bank."

"He's required to file a report," Franklin said. "There's been a crime committed."

"We don't know that for a fact," Rhostok murmured, as he ran his fingers along the rust marks. "We have no actual proof of any crime."

"You've got a goddamn human hand in a safe-deposit box," Franklin shouted. "You don't call that a crime? What kind of proof do you need? At the very least, you've got a case of human mutilation here. You should be calling the coroner."

"Plenty of time for that," Rhostok said. "Until we find out whose hand this is, and how it got here, we won't know what sort of crime was committed, if any. I'd just as soon keep it quiet for now."

"The less said the better," Zeeman happily agreed.

"Well, I won't be a party to any cover-up," Franklin said. "Maybe that's the way you do things in this town, but it's not the way I operate. I'm going to file a report, even if you don't."

Rhostok turned his head slowly, until the tax agent was fixed in the sights of his glare.

"Let's get this straight, Franklin. I'm conducting this investigation. I don't want any information about what we found here revealed until I'm ready. In other words, you keep your damn mouth shut. You understand?"

The now profusely sweating tax agent stared back at him without responding.

Rhostok sent the other policeman out to the car for evidence bags and latex gloves.

The evidence bags turned out to be gallon-sized plastic freezer bags. Nicole watched Rhostok don the latex gloves, reach into the safe-deposit box, and carefully lift out the severed hand. He put the hand into the evidence bag, bloody stump downward, and sealed the bag. The giant policeman made no attempt to hide his disgust when Rhostok gave him the bag. Rhostok instructed him to put it in a freezer at the police station before it started to decompose, then come back to the bank to dust for fingerprints around the open metal box.

Separately, Rhostok carefully folded the thick wrapping paper and placed it in a second plastic bag. Nicole noticed he didn't give this bag to the other policeman.

At last they could leave the vault. Rhostok cautioned them not to touch anything on the way out.

The bank president was the last one to exit. As he closed the steel gate, a low growling noise started somewhere deep within the bowels of the building. It was a monstrous, low-throated rolling sound that grew in intensity until Nicole could feel the floor of the bank trembling beneath her feet.

Through the bars of the gate, she could see the safe-deposit box shaking in its half-open position.

The top of the box slammed shut.

The empty box vibrated until it came out of its slot and fell to floor.

Wendell Franklin's face went white with fear.

Nicole reached out in panic to Rhostok, who for some reason didn't seem frightened.

Eighteen

"What the hell's happening?" Franklin backed away nervously.

The rumbling continued, deep and menacing, until it finally expired with what seemed like a long sigh.

"It's just the earth settling," Rhostok said. "Another old mine tunnel collapsing."

"Mine tunnels?" Franklin asked. "The mining companies went out of business fifty years ago. All that stuff was supposed to be filled in by the State."

"You're talking hundreds of miles of tunnels on nine different levels under the Lackawanna Valley," Rhostok explained. "There's no way they could ever fill them all."

"They filled the ones under Scranton."

"Well, I guess they missed the ones under Middle Valley," Rhostok said. "So nature's doing the job for them. The tunnels fill up with water, the timbers rot, and they collapse."

"It felt like a small earthquake."

"Same principle. Usually the settling doesn't do any damage, but once in a while a building foundation cracks or a gas line breaks and we get an explosion."

"A hell of a place to live," Franklin muttered. "Right on top of an environmental disaster zone. You're lucky the EPA doesn't come in and condemn the whole town."

"It's not that big a deal," Rhostok shrugged.

He instructed Zeeman and the bank guard to wait for Bruckner to come back and take photos and do the fingerprint work. The rest of them were free to go.

Nicole was glad to get outside. Although the sun was setting, it would take a few hours before things cooled off. But the fresh evening air was a wonderful relief after the cramped and sticky confines of the vault. She paused on the front steps, still shaken by what she had seen inside. Wendell Franklin was rewinding the handkerchief around his finger.

"You'd better have a doctor look at that finger," Rhostok advised him. "You might need a tetanus shot."

"It's just a little cut," Franklin responded as he headed for his car. "An ice cube will stop the bleeding."

Nicole was leaning against one of the marble entrance columns, sucking the fresh air deep into her lungs.

"Are you okay?" Rhostok asked her.

"Not really," she admitted. "For a while there, I thought I was going to faint."

"Maybe you should sit down for a minute. Catch your breath."

"All I want to do is go home," she said, fumbling in her purse for her car keys.

"You shouldn't be driving," Rhostok said. "Not in your condition. I don't think it's safe."

"I'll be all right. Really, I feel fine now."

"I'm not so sure. You look pale, and your hands are shaking." Rhostok took away her car keys. "Come on, I'll take you home you in the patrol car."

Nicole was suddenly wary, having learned long ago that a police car wasn't necessarily a safe place for her to be.

"Give me back my keys," she demanded.

"You'll be safer in my car."

She looked around, hoping for an excuse not to go with him. But he had her keys, the streets were empty, and she certainly didn't want to go back into the bank.

"You'll take me straight home? No detours, no stopping at the police station?"

"No detours," he promised. "I'll take you straight home."

She entered the vehicle reluctantly, sitting as far away from him as she could. As if the short span of the front seat offered some sort of protection from him.

"You shouldn't be ashamed to admit you're scared," he said as he started the car. "Most people in your situation would be begging for protection."

"Why should I want protection?" She was accustomed to police officers offering "protection" when they really had something else in mind.

"Finding a human hand locked up in a safe-deposit box, I'd say that would frighten the average person."

She tugged at her skirt in a futile effort to cover her exposed knees. If she had known she was going to be riding in the front seat of a police car, she would have worn something a little more modest.

"Okay, I was shocked," she admitted. "Maybe disgusted is a better word. But why should I be frightened?"

"Didn't you think that what you found in the vault might have something to do with your husband's death? Be honest now. Wasn't that your first thought?"

It had been, of course, but she refused to admit it.

"Didn't it occur to you there might be a connection?" he persisted.

"My husband died of a heart attack," Nicole replied.

"You don't know that for certain."

"That's what the coroner said."

"Without an autopsy, he's just guessing at the cause of death."

"Don't you believe your own coroner?"

"Normally I would," he said. "But in this particular case, let's just say I'm still suspicious."

"You think I killed him? Okay, I admit it. I killed him."

She recalled those last feverish moments of lovemaking, Paul suddenly gasping for air, his head thrown back, and she, to her everlasting shame, mistakenly thinking it was merely the moment of ejaculation. Instead of stopping and possibly saving his life, she greedily squeezed her sweaty thighs tighter around his hips until his body went limp and he collapsed in her arms. Could she have saved him? Probably not. But she knew the question would haunt her for the rest of her life.

"He died in my arms." She turned away so he wouldn't see the tears in her eyes. "We were making love. He was on top of me. If anybody was responsible for my husband's death, it was me."

"That's probably how it was supposed to look," Rhostok said.

She spun around to slap him, but he grabbed her hand in midair and squeezed it until the pain made her forget her anger.

"I'm sorry." Rhostok let go of her hand. "That wasn't meant to be an accusation. I was just thinking out loud."

"Don't you think I feel guilty enough about what happened?" Nicole massaged her reddened wrist.

"I said I'm sorry."

"I know what you're doing. It's one of your police tricks. You think I murdered my husband and you're trying to act like we're in a private conversation to see if you can get me to say something incriminating. You're afraid if you took me in for formal questioning, I'd want to see a lawyer."

"If you had a lawyer, he'd be advising you to ask for police protection."

"I don't need police protection. I don't need anybody watching me. I can take care of myself."

Rhostok was driving slowly, picking his way along a circuitous route that wound through quiet, tree-shaded streets. He kept checking the rearview mirror, seemingly watching whether someone was following them. It was absurd behavior for a small-town policeman, she thought.

"Now what?" she asked. "You think we're being tailed?"

"You never know."

"You're really a piece of work," she said. "You don't trust anyone, do you?"

"It's the Russian way," he said. "We're a naturally suspicious people."

"Too suspicious, if you ask me." She folded her arms and slumped down in the seat. "This town gives me the creeps. Ever since I came here, I feel like every move I make is being watched. Like there's always somebody just out of sight, spying on me to see what I do."

"Really?" He kept checking the rearview mirror. "Did you ever actually see the person you think is watching you?"

"I didn't say it was just one person. Sometimes I think it's the whole damn town. Then again, maybe I'm just being paranoid."

"Not necessarily," Rhostok said. "Your instincts might be right."

"It's probably just my imagination. Maybe the real problem is that I feel so out of place here. It's so damned . . . Russian. I just don't fit in."

"But your background is Russian, or at least the name on your driver's license."

"Baronovich was my mother's family name. I never knew my real father." Seeing the question on his face, she quickly added, "I'd rather not talk about it, okay? Let's just say I thought coming here would be good for me, and it turned out to be a disaster. All I want to do now is get out of town."

"And go where? Back to Las Vegas?"

"How did you know about Vegas?"

"That's where Paul met you, wasn't it?"

"Yes, well, I definitely won't go back there. Maybe L.A., maybe San Francisco. Someplace where nobody knows me."

"I'm afraid that wouldn't do much good. They'd track you down and find you."

"They? Who are *they?*"

"The people who killed your husband. The same people who killed his father."

"Look, I know how my husband died. I was there, remember? Nobody else was in that room but the two of us. And I'm telling you he wasn't murdered."

"Things could have been done to him before he went into the bedroom."

"You're really incredible," she said.

"I don't want to frighten you, but you might be involved in something far more dangerous than you realize."

It was dark by the time they reached her house. Rhostok pulled up in the driveway and turned off the headlights. The neighborhood was quiet, except for a dog barking somewhere in the distance. The elderly owners of the house next door, Bogdan Spiterovich and his wife, Olga, were sitting on the swing on their front porch as they did every night. What would they think, she wondered, if they could hear the incredible conversation she was having with this policeman? Nevertheless, she made no move to leave the vehicle.

"Do you know how Paul's father died?" Rhostok asked.

"I heard you arguing with O'Malley about that. You think he was pushed, but O'Malley said it was suicide. I prefer to believe Paul. He said it was probably an accident. His father was eighty years old, and he had Alzheimer's. He might have stepped off the roof of that nursing home without even knowing where he was."

"In the first place, it wasn't a nursing home," Rhostok said. "It was a mental institution. In the second place, Vanya's Alzheimer's wasn't that bad yet. He was in there because he had a violent psychotic breakdown. He got up one morning, went outside, and pumped five rounds from a deer rifle into a car that was parked in front of his house."

"Paul never mentioned anything about the gun," she said.

"Vanya was being held in a high-security lockdown ward reserved for violent patients. On the night he died, he managed to get out of his locked cell, past the guards, and up onto the roof. Now how do you think an eighty-year-old man with Alzheimer's did that?"

"You're the cop. You tell me."

"I don't think he did it by himself. I think someone took him up there, the same person who threw him off the roof."

"But the coroner said it was suicide," she insisted, as if repeating it would make it so.

"The fingers on Vanya's right hand were broken before he died. A man doesn't do that to himself if he's going to commit suicide."

As Rhostok spoke, Nicole stared at the house that had once contained her dreams for the future. The two-story wooden frame building had a wraparound front porch and overhanging eaves, on a street where the "company houses" were once identical. Over the years, new additions, siding, paint, and landscaping had given each of the houses its own individual character. Paul's father had added elaborate gingerbread detailing to the house. It gave the structure a distinctly European character. But what seemed ornate and charming in the daylight took on an ominous dimension in the darkness.

"Your husband and his father are dead," Rhostok continued. "Now you open a safe-deposit box and find a human hand inside. Don't you think that's a warning of some kind? A sign that your life might be in danger?"

Nicole continued to stare straight ahead. The ghostly light of a full moon illuminated the front lawn but created deep black shadows on the side of the house. She was starting to imagine she could see some movement in those shadows. But every time she focused on the place where the movement seemed to occur, it stopped. Nicole was beginning to have second thoughts about spending the night alone. Although she didn't want to admit it, she was warming up to Rhostok's offer of police protection.

"Why would I be in any danger?" she asked, trying to keep her voice from betraying the fear that was growing inside her. "I didn't do anything wrong. I don't know anything about that hand or who put it in the box. I don't see what any of it has to do with me."

"Did you ever hear of a man named Ulyanov?" he asked. "Florian Ulyanov?

"No."

"What about Boris Cherevenko?"

"No."

"You're sure? Paul never mentioned their names?"

"Never. Names like that, I certainly would have remembered. Why?"

"They were friends of Paul's father. Good friends. They went to school with Vanya, right here in Middle Valley, and they all went through the Second World War together. In the same outfit."

"I never heard of them. Why?"

"Because they're dead. They were both murdered . . . in the five weeks before Paul's father was killed."

"That's terrible. But what does that have to do with me?"

"The right hands of all three men were mutilated."

Nicole knew where this was heading, but she refused to acknowledge it, hoping there was some mistake.

"What you found in the vault was a man's right hand," Rhostok said. "That can't be a coincidence. It's a warning."

"Why? Why does it have to be a warning?" She couldn't keep her voice from trembling. "Why are you trying to scare me?"

"If anybody's trying to scare you, it's whoever put that hand in the safe-deposit box. Since Paul and his father are already dead, the only person that warning could have been aimed at was you."

Nineteen

"If it was a warning, it couldn't have been intended for me," Nicole argued. "I didn't even know about the safe-deposit box."

"Then how did you get the key?"

"I . . . I found it on my bedroom floor." Seeing the skepticism in Rhostok's face, she quickly added an explanation. "It was under the dresser. It was in a little yellow envelope that looked like it had been taped to the bottom of the dresser years ago. But I didn't find it until the morning after Paul died."

"You didn't think the timing was a little too convenient? After being there for years, the key suddenly drops to the floor the day after your husband dies?"

"I can't explain it. Sometimes things happen like that. It's Fate."

"That's possible," Rhostok agreed. "It's also possible that someone slipped into your house during the night and put the key where they were sure you'd find it."

"Someone? Like who?" This was unbelievable, she thought.

"My guess is the same people who killed those three old men. The same people who ransacked the house."

"Paul said that was just vandalism," she recalled.

"That might be what it looked like to him. But to me, it looked like a search. Whoever it was, they went through the house very carefully. They went from the attic to the basement. They even dug holes in the cellar floor. I have no idea what they were looking for, but my guess is they found the safe-deposit key taped to the bottom of the dresser."

"But . . . if they found the key, why return it?" she asked, still fighting the idea.

"I assume they wanted you to open the box. Somehow they got into the bank, took whatever they found in the vault, and left the hand there. They left it as a warning to you."

"How could that be? At the bank, they said the vault hadn't been opened in fifty years."

"I don't care what they said. Based on the condition of the hand, it couldn't have been in there longer than a few hours. Somebody must have got in there this morning, maybe before the bank opened, and emptied that box. And if it wasn't meant as a warning, why else would they leave a severed hand behind? Why not just empty the box and leave? Someone wanted you to open that box and find that hand."

"But why pick on me?" she moaned. "I hardly know anybody in town. I never even heard of Middle Valley. What does all this have to do with me?"

"It might have something to do with you being married to Paul, or the fact that you're living in this house."

"No. I don't want to . . . I can't . . . believe you."

"There's a trail of death that leads from Arizona to Florida to Middle Valley and right here to this house. The house belonged to Paul's father. When he was killed, Paul inherited the house. Now he's dead, and you've inherited the house. That could mean you're next in line."

The fear and tension that had been building inside her finally erupted.

"Stop it!" she shouted, her voice almost choking on the words. "Stop trying to frighten me! I don't want to hear anymore. Just stop it! Stop it and leave me alone!"

She threw open the car door and ran up to the porch. Eyes blinded by tears, she fumbled in her purse to find her house keys. She felt Rhostok's powerful hand on her wrist and tried to pull away again, but his grip was too strong.

"I'm trying to help you," she heard him say.

Nicole struggled to free herself. She pounded her fists against his solid chest and tried to scream, but all she could manage was a pitiful whimper.

Finally, she fell against him. He absorbed her grief in silence, allowing her to surrender and cry herself out against his chest.

All the shock and tension of the last three days, the horror of Paul's sudden death, the awful disintegration of her hopes for the future, the horror she felt at the bank, and now the fear that her very life might be in danger, all spent itself and left her quietly whimpering and wanting him to hold her.

"I'll try to keep this quiet," he said. "The less anyone knows about what happened at the bank, the safer you'll be."

At first he kept his hands at his sides, as if he were afraid to embrace her. She pressed her body tighter against him, seeking protection in his strength. Her rich breasts flattened themselves against the solid wall of his chest. She could feel the leather of his pistol belt against her stomach.

Any other man would have swept her up and taken her inside, she thought. But Rhostok wasn't like any other man. All he did was stroke her hair and murmur a few soft words to comfort her. She felt safe in his arms.

"I'll send Otto Bruckner over when he gets done at the bank," he said gently. "He'll keep an eye on the house."

She held tighter to Rhostok, afraid to let go in the darkness, wishing desperately it could have been Paul, and feeling ashamed of the way her body was responding.

Twenty

Nicole was not a woman who frightened easily.

But she had never before been warned that a killer might be after her.

She insisted on Rhostok going through the house before he left, checking for any sign of intruders. She followed him from room to room, watching him test the locks on the doors and windows and peer into the closets. He paid special attention to the cellar, inspecting the door to the backyard to be certain it was secured from the inside. The strange holes that someone had dug in the dirt floor looked more ominous to her now. They were haphazard in location and shape. Some were narrow and deep, others resembled shallow graves. Seeing them now, after Rhostok's warning, she wondered if one of them was intended for her.

When Rhostok was satisfied the house was secure, he warned her not to open the front door to anyone except him or Otto Bruckner.

As soon as he left, she slid the deadbolt into place. She turned on all the downstairs lights, including the security spotlights that illuminated the backyard. For good measure, she propped a chair against both the front and kitchen doors. Then she hurried upstairs and locked herself in the master bedroom. Unwilling to lie down on the bed where her husband had died, she huddled in a corner where a window gave her a good view of any intruders approaching the house.

Locking the doors had brought her little comfort. No deadbolt could protect her from the inevitable questions a frightened mind asks itself.

The policeman had warned her that her life was in danger. Yet he didn't want her to leave Middle Valley.

Why not?

And how much of what he said was true?

Normally, she could tell when a man was lying. But this policeman had a face that was impossible to read, an expressionless mask that revealed nothing of his inner feelings. He had delivered a frightening mixture of fact and suspicion, but there was no anxiety in the way he spoke. Just that dispassionate voice and that earnest, strong-jawed face. He could have been talking about the weather, for all the emotion he showed. And yet, he had been telling her a tale of brutal murders that led right to her doorstep.

What reason would he have to lie to her about such awful matters?

His words, she realized, had turned her into a prisoner in her own house, so frightened she was hiding behind locked doors.

The house was all that she had left to show for her marriage to Paul. It was the one safe refuge she had found in her life, the one place where she had been able to hide from the past that haunted her.

Now even this haven was becoming simply another way station on the dreadful journey Fate had chosen for her. Was there a curse on this house, and was she, as the current owner, doomed to become its next victim? If that were so, she thought, perhaps she could break the curse by leaving. Tear up the will and get out of town as soon as possible. It seemed the rational thing to do.

And yet, deep down, she knew fleeing would solve nothing. She had done that too many times before, only to discover further misfortune awaiting her. If there were a curse, she was convinced, it was a curse that Fate visited upon her when it endowed her with features that men found irresistible. And now, cowering in the corner of the room where her husband had died, she was convinced there was no other explanation.

She never had trouble attracting men; there were those who would pay any price to be near her. Yet it was that very beauty, the flesh desired by so many men, that entrapped her, condemning her finally and, she thought, eternally to the hell her life had become. One man after another had plied her with false promises, leading her on journeys from New York to Miami and finally to Las Vegas, journeys that always ended dismally in a progression of shabby hotel rooms from which there seemed no escape.

Other women who worked with her sought temporary refuge from their similar plights in the sweet embrace of mind-altering substances: selecting, like delighted diners studying a menu, from the wide variety of pharmaceuticals always available from their patrons. It would be much cheaper and faster, she used to think, to escape by cutting her wrists in a warm bath; a bubble bath, perhaps, piled high with foam so she wouldn't see the hideous discoloration of the water. She was unable, however, to face the finality of that decision.

Nicole had been trapped in a life she didn't want, but one she had dared not end. Which was why, when she woke up one morning and found herself married to a man much older than she, a man with a long, deeply lined face and hair already turned gray, she didn't protest. She saw it as the blessed hand of Fate, intervening in her life to offer her a second chance. Until that morning, she thought of marriage as something eternally forbidden to her, a ritual and a way of life only normal women were destined to enjoy. Her new husband had oversized ears and watery eyes, and only a union pension for income. But he had a soft voice and a friendly smile and he was gentle and caring towards her.

Given the circumstances of their marriage, it was impossible for Paul not to know about the kind of life she had been living, but he didn't seem to care. All he wanted to do was take her with him to his hometown in Pennsylvania where he had inherited his father's house. She wasn't in love with him then; that would come later. Nevertheless, it seemed like the answer to her dreams: the chance for a fresh start, the opportunity to wake up in the morning without feeling disgust for what she had done the night before.

But now it appeared that she had once again run away from a bad situation only to find herself trapped in a worse one. At least in Las Vegas no one was trying to kill her.

What finally drew her out of the corner was an ugly, yet familiar smell creeping into her nostrils.

At first, she thought it was her imagination playing tricks. She tried to ignore it. Tried to forget the bitter memories it brought to mind. Yet the acrid aroma grew stronger until its presence was impossible to deny. She looked out the window. The policeman Rhostok promised had already arrived, but he was still in his car out front, probably filling out some forms. He was close enough, however, to respond quickly to any cries for help.

Quietly, she unlocked the bedroom door and made her way downstairs, dreading what she was certain she was going to find.

Sitting in her dead husband's favorite chair was Vassily Zhamnov, smoking one of those foul-smelling Red Star cigarettes that could be purchased only in the Russian-owned grocery stores.

Vassily was a lean man with a narrow face. His black hair was combed straight back from his forehead, curling slightly at the ears. As usual, he wore expensive yet strangely ill-fitting clothing: a pale blue silk shirt and gray slacks that belonged on a man much heavier than he.

He was the very last person she wanted to see at this particular moment in her life.

The man she thought she had finally escaped.

"How did you get in here?" she asked in a trembling voice.

Vassily's smile was more brutal than friendly. That he had somehow managed to enter the locked house without a sound didn't surprise her. Nor was she surprised that he had managed to slip inside without alerting the policeman outside. This was a small town, unaccustomed to men like Vassily.

"I come to offer my condolences on the death of your husband," he said.

"You came here all the way from Las Vegas just to tell me that? How did you find out?"

Vassily shrugged, dismissing her questions with a wave of his hand. He inhaled deeply on his Russian cigarette and let out a slow stream of smoke before speaking.

"You will please to tell me exactly what you are finding in the safe-deposit box."

Twenty-One

Proper police procedure would be to photograph the hand and send it down to the county morgue, where body parts were normally stored until they could be reunited with the appropriate corpse. But it was the first solid clue that Rhostok's murder investigation had turned up. And coming so soon after he had learned about the murders in Florida and Arizona, he wasn't about to give it up that easily. He spent the next few hours contacting local hospitals and checking regional accident reports. He could find no record of any recent amputations or accidental dismemberments, no logical explanation for the gruesome discovery.

As the evening progressed, he was haunted by the thought that the hand looked familiar. He was convinced he had seen the odd curvature of the misshapen finger somewhere, on someone before. Was it someone he knew? A local resident? A man he had seen in a photograph?

Finally, exhausted, he left the hand in a freezer at the police station and took the oilskin wrapper home, where he could study the strange message it contained without anybody asking questions.

Twice during the night, he turned on the light to study the words. Although the lettering was Cyrillic in style, it wasn't standard Russian. It was Old Church Slavonic, the antiquated language now reserved for use in Orthodox churches. Although the spoken version was quite similar to modern Russian, the written version was unintelligible to the uninitiated. He studied it carefully to be certain he had read it correctly. To confirm the name he remembered from stories his grandfather had told him.

He wondered what his grandfather would have thought of the contents of the box. Probably he would have buried it all in the Russian cemetery: the hand, the paper, and maybe even the box itself, consigned it all to the earth, perhaps with a prayer. It would have been a perfectly understandable, even predictable reaction for someone who followed the old ways.

And later, perhaps, over a glass of tea and a fresh pipeful of tobacco, his grandfather would once again tell the bizarre story of the "Holy Devil" who emerged from the Siberian wilderness to exert his strange power over the Imperial throne. It was the tale of a crude, semiliterate monk who became for a time the most powerful man in Russia. They called him a holy man and a whoremonger, a drunkard and a prophet, a miracle worker considered by many to be the Antichrist and revered by others as a saint.

The old Cossack would have speculated that the hand might belong to that infamous figure, the man whose name was inscribed in thick pencil strokes on the oilskin wrapper.

And perhaps somewhere in there, in the complicated mixture of myth and history so typical of the old man's reminiscences, would be an obscure detail or clue that might eventually lead to an answer to the question that kept Rhostok awake.

But the old man was gone, dead and buried and unable to offer any insights. And Rhostok, although raised in the Russian tradition of mysticism and superstition, had a logical mind that sought rational answers. Given the condition of the hand in the vault, it was impossible for him to believe that it could ever have belonged to the legendary Mad Monk, in spite of what the Cyrillic lettering on the wrapping paper said.

After all, Grigorii Effimovich Rasputin was murdered in Russia nearly a century before, on a snowy December night in 1916.

"But how could Rasputin become the most powerful man in Russia?" the boy asked. *"Surely the Tsar was more powerful. Didn't the Tsar command the armies, the people, and all the lands of the Russian Empire?"*

The old man smiled. The boy was learning his lessons well.

"The Tsar's power was only over things of this world," the old man explained. *"Rasputin had powers that went beyond the ability of mortal men to comprehend. He could predict the future. He could read minds. He was able to cure the sick. He experienced apparitions of Our Lady. He had the power to control people's thoughts, and make them do his bidding."*

"There were other men in history who had those abilities, too," the boy said. *"Nostradamus and the saints. They had such gifts, too, didn't they?"*

The old man welcomed the boy's comments. It showed the young lad was developing the capacity for independent thought.

"But each of those was given only a single gift from God," the old man said. *"Nostradamus was given the gift of prophecy. Saint Bernadette was blessed with visitations by the Virgin. Saint Francis was granted the ability to cure the sick. But Rasputin had all those gifts and more."*

"Was that how he became so powerful?" the boy asked.

"That was what first brought him to the attention of the Tsar and the Empress," the old man said. *"They recognized him as a holy man. But what made them kneel before him was a very special gift known as the* zagovariat krov."

"The power to talk to the blood?" the boy asked, eager to show off his growing command of the Russian language.

"Yes," the old man said. *"The* zagovariat krov. *Rasputin could stop*

the flow of blood by talking to the victim. And that was what gave him such influence over the Russian throne."

Twenty-Two

After a restless night, Rhostok wasn't happy to see the Channel One Action News van waiting for him at the police station in the morning.

It was never good news when the TV people came to Middle Valley. The last time they showed up was to interview the families of four high school seniors who died in a car accident on prom night. Before that, it was to videotape the wreckage of a house that was blown apart in a gas explosion. Since he had had no reports of anything so disastrous happening overnight, he could only conclude that the reporter had somehow, in spite of his efforts to keep it quiet, found out about the contents of the safe-deposit box and wanted to pursue the story.

The van was parked in a police slot, right below the Official Use Only sign. Whoever left it there would probably claim they didn't notice the sign. He debated writing a ticket, but decided against it. There was no point in making enemies with the media.

He took a deep breath and squared his shoulders before entering the building.

Fortunately, there were no cameramen inside.

Just a stunning young blonde, immaculately dressed in a bright red jacket and skirt, the hemline of which ended halfway down her thighs. She turned and gave him the same dazzling smile he had seen her use on TV.

He recognized her immediately. Her name was Robyn something . . . Robyn Cronin, that was it. She wasn't one of the anchors, or even one of the first-string reporters who filled in for the anchors on weekends. She had first shown up on camera a few months ago, doing special features. Sometimes spooky things, like that story about the little girl who was revived after being clinically dead for sixteen minutes and later told the doctors about going through a tunnel of light and visiting her dead grandmother.

He greeted her by name, which increased the brilliance of her smile.

She was shorter than he expected. On TV she looked taller. But then he remembered reading that a lot of movie and TV personalities were short. It was all camera tricks that made you think they were normal height.

He led the reporter into his office, a small room filled with mismatched wooden and metal furniture that looked like it came from the Salvation Army. The only personal item he had brought with him when he inherited the office was the wire cage in the corner that housed the two yellow mine canaries, which Rhostok maintained as a memorial to his father's unnecessary death. The canaries, whose ancestors' sensitivity to explosive gases had saved the lives of generations of miners, burst into frantic song at Rhostok's arrival.

He unzipped his jacket and tossed his hat on a display case that was filled with dusty old Commonwealth of Pennsylvania law books, and motioned the reporter to a heavy chair in front of his desk. She placed her purse on the desk between them. It was an expensive black leather bag with a gold chain, the top flap left carelessly open.

Just as he feared, she immediately asked about yesterday's events at the bank. The sudden alertness in her eyes warned him to be careful. She was looking for a story, and probably ready to make him part of it if he stood in the way.

"How did you find out about it so fast?" he asked.

"A confidential source."

She was giving him that bright perky smile she used on TV, tilting her head towards him like they were supposed to be buddies or something.

"Probably the bank guard," Rhostok muttered. "Either him or that idiot from the Department of Revenue."

He turned his back to her and poured some birdseed into the plastic feeder for his canaries.

"I hope you're not planning to put anything about it on TV," he said, his back still turned.

"Why not?" she asked.

"Middle Valley's a small town," he said, trying to keep it low-key. Hoping maybe she'd lose interest and go away. "I'd hate to see people getting worked up over nothing."

"You haven't contacted the coroner's office yet," she challenged him. "Why not?"

"Because as far as I know, nobody's dead. We don't have a body."

"Just part of one."

"That's right. Anyway, there's nothing unusual about it." He was doing his best to sound casual, to make the discovery seem less than it was. "We find all kinds of things around town. Especially in the spring, when the thaw comes. You'd be surprised what gets lost in the snow. Wallets, jewelry. For Christ's sake, even missing animals. We had a championship

Labrador retriever go missing two years ago. The owner claimed it was stolen, it was supposed to be worth three thousand dollars. A show dog. They found it at the end of his driveway when the snow melted. The dog must have been out taking a leak and a snowplow came by and buried it."

After assuring himself that the canaries were happy and healthy, Rhostok walked around behind the reporter, where he opened the top of the coffee maker and put in a new paper filter. She turned in her chair to face him. Her bag was now on her lap.

"This isn't springtime," she said. "And we're not talking about finding some lost object in the snow. We're talking about a human hand, found inside a locked safe-deposit box in a bank vault."

Rhostok poured four heaping scoops of coffee into the filter, added a spoonful of chicory, and measured in two cups of water.

"Well, you see, that's why we were able to find it," he said, attempting to make a joke out of the discovery, still hoping to convince her not to take it too seriously. "If it was outside, the raccoons would have gotten it. Or the skunks, or somebody's dog. There wouldn't be anything left for us to find." He turned and smiled. "I hope you like your coffee strong. I make it Cossack-style, double-strength with some chicory."

She was a pretty woman, Rhostok thought, if you ignored the fact of how short she was, no more than five feet or so. She wasn't a natural beauty like Nicole Danilovitch, but like most of the women he saw on TV, the skillful use of cosmetics enhanced her best features. Her eyebrows were carefully plucked and shaped. The application of bluish-gray shadow made her eyes appear larger and more inviting than they did on TV. A brush of facial powder highlighted her cheekbones and gave the illusion of a slimmer face. The bright red color on her lips looked like it was painted on, with the upper lip almost imperceptibly lighter than the lower one. It was a lot of makeup for early morning, he thought. But she probably had to keep herself ready to go on camera at any time. He assumed her blonde hair was dyed, because nobody he knew had hair of so golden a shade. He took an odd delight in being this close to a TV personality, so close that he could smell the delicate and probably very expensive fragrance that lingered about her.

The coffee machine sputtered and hissed as the water boiled and dripped through the coffee grounds, the coarse aroma quickly overpowering her perfume.

Rhostok let out a heavy sigh and slumped down in his chair. He had a long day ahead of him, and he wanted to get her out of here without revealing any more than he had to.

"You think I'm trying to cover up something, don't you?" he challenged her.

"I didn't say that."

"I know you're looking for a story," he said, with what he hoped was a friendly smile. "That's your job. But the fact of the matter is, there's no story here." Sensing that she wasn't buying into his denials, he made one last effort. "At least, no story worth putting on TV."

"I'd like to see the hand," she said.

"Coffee'll be done in a minute."

"Thanks, but I want to see the hand."

"You think that's going to tell you something? It's just a piece of meat."

"It's a place to start."

"There's no law that says I have to show it to you."

"If you refuse, it's a better story," she parried. "I could have a camera crew here in half an hour. We'd be on the news at noon with your refusal to cooperate."

Her voice was flat, as if she didn't give a damn whether he cooperated or not. He felt like telling her to go to hell, but he was afraid she might quote him on that. And then go snooping around town to see what she could find out from someone else.

It didn't take a genius to figure out what she'd do next. Nicole Danilovitch was up there in the house on Dundaff Street with Otto on guard outside. She was probably scared and lonely, even though she tried not to show it. If this reporter went up there, the widow would probably think Rhostok went back on his word to keep it quiet, and she just might blurt out the whole story about how he had told her that her husband and his father were murdered, and how the hand was supposed to be some kind of warning from the killer.

Jesus, he could see it on the TV now: *The Middle Valley Murders, Details on the Six O'Clock News.* Or maybe: *Serial Killer Stalks a Local Russian Community! Tune in to an Exclusive Action News Report.* The town would go into a panic. The shotguns would come out of the closets, ready to cut down the Federal Express guy if he didn't properly identify himself. Reporters from *America's Most Wanted,* maybe even *Dateline* or *48 Hours* would show up and start interviewing the old people, play on their fears and superstitions until they'd lock themselves up in their houses.

He had already tried lying to the reporter. The only remaining option, as far as Rhostok could see, was to pretend to cooperate, give her a few meaningless facts, and ask her to hold off on any story until he could investigate further. It was worth a try.

He retrieved the hand from the freezer compartment of the refrigerator in the back room. Some ice crystals had formed inside the plastic evidence bag, partially obscuring the contents. The hand was frozen brick-solid now, its pink skin covered with a patina of white frost.

"I put it in the freezer to preserve it," he explained. "Seemed silly to send it to the morgue. The coroner's office is already overworked. It's not worth bothering them about a little thing like this."

He offered her the plastic bag for closer examination, but at first she declined. It made an icy clunk when he dropped it, a little too casually, on the desk in front of her, right next to her purse. He watched her try to hide her disgust. He adjusted the position of the freezer bag so she could see the hand better.

"Is that how it was when you found it?" she asked. "The fingers partially bent like that?"

"That's the normal position of human fingers when death relaxes the muscles. You'll see them curling up that way on corpses."

The ice crystals quickly started to melt in the warmth of the room, fogging up the plastic.

"You want me to open the bag so you can see it better?" he asked.

The reporter made an unpleasant face and shook her head, apparently unprepared for his offer. Rhostok leaned back in his chair and smiled.

"What are you planning to do with it?" she asked.

"I don't know," he shrugged. "Keep it and see if anybody claims it, I guess."

"You make it sound like Lost and Found."

Her eyes never once moved from the freezer bag. He was surprised by the intensity of her focus.

"There's not much else we can do," he said. "After a reasonable time, if we can't figure out whose hand it is, we'll get rid of it. Cremate it, maybe, or else bury it in the cemetery, where it belongs."

"Have you done any tests?"

"We lifted some fingerprints before we froze it. We'll check the prints with the FBI, see if they can find a match."

"How long will that take?"

She edged closer to the bag. You'd think the damn thing was alive, the way she acted. Rhostok watched with mild amusement, waiting to see what she was going to do.

"Running the prints would only take fifteen minutes, maybe, the way they're computerized. But the chances of finding a match are pretty minimal. The only prints they have on file are criminals, veterans, civil servants like me, people who have a reason to be fingerprinted. You're talking very small numbers, compared to what the FBI would like you to think."

She was working up her courage to open the bag, he could tell. Her mouth was set in a grim line, those cute little red lips suddenly narrow and determined.

"It doesn't smell," he assured her. "It's frozen solid."

She was young for a reporter, he thought, but then TV is different. Most of the reporters he met were from the *Scranton Times and Tribune*, older guys who tried to act like they had seen it all, like they were too important to get excited over a fire or a car crash or somebody committing suicide. All they wanted was the name and the age, the time it happened, and the cause of death, and they had to get back to Scranton, like some major news event was about to happen down there. But this girl, no older than her mid-twenties, was sitting here and swallowing her disgust and looking at the hand like it was going to reveal something about itself.

He had to respect her for that.

"Is this normal?" she asked. "I mean the way the wrist is cut? It looks almost surgical."

"That depends on how it happened," he said. "Say it was caught in a lawn mower. Guy reaches in to clear the blade, and zap, there you go. A power mower would slice it off nice and clean."

She still didn't open the bag, as if she were afraid she'd somehow be contaminated by the contents.

"Cut off by a lawn mower and it ends up in a bank vault?" She shook her head. "You'll have to do better than that."

"You're wrong there," he said. "I don't have to do anything. I have no indication there's been a crime committed. It could have been an accident. But unless somebody shows up missing his right hand, we'll never know. I'll just bury it and forget about it."

The coffee was finished dripping, so he filled two styrofoam cups.

"You take sugar?" he asked.

"A little Equal, if you have it."

"Cream?"

"No, thanks."

He sprinkled a spoonful of Coffeemate into his cup, just enough to take the edge off the thick black liquid. He put the other cup in front of her and took his seat again, where he awaited her next move.

She turned the freezer bag over and examined the hand from different angles. The frost quickly melted, giving her a better view of the details. He watched her while he sipped slowly on his coffee, careful not to burn his tongue. In the background, the canaries chirped happily while they hopped from their perches to the feeder and back again.

"You better let me put it away," he finally said. "I don't want it to thaw out."

Reluctantly, she handed the bag back to him. He ran his fingers along the top, to be sure she hadn't accidentally opened the airtight plastic ridges.

"It's a big hand," she said. "The hand of a strong man, I'd imagine. Fingers are thick, there's some sort of pockmarked scarring on the back. It looks like he did manual labor at some point, but not recently. There aren't any calluses on the palm, and the fingernails are carefully manicured."

"You sound like a cop," he said. "Did they teach you that in journalism school?"

She looked up at him and blew across the top of her coffee to cool it off. With her lips puckered up like that, she looked like she was blowing him a kiss. Cute.

"Of course, you saw those little details, too," she said. "You probably have them all written down in a report somewhere."

She was fishing again, he thought.

"I took some notes," he responded cautiously.

He was taking another sip of coffee, feeling good about the way he was able to handle the reporter, when she gave him that perky little smile again.

"I understand the hand was wrapped in a piece of brown paper," she said. "There was some strange writing on the paper. Was it in Russian?"

He stopped with the cup resting on his lip. Trying desperately to think of an answer that would stop any further questions, and knowing there wasn't any.

Twenty-Three

"I can't discuss that," Rhostok said.

The sudden gleam in her eyes warned him it was the wrong thing to say.

"So you confirm there was some sort of message on the wrapping paper?"

He remained silent, afraid to deny it, because he wasn't sure how much she already knew.

"I'll take that as a yes," she said, and abruptly changed the line of questioning. "Let's talk about Nicole Danilovitch, the woman who found the hand."

"What about her?"

"Well, she's the central figure, isn't she? Kind of a mystery woman, too, from what I hear. Showed up as a new bride around four weeks ago. Suddenly she's a widow, checking out the contents of her late husband's safe-deposit box. Where'd she come from? I'm assuming you did a background check on her." The blonde reporter leaned closer across the desk and gave Rhostok a conspiratorial smile. "Come on, tell me about her."

Rhostok pushed himself back in his swivel chair until the wheels rolled off the plastic carpet protector. He wanted to keep a distance between himself and the attractive reporter, to give himself some time to think.

"There's no law that says I have to tell you anything," he muttered.

"A Las Vegas showgirl marries a local citizen, and a month later he's dead," she continued. "What was your feeling about that?"

"I felt sorry for her."

"What about him? The way he died, that was kind of . . . well, unusual, wasn't it?"

"Not particularly. A lot of men go that way. Women, too."

"But still, you were suspicious. You wanted blood tests done."

"A standard toxicology test. Nothing unusual about that."

"That was the second death in the family in a couple of months," she pressed on. "What about the way the husband's father died? You thought there was something suspicious about his death, too, didn't you?"

Her line of questioning, the amount of information she had, and the way she was already connecting the information took him by surprise. Rhostok had some experience with the media, but it was all on routine matters. He had never before encountered a reporter like Robyn Cronin.

"How did you come up with all this stuff?" he asked.

"That's confidential."

"Baloney. You found out from someone at the coroner's office."

"We can't reveal our sources," she said in a smug voice. "We're pledged to keep their identities confidential, unless they tell us otherwise."

"You want to keep your sources confidential, but you don't want anybody trying to hide anything from you. Shouldn't it work both ways?"

"So you admit you're trying to hide something?"

She rose and came around the side of the desk, effectively trapping him against the wall. She sat on the edge of the desk, the soft flesh of her buttocks molding itself against the sharp angle of the wood. The movement pulled her already-short skirt dangerously farther up her thighs. She didn't seem to notice. Or then again, he thought, maybe it was intentional.

"Just because I don't tell you something doesn't mean I'm hiding it," he said.

"Now you're pulling a Clinton on me."

She was smiling and acting playful, maybe even flirting a little, like it was some kind of game. She was so near, he could have reached out if he wanted to and put his hand on the glossy black stockings that encased her legs. So near that he could smell, mixed in with the flowery aroma of perfume, the musky smell of female flesh. He tried to keep from staring at the hemline of her skirt. Concentrate on the face, he told himself. This was no time for sex fantasies. He could see a thin film of perspiration above her upper lip, glistening on her powdered skin. She seemed a little nervous, he thought. She moved her purse again, keeping it between them. As if she were worried someone was going to steal it in here.

"We don't seem to be making much progress here, Chief Rhostok. Let's start over again, okay?"

"Now don't go calling me chief," he said. "I'm just the acting police chief. It's strictly a temporary appointment, and I don't want anybody to think I'm claiming otherwise. Just call me Rhostok, like everybody else does."

"All right, Rhostok," she said, impatiently. "Let's get back to the beginning. Do you know whose hand it was?"

"No."

"Do you have any hunches or suspects?"

Hunches? For God's sake, where'd she get this language, from old movies?

"No."

"Do you have any idea why the hand was locked up in a bank vault?"

"No."

The smile disappeared from her face.

"You're not making this easy," she said.

"I'm being honest."

"Okay, what about the woman who had the key to the box?"

"What about her?" he shot back. "She just buried her husband. You want to go up there and stick a microphone in her face? Ask her, 'How do you feel about your husband now, Mrs. Danilovitch?' See if maybe you could get her to cry in front of the camera?"

"I'm just trying to get at the truth," the reporter said.

"You're trying to make something out of nothing."

"The truth never hurt anybody," she said.

"You're wrong there," he said. "People get shot, they get divorced, they go to jail, they even commit suicide, because somebody found out the truth about them. Sometimes it's better to keep the truth to yourself, like the priests do in confession."

"You're not a priest. You're a cop. And I'm a reporter. Now look, I know there's a story here. There are two ways I can handle it. I can make you look good, like you're a smart cop, doing a great job. The kind of problem-solver who deserves to be promoted to chief of police."

She shifted her position on the desk to get closer to him. He could hear the smooth rustle of her pantyhose as she moved. Focus, he warned himself. Keep focused and don't be distracted by her movements, which were probably part of her technique for getting the information she wanted.

"What's the other way?" he asked.

"The other way isn't very good. I can make you look like you're conducting a cover-up, that you're sitting on the investigation, hoping it'll all go away."

See now, there it was: the threat. That's the way they always operate, he thought. Just like *60 Minutes*. Don't cooperate with them, and they threaten to make a fool of you on TV.

"Why are you pushing so hard on this?" he asked. "Why don't you just wait till I find out what's going on? You think some other reporter is going to come in here and get the whole story before you do?"

"I could go on the air right now with what I have," she said. "The hand in the vault, the mysterious widow, the suspicious deaths of the husband and his father. It's a hell of a story."

"You don't have a story. All you have is a couple of unconnected facts."

"I don't need to have the whole story. That's not the way TV works. All I have to do is ask the same questions on the air that I've been asking you here. And then report that you refused to answer me."

"You get an idea in your head, you don't give up, do you?"

"I never give up," she answered, pulling herself farther up on his desk and crossing her legs. "But I could keep this story off the air for the time being, if you cooperate with me."

"You could do that?"

"If I tell my boss you're cooperating with me, I'm sure we could work it out."

"What sort of cooperation did you have in mind?"

She leaned towards him. Her proximity was starting to annoy Rhostok.

Ever since she showed up, she had been getting too damn close to him, walking around the desk when he pushed his chair against the wall, and now perched on his desk so close her knees were almost touching him.

"You tell me everything," she said. "Absolutely everything you know about this case."

"I tell you everything. And then what happens?"

"Then you keep me up to date on your progress, and I keep the story off the air until you're ready to go public. And of course, I get the exclusive on it."

She fixed that perky little smile on him and gave her shoulders a shrug, as if it were all so simple that he should agree immediately.

He reached for his coffee cup. The sudden move seemed to startle her. She quickly slid her purse out of his reach. He looked up at her. Something funny in her eyes, he thought. She had been looking directly at him all this time, eyeball to eyeball, trying to look sincere and honest, and then she suddenly shifts her eyes and she's worried about her purse.

"I don't know," he said, cautiously. "I don't know if I can trust you."

"I give you my word."

"Your word."

"You won't accept my word?"

"I'm not sure," he stalled. "Maybe I should consult my canaries."

"Your canaries?" She frowned, looking confused.

He nodded at the cage behind her.

"Those are mine canaries. In addition to detecting mine gas, they're very sensitive to changes in sound frequencies. That makes them natural lie detectors. If there's any stress in your voice, any tension that suggests you're lying to me, they can detect that. It strikes some kind of harmonic resonance in their inner ears, and it makes them nervous. They start jumping around."

The reporter turned to look at the canary cage. Rhostok had to smile, it was so easy. While she was distracted, he reached over and grabbed her purse.

"That was just bullshit about the canaries," he said, when she turned back and saw him pawing through her handbag. "You're pretty gullible for a reporter."

She gave him a shrug and that what-the-hell look that told him she wasn't going to fight it, she was too much of a professional for that.

"I assume you have a permit for this," he said, pulling a small flat .25 caliber automatic from her purse. He removed the clip and ejected a bullet from the chamber before placing it on the desk.

Twenty-Four

He was more interested in the other item, the reason she had been moving the purse around so that it stayed in front of him. It was a slim black Japanese tape recorder, no longer than a pack of cigarettes and only a third as thick. The small silver lettering said it was voice-activated. A narrow window revealed two circular cores of tape.

"Amazing how they design these things," he said, watching the way the tape started turning at the sound of his voice and stopped when he stopped talking.

Without another word, he fumbled at the tiny buttons until he found the EJECT, popped out the cassette, and dropped it into the remnants of her coffee.

"There's a law against that, taping a conversation without the other person's knowledge," he said.

"You just destroyed the evidence."

"It's not worth making a big deal about," he shrugged, rising and crossing the room. "I'll fix you another cup of coffee."

He took out the soggy brown filter, put in a new one and soon the room was once again filled with the pleasant aroma of brewing coffee.

"I'm surprised you're not throwing me out," she said. "Most cops would."

"There was a time when I would have," he said. "But being the acting police chief, I've got to be more diplomatic."

"It wouldn't hurt you to be more cooperative, too."

Rhostok watched while the coffee machine coughed and gasped and once again began to spew its narrow stream of dark fluid into the glass pot.

"I'd like to explain something to you," he said, without turning to face her. "Why I'd like to keep this business about the hand quiet for a little longer, at least until I get a few more facts."

"I'm listening."

"You've got to keep in mind the mentality of the people here. Middle Valley is a different kind of town. Most of our residents trace their roots back to Russia. They're either immigrants themselves, or the children or grandchildren of immigrants. And new immigrants are still coming over. Mostly relatives of the people already here. If anything, the town is getting to be more Russian every year."

"I already know that," she said in a bored voice. "Our station did some interviews up here when the Soviet Union was breaking apart."

"If you go back and look at those interviews, you'll see the kind of attitudes I have to deal with." He filled two styrofoam cups with fresh coffee and brought them back to his desk. "The Russians have always been a mystic people. They believe in miraculous icons and omens that foretell the future and in holy men who can cure illnesses by the laying on of hands. When the Russian immigrants came to Middle Valley, they brought their superstitions and religious practices with them."

He took a long sip of coffee. He noticed she wasn't drinking hers.

"We've got three different Russian churches here, each of which practices its own version of the Orthodox faith. And we've also got some splinter groups who worship in empty storefronts and private homes. The *Khlysty* believe they can reach salvation through wild sex orgies. The *Molakane* are pacifists. The *Dyriniki* worship the sky through a hole in the roof. And the *Bozhe Lyudi* call themselves the Children of God and supposedly performed ritual mutilation of their women in the Old Country. Now those sects might seem strange to outsiders, but they're just a few of the underground cults that exist in Russia. And we've got them here, just like any other Russian immigrant community."

"You said something about priests who cure illnesses," she said, still not having touched her coffee. "Are there any of those in Middle Valley?"

"The most famous would be *Episkop* Sergius," Rhostok said. "He claims to be carrying on what's known as the *starechestvo* tradition." Seeing her questioning look, he explained, "Those were the holy men who wandered through the Russian countryside in the old days, preaching the word of God and curing the sick."

"Did they really . . . I mean, cure the sick?"

"From everything I ever heard, yes. My grandfather used to tell me stories about them. In those days, there were no doctors in the country-side. When people got sick, they depended on folk remedies, or waited for a visiting *starets* to cure them."

"And this . . . what did you call him . . . *Episkop* . . . ?"

"It means Bishop."

". . . this *Episkop* Sergius, is he still here? In Middle Valley?"

"He's still here," Rhostok said. Somehow the conversation had taken an odd turn, he thought. Her questioning now seemed less aggressive, less confident. But as long as she wasn't pressing him about the mysterious hand, he was happy to answer her questions. "Sergius is in charge of the Old Ritual Russian Orthodox Church of Saint Sofia. It's kind of run-down now, but it's still a beautiful church."

"I'd like to know more about him . . ." she started to say, and then seemed to find a need to explain her interest. "There might be a story in it."

"Well, in the first place, he's not a real *Episkop*. At least not of the established Orthodox faith."

"But he has a church . . ."

"It's an autocephalic church," Rhostok said. "That means it's self-governing, which gives Sergius the right to give himself any title he wants. He came here from a monastery in Siberia, and when he discovered that Saint Sofia didn't have a resident priest, he moved into the rectory and installed himself as head of the church. Saint Sofia wasn't much in those days. The church was built by the Old Believers, a fundamentalist group that was run out of Russia by the mainline Orthodox Church. According to my grandfather, all the Old Believers wanted to do was worship the way their ancestors did. When they refused to accept changes in the liturgy, their homes were destroyed, their villages leveled, and their priests were burned alive. Twenty thousand Old Believers were slaughtered in the name of reform. The survivors went underground. Some came to America. They settled around Erie and Pittsburgh, and here in Middle Valley, where they built Saint Sofia.

"But by the time Sergius showed up, the building was falling apart. The Old Believers who built the church were dying off, and their children were moving away. There was only a handful of parishioners left, barely enough to support a priest. Yet within a year, Sergius managed to turn things around and developed a thriving parish."

"How?"

"By working miracles. Curing people."

"A faith healer?"

"He preferred to call them miracle cures. He claimed to have the power to cure any illness."

"And the people believed him?"

"Not after the first cure," Rhostok said. "Russians may be superstitious, but we're also cynical. It took three or four cures before the parishioners began to believe in him. Pretty soon, people were coming from as far away as Reading and Philadelphia. They claimed he was able to cure them of cancer, lung disease, leukemia, diabetes, almost anything you can name."

"Was it true? I mean, did he really cure people?"

"There was never any careful investigation, not the kind you'd get in the Catholic Church or the traditional Orthodox Church. Some of the so-called cures turned out to be cases of wishful thinking, temporary remissions like the kind that happen with any illness. But others . . . others were people on their deathbeds, people with terminal illnesses, who got up and walked after he prayed over them. And I know at least five of those people who are still alive today, twenty years later. They still go to his church, every single morning.

"There's an old woman who lives in his rectory now; she works as his housekeeper. When she was living with her husband, she was diagnosed with inoperable cervical cancer. She was given four months to live. That was twenty years ago. Sergius supposedly placed his hands on her abdomen and prayed over her all night. In the morning, they found him slumped on the floor, exhausted. But the woman was cured. She left her husband and devoted her life to Sergius."

"That's incredible."

"Apparently not for a *starechestvo*," Rhostok said. "According to the old legends, the *starechestvo* had the power to heal the sick, to look into the future, and to see into the minds of men and read their thoughts."

"You're not just making this up, are you?" she said, some of her former cynicism creeping back into her voice.

"The *starechestvo* is an old Russian tradition," Rhostok went on. "Dostoevski wrote about a *starets* named Zosima who made his disciples stronger with the gift of self-knowledge and helped them in their struggle for spiritual improvement. It all sounds well and good, all that business about healing the sick and guiding the way to spiritual improvement, but there's a dark side, too. The *starets* requires complete obedience from his disciples. He exerts total authority over their minds. The legends say that a true *starets* can read the thoughts of other people and eventually absorb their will into his own, taking absolute control over their thoughts."

"But if he can cure the sick . . ." Robyn whispered. "Does Sergius still perform cures?"

"I'm not sure," Rhostok said. "He hasn't performed any public healings for a long time. Attendance at his church has dropped off, almost to the point it was when he first arrived. Some people who know him, the few that will talk about what goes on in the church, say he's desperately looking for a way to restore his powers."

He caught himself, afraid that he might already have told her too much. She was clever, the way she went about drawing out all these details, sounding as if she were fascinated by the faith-healing ability of Sergius and the *starets* legends. Was it possible, he wondered, that she might already suspect that the man whose name was on the brown wrapping paper was once a *starets* himself, and one of the most famous miracle healers in Russian history?

"All I'm trying to do is point out what might happen if you put the story on TV before we have all the facts," he said. "People around here still have Old World attitudes and superstitions, even the ones who are first- and second-generation."

"Like you?"

"The old ways die slowly," he said, ignoring her comment. "People hear about a hand in a locked vault, and if I can't tell them why it's there or whose hand it is, they're going to come up with their own supernatural explanations. They'll say it's a sign from God, or a miracle, or maybe even the work of the Antichrist."

"That's absurd," she said.

"To you, maybe. But that's the way people think up here, especially the older ones."

"A sign from God," she murmured. "The work of the Antichrist . . . it's starting to sound like an episode of *Unsolved Mysteries*." He could see her mind calculating how it would play on TV. "Then again, the religious over-tones could give the story an extra dimension. I could interview some of the Old Believers and that other group, what did you call them, the *Khlysty?* Maybe shoot some footage inside their churches." She was responding exactly as he feared she would, her voice rising with excitement. "And that subtext of the Russian immigrants and their superstitions adds a fascinating ethnic angle. It might even get picked up by the network."

"See now, there you go, all you care about is your damn story. Believe me, it's just a hand in a safe-deposit box. There's nothing mystical about it."

"You're the one who put the mystical spin on it," she pointed out. "And frankly, I find it intriguing."

"Look, I'm willing to cooperate with you, help you in any way I can. But before you do your story, give me a chance to find out what's going on. Whose hand it is. How it got there."

"But you're not doing anything in that direction," she argued. "You're sitting on the case. You're keeping the hand in the freezer. You haven't run any tests. You haven't even called in the coroner. What are you doing, waiting for some kind of omen yourself?"

"If I called the coroner, every TV station in Scranton would have their camera crews waiting outside. The newspaper people would be here, maybe even the *National Enquirer*. It'd be a real circus. I'm trying to avoid that. I wish you'd help me out."

She was cool about it. No change of expression on her face, except for a slight narrowing of her eyes.

"There's got to be something in it for me," she said.

He waited while he watched her mind work it out.

"Will you promise me exclusivity on this?" she asked.

"I can't do that," he said. "Only because I don't know if the bank guard told anyone else. But I can protect you on it. I can let you know if any other reporter comes snooping around. At least you'll have a head start."

"Not good enough. I need information. Details. I need to know everything you know about this case, and I want to be able to quote you on it."

"Give me seventy-two hours," he countered. "You come back in seventy-two hours and I'll share everything with you."

"You really expect me to sit on the story for three days?"

"And that means no interviewing anybody who was at the bank."

"That's completely unacceptable."

"That's the deal," he insisted.

"Come on, Rhostok, you've got to give me something. I can't go back to the station without anything to report."

"Tell them I showed you the hand. Tell them I won't show it to any other reporter, as long as you cooperate."

"Can I come back with a cameraman, take some video?"

"Not for seventy-two hours."

"You're really a difficult person, you know that?" she said. "How about giving me some deep background stuff, totally off the record?"

"Do we have a deal?"

"All right," she sighed. "No story for seventy-two hours, but you've got to give me some deep background stuff to make up for that tape you destroyed."

"Strictly off the record?"

"I promise."

He was surprised at how easily she agreed. He wasn't sure he could trust her to keep her word, but she was asking too many questions, and he wanted to get her out of his office before he accidentally revealed more than he wanted to.

He was careful to give her no privileged information. He offered only those facts that she could have gotten from Zeeman or Franklin or anyone else who was in the bank when the vault was opened.

He didn't tell her why he suspected that Vanya Danilovitch was murdered, or exactly how Paul Danilovitch died.

He didn't tell her that he had assigned Otto Bruckner to protect Paul's widow.

And most important of all, he managed not to reveal what she was most curious about: the name that was written on the brown paper in which the hand was wrapped.

High up on the rock ledge, the old man unfolded a lunch of dark rye bread, a chunk of butter, a length of sausage which he cut with a pocket knife, beer for him, and sweet orange soda for the boy.

"The Emperor Nikolas, like all the Tsars before him, had absolute control over the lives of millions of people," the old man said. "But when his little son Alexei was dying, the Tsar was helpless."

"Why was his son dying?"

"The little Tsarevich was born with a condition known as hemophilia," the old man said, knowing from the boy's eyes that the information was being immediately filed away in his memory. "The illness causes uncontrollable bleeding from any wound or injury. There was no cure for it at the time, which meant that even a small scratch could be life-threatening. Somehow, the little Tsarevich managed to survive until he was four years old. That would have been in, let's see" (the old man counted on his fingers) "around early 1908. Yes, in 1908 he fell while playing with his sisters. Blood immediately began to pour from his mouth and nose. He was soon in terrible pain. He started bleeding internally, and overnight the little boy's leg swelled up to twice its normal size. The finest doctors in Russia could not stop the bleeding. The Tsar and the Empress were told he would soon die. An official announcement of the boy's death was being prepared, and the ringing of church bells was ordered in the capital."

"But Rasputin had the power over blood," the little boy shouted excitedly. "He could save the life of the Tsarevich, couldn't he?"

The old man smiled at the speed with which the little boy's mind jumped ahead.

"Yes," he said. "Rasputin arrived when everyone had given up hope. He knelt at Alexei's bedside and prayed for a long time. Then he touched the Tsaverich's leg with his right hand and told the boy he would be all right. And almost immediately, the little Tsarevich opened his eyes and smiled. The bleeding stopped. The next day he was dancing in the palace hallway."

"Did it really happen that way, Grandfather?" For a moment, the boy forgot his food. "Dying one moment, and alive the next?"

"There were many witnesses to what happened, including the Imperial doctors. No one could explain it then, and no one can explain it even now."

"And all Rasputin did was pray? He didn't give any medicines?"

"No medicines. Only his prayers and the laying on of hands."

"Then it was a miracle," the boy declared.

"Oh, yes," the old man said. "A miracle, all right. And by saving the Tsarevich, Rasputin demonstrated his mystical powers to the Imperial

Family. *After that, whenever the Tsarevich took ill, the Empress sent for Rasputin. And every time, he was able to stop the bleeding."*

"But if his powers were so great, why did the bleeding come back?" the boy asked. "Why did he not perform a permanent cure?"

Twenty-Five

Rhostok had first met Professor William Altschiller when he attended a series of lectures, "Scientific Procedures for Identification of Human Remains," which had been offered to local police units the previous year.

Altschiller was professor of forensic anthropology at the University of Scranton. He was a nationally recognized authority in his field and did occasional work for the Defense Department. A dozen years before, the department had flown him into Cambodia to identify some recently discovered human remains from the Vietnam War.

The way the *Scranton Times* reported the story, some Montagnard tribesmen found the wreckage of a helicopter that had crashed in the Parrot's Beak region, just over the border from Vietnam, during the war. Markings identified it as an Air Cav MedEvac unit, probably carrying wounded marines. According to the military officers who accompanied Altschiller, the chopper was brought down by ground fire from North Vietnamese who were based in Cambodia. They pointed out the rusted holes that were stitched along the belly of the helicopter in a straight line, evenly spaced, like a row of empty rivet holes. It was machine-gun fire that made rows like that, Altschiller was told. But either the helicopter kept going for a while or the North Vietnamese were driven off by a bombing run, because no one found the wreckage until more than thirty years after the war ended.

The bodies of the soldiers had remained in that ravine all those years, with generations of jungle parasites feeding, maturing, and planting their eggs in the decaying flesh until the bones were stripped clean under the flak jackets and it was time for the bugs and worms to move on in their eternal search for food.

By the time Altschiller arrived, all the fabric and leather at the crash site had disintegrated or been consumed by humidity and mold, and some unknown microbe was halfway done with the rubber parts. The bones were scattered, some carried away by jungle animals. From twelve casualties, there were only two complete skeletons. The rest were partials. Some of the partials amounted to only a few dozen bones out of the two hundred that make up a complete human skeleton.

Despite these problems, Altschiller managed to make positive identifications of eight marines and supplied physical descriptions based on the remaining bone fragments that led to eventual identification of three others after a computer scan of MIA records led to family members from whom DNA samples could be obtained.

Altschiller frowned when Rhostok complimented him on the story the *Scranton Times* had done on that mission.

"I try not to talk about those assignments anymore," he said. "Especially to the press. Some of the faculty members still don't like the idea of Defense Department contracts, no matter how humanitarian the work might be."

"How do they feel about police work?" Rhostok asked.

"I'm sure they'll eventually get around to criticizing that, too. And when that day comes, I'll be out of work. Now, what do you have for me?"

Altschiller eyed the cardboard shoe box that Rhostok carried under his arm. They were in the professor's office at the university, which consisted of a small desk and two chairs wedged into a windowed corner of a huge laboratory on the top floor of the science building. It was shortly after the morning classes ended at the university. The professor was still wearing his white lab coat, but now that he had a few hours to relax, he had unbuttoned the front to allow his stomach to expand to its normal girth. A quirk of nature had endowed him with a peculiarly pear-shaped body. A few strands of fine brown hair atop an otherwise bald head served as the stem. His face was round, with a bulbous lower lip that hung down in a perpetual pout. His shoulders were narrow, as was his chest, but his stomach and hips ballooned far out of proportion to the rest of his body. He tended to waddle when he walked, and Rhostok wondered how he could possibly fit his bottom into the chair behind the desk. The man would have been more comfortable on a sofa, he thought.

When Rhostok opened the cardboard box, he expected Altschiller to show some surprise at the contents. Instead, the professor curled his lower lip into a pleasant smile, as if he were being presented with a charming curio rather than a severed human hand in a plastic evidence bag.

"Where did you find this?" Altschiller asked.

"It was locked up in a vault at the Middle Valley State Bank."

"They're depositing human parts up there?" Altschiller chuckled at his own humor. "Or was it security for a loan?"

Rhostok didn't laugh.

"In a vault, you say?" Altschiller's eyes remained fixed on the contents of the box.

"Actually, in a safe-deposit box inside the vault."

"But why bring it to me? This is obviously evidence of some sort of crime. Shouldn't you be taking it to the coroner's office?"

"I'd rather not go through official channels on this," Rhostok said. "Not just yet, anyway." Seeing the professor's skeptical glance, he quickly added, "Besides, O'Malley can't give me the kind of answers you can. He's more of a politician than a coroner. If I turned the hand over to him, he'd use it to get himself on TV, get some more name recognition before the next election."

Altschiller nodded his agreement. "What do you want from me?"

"First, I want your promise to keep this quiet. I don't want anyone knowing about the hand, or knowing that I brought it to you."

"If it's the press you're worried about, I already learned my lesson," Altschiller said. "I don't do interviews anymore."

"Good. Because I'm going to leave the hand with you. I want you to examine it, test it, do whatever it is that you do to find out as much about it as you can. I've already taken fingerprints and faxed them to the FBI, but their computer search came up negative. I'm hoping you can come up with something."

Altschiller snapped on a pair of latex surgical gloves and lifted the evidence bag out of the box. The hand inside had thawed out on the drive to Scranton.

"Well, it's obviously fresh," the Professor said, carefully tilting the bag to better examine the bloody stump. "You can tell that just by looking at it. The blood still hasn't fully coagulated. It can't be more than an hour or two off the body."

"It was discovered about five-thirty yesterday afternoon."

Altschiller's lower lip curled into a frown.

"Impossible. That's almost twenty hours ago."

"Take my word for it," Rhostok said. "I was there. And it's been in my possession ever since."

"But look at the color." Altschiller opened the bag to examine the hand more carefully. A wheaty odor arose from the bag, the same odor Rhostok remembered from the bank. "A hand that's been severed at the wrist would lose all its blood and turn gray in a matter of minutes. But in this case, the flesh is still pink. The veins haven't collapsed. That means it still retains the full complement of blood. And look at the condition of the blood at the stump. Under normal conditions, any remaining blood should have clotted and started turning brown after a few hours. By this time, my God, the blood should be totally dried and crusted, with necrosis setting in on the flesh."

"Maybe that's because I froze it," Rhostok said. "It's fully thawed out now, but I kept it in the freezer overnight so it wouldn't deteriorate."

"Did you ever notice what happens to a fresh steak when you freeze it?" Altschiller asked. "It loses that bright red color because the blood crystalizes and undergoes molecular changes. But look here," he indicated the gaping wound at the wrist. "The raw flesh is a deep red, the blood is bright and viscous. There doesn't appear to be any degradation of the wound whatsoever. This is how your wrist would look if I cut it open right now. The condition of this specimen is totally inconsistent with an overnight time span."

Rhostok decided not to confuse Altschiller with any speculation about how long the hand might have been in the safe-deposit box before its discovery. He especially didn't want to mention the bank president's claim that the box hadn't been opened in more than fifty years. Altschiller had enough of a problem with an overnight time span. Let him go on that, see what he comes up with, Rhostok thought.

He followed Altschiller across the laboratory. It was a large room, containing two rows of slate-covered student worktables, each of which had a sink, four Bunsen burners, two microscopes, an assortment of glass vials and test-tube racks, and a computer. The walls of the room were lined with glass-fronted cabinets and shelves that were filled with large glass jars, cans, and cardboard cartons, all of whose contents were identified by chemistry symbols or Latin names. Some of the large jars contained preserved human organs.

A stainless-steel table, its edges curved up to prevent any liquid from spilling over, occupied the center of the room. It was long enough to accommodate a human body without squeezing it to fit, depending on how tall the person was. It was to this table that Altschiller proceeded.

He gently removed the hand from the evidence bag and placed it on the table, with the fingers curling upwards.

"Interesting," Altschiller said. He poked at the hand with a hooked metal instrument that resembled a dentist's probe. He pulled at the skin, flipped the hand over, and poked the tip of the probe against the bloody stump. A sticky drop of blood clung to the tip. "Yesterday afternoon, you said? You're not being facetious, are you?"

"There were other witnesses to the time it was found, if that's important."

"How long can I have to examine it?"

"How long will it take?"

"I'll start working on it right away." Altschiller flipped a switch on the side of the table, turning on powerful overhead floodlights. He hooked the sharp end of his probe under the thumb, slowly repositioning the hand under the lights. "I wouldn't want to freeze it again. The freeze-thaw cycle is bad for specimens."

"How much will you be able to tell me about the person it belonged to?"

"Quite a bit," the professor said confidently. "Working with a whole hand, I can draw you a pretty good picture. Normally, you want larger bones for determining height, but I can work well with what we've got here. I can give you approximate weight, physique, musculature. It's just a question of extrapolation. Distribution of fat and muscle in the palm of the hand is pretty indicative of what we'd find in the rest of the body. And serum protein analysis can tell us about diet, sometimes even ethnic background, depending on the type of abnormalities that show up. That's what we look for, abnormalities. It's in the deviations from the normal that identity can be proven."

He poked his probe under the nail of the middle finger. A tiny flake of black soot fell to the table. With a pair of tweezers, he carefully placed the speck of dirt on a glass microscope slide.

"I might even be able to tell you where the victim was before he died, if we find any markers in the dirt sample. As far as general health, that could take a little longer. Can I use some of my students? I've got some young research assistants who absolutely love this sort of stuff. They can do the tissue tests and fraction analysis while I work on the rest of it."

"Only if you can trust them to keep quiet," Rhostok said.

"I know, I know, you don't want to be reading about this in the newspapers tomorrow."

"I've already had a TV reporter snooping around."

"That's even worse," Altschiller muttered.

"Maybe you could make it a blind test," Rhostok suggested. "Just give them the samples and not let them see the hand."

Altschiller used another instrument, one with a tiny scoop on the end, to remove a drop of blood from the hand. He carefully placed it on a glass slide.

"Is it really all that confidential?" he asked.

"I'm already having problems with the coroner," Rhostok said. "He's pissed that I'm questioning one of his findings. If word got back to him that I was going around him by having you conduct this examination, he could make trouble, call the D.A., maybe even get me charged with obstruction, if he wants to push it that far." After a pause, he added, "It could be trouble for you, too."

"You don't have to worry about my assistants," the professor said. "They work with me on some of my Defense projects. They know how to keep secrets."

All this time, Altschiller had continued his preliminary examination of the hand. He poked at it with another instrument, a sort of reverse-action scissors that spread apart the raw flesh at the stump.

"It looks as if this hand was removed by a doctor," Altschiller said. "Or at least someone with a knowledge of anatomy. The cut was made right at the end of the carpal bones, where they articulate with the radius and ulna. Whoever performed the amputation left a small scratch on the scaphoid bone, but otherwise did a very neat job of it, with minimal destruction."

He snipped a tiny bit of flesh from the wrist.

"Okay," he finally said, straightening up. "I've got one student I trust with my most secret projects. Michael Chao already has a top-secret clearance from Defense. I'll use him. It'll be just the two of us, but he'll have as much access to the hand as I will. Now is there anything else you can tell me, any other information you might have about the hand or how it found its way into the vault? Anything that might help my investigation?"

"I've been checking area hospitals within a fifty-mile radius," Rhostok said. "And also area police departments. I tried not to be too specific about what I was looking for, but none of them reported any accident or crime victims with arm injuries other than a couple of broken bones and a mangled elbow."

He felt guilty about not being completely truthful. There was, after all, the Old Church Slavonic inscription on the wrapping paper to consider. But he rationalized not telling the professor about it on the grounds that it identified a man who could not possibly have any relation to the hand. Not unless the laws of time and physics were repealed.

One of the things the boy enjoyed about these picnics with the old man was eating "muzhik style." Instead of making sandwiches, they would tear off chunks of bread and meat and dip them into the soft butter, just as the peasants in Siberia did.

"The Tsars of Russia felt they derived their powers directly from God," the old man continued. *"Like the Tsars before him, Nikolas ruled not only the nation, but also the Russian Orthodox Church. Rasputin, on the other*

hand, came from the lowliest poverty and spent most of his life preaching humility. That was why he continued to wear peasant clothing and eat with his hands, even at the banquet tables of the Imperial Palace. The muzhiks believe God sent Rasputin to remind the Tsar of the limits of his power. It was God, after all, who visited the terrible illness on the heir to the throne. To have a muzhik, a peasant, cure the son of the Tsar was meant to be a lesson in humility."

"But you haven't answered my question, Grandfather," the boy persisted. "Why not a permanent cure?"

"A single cure, a single healing of the Tsarevich could too easily be dismissed by the courtiers as coincidence, or explained away by clever doctors," the old man said. "But to repeat those cures in front of different witnesses and sometimes in the most incredible circumstances, that convinced even the most skeptical that they were truly witnessing miracles. And more important, it served as a constant reminder to the Imperial Family that God could withdraw His approval of them at any time."

"So the Tsar was placed at the mercy of a muzhik," the boy said. "Without Rasputin's intercession, he knew his son would die."

"The muzhiks say that was God's plan."

Twenty-Six

"I don't know if I can do this," Nicole said.

Vassily shrugged. "You have done such things for me before."

"I was a different person then."

"No. You are the same Nicole as before. People like you do not change."

She wanted to argue with him, wanted to tell him how her marriage, as brief and doomed as it was, had changed the way she felt about herself, about men, about life and the way she wanted to live it. But she knew it was pointless to try to discuss such things with Vassily. To him, she was simply a possession, a beautiful and valuable piece of property to be used for his own pleasure and rented out for profit when the price was right. A piece of property that he had reclaimed as soon as Paul was dead.

"After this, it's all over?" she asked. "You won't bother me anymore?"

"I give you my word," he said.

She didn't believe him, of course. He had already promised her freedom once before. And now here he was, back again, having managed to slip her out of the house without alerting the policeman assigned to guard her. Now they were parked on a busy street in Middle Valley, in a four-year-old Buick Century, one of those barely noticeable gray cars Vassily seemed to prefer. The bitter fumes of his Russian cigarettes filled the interior of the car as he studied the entrance of the building farther up the block.

"How do I know you won't go back on your word again?" she asked.

"You have no choice," he shrugged. "But I tell you the truth this time. If you do what I ask, you will never see me again."

They were parked with a clear view of the Middle Valley Police Station, an old red brick building. She felt nauseated at the thought of what Vassily wanted her to do. He had forced her to perform bizarre and even perverted acts in the past, but trading her body for a dead human hand seemed unimaginably degrading. She toyed with the idea of telling everything to Rhostok, telling him about Vassily in the hope that . . . what? That the policeman would somehow save her from the man who controlled her life? Not likely. Vassily was too smart for that. He hadn't struck her, hadn't left any incriminating marks on her, hadn't even made any serious threats. He had broken no laws by showing up here. There was nothing the police could do. And it would be pointless to run. There was no escaping Vassily.

"It is a good offer I am making," he said. "Your freedom for performing this service for me."

"And if he refuses?"

"But I think you know how to convince him." Vassily smiled and stroked her cheek. His fingers were cold and bony and smelled of nicotine. "What man could resist a woman so beautiful like you?"

She had heard him describe how he had once killed a man with those fingers. He explained how, by carefully placing two fingertips against the carotid artery, he was able to cut off the flow of blood to the brain without leaving any bruises or other telltale marks that might arouse police suspicions.

Nicole stiffened as she felt his fingers move down to the side of her neck. He was smiling almost playfully, as his fingertips sought out the pulse that revealed the location of the artery. How easy it would be, she thought, to let him end it all right now. Send her into the blessed void where she would finally find the peace that had eluded her on Earth. But knowing Vassily, it would not be that simple. He was a purveyor of pain, not peace. He would find a way to force her to do his bidding, as he had done in the past.

"Are you prepared now to do this for me?" Vassily asked.

She had no idea why the ugly piece of dead flesh was so valuable to him. She certainly never wanted to see it again. All she wanted was to free herself from him, and if accomplishing that meant debasing herself one last time, she was prepared to do it.

"Yes," she sighed, resigned to her fate.

Vassily opened the top button of the pink dress he had selected for her and watched her breasts surge against the loosening of the tight fabric.

"You will work your charms on him. And what will you say if he questions your right to claim it?"

"I'll tell him the hand was taken from my husband's safe-deposit box. Legally, whatever was in the box is now my property, and I want it returned to me."

"Correct," Vassily said. "But he will argue it is a human hand. He will say it is not like an heirloom or a piece of jewelry. He will claim it isn't ordinary inheritable property. It is evidence."

"And I will tell him that unless they can prove a crime was committed, unless they can prove that a living human being was mutilated or murdered to obtain the hand, it can't be considered evidence," she said, repeating the words they had so carefully rehearsed. "Lacking any proof of a crime, the hand is simply a hand. As long as the proper health laws are observed, a body part can be considered personal property. And that makes it my property, as the sole heir to my husband's estate. I intend to turn it over to the Old Ritual Russian Orthodox Church of Saint Sofia, so that it can have a proper burial."

"Very good," Vassily said, as he motioned her to get out of the car. "Very good. If you succeed, you will be done with me."

Twenty-Seven

Rhostok had always harbored a vague mistrust of beautiful women. God had not placed them on Earth for men like him, he was convinced. They were exotic creatures who traveled on a different plane, who thought differently from ordinary people, with goals and ambitions he could never hope to discern. Most of the beautiful girls who grew up in Middle Valley inevitably left town at the first opportunity. He knew little about the kinds of lives they led. All he knew for certain was that the ones who didn't have successful careers married doctors and lawyers and wealthy businessmen, never policemen like him.

Those he encountered during his career in law enforcement often sought small favors or expected preferential treatment, in return for a warm smile and the opportunity to bask in their beauty for a few moments.

When the Danilovitch widow showed up, however, the "favor" she sought was neither small nor anything he could have expected. She came for the hand, and although he explained that it was no longer in his possession, she seemed willing to offer a lot more than just a smile in return for his help in getting it for her.

She wore a simple pink dress that on any other woman would have been considered modest. The body contained within that dress, however, was so well endowed that Rhostok had to force himself to keep his eyes on her face. She was the stuff of erotic fantasies, and her body language suggested she would be his if only he would do this one simple thing for her. As she pleaded her case, he found himself agreeing with her logic, with the common sense of what she was saying.

On a purely legal basis, if no crime could be detected, whatever was found in the vault, human remains or not, belonged to her. But the more determined her pleading, the more puzzled he was that she would want possession of so grotesque an object.

Every movement, from the way she ran her hand through her hair to the way her tongue occasionally moistened her lips, seemed to be sexually charged and aimed directly at him. He had never been the object of such sexual intensity before. Here was this stunningly beautiful woman making him feel as if he were the most important man in her life, the man she had been waiting for. She was the answer to all his lonely nights, all the libidinous dreams, all the erotic fantasies he had ever had. She was his for the taking. All he had to do was reach out and touch her.

And yet, he held back.

He ached to take her in his arms, to feel the softness of her flesh beneath the smooth dress, to caress the warm curves of her body, and yes, yes, yes to press his mouth against those lush painted lips.

And yet, he held back.

He was perspiring under her gaze. His nerve endings tingled in response to some unseen message her body was sending. His loins ached with desire. Why did he not take her, he wondered? She had come here prepared to exchange her body, if need be, for the object found in the vault. Yet he felt frozen in place. Unwilling to allow such an exchange to occur.

Why? Why was he willing to suppress the hormonal storms she aroused in him? He knew she had done such things with other men. The vice cop in Vegas had told him all about the life this beautiful "showgirl" had lived. But he could not bring himself to take her.

She came closer to him. Close enough for him to smell the warmth of her body. To feel her breath on his face. To see the thin line of mascara on her eyelashes. And . . . what else was that in her eyes . . . tears?

Some of her mascara began to melt. Suddenly, as if embarrassed by what she was doing, she stiffened and pulled back, turning away from him.

"I'm sorry," she said. "I can't . . . I can't . . ."

He thought he heard her sob. With one hand blocking her face from view, she hurried to the door.

For long moments after she left, Rhostok remained motionless in his chair.

He wanted her, wanted her desperately enough to go running after her. But it was his grandfather's words that held him back.

"Trust no one," the old man always said. *"Expect betrayal."*

Twenty-Eight

The Scranton police didn't provide many details over the phone about the dead man. Although the death scene was outside his jurisdiction, they told Rhostok the coroner wanted him to identify the body.

"The body's upstairs," the policeman told Rhostok when he arrived at the Laurel Avenue Apartments. "O'Malley's up there, too. I thought you might like to see this first." He pointed to what looked like dark-red latex paint dripping through the plasterboard ceiling. "Hell of a ceiling leak, isn't it?"

A three-foot section of wet ceiling sagged downward from the weight of the blood trapped above. It appeared ready to collapse at any moment. Someone had placed a turkey roasting pan on the floor. About an inch of blood was already collected in the pan, but it was too late to save the carpeting.

"Must have scared the hell out of the tenants," Rhostok said. "You'd better poke a hole in that ceiling and let it drain, or the whole thing will collapse."

"They'll have to rip it all apart anyway," the policeman shrugged. "You ask me, they should tear the whole building down. I don't know why a guy making his kind of money would live in a place like this."

The narrow, three-story building occupied a piece of property too small to allow for even a patch of grass to soften the appearance of the entrance. White aluminum siding covered the poorly fitted joints on the outside. Inside, the floors were starting to separate from the walls.

"Maybe he was trying to save money," Rhostok said.

"Whatever he saved won't do him any good now," the policeman responded.

The main pool of blood was in the apartment upstairs, where Wendell Franklin was lying on the bed, wearing a pair of faded blue pajamas. He was on his back; one hand hung over the side. The pool of blood started beneath the hand and followed the uneven pitch of the floor to the wall, where it seeped through a crack in the baseboard. A green fly was ignoring Franklin's body, buzzing instead around the fringes of the blood. Rhostok raised a hand to his nose in a vain attempt to block the sickly smell of death from climbing up his nostrils.

"O'Malley doesn't want the windows open," the policeman said. "He doesn't want any more bugs coming in."

Franklin's thick eyeglasses were on the nightstand, where presumably he left them before going to sleep. Some of the puffiness Rhostok remembered was gone from Franklin's face, drained out with the blood. The florid complexion was gone from his cheeks, too. Franklin actually looked healthier in death than he had when alive.

The coroner sat on the edge of Franklin's bed. He had his briefcase on his lap, using it as a desk on which to fill out some forms. His withered right leg, the result of Lackawanna County's last recorded case of polio, stuck out at an odd angle. The edges of the metal brace were visible around his ankle.

O'Malley nodded to Rhostok without getting up.

"I know it's out of your jurisdiction," he said. "But when we found the deceased's appointment book, it listed a trip to Middle Valley yesterday. You might be one of the last people to have seen him alive. Did you know him?"

"Wendell Franklin," Rhostok nodded. "He's a state revenue agent. What happened to him?"

"Bled to death," O'Malley said, turning his attention back to the form. "You can see that just by looking at him."

Rhostok bent down to examine Franklin's hand, particularly his index finger, which had been injured at the bank. Three flesh-colored Band-Aids, drenched with blood, hung loose from the tip.

"I'm looking, but I'm not believing what I'm seeing," Rhostok said.

"Believe it," O'Malley shrugged. "The man bled to death from that wound on his finger. He just laid down on the bed and went to sleep and bled to death. Didn't even wash the dishes. If you look in the sink, you'll see there's blood on his dinner plate, too. He had two servings of Weight Watchers frozen lasagna. The cops checked the garbage and came up with that."

"You've got to be kidding," Rhostok said. "He bled to death from that little cut on his finger? It's just a scratch. It happened at the bank. He cut himself on the edge of a safe-deposit box."

O'Malley finished his paperwork. The corpse's arm swung loosely when the coroner got up from the bed.

"Actually, it's a fairly deep cut," O'Malley said. "It severed two capillaries and one small vein. But you're right. It's not what you'd consider a mortal wound. Unfortunately, the guy was obviously a bleeder. A hemophiliac. You know what that is?"

"Yeah, I know," Rhostok said. "Every Russian knows about bleeders. They don't have a clotting factor in their blood like the rest of us do." He waved away the green fly, which couldn't seem to decide where to settle to begin its feast. "The last Tsarevich was a bleeder."

"Then you know hemophiliacs can bleed to death from the simplest wound."

"The way the little Tsarevich bled to death was from about two dozen gunshot wounds to the head and chest during the Revolution."

"Usually bleeders take good care of themselves." O'Malley ignored the Russian history reference. "This fellow should have checked into a hospital instead of coming home and trying to treat himself. There are medicines now that can restore the clotting factor. At least temporarily."

Rhostok left the bedroom and decided to check out the tiny kitchen. There were bloodstains on Franklin's dinner plate, just as the coroner had said. The Weight Watchers lasagna packages were in the garbage. So was an empty one-pint carton of Sealtest Fat-Free Strawberry Swirl ice cream. Franklin sure took his good-natured time eating before laying himself down to die.

"I'm surprised there aren't more uniforms around," Rhostok said to the policeman who followed him into the kitchen.

"You should have been here a half-hour ago," the policeman said. "There must have been about a dozen of us here. Three or four squad cars. When the downstairs tenant called 911 and described what was coming through his ceiling, we thought we had a mass murderer or some-thing. We had the whole works here, photographers, crime lab, assistant commissioner . . . you know how that works."

Rhostok nodded.

"But once the coroner said it was natural causes, everybody disap-peared. That's when O'Malley called you. He didn't want the body removed until you got here. The two of you must be good friends."

"Not really," Rhostok said. "It's all politics. He thinks maybe I can help him with the Russian vote in Middle Valley, so he's trying to stay on my good side."

The policeman readily accepted the explanation. But Rhostok knew it wasn't the real reason he had been summoned. He was sure the coroner had something else on his mind.

"I'm about ready for the body-bag boys," O'Malley said when Rhostok returned to the bedroom. He had been leafing through the papers in Wendell Franklin's attaché case. "This fellow's been running some real nickel-and-dime tax audits." He waved a folder to illustrate his point. "Here's an ironworker making twenty-five grand a year. He was going to nail the poor guy for travel expenses. Why don't they go after the big fish instead of the little ones?"

"Not many big fish in Scranton," Rhostok said. "He was probably doing the best he could."

"Maybe that's why the safe-deposit box was such a big deal for him. He took a lot of notes on that, Rhostok. The widow's name, her address. Here it is, Mrs. Nicole Danilovitch." O'Malley made a point of reading the name from the notebook, as if he didn't remember her. He waited for a response from Rhostok. When none was forthcoming, he flipped through a few more notebook pages. "He made a lot of notes about what they found in box number fifty-two. Must have scared the hell out of him, finding a human hand in a bank vault."

So O'Malley knew about the hand, Rhostok thought. That and the widow's involvement. He had noticed the way O'Malley had looked at Nicole the other night. The man had a reputation for chasing after newly widowed women. Maybe he was looking for an excuse to give her a call. Rhostok put the thought out of his mind and changed the subject back to Wendell Franklin, wanting to settle something that puzzled him.

"Is it possible he could have been a bleeder and not known about it?" he asked. He recalled the way Franklin had reacted to the cut on his finger. He hadn't shown any fear or panic, or even nervousness. He was very casual about the cut, treating it as nothing more than a minor annoyance.

"Hemophilia is an inherited disease," O'Malley said. "It usually comes from the mother's side. Your friend here would have been a bleeder from the day he was born. When he was a child, his parents would have watched him carefully, kept him out of any sports where he could get cut or bruised. They would have drilled into him the fact that any injury could trigger uncontrollable bleeding. He must have known about it. All bleeders do."

"But that's the strange part," Rhostok said. "If he was a bleeder, why didn't he get upset when he cut himself? He acted like it was nothing. Said he was going to put an ice cube on it to stop the bleeding."

Rhostok bent over to examine Franklin's finger more carefully. It was cold and rubbery to the touch. The wound was deeper than it seemed, just as O'Malley said. But it still didn't seem that bad. On someone who didn't suffer from hemophilia, a butterfly bandage should have been able to stop the bleeding. Or a little extra pressure. Just press the finger against the thumb and hold it there for ten, fifteen minutes. Rhostok had done that himself for similar cuts. The tip of the finger was dark, almost black. The other fingers on the hand had darkened tips, too.

"I don't pretend to know what goes through people's minds," O'Malley said. "That's not part of my job. Maybe he wanted to commit suicide. Who knows? After all, bleeding to death isn't a painful way to go. It's like taking a tranquilizer. When you lose blood, you lose energy. Imperceptibly at first, but it keeps going and first thing you know, you're feeling sleepy. The heart keeps beating, doing its best to supply the brain. But all that does is keep pumping the blood out of the body. With less blood to the brain, the neurons start shutting down, and you feel like you're drifting off into sleep. It's not as if he was in any pain, the way he went. It's actually a very pleasant sensation, as long as you don't realize what's happening."

The green fly settled on the side of Franklin's nose. It rubbed its forelegs hungrily together and started searching for some nourishment. Probably feeding on dried-up sweat. Rhostok waved it off before the fly reached Franklin's glazed eyeball.

"Why are his fingertips turning black?" Rhostok asked.

"He's been dead awhile."

"I've seen corpses before, but I never saw that happen."

"Every human being is different," O'Malley said. "Could be his metabolism or any of a dozen other things. Could be just newsprint, too. Maybe he was reading the paper."

"Are you going to do an autopsy?" Rhostok asked.

"The man bled to death. I don't need an autopsy to determine that."

"What about a blood test?"

"What for?" O'Malley responded.

"To see if it was hemophilia."

"I already told you it was hemophilia."

"And you told me Paul Danilovitch died of a heart attack. You didn't want to do any tests on him, either. I'm still waiting for those results."

The weight of O'Malley's leg brace tugged at the side of his body and made a heavy noise with every step he took.

"I've got the Danilovitch results in my briefcase," he said. "But this guy on the bed, he's a different case. And this isn't your jurisdiction. We're in Scranton now, not Middle Valley. What do you care if he's a hemophiliac? It's got nothing to do with you."

"I'd like a blood test, just to be sure about the hemophilia."

"What's to test? You're a policeman, look at all the evidence. Blood all over the floor. Goddamned blood soaking through the ceiling downstairs. How else would all that blood drain out of a little cut on his finger? He had to be a bleeder."

"Most corpses I see, even auto accidents where the victim's chest is ripped open, there's always some blood left in the body," Rhostok said. "It settles and leaves purple marks where it collects."

He partially pulled down Franklin's pajama pants. The top of the dead man's buttocks, where they rested against the bed, were as pale as the rest of him.

"No purple marks. No indication of blood settling. Looks like Franklin doesn't have any blood left in him at all."

"So he lost all his blood," the coroner sneered. "That only proves he was a hemophiliac. So what's your point?"

"I don't know much about medicine, but once his heart stopped pumping, shouldn't the blood have stopped flowing?"

"Not necessarily. It's a question of physics. Look at the position of the body, with the hand hanging off the bed. If the blood was thin enough, if the absence of clotting factor was complete, the force of gravity could go to work. Sort of like when you leave water in your garden hose and it drains out. That's probably what happened here. It's certainly unusual, but not impossible."

It sounded to Rhostok like something the coroner made up on the spot, as if he didn't have a valid medical explanation. Rhostok watched a cockroach dart out from under the bed, where Franklin kept his dirty socks. The bug ran up to the pool of blood, felt it with his antennae, and must have decided it was too sticky for him. Or too fresh. He moved in an irregular start-and-stop search pattern until he found a dried-up section of blood where he settled down to feed.

"I'd like you to do a blood test anyway," Rhostok said. "You've got plenty of blood here. Take a sample before it dries out."

O'Malley took a step towards the cockroach, sending it darting back to the safety of Franklin's socks.

"The blood's probably contaminated from coming into contact with any dirt on the floor."

"Jesus, what the hell is it with you, O'Malley? It's bad enough you're trying to avoid an autopsy on this guy, just like you did with Paul Danilovitch. Now you're pulling the same kind of crap about a blood test. I mean, how much does it cost? You want me to pay for it out of my own pocket?"

"Okay, okay, I'll draw a sample if you want, but I know what I'll find. Get my bag, will you?"

The metal brace made it awkward for O'Malley to get down to floor level to take the sample. He had to place one hand behind his withered knee and, using the bed as a support, lower himself slowly until he was kneeling on his good leg with the other extended out at an awkward angle. He slipped on a pair of protective latex gloves and selected a thick part of the puddle to draw a dark sample up into a syringe.

From beneath the floor came a low growling noise.

Small ripples ran across the glossy surface of the blood. A picture frame rattled on the wall. O'Malley stopped what he was doing and clutched the bed in fear. His eyes watched the ceiling, where a small crack had appeared.

"It's just another tunnel collapse," Rhostok said. "Same thing happened yesterday in Middle Valley."

They waited until the earthen growling passed. When it was over, O'Malley let out a sigh of relief.

"It always makes me nervous," he explained. "With this leg of mine, I worry about getting trapped in a collapsing house."

"You'd have more of a problem if we were in a brick building," Rhostok said. "With a major cave-in, it's the big stone buildings like the courthouse and the churches that'll collapse first. A wooden building like this, it'll stretch and give when the ground shifts. The joints will pull apart, like that section over there." He pointed to a corner where the molding had pulled a half-inch away from the wall. "A house like this is fairly safe. The only thing you'd have to worry about in here would be the possibility of methane gas seeping up through the cracks. Then you light a cigarette and the whole building explodes."

Twenty-Nine

O'Malley lifted himself back up to a standing position. He removed the plastic insert from the syringe tube and labeled the blood sample.

"Are you going to hang around and stare at the corpse much longer?" O'Malley asked. "I'd like to get it back to the morgue before it starts going bad."

"I'm done," Rhostok said. "I appreciate your calling me down to see this. I know you didn't have to do it."

The cockroach was back, feeding at the edge of the blood again. This time it was joined by another. The cockroaches didn't bother Rhostok. It was the fly, the way it kept crawling on Franklin's nose, that annoyed him. It was making his own nose feel itchy.

"According to Franklin's notes, a human hand was found in the bank yesterday," O'Malley said. "When do I get a look at it?"

He nodded to the policeman at the door, who went outside to summon the body-removal crew.

"Is that why you got me down here?" Rhostok said with a smile. "So you could ask me about the hand? And here I thought you were just being nice to me."

"You should have called me yesterday, Rhostok. Anything like that, you're supposed to call the coroner's office."

"It wasn't a body, just a part of a body. I didn't think it was worth bothering you about."

Two morgue attendants entered with a tubular stretcher. They barely glanced at the pool of blood on the floor. That was a job for the police or the building superintendent or someone else. Their job was strictly body handling.

"You were trying to keep it quiet, trying to help out the widow, weren't you?" O'Malley asked, apparently offering him an excuse.

"I planned to call you," Rhostok lied. "But first I wanted to investigate a little on my own, see if maybe I could find the guy it belonged to."

He watched the attendants unzip the black body bag and roll Franklin inside.

"What about Franklin's next of kin?" Rhostok asked, hoping to change the subject.

"His parents live in Newark, according to some letters that were on his dresser. A sister in Syracuse, and that's it. The Scranton police will contact them." O'Malley bent over his briefcase, searching for more forms. "From what I read, the hand was locked up in a safe-deposit box. Is that true?"

"That's why Franklin was there," Rhostok said. "It seems that part of his job was to supervise the opening of dead people's safe-deposit boxes."

"According to his notes, the box was originally rented in the name of Vanya Danilovitch. He was that suicide we had up at Lackawanna, wasn't he?"

"You were the one who decided he committed suicide, not me."

"And that was his son who died last week?"

"Just a coincidence, that's what you said."

"And the woman who opened the box, that was the widow?"

"Fascinating, isn't it?" Rhostok said. "You want to change your opinion about how those men died?"

"No, no, I don't. I was just thinking . . ."

"What?"

"Nothing important. You said he cut his finger at the bank?"

"That's right. He cut himself on a sharp piece of metal when he was opening the box."

The doorway was too narrow for the usual gurney, so the attendants were using a metal-frame stretcher to take the body out. They worked in silence until the attendant in front caught his finger between the metal stretcher and the edge of the door frame. He started swearing and shifted the weight of the stretcher to his other hand, nearly sending Franklin rolling to the floor.

"The one I feel sorry for is the widow," O'Malley sighed.

"Maybe you should send her flowers."

"Come on now, have some sympathy for her. Look what she's been going through. First her husband dies, then she finds a human hand in the family's safe-deposit box . . . I've seen things like that before, but for her it must have been a hell of a shock . . . and now she's going to hear about this poor guy's death. I hope you're not going to try to turn this into something it isn't."

"What do you mean?" Rhostok asked innocently.

"I know the way you Russians think. But these are isolated events, Rhostok. I hope you don't try to turn it all into some grand conspiracy."

Rhostok remained silent.

"I've got an election coming up," O'Malley continued. "The last thing

I need is any kind of distraction or second-guessing right in the middle of my campaign. You know how the media likes this kind of stuff." His voice turned suspicious. "You haven't been talking to the media, have you?"

"There was a reporter who came snooping around today. A little blonde from Channel One."

"Oh, Christ! What did you tell her?"

"Nothing much. She seemed to know a lot already about what happened. Probably got the story from the bank guard."

"Damn!"

"She also seemed to know an awful lot about how Paul Danilovitch died, and about old Vanya. As a matter of fact, I thought she got that information from your office."

"Not from me," O'Malley assured him. "But I'll sure as hell find out if any of my people are talking to the press and put a stop to it."

"Anyway, everything ended up fine. She promised to keep the story off TV for a couple of days, so I can investigate further."

"Be careful, Rhostok. You don't know the first thing about working with the media. They'll promise you anything, as long as it helps them get their story."

O'Malley removed a paper from his briefcase. He asked the other policeman to leave the room before he pivoted around on his steel brace to face Rhostok.

"You know, Rhostok, if you don't cooperate and help me keep this quiet, I can turn it all back on you. Technically, you violated the law by not notifying me about the discovery of a human body part. And you're still in violation by not turning it over to me."

"I didn't want to make a big deal out of it. The widow was upset. I thought it would be better to keep it quiet for a while."

"I know, I know. You were just trying to protect the widow. I can't blame you for that. She's really a beautiful woman. But the law's on my side in this situation. I want that hand. I can force you to produce it. I just hope it doesn't come to that."

"Why are you getting so upset?"

"Because you're stepping on my turf. Human remains belong in the morgue. You can't go circumventing procedure. We've already had two phone calls asking about the hand, and we had to tell them we hadn't received it yet."

"Two phone calls? From who?"

"I don't know. John Q. Public, I guess. They didn't identify themselves."

"Didn't your people ask them for their names?"

"Why would we do that?"

"Don't you have caller ID on your lines?"

"I guess. I don't know. What does it matter?"

"Jesus, don't you get it? If they know about the hand, maybe they could help us identify it."

"Well, if you sent the hand down to the morgue when you should have, then maybe those callers would have come down and done just that. But now, we'll never know, will we?" O'Malley looked at him with a quizzical expression. "I think you're hiding something, Rhostok. Not just the hand. Something else. What is it?"

"It's nothing that concerns you."

"Well, maybe it doesn't. But maybe it does." He handed Rhostok the paper he had been holding. "This is the blood chemistry report on Paul Danilovitch. Do you know if he was taking any medication?"

"What did the widow say?"

"She said all he was taking were some supplements. But the report indicates an abnormally high level of serum potassium. More than twice the normal level. The only way the level could be that high would be for him to be taking oral doses of potassium chloride. Do you know whether he had a weak heart?"

"Not that I knew about. I saw him out jogging almost every day after he got back to town."

"Potassium chloride is usually prescribed for patients with weak hearts. Usually older people or patients with specific cardiac problems. What it does is make the heart work harder. It increases the heart rate and raises the blood pressure. If you've got a weak heart, it could save your life, but if your heart is fine, you wouldn't want to take it. With an elevated level of potassium, any kind of physical exertion could trigger cardiac arrest in someone with an otherwise healthy heart."

"That's what killed him?" Rhostok stared at the numbers on the sheet. "He was taking potassium chloride?"

"That's not exactly what I said," O'Malley corrected him. "What I said is his blood contained a very high level of serum potassium. We'll never know if he was taking potassium chloride, because his body would quickly metabolize it into serum potassium. And serum potassium is a chemical that's always present in the blood, although normally at much lower levels than we found in this case."

"Did you check their medicine cabinet?"

"Of course. It's part of our routine in a case like this. All I found was the usual aspirin, mouthwash, and vitamins. No supplements except a multivitamin for senior citizens."

"What about an autopsy?" Rhostok asked. "You could still dig him up."

"What are you looking for, a murder? An autopsy wouldn't tell us anything. Long-term use of potassium chloride could possibly cause gastrointestinal lesions. If it were medically prescribed, that's malpractice maybe. Not murder. A quick single dose, on the other hand, would be masked by the body's own production of serum potassium. No way could I prove foul play. In any event, the high level of potassium was simply a contributing factor. I don't need an autopsy to tell you who killed Paul Danilovitch."

"I'm waiting," Rhostok said.

"Well, hell, it's obvious," O'Malley grinned. "It was that beautiful young wife of his. With all that potassium in his system, his heart couldn't take the exertion. To put it crudely, she screwed him to death." He chuckled at his little joke. "And as far as I know, there's no law against killing a man that way."

Of course he was right, Rhostok thought. Even if the act were premeditated, done with full knowledge of the fatal effect fornication could have on an individual with a weak heart, no one in the history of law enforcement had ever been charged with murder by sex. He wasn't sure that was what had happened, but if it were, it would be the perfect crime.

Thirty

Robyn Cronin's instincts told her not to open the door.

Just turn around and get as far away from this room as she could. Forget the assignment she had been given and the reason she took the job at Channel One in the first place. Just get the hell out of there.

But as she had done so many times before in her broadcasting career, she ignored her instincts. She told herself this was a time to be calm and logical, not emotional.

She was late for the staff meeting and the others were already inside. A rush of overheated air and acrid smoke greeted her when she opened the door. She paused for a moment in the doorway, trying to adjust her eyes to the dim light. The conference room, which the ratings consultant had converted into his personal office, was windowless and dark, except for a small green-shaded desk lamp in front of him and the red-hot coil of a portable electric heater humming in the corner beside him. There was no ventilation in the room, the air conditioning having been turned off when the consultant moved in. Jason, Mary Pat, Lee, Don, and the camera crews were all there, perspiring heavily. The heater's red glow was reflected on the sheen of their sweat-soaked faces.

The only person in the room who didn't seem uncomfortable was the ratings consultant.

He sat at one end of the conference table, which now served as his desk. He wasn't the well-groomed product of the East Coast media establishment they had all expected when the announcement had first come through. He was a shriveled old man wearing a heavy tweed jacket over a crewneck sweater. In spite of the stifling heat in the room, he appeared to be shivering.

"Close the door," he commanded in a raspy voice. "You're letting in a draft."

Robyn did as she was ordered, crossing the threshold and finding a place against the wall. The small desk lamp cast just enough of a glow to light up the consultant. His tiny figure was almost hidden behind a pile of computer printouts and ratings books. His white hair was an uncombed thicket that hung over the tops of pendulous ears. His face was pale and wrinkled, his eyebrows overgrown, his cheeks sunken. Two arthritic hands curled around the huge bowl of an antique pipe, as if trying to draw warmth from it.

"You're late," the consultant said.

His name was Hamilton Winfield, but they often referred to him simply as the consultant. As if his role at the station provided all the identification he required.

"I was on the phone with my contact at the coroner's office," she explained.

"Does he know about the hand?"

"Apparently he does now."

"That's too bad. Too bad. I don't know how much longer we can keep it quiet."

The consultant took the pipe from his mouth. The smoke wasn't the aromatic kind most men seemed to prefer. This smoke was bitter and dense. It reminded Robyn of smoldering autumn leaves. She took a handkerchief from her purse. She wanted desperately to leave, to get back out in the cool sweet air conditioning of the outer office. But it was too late for that now.

"What happened in Middle Valley this morning?" he asked. "Did you see the hand?"

"Yes. They're keeping it in a freezer at the police station."

The consultant chuckled.

"They probably think they're preserving it. Did you get a close look at it?"

"After some arguing with the acting police chief, yes. Rhostok is a stubborn man, just like you said he'd be. But when I threatened to put the story on the air, he finally took the hand out of the freezer to show me."

"Describe it."

"It was kind of gruesome, but other than that, there didn't seem to be anything unusual about it. It was a man's right hand. Fairly large, looked like it came from a big man, maybe farmer or laborer. Thick fingers, yet strangely, no calluses. The flesh was cut cleanly at the wrist bone. I couldn't see any sign of decomposition. I'm not an expert on severed hands, but I've seen dead bodies before. I'd say the hand couldn't have been in the vault for more than a day."

"What about the blood? Was it still fluid?"

"No way to tell. It was frozen solid."

"Why didn't the policeman send it to the coroner? Isn't that the law around here?"

"He said he wants to investigate further. He also doesn't want any publicity. He's trying to keep it quiet, to avoid any sensationalized media stories, which he says will upset the local citizens, most of whom are Russian and very superstitious."

"That's wise of him. At least he's keeping it quiet. I assume then that he welcomed your offer to keep the story off the air."

"He thought it was his idea." Robyn smiled.

"Very good," the consultant said. "Very nicely handled."

"We agreed on a seventy-two-hour delay."

"And he agreed to keep you informed of any new developments?"

"Yes. But frankly, I don't see why we're wasting so much time on this, playing around like it's some major story, and why it's so important that we get an exclusive. Jason used to call this kind of thing spook stuff, and would have put me on the air with it at noon, instead of wasting time cutting a deal to keep it quiet."

It was the first time she had worked up the courage to challenge the consultant. His arrival at the station had been preceded by a letter from the holding company that owned the string of stations of which Channel One was among the smallest. The letter gave the old man total operational control over news programming. He was a veteran newsman, according to the letter, and now worked as a specialist in boosting ratings, having revitalized the news departments of failing TV stations in New York, Seattle, Boston, and other major markets.

"That's why Jason is no longer in charge of the news department," the consultant said. "And I'm afraid you still have a lot to learn about what makes a good news story, and how to handle it."

She looked to Jason for support, but he avoided her eyes.

"This isn't real news," Robyn insisted. "It's a curiosity. A mystery. But not real news."

"The curiosity is that a person is dead, and the police apparently can't identify the victim. Or perhaps they don't want to. When you spoke to this Rhostok, did he have any idea how or where the owner of the hand died?"

"You're jumping to a conclusion," Robyn said. "Just because they found a hand, doesn't mean the person is dead."

She could see she was getting him angry. He sucked in short bursts of air until the bowl of his pipe glowed red. His root-like hands clutched it tightly, relishing the heat.

"You think this is some innocent affair?" the consultant growled. "You know nothing of why it happened, or what terrible events it might foretell. Your job is to uncover the news, not to make excuses for it or try to minimize it."

"A good news story is based on fact," she said. "Not conjecture."

"We already have a fact. A human hand. That is enough of a fact."

"But that's all we have. Anything beyond that single fact is conjecture. Not news. Just conjecture."

"You're wrong. We know that something evil has happened. We may soon be forced to share that fact with our viewers, and warn them that more evil is yet to come."

He puffed deeply on his pipe, sending sparks into the dark air, flooding the room with more of the bitter smoke. Robyn coughed into her handkerchief. Her cheeks were feeling flushed with the heat.

"How do you know what's going on?" She challenged him. "You didn't talk to anyone in Middle Valley like I did. You don't know anything about the hand except what your mysterious source told you."

"But I know about evil," the consultant growled. "I know the power of evil to affect the ratings. If you studied news ratings the way I do, you'd know beyond any doubt that it is a fascination with evil that draws viewers to the news."

The pipe was forgotten for a moment. In its place, the consultant's eyes took on the red glow of the heater in the corner. But that was impossible, Robyn realized. The heater was behind him and couldn't be casting its image on his pupils. She rubbed her own eyes, trying to clear her vision. It must be the heat, she thought, when the strange glow in the consultant's eyes didn't disappear.

"Think of the major news stories of your generation, the ones that continue to haunt us," he went on. "The World Trade towers, Oklahoma City, ethnic cleansing in Kosovo, the Kennedy assassinations, and before that, Hitler and the Holocaust and Nagasaki . . . they are all stories that illustrate the dark side of human experience. The public is infatuated with evil. No matter how you try to deny it, the most successful news stories are those that put on display the greatest measure of inherent evil."

The silence in the room was so great, Robyn could hear the hot air being sucked through the stem of the consultant's pipe and the smacking of his lips as they opened to expel more of the hateful fumes.

"You may laugh and think the old fool is being dramatic." He looked away from her for a moment, turning his reddish eyes on the others in the room. "But it is my understanding of this basic truth that has made me one of the most successful ratings consultants in America today. And I am here to implement all that I have learned."

Robyn coughed weakly and put her hand to her mouth, trying to prevent the smoke from entering her lungs. The old man glared at her. Damn, she thought. He thinks I'm laughing at him.

"I'm sorry," she apologized. "It's the smoke."

He made a point of blowing an extra mouthful of fumes in her direction. She could feel the trickles of perspiration rolling down her back, soaking her seventy-dollar silk blouse. She worried about the smoke ruining her clothing. And she worried that the consultant was singling her out for his wrath.

"You may resist my methods at first," he said. "But when you see the ratings increase, you'll come around to my way of thinking—yes, you will."

She didn't like the way he directed his smile at her. Smiled and sucked on the end of his pipe as if he drew nourishment from the foul-smelling instrument.

"And you, Miss Cronin," he continued. "I can make you famous. If you handle this story the way I instruct you, the news departments of all three networks will be bidding for your services. Would you like someday to be working at the network level?"

What else could she say?

"Yes."

"Very well, then. Now that we know where the hand is, we have to find a way to get it into our possession."

"What?" She couldn't believe she had heard him right.

"I want that hand," he said. "I want you to get it for me." He reached under the conference table and withdrew a stainless-steel case, which he slid across the table towards her. "I want you to bring it to me in this container."

Thirty-One

It wasn't until she reached the privacy of Jason's office that she allowed her anger to boil over.

"He's crazy," she shouted. "Absolutely crazy! All that talk about evil and the ratings. And everybody sitting there like they believed it, including you! I never saw anything like it."

"I think you're overreacting," Jason said.

He was a tall, slender man with sandy hair and a loose grin that pulled his mouth to one side. He wore pleated chino slacks, Gucci loafers, and a Rolex watch and walked with a perpetual slouch, as if he were self-conscious about his height. The consensus around the station had been that he was too soft for the job of news director. Too flexible. Too easily manipulated. She saw that at their first meeting, when she charmed him into hiring her over Lee Montgomery's objections. Thanks to Jason, she had been successful so far at getting enough face-time on the newscasts. But now she was worried that his diminished role at the station could be a threat to her career goals.

"Doesn't it bother you, having a nut like him running the news operation?" she asked. "I know we've got a problem with the damn ratings, but my God, the man looks like he stepped out of an old horror movie. He's got that heater on all the time and the room closed up and dark, and that stinking pipe . . . I don't know how I'll ever get that odor out of my clothes."

"He's an old man," Jason said. "He's probably got circulation problems. Maybe arteriosclerosis, like my father had. Dad always kept the house so hot, we couldn't sleep at night, even in the winter."

Built into the wall of Jason's office was a bank of Sony TV monitors, each with its own video recorder mounted below. They were programmed to record the news broadcasts of all six local channels, including Action News. Jason pressed a single master control button and all six monitors flickered to life, simultaneously replaying last night's ten o'clock news segments.

"But he's weird, Jason. He gives me the creeps."

"The way he presents himself is unusual, I'll grant you that." Jason stretched out his six-foot-six-inch frame on the black Spanish leather couch. His legs, too long for the couch, extended over the arm. He crossed his hands behind his head, snuggling his shoulders into a leather pillow. "He's certainly not what I'd expect a ratings consultant to look like. He must be terrific at what he does to be able to get away with that routine of his."

The video replay on the top right monitor showed the Action News logo dissolving through to gray-haired Lee Montgomery, sitting at the prop news desk with the usual blank sheets of paper in his hand. Faking an expression of surprise at the intrusion of the camera, Lee looked up from the papers, raised his left eyebrow, and smiled as he started to read the news from the teleprompter. The optics of the TV camera had the usual flattering effect on his face. As everyone at the station knew, the camera loved Lee.

"You're just going to roll over and accept this?" Robyn asked. "You're not going to call the owners and protest?"

"What good would it do? He's already here. You saw the letter. He's officially in charge, at least for a while. And if I were you, I'd be careful how I speak to him. I don't think he likes people to disagree with him."

While he talked, Jason was watching the monitors. He was always watching the damn monitors, she thought. As if he were going to find some secret in them. As if they were going to reveal how to stop the ratings slide at Channel One.

"The man is a disaster," Robyn insisted. "He's going to run this station right into the ground."

She purposely stepped between Jason and the TV.

"Come on, Robyn, honey. Give the old guy a chance. He makes some good points."

"You're actually on his side?"

Jason shifted to a sitting position so he could continue watching the news replays.

"The man obviously has experience. He was a foreign correspondent for the *Herald Tribune* in the 1930s, before he switched to radio. He covered the Second World War for the Blue Network. Christ, he did a live broadcast from Hitler's bombed-out bunker in 1945. The man knows how to cover a story. And give the owners credit for some brains, too. They wouldn't have sent him here if they didn't think he could turn the station around."

She moved her body closer to him, until it was impossible for him to see around her anymore.

"Guts and gore," she said. "That's all he wants."

Jason reached out to wrap his arms around her waist. She tried to suppress a shiver.

"People like to see those things on the news," he said. "Morbid fascination. It's the same reason people slow down on the highway to look at a car wreck. How do you think the *National Enquirer* got where it is today?"

"If I wanted to work at the *National Enquirer*, I would have gone there. And I would have been the best damn reporter they have."

He started pulling her in closer.

"I'm sure you would," he said. "You're a terrific reporter, Robyn. You've got a great future. That's why I think you should get out there and show the consultant what you can do. This is your big chance. He wants that hand. Go get it for him."

She tried to hold back, to avoid yielding, but he was too strong. He pulled her down to him, as he had done so many times before. The warmth of his body melted her anger. She let herself relax, to be molded and shaped to his contours. She rested her head against him, nuzzling her cheek into the hollow of his chest. She felt comfortable and secure with the familiar smell of his body.

"He scares me, Jason," she said in a quieter voice. "I'm afraid of him, but I don't know why."

"You're a tough little cookie. You'll find a way to cope."

She felt the warmth of his breath against her hair.

"I've never met anyone so strange," she said.

Jason kissed the top of her head.

"Mmmmm, that feels good," she murmured, snuggling in closer to him. She shivered at the feeling of his lips on her scalp. He was touching some forgotten feminine nerve that sent its primitive signals throughout her body.

He kissed her again, moving his lips to the top of her forehead, brushing the tip of his tongue ever so lightly along the sensitive edge of her hairline. Finally, he stopped at her temple, where he gave her a kiss so tender and delicate, she let out a sigh. She turned to raise her lips to his.

But their eyes didn't meet, because he was still watching Lee Montgomery on the monitor. Apparently, he hadn't taken his eyes away from the TV the entire time he was caressing her. Irritated that she wasn't getting his full attention, she pulled away from him.

"Hey, what's the problem, Robyn?"

"I thought I could depend on you."

He laughed and tried to pull her close again, but she resisted, struggling out of his arms.

"Why won't you back me up?" she demanded.

"You take these things too seriously," he said. "You'll get your big break, you'll see. Why don't you just relax and let it happen for you?"

But the moment was gone. And with it, she realized, something more. She pulled farther away from Jason, out of the reach of his long arms.

"You won't stand up against the consultant, will you?" she asked. "Not for me. Not for the station. Not even for yourself."

He wasn't going to be much help to her anymore, she realized. There was no longer any need to hide her scorn.

"This is nothing for us to fight about, Robyn." He gave up trying to reach her and settled back down on the couch, keeping his eyes on the monitors while he talked. "I've been in situations like this before. The best thing to do is to go with the flow, let the scenario play itself out. If the old fart makes a mistake, I'll be ready to step right back into the picture."

"That's fine for you," she said. "But what about the rest of us?"

"Why don't you admit what's really bothering you, Robyn? You're just upset because you haven't been getting much on-air time since the consultant showed up."

"Correction: I haven't been getting *any* air time since he showed up. Zip. Zero. What kind of message is that supposed to send to me?"

"The man as much as promised that you'd get your big break if you do what he tells you. Why don't you accept him at his word?"

"Because what he's doing doesn't make any sense. He claims this business with the severed hand is going to be a big story. But he sends me up to Middle Valley without a camera crew. And he tells me to make a deal with the police, can you imagine that? Even before we get the story, he wants me to promise the police that we won't go on-air with it. Now he wants me to get the damn hand for him. Not the story. Just the hand. Now how am I supposed to do that? The police won't even release it to the coroner."

"Knowing you, I'm sure you'll think of something."

"I'm sure I will," she muttered.

And if she didn't, she wondered, what then? Start over at another small station? Waste another two years trying to win a regular on-air position? In an industry that prized youth and attractiveness, she wasn't sure how much longer she could wait for that fabled "big break."

It was four years since she had graduated with honors in journalism from the University of Pennsylvania. Urged on by enthusiastic professors, she entered the workforce convinced that she was on the fast track to a high-profile career in television. The professors had told her it was the golden age for women in broadcasting. They had told her the male monopoly on the news had finally been broken. They had shown her a recent study of the five major markets that indicated female reporters dominated the midday and early-evening newscasts by a ratio of six to four. For a woman as intelligent and with as attractive an on-camera personality as Robyn, the future couldn't be brighter. Or so she was told.

But those professors had no experience in the real world. For every opening Robyn learned about, there seemed to be dozens of women applying who were more attractive than she. She thought of them as empty-headed blondes lured by the glamour of high-paying media jobs, the kind of women who probably thought being on a network news-magazine was almost as good as being a movie star.

Of course, being empty-headed had nothing to do with it. She realized there was a particular personality news directors seemed to prefer. In men, it was the authority figure, an individual with a mature voice and calm demeanor, who was the prototypical anchor. At his side, it was usually a cheerful blonde with a perky smile who often wore a red outfit and would always end the newscast with an almost flirtatious wink and nod at the camera.

With that insight, she immediately changed her hair color from its natural brunette to blonde. Not just standard blonde, but a pale straw-blonde, blonder than any other woman she encountered on her interviews. She changed her makeup to emphasize her eyes and mouth, mimicking the cosmetic techniques that were common to all the major female news personalities. Five-inch heels and a carefully teased hairdo made her height seem almost normal.

Two weeks after her makeover, she was hired for her first job in broadcasting. It was a small UHF station in Altoona, Pennsylvania, where she did mostly off-camera work. It wasn't very satisfying. She did a lot of rewriting of stories from the *New York Times* and *Wall Street Journal,* condensing them to five- and ten-second segments that she often had to type into the teleprompter herself. She went out with a cameraman to interview the families of accident and crime victims, although skillful editing back at the station made it appear as if the anchor had done the interview.

She did get one or two on-camera opportunities, human-interest stories that she parlayed into her next job in Donora, in southeastern Pennsylvania. A year there, and she had the interview with Jason, which brought her to Channel One. She was soon doing fill-ins on the weather and occasional human-interest segments, plus of course, the usual off-camera reporting. Things finally seemed to be going well. Each week she was getting more face-time on camera. And with her new situation came immediate acceptance in the local community. She could go anywhere, interview anyone, pursue any story, and find that people accepted and even respected her. She was getting a reputation as a local TV personality. She put in the extra hours, the weekends, answered the calls in the middle of the night to cover accidents or fires or crimes in progress. She was happy and, perhaps inevitably, drifted into an intimate relationship with the man who hired her. The next step would be a regular on-air slot, he promised, and then she could parlay that into a co-anchor slot or else move on to a station in a bigger market.

It was all coming together for her. But the arrival of Hamilton Winfield threatened her career plans.

"I don't think the staff should panic," Jason said. "Usually what happens in a situation like this, the ratings people go for a quick fix. That's what I expect Winfield to do. Change the face on the tube. Bring in a new anchor, maybe dress up the set, and go for more sensational stories. It's purely cosmetic, but it's the single fastest, cheapest, and most visible action he can take." Jason chuckled as he watched the end of Lee Montgomery's traditional salute to the viewers. "If I were Lee, I'd be a very nervous anchorman right now."

"You hired Lee," she said. "I thought the two of you were friends."

"Sure, we're friends," he said with a shrug. "But it's out of my hands now. In any event, this could be a terrific opportunity for you, Robyn. You always wanted your chance at the anchor slot. Well, it might be a long shot, but be nice to the man, do what he tells you, and it might happen."

"Do you really believe what he said, about the way to build ratings?"

"I'm not sure what I believe anymore. I've been watching these taped news replays for six years now. Watching and analyzing and trying to make our news coverage better than the competitors. And where did it get me? Last place in the ratings. And an outsider who comes in to change our format without even consulting me."

He got up and turned off the monitors. He tried to take her in his arms again, pick up where they left off, but she pulled away.

"Well, what the hell," he said. "Maybe the old man is right. A little evil might be the best thing for Channel One right now."

Something in his voice frightened her.

"What harm could it do?" he asked.

"I don't know," she answered quietly, rubbing her arms to get rid of the chill that had suddenly come over her.

She was worried about Hamilton Winfield.

She was afraid that the real reason for the sudden arrival of the strange old man might have nothing to do with the ratings.

Thirty-Two

It was close to midnight when Nicole heard heavy footsteps coming up the stairs. She drew the yellow nightgown tighter around her and waited with dread as the footsteps came closer. The giant policeman, for she was sure it was him, made no attempt to hide his approach. At the top of the stairs, he apparently stumbled in the darkness. She heard a loud, almost painful groan, and she imagined him picking himself up and heading for her room. Probably drunk, she thought.

He was supposed to be spending the night downstairs, protecting her from any intruders. She had resisted the idea of having a man, even a policeman, in the house, fearing exactly what she was certain was now going to happen.

The bedroom door trembled against the weight of his fist.

She jumped out of bed and turned on the lights, looking around the room for anything she could use as a weapon. She wasn't going to give in to his drunken sexual demands without a fight.

"Open up!" he shouted.

"Go away!"

"No . . . please . . . open up!" Pleading now, his voice sounded unnatural, almost liquid.

"Go away!"

She heard him throw his weight against the door. It shuddered violently. The lock strained for a moment, holding onto the wooden frame, but finally surrendered its grip in a burst of wooden splinters. The door exploded inward. Otto Bruckner's massive body crashed to the bedroom floor.

Nicole screamed.

Bruckner raised his head, and she could see that something awful had happened to him.

Blood was pouring from the big policeman's mouth. His face was flushed, his eyes streaked with red. His breathing made a wet sucking sound. He seemed to be struggling to speak, but the flow of blood from his throat was making it impossible.

Helpless and frightened, Nicole drew back into the corner by the closet. She watched in horror as Bruckner tried to rise, then collapsed, and began to pull his way across the floor to her, his fingernails scratching against the oak planks.

"Get . . . out . . ." he finally gasped. "Go . . ."

His last heavy breath expired in a spray of blood. His body fell still. The spattering of red on the floor quickly turned into a small pool, fed by the stream of blood that poured freely from his mouth and nose.

She watched the policeman's blood spread across the floor to engulf his shirt and pants.

It was the second time in a week she had seen a man die in her bedroom.

But this death was more frightening than her husband's. This was no heart attack, no normal death from natural causes. The amount of blood that poured from Bruckner's body suggested some terrible injury. The way he pounded at her door . . . his dying words . . . it seemed a desperate attempt to warn her . . . about what? The man was a giant, almost seven feet tall and probably close to three hundred pounds. Yet something . . . or someone . . . had killed him. But how? And who?

Was there an intruder in the house?

She listened carefully, but couldn't hear anything except her own nervous breathing.

That didn't mean no one was there, of course, waiting for her in the darkness.

There was only one man she knew who would have wanted to enter the house at this time of night.

Only one man she knew who had the strength and the cunning to kill the huge policeman.

That man was Vassily.

She remembered how he had shown up the previous night, and how frightened she had been to see him there, calmly smoking his Red Star cigarette. Life with Vassily was always an uneasy combination of intimidation and shows of affection, with Nicole never knowing from one moment to the next which face he would show. She had expected one of his more brutal forms of punishment for her allowing herself to get married, however unknowingly, to a client. But he had smiled, endorsed the union, and, acting in an almost fatherly manner, took them both out to an outrageously expensive dinner at the Bellagio, and even paid for the lawyer who drew up Paul's will. He had wished them good fortune in their new life, and when they left Vegas, she thought she was finally free of him. And then last night he was back to take control of her again, alternating promises of money with his usual threats if she would perform one last assignment for him.

She had failed in that assignment, failed to get him the object that he said would bring him great riches. He had been angry when she came out of the police station, telling her to walk home because he didn't want to be seen with her. She knew the anger would continue to boil in him, so when she got home, she invited the big policeman to take up residence in the downstairs living room. She felt safer with the policeman inside the house instead of outside in the patrol car. He was a big man, a bald-headed giant who could take on almost any adversary.

Except Vassily, she thought, as she stared down at Bruckner.

There would have been no reason for him to kill the policeman, unless . . . unless in one of his sudden and violent mood swings, he decided to exact retribution for her failure.

She stared at the dead policeman at her feet, remembering his last words. He had climbed the stairs and knocked down her door to warn her to get out of the house . . . to go. Yes, that was what she had to do. Get out of the house. Go, go, go . . .

But go where?

She didn't know any of the neighbors well enough to trust them. Vassily, with all his cunning, might even have made allies of them. No, it would be too risky for her to go to the neighbors.

And calling 911 was not an option, either. When they found the dead policeman in her bedroom, the second man to die in her bedroom in a week, nobody would believe she hadn't played some part in his death.

She had to find a place to hide out for a few days. She couldn't go to the police, couldn't think of anyone to shelter her. But she had to find a place to stay, a place where she would be safe from Vassily.

But first, of course, she had to get out of the house alive.

Thirty-Three

Nicole stepped carefully around the spreading pool of blood, around the policeman's body, and to the top of the stairway. There she hesitated.

Why wasn't there any light downstairs?

Had the policeman been sitting there in the dark, hoping to surprise any intruder?

Or had Vassily, if it were he, turned off the lights after surprising his victim?

Either way, the staircase led down into darkness, a descent into danger. Nevertheless, it represented her only hope of escape. The darkness might give her an advantage over her unseen adversary. After all, she knew the entire layout of the house, knew where every piece of furniture was located. Like in that film she had seen about the blind girl escaping a killer by turning out the lights, Nicole thought she might be able to navigate her way around the chairs and tables and lamps in the darkness. If Vassily tried to attack, he was sure to stumble over some piece of furniture or bump into the wall of one of the small rooms, maybe allowing her enough time to escape.

Trembling with fear, she started down the stairs. Her bare feet searched out each step, feeling for the squeaky treads, moving slowly and quietly.

When she reached the bottom of the stairs, when she was standing vulnerable and frightened in the darkness, she suddenly realized the folly of her plan.

At any moment, Vassily could simply turn on the lights. For all she knew, he could be sitting in the front room, waiting for her to walk into his trap. How could she have been so stupid? She stood motionless, not daring to breathe, listening for the slightest sound, expecting an attack at any moment.

The front door was less than ten feet away, but it seemed an impossible distance to cross. She'd have to pass between the entrance to the living room on one side and the dining room on the other. And she had already made certain both the front and back doors were locked and double-bolted. If Vassily was already in the house, any attempt to open either door would be noisy and cost her precious time.

Instead, Nicole backed slowly down the hall towards the kitchen, sliding her hand along the wall until she felt the wooden door that led down to the cellar.

With agonizing slowness, she opened the cellar door, praying that no sound would give away her location. Cool, damp air welcomed her as she descended this steeper, rougher stairway. She shivered as her bare feet slid across the cold earthen floor at the bottom. It was an old-style cellar, with foundation walls constructed of round stones joined with rough cement. She felt her way along the wall, moving cautiously to avoid stumbling over the clutter that lined the sides. The cellar was a part of the house she seldom visited. It was used as a storage area for old furniture, tools, and work clothes. The dank air was filled with the aroma of moldering fabrics and rusting metal and moist earth.

She hesitated when her feet struck a mound of soft dirt. It warned her she was near one of those mysterious craters someone had dug in the cellar floor.

She continued moving along the wall, away from the stairway. She wished desperately that she could see something: a shadow or an outline or a gradation of darkness, anything to help her see where she was going. But not even the faintest rays of ambient light existed down here. She could have been stumbling through one of the abandoned coal mines below Middle Valley and it wouldn't have been any blacker.

Her foot felt another pile of soft dirt. She felt for the edge of the dirt with her toes and stepped around it.

And suddenly she was falling.

Nothing beneath her feet.

Hands grabbing instinctively in the air.

Unable to save herself from falling in the blackness, but remembering at the last moment not to scream.

And landing at the bottom of what seemed to be one of the largest of the holes. It was the length and depth of a shallow grave. She lay motionless for a while, listening for any sounds upstairs. She thought she heard the front door open. Thought she heard gentle footsteps. Yes. That was definitely a floorboard squeaking. Someone was moving around upstairs. There wasn't any time to waste. Nicole raised herself to her knees. She groped her way out of the hole and crawled through the blackness to the back of the cellar, blindly feeling for the steps that led up to the backyard.

At the top of the stairs was a set of horizontal double doors. They were secured from the inside with a wooden bar, which she easily removed. But the doors had to be pushed upwards and were too heavy to move with her hands. She bent over and pressed her back against them. The rough wood bit through her silk nightgown. She pushed slowly, fearful of making any noise, straining against the weight, until she was finally able to raise one of the doors. She held it open a few inches while she listened for any sound. All she could hear was the noise of a car's tires squealing in the distance, some teenage driver probably.

She waited, still listening.

The next sound she heard came from behind her. It was the hallway door, the one she had opened so carefully, the very door that led to the cellar. Someone was opening it and trying to be quiet, but not being as successful at it as she had been. The opening of that second door created a draft that blew gently across her face and down the front of her nightgown.

She had to get out now! No more worrying about being quiet. She shoved the door up with all her strength and stumbled out into the backyard.

The cool night air washed over her. In the bright moonlight, she could clearly see the line of hedges, the white utility shed in the back, the lights of the windows in the neighboring houses. The moonlight made it easy to see where she was going, but she knew it also made her bright yellow nightgown easier to spot. She hurried to the side of the yard and crouched in the shelter of the hedge.

She was breathing in short, nervous bursts. Trying to listen for any further sounds from the house. All she could hear was the sound of a television set, maybe Jay Leno's voice, coming from the house next door.

None of what was happening made any sense to her. Was it all her imagination? Had she really heard the sound of footsteps in the house? Maybe she hadn't quite closed the hallway door and the draft from the cellar door caused it to squeak open? Was it her own panic that chased her out of the house, sending her scrambling through the cellar and the dirt and the dew-soaked grass to leave her trembling and wet and crouching in the hedge like a madwoman?

No. The policeman breaking down her bedroom door wasn't a product of her imagination. He was real. His death was real. The blood on the floor was real. The danger in the house was real.

But where could she could go now?

Not to the neighbors. Even if she could trust them, they'd think for certain she was crazy, pounding on their back door in the middle of the night in her dirt-smeared nightgown.

And even if they did take her in, what then? They'd call the police, and she'd end up in jail. She'd have to think of something else. But first, she'd have to get away from here. She was halfway across the backyard when a dog started barking in the house next door. Across the alley, another dog heard and joined in.

Nicole slipped into an opening in the hedge and waited. She had made no noise at all since leaving the cellar, she was certain. Was there someone else out here? Someone waiting in the alley?

Oh God, no, she prayed, drawing herself deeper into the prickly hedge, feeling her nightgown catch and tear on the branches.

From her hiding place, she watched a searchlight beam click on and then off inside the house. A shadow appeared on the back porch. It separated itself from the shadow of the house and crossed the yard, where she thought she heard a muffled conversation. The dog on the other side of the alley grew more agitated.

The shadow came back into the yard, pausing at the hedge no more than an arm's length from where she huddled. The hedge rustled above her. At any moment a hand would reach out to seize her. There was no escape.

The sudden white beam of a searchlight blinded her. It shot over her head into the neighboring yard, dancing along the lawn, past the children's swing set, pausing to inspect the garbage cans lined up against the back fence, and exciting the dogs into a frenzy of barking.

The porch lights went on at the neighbor's house. The flashlight clicked off. The shadow detached itself from the hedge and started towards the house. The neighbor's dog came running out to investigate, a small white poodle barking furiously. The dog darted through the hedge, ignoring her, and headed for the man with the light. Nicole watched as it approached him, snapping and snarling. She saw a sudden movement, heard a sickening crunch of bone and flesh, and shuddered at the dying screams of the little dog.

In that moment, she knew with terrifying certainty that Rhostok's warnings were true.

Someone was after her.

She took advantage of the dog's pitiful yelps to slip the rest of the way through the hedge. She moved quickly through the next yard, keeping away from the open lawn area, picking her way past a wheelbarrow, a coiled garden hose, a stack of flower buckets, and a parked car. By the time she heard the dog's owner shouting from his back porch, she was four houses away.

The wet grass soaked the bottom of her nightgown. Driveway gravel stung the bottoms of her feet, and she had a dull ache in her thigh from falling into the strange pit in the cellar.

She kept going, not knowing where she was headed.

She had no choice.

Just keep moving.

Get out of there, for God's sake. Run away. Find a place to hide. Find shelter.

But where?

Who could she possibly trust in this town where she was still considered an outsider? She barely knew anyone, unable to penetrate the closed minds of these people to whom any newcomer was suspect. Where could she possibly find refuge in a town so alien to her that she didn't even feel part of her own husband's funeral?

Gradually, an idea took hold.

On painful feet (oh God, why didn't she think to put on some slippers?), she hurried through a half-dozen backyards, then across a street and through another series of yards and alleys where she roused other dogs for brief moments, and finally headed up into the older part of Middle Valley.

At the top of a small hill, outlined against the thin silvery clouds, rose the silhouette of a massive brick building. It was crowned with an onion-shaped dome. Atop the dome was a Cyrillic cross. It was the Old Ritual Russian Orthodox Church of Saint Sofia, the site of her husband's funeral service.

Standing beside the church was the residence of the *Episkop*, a two-story building made of the same brick as the church itself. And like the church, the rectory was also in a state of disrepair. Nicole stumbled on the front sidewalk, which tilted at unplanned angles. The iron gate was off its hinges, resting against the fence, which was propped up with reinforcing pipe.

She felt safer once she entered the church grounds. Sanctuary was an old tradition with churches. She knew that from watching an NBC *Dateline* story about Haitian refugees. Well, she was a refugee tonight. And the bearded priest had already demonstrated how deeply he believed in the old traditions. She hoped he wouldn't turn her away.

She went around to the back door. A light in the kitchen revealed a tiny figure seated at a bare wooden table. It was a crone, stitching an ornate piece of church tapestry. The woman wore a long-sleeved, high-collared black dress that left only her bony hands and wizened face visible. A white lace skullcap covered her gray hair.

Nicole tapped at the window.

Startled, the old woman's head snapped erect.

Nicole tapped again, and the woman darted out of the room. Moments later, she returned with *Episkop* Sergius and nodded towards the door.

Instinctively, Nicole pulled her nightgown tight around her body, brushed some of the dirt from her hair, and wiped her bare feet on the porch. Knowing how dreadful she must look, she smiled bravely when the *Episkop* opened the door.

He seemed transfixed, as if seeing her for the very first time.

"Mother of God," he murmured. The same words he had used at their first encounter.

His breath smelled of sacramental wine.

A few days ago, she had felt only scorn for the coarse, unkempt priest and the religion he represented, dismissing him as another Russian immigrant with a peasant background who was unwilling to accept modern ways. Her current state of desperation had changed her image of him to a possible protector, a man whose vows would require him to defend her from evil.

"Please, please can I come inside?" Nicole begged.

After a moment's hesitation, the *Episkop* stood aside to let her enter. He closed the door behind her and motioned for the old woman, who watched suspiciously from the hallway, to draw the shades.

"Do they know you came here?" Sergius asked.

Nicole looked up at him, surprised by the question.

"You know who's after me?" she asked.

"You are running from someone," he said. "To be dressed the way you are, obviously you fear for your life."

The *Episkop* stared down at her with those cold gray eyes that seemed to peer deep inside her, as if searching for some hidden truth. She trembled, suddenly aware of her nakedness beneath the nightgown and the way her nipples, stiffened by the cold, pushed embarrassingly against the smooth silk.

He spoke in Russian to the old woman, who waved a bony hand for Nicole to follow her.

"Svetlana will cleanse you, *malyutchka,*" the *Episkop* said. His cavernous voice filled the room, leaving no space for her to object. "And then we will talk of your problem."

Svetlana led Nicole down the dark hallway. The floor was bare and uncarpeted, the air filled with the stale smell of years of neglect. Nicole followed the old woman up the stairs to a small bathroom at the end of another hallway, where a single bare bulb provided the only illumination. The room contained an ancient cast-iron tub and an antique toilet whose tank was positioned high up on the wall. A large white ceramic bowl and a pitcher of water waited on a small table beside the sink. A bar of white soap, a washcloth, and a folded towel lay next to them. Neatly laid out over the back of the only chair in the room were a black cotton slip and a white terry-cloth robe, a pair of bedroom slippers on the floor beneath.

The way the room was prepared made it almost seem as though her arrival had been anticipated.

Svetlana quickly stripped Nicole of her nightgown and ordered her to squat in the tub. Before Nicole realized what was happening, the woman poured cold water over her head and began soaping her. Nicole tried to resist, but she was too tired and the woman was surprisingly strong.

"You must be properly cleansed before approaching the holy *starets,*" Svetlana said. Her voice was heavily accented and gravelly with age.

Her hands moved expertly over Nicole's body. She rubbed the flesh, roughly at first and then more smoothly, and finally, after toweling her off, applied a thin coating of perfumed oil to every inch of Nicole's skin.

Wrapped in the warm terry-cloth robe and shod in slippers, Nicole was led back downstairs to a small chapel, a windowless room filled with glittering icons of the Madonna and Child, various martyrs being tortured and mutilated, and Christ ascending into Heaven on a cloud of angels.

The *Episkop* rose from a red velvet kneeler in front of the icons.

He locked his gray eyes on hers.

"You will be safe here, *malyutchka,*" he said, answering her question before she could ask it. "There is no one here but the three of us. What was once a thriving rectory is now an empty building for a single priest and his housekeeper."

Svetlana let out a sudden torrent of Russian words.

"Speak English for our visitor," the *Episkop* commanded, as if he could sense what Nicole was thinking. "She is frightened and fears that which she does not understand."

Nicole couldn't take her eyes away from the *Episkop*'s mesmerizing gaze.

"A single priest and a woman like her." The crone spat out the words. "Together under the same roof. It would be a serious scandal. What would the parishioners think?"

Sergius smiled at Nicole, ignoring the criticism.

"I follow the old ways," he told her. "You came here out of the night seeking shelter. I offer you the sanctuary of my house. But it can be done only in a way that protects my dignity."

"Which is . . . ?" Nicole asked.

"Svetlana," he called over his shoulder to the crone. "You will leave us now. Go to your room."

The old woman scowled at Nicole, but obediently gathered up her needlework and left without uttering another word.

"You will stay in the room next to mine," the *Episkop* said.

Nicole took a step backward, suddenly unsure of the situation.

"The door to your room will remain open," the *Episkop* said, "as will mine."

"I'm grateful for your help." Nicole's voice was hesitant. "But I'd feel better if my door was locked."

"If you will stay here the night, all doors will be left unlocked and open," he said. "I am a man of God. To have a woman hide from me behind a locked door is an insult to the vows I have taken." He wrapped his hand around the wooden crucifix in his sash. "There is an ancient tradition among the holy men of Russia. It is a belief that devotion to God can only be considered strong if it is tested over and over again. Otherwise, it becomes weak, like a muscle that is never used. To spend a night with a woman in the room next to mine, that will be a test of my faith. Especially when the woman is as beautiful as you, *malyutchka*."

Nicole heard a noise in the hallway and assumed the old woman was still on the other side of the door, listening.

"You have been sent here by God, *malyutchka*," said the *Episkop*. "Sent here to test my faith. To prepare me for the terrible events that are yet to come."

Thirty-Four

Nicole waited in the darkness for *Episkop* Sergius to come to her, as she knew he would.

It didn't matter that he was a priest, a holy man who professed a devotion to God and the old rituals of his church. As long as he was still a man, he would come to her.

They always did.

He had taken her to an upstairs bedroom, opened the window to allow the night breeze to enter, and then made a show of blessing her, bidding her good night, and retiring to his own room. Through the open doors, she heard him muttering in Russian. Whether he was praying or talking to himself, she had no idea. His heavy feet paced back and forth as the night grew later.

She was starting to fall asleep when a creaking board in the hallway snapped her back awake.

That would be Sergius, she thought, having finally made up his mind.

In the end, he wasn't any different from the others.

In spite of all his protests about his faith and devotion to God, he hadn't been able to resist the temptation of a beautiful woman lying in a nearby bed. She waited under the bedsheet, listening as his footsteps drew closer.

The door swung open the rest of the way. Blocking the dim light of the hallway, cutting off any possible avenue of escape, stood the massive figure of the bearded priest.

Nicole pulled the sheet up to her chin.

Sergius came slowly to the side of the bed.

"Is this how they come to you?" he asked. Even in a whisper, the resonance of his voice filled the room.

"What do you mean?" Nicole asked.

"The men. The men who have come to you and abused you all these years. Is this how they come to you?"

The tone of his voice made her shiver. She had learned long ago that every man had his own particular demons. Those who began by asking questions were often the ones to fear the most.

"What do you want with me?" she asked, although she was certain she already knew the answer.

"Do not be afraid," he said.

He sat down on the edge of the bed. The old mattress sagged under his weight, shifting her body closer to him, until their hips touched. She pulled back to the other side of the bed.

"Men have been coming to you for many years," he said.

"That's none of your business," she responded. She didn't like these kinds of conversations. Too often they led to violence.

"It wasn't your doing," he said. "It was the sinful nature of the men who have been forcing themselves on you. Evil men. Old men and young. Even the man who lived with your mother."

Nicole let out a startled gasp.

"Who told you that?"

"I can see it in your eyes."

"The room is dark."

"The way I see requires no light," the *Episkop* said. "The images I see are not of the present."

"What do you know about my stepfather?"

Mistrustful of the bearded holy man, she clasped the bedsheet tighter to her.

"He came to you when you were but a child," Sergius whispered. "Beauty laid its curse upon you at an early age, *malyutchka*." Frighteningly, he used the same words she often used to describe what Fate had done to her. "And you have suffered from that curse ever since. You have been unable to escape its consequences."

"I don't want to talk about him."

"When your mother was away from home, he took you on her bed. You screamed out in fear and pain at first. But then you learned to please him."

"No one knew about that," she gasped.

"But your mother knew. She saw it in your eyes, just as I see it in your eyes. Yet she never left him. Even after you lost his child."

"It . . . it wasn't a child yet. Just tissue. Blood and tissue."

"We are all just blood and tissue," Sergius said. "It was a child. A girl."

"A girl? How could you . . . the doctors never . . ."

"She would have had blue eyes, like yours, *malyutchka*. And soft, silky blonde hair. She would have been a happy little girl, laughing and full of mischief the way you once were."

The image of a child flashed through Nicole's mind. A little girl in a white dress jumping rope and singing some childish song. Perhaps an image of herself in those happy days before losing her innocence. Or maybe a wishful fantasy of the child she would never have, conjured up in the mind of a woman with a damaged womb.

The image brought tears to her eyes. Her body began to tremble.

"Do not cry, *malyutchka*."

"He was a pervert," she spat out the words.

"The other men came soon after, when you left home," he said. "So many of them, attracted by your beauty, that after a while you stopped resisting."

"Is that why you're here?" she cried. "Because you think I won't resist?"

If that was all it was, just another man looking for sex, she could deal with it. The rest of it, however, his apparent knowledge of the most personal secrets of her adolescence, was the part that frightened her. Nicole moved farther away from him, until she was at the edge of the bed.

"Take off your clothing," he commanded.

"You're a priest," she said, wiping away her tears.

"Take off your clothing and lie back on the bed," he insisted.

She wanted desperately to resist. She wanted that part of her life to be over. But this strange priest was opening it up again. Frightening her by speaking of secrets so intimate that she had never shared them with anyone, including her husband. How could a stranger possibly know such things?

"Do as I tell you, *malyutchka*."

She wanted desperately to refuse. She knew it was terribly wrong. Even in her most depraved moments, she had never been involved with a priest. Yet there was something in the power of his voice that seemed to render her helpless. Despite the shame she felt, she obeyed his command. She slipped out of her nightgown and lay naked on the bed, her flesh exposed to the cool night breeze. Her breasts shivered. Was it from the breeze, or the anticipation of the first touch of his coarse fingers?

"I know all about your stepfather," he said. "I could tell you about the others and what they did to you. I know why you left your mother and ran away from home."

"You can't possibly know that," she said, thinking back to the horror of those days.

"You lost the baby, *malyutchka*. You lost the baby and you were left barren. The doctors who saved your life said you would never have children and your mother said it served you right. Instead of protecting you, your mother resented you."

"She hated me," Nicole said, her voice breaking.

"You were ashamed of yourself when you left home. You thought you were evil."

"Yes."

"And that was why you allowed those men to do with you as they did."

"Yes."

"In return, you thought they would protect you."

"Yes."

"But your sinful actions exposed you to greater dangers."

"I'm ashamed of what I did," she moaned, shivering as the night breeze bathed her naked body. "If you know as much about me as you claim, you'd know how much I've sinned. But I had no choice."

"Your sins are not unique," the *Episkop* said. "All mankind is immersed in a sea of evil. But it is this very evil that makes salvation possible. For without sin, there can be no redemption, and without redemption there can be no salvation."

She trembled at the first probing touch of his hand on her naked stomach.

It was a heavy hand, with rough fingers. Yet he moved it delicately along her skin, barely touching the surface. His fingertips moved in circles around her navel. Her stomach muscles tensed in an involuntary response.

"Without evil, there can be no good," he said.

The circles grew wider, his hand exploring more of her body.

"Yes," she whispered.

"Just as without Hell, there can be no Heaven."

"Yes."

"The Old Believers of the Holy Mother Church know that only through confronting sin can the faithful be saved. Do you believe that?"

"Yes."

Despite herself, her body heaved and quivered with pleasure as his fingers danced along her stomach and moved up into the hollow between her breasts.

"A holy man who has never faced temptation can never expect to see the face of God," he continued. "On the Holy Mountain in Athos, home of the great Orthodox monasteries, all females were banned to avoid temptation." His fingertips teased at her nipples, which immediately came erect. "The ban included females of all species, including the lowest animals. But it was all done in error. Temptation itself is the true source of moral strength. Only by pitting oneself against evil can one achieve salvation. That was why Jesus went into the desert: to confront Satan's temptations. Like Him, we must constantly confront evil in all its forms."

His hand came to rest on her right breast, completely enveloping the soft mound of flesh within his grasp.

"You think I am here to seduce you," he said. "But I am merely here to confront temptation. I am proving my strength over evil at this very moment, and in so doing, I am building my resistance for the future."

She felt his breath coming more rapidly, his body heat increasing. When he leaned over her, the cloth of his robe rubbed coarsely against her smooth skin. The contrast sent tremors through her body.

"You must not give yourself to me," he said.

The bristle of his beard scratched against the side of her breast.

"Promise you will not give yourself to me."

"I promise." He wasn't the first man who wanted her to pretend to resist.

She felt the warmth of his breath hovering just above her right nipple. She waited for him to take it into his wet mouth, for his teeth to nibble against its nubby surface as so many men had done before him.

"I am not like those other men," he suddenly said. He pulled away from her, withdrawing his hand from her flesh. "I am a soldier of God," he said, as he rolled away from her.

The night air quickly cooled Nicole's nipple, which remained erect, waiting for the arrival of the *Episkop*'s lips.

"A priest is like a soldier sent into battle," he went on. "The soldier cannot be certain of his courage until he finds himself locked in combat with the enemy. Likewise, a soldier of God cannot display his holy valor until he is locked in combat with the *Diavol*."

The bed groaned as he rolled back to face her once again. She sensed his hand moving towards her.

"I am here to offer you redemption," he said. "To show you the way to salvation."

She could feel the heat of his hand even before it touched her skin. He held it above her navel for what seemed a terribly long time. Her body quivered with anticipation. Slowly, ever so slowly, his hand moved towards her navel. She could sense the heat increasing, and with it some strange sort of energy, not quite electric, certainly not human, yet definitely emanating from his hand. In response, she felt her flesh begin to tingle. The microscopic hairs that cover all human skin seemed to rise, drawn from their pores by whatever animal magnetism his flesh possessed. And when his hand came to rest on her navel, she was unprepared for the violent reaction of her body. The contact sent her into a sudden series of actions so shocking that she threw her neck back and her legs wide apart and couldn't control the violent convulsions of her body pounding against the bed. Her hips bounced wildly on the mattress. Her legs strained and stiffened until they ached. Guttural, almost subhuman sounds came from deep within her throat.

The mere touch of his hand had transformed her into a thrashing sexual creature who felt more animal than woman.

And just as suddenly, his hand withdrew.

Yet its impact remained. All restraint, any notion of feminine modesty and bodily privacy were gone from her thoughts. She moaned and whined and called his name and begged him for more.

None of the men in her past, not even Paul whom she loved so dearly, or Vassily with whom she lived so long . . . not one of them ever was able to trigger so primitive a response inside her.

And still it wasn't enough.

She hungered for more.

Her body trembled, her stomach ached, her legs shook, her mind lusted for more.

And he had done nothing more than touch her.

She reached out to the *Episkop* in spite of her earlier promise. She wanted to bring him close and give herself to him. She wanted this bearded creature inside her.

But Sergius pulled himself away.

"You must resist me," he said.

"But why?" she cried out.

"To make yourself strong."

Her eager hands reached out into the darkness, but he was already beyond her grasp.

"Do you want me to beg?" she asked. "Is that what you want from me?"

She needed him on top of her, inside her, to finish what he had started. What no man had ever been able to ignite in her before.

"Please, my *Episkop*, I need you."

"No. You shall not have me."

She tried to locate him by the sound of his voice. There he was in the corner. But when she ran naked across the room, he was gone.

"Why are you doing this to me?" she whimpered. "Why torture me like this?"

His voice, when it came, was from the other side of the room, back near the bed.

"I do it to strengthen you in the Lord *Khristos*."

She spun around, and moved again towards him.

"How can you speak of religion at a time like this?" she asked in an angry voice. "After what you were doing? What kind of priest are you?"

"I am not one of your modern priests who have given themselves up to comfortable ways. In Russia, I was known as a *starets,* a prophet with the ability to see into men's souls." The resonance of his voice echoed through the room. It was everywhere and nowhere, impossible to locate. "I am a prophet, a healer, a holy man sent here to await the miracle that will light the way for the faithful to return to the church."

"What kind of holy man would treat a woman like this?"

"It is only to teach you discipline. If you are to follow me to the rebirth of our faith, you must have total control over yourself."

"Follow you?" she asked in disbelief. "Why should I follow you?"

"Because you see how strong I am. All those men who have taken you, unable to resist your beauty, they did it merely to satisfy their own animal needs. But my faith allows me to touch you without surrendering. You have never met a man like me. You need my strength, *malyutchka*. You need what I can teach you."

"I don't need anything from you," she shouted, turning from one dark corner to another, hoping to catch some hint of his location.

"I can see into your soul," he said. "You hunger for my strength."

"I hunger for your body."

"My body belongs to the Lord *Khristos,* not to you."

"Get away from me, then," she shouted. "Leave me alone."

She wrapped herself in the bedsheet and ran for the door. He stopped her in the middle of the room, tearing the sheet from her body with such force that she spun to the floor.

"Get back into bed," he commanded.

Meekly, she obeyed, crawling on her hands and knees until she reached the bed. She was ashamed of her nakedness now. Ashamed of the way she had begged for him. Ashamed of how she had defiled the memory of her husband so soon after his death. With tears streaming from her eyes, she pressed herself against the wall on the far side of the bed.

The weight of the *Episkop*'s body lowered itself once again upon the mattress. Not sitting this time, but lying down. He pulled Nicole's naked body against him. The crucifix in his sash poked against her ribs. She felt small and helpless in his arms. Vulnerable and frightened.

And something else.

Something that surprised her.

She felt grateful to him.

Grateful to be able to curl up like a child in his protective arms, without fear of being violated during the night.

"There is an old custom in Russia," he said in a gentle voice. "The *starechestvo* of the Old Church would lie down with women to prove their sanctity. Makari and Phillipov did it. And even the great saint Rasputin was said to have lain beside the Empress Alexandra. Tonight, we will follow the Old Ritual and lie here together to prove our strength and sanctity."

He placed a hand on her bare hip. This time he made no effort to explore her body.

He simply rested his hand on her soft flesh. A curious warmth continued to radiate from his hand, a warmth that she could feel penetrating the tissue beneath and entering her bloodstream, where it was carried to her heart and from there diffused through the rest of her body.

A peaceful feeling came over Nicole. She could feel her heartbeat slow, her breathing grow deeper, and her muscles relax. The *Episkop*'s clothing and beard exuded an odor of stale incense and perspiration. She breathed it in, taking his odor down deep into her lungs. She was glad to possess even so little of this holy man.

"I tremble at what awaits us, *malyutchka*." His voice was heavy and sad. "The holy place will be destroyed. The saints will burn in the fires of Hell."

"I don't understand."

"When the policeman Rhostok rises up, the church will fall. The dead will kill the living."

Nicole sat up in bed, stunned and bewildered by his pronouncement. Sergius reached out and pulled her back down beside him.

"It is all right, *malyutchka*. There is nothing I can do to change the future."

"Why would Rhostok do such a thing?"

"I am not able to see his motive," Sergius said.

"Use your vision to look inside his soul, as you did with me," she whispered.

"Some men have the power to close their minds to the *starets*. Rhostok is one of these. His grandfather taught him to trust no one, to expect betrayal, and so he closes his mind."

"But he was trying to help me. He sent someone to my house to guard me."

The *Episkop* let out a deep sigh.

"The bald giant can help no one now," he said in a tired voice. "He is already dead."

After a long silence, he added ominously, "Now tell me what you found in Vanya's safe-deposit box."

Thirty-Five

The president of the Middle Valley State Bank died at his desk at 9:42 A.M. the following morning.

According to a customer who was discussing a loan with him, Harold Zeeman suddenly frowned, raised his left hand to his forehead, opened his mouth as if to say something, and fell face down on the green blotter that covered his desk.

According to his personal physician, who arrived shortly after the paramedics, Zeeman was probably dead before his head hit the desk. The cause of death appeared to be a cerebral hemorrhage. It was a severe form of stroke, the doctor explained to Rhostok, who rushed to the bank as soon as he heard about it. Stroke was a not uncommon cause of death among men Zeeman's age, the doctor said, particularly given the banker's history of hypertension. In addition, Zeeman had complained about a headache and seemed mildly confused earlier in the morning. Taken together with the sudden nature of his death, he presented the classic stroke symptoms. The fact that there was no indication of shortness of breath or chest discomfort prior to his collapse ruled out the only other possibility, which would have been a massive heart attack.

But the doctor's explanation made Rhostok uneasy.

"A hemorrhage?" The word reminded him of the way Wendell Franklin had died. "You mean bleeding."

"Basically, yes," the doctor said. "A cerebral hemorrhage is bleeding that takes place within the brain. It could be caused by a weakness in an artery wall, an aneurysm, maybe just a spontaneous rupture. In any event, an artery gives way and releases blood into the brain. In Harold's case, the bleeding probably started sometime earlier this morning, which would account for his headache and confusion. Unfortunately, once the hemorrhaging started, nothing could have been done to save him."

"You're sure of that diagnosis."

"Well, obviously, it would take an autopsy to confirm it one hundred percent. But I've seen dozens of these cases, Rhostok. There's nothing particularly unusual about this one. Except maybe for the fact that his eyes are heavily bloodshot, which suggests the hemorrhage was quite severe. That would account for the sudden death."

"Are you going to do an autopsy?"

"I don't see any reason to request one. There's absolutely nothing suspicious about Harold's death. And I certainly don't want to subject his widow to the emotional trauma."

"What about a blood test?"

"What for, Rhostok?" There was a touch of irritation in the doctor's voice. "The man died of natural causes. Don't try to turn it into something it isn't."

Thirty-Six

When the first rays of the sun awakened Nicole, she was too ashamed to open her eyes.

What was happening to her?

There was a time when she thought she had power over men, was able to use her beauty to manipulate them into doing her bidding. As a showgirl at the Mirage, she could see that power reflected in the faces of the audience, the yearning in the men's eyes, the envy in the women's. Even when she worked as an escort, a job she despised, she was considered so desirable her clients included wealthy high-rollers, corporate CEOs, and even on one occasion a Hong Kong movie star.

How could she possibly have been reduced to crawling naked on all fours around the room like an animal in heat, begging a foul-smelling small-town priest to satisfy her lust? And feeling such disappointment when he rejected her?

She had heard about men like Sergius, religious zealots who exert total domination over their followers, turning them into disciples incapable of free will or independent thought.

Until last night, she had thought she could never fall victim to such bizarre forms of mind control. Yet, incredibly, she feared that was exactly what was taking place. What he had done to her, even though it had not reached the level of sexual union, had sucked the strength from her body and left her both physically and mentally exhausted.

When she awoke, she couldn't hear the *Episkop*'s heavy breathing or smell his body odor, so she knew she was safe from him. At least for the time being.

He hadn't harmed her last night. Not physically. Had not even coupled with her, although he spent the night in her bed. What he did was far more frightening: Somehow he had inserted himself, against her will, deep into the most private areas of her consciousness. As she lay beside him, she could feel him invading her memory, penetrating the most intimate secrets of her womanhood, entwining his own thoughts with hers until their two minds were conjoined in some strange way she didn't understand. Unable to resist the intrusive power of his will, in the end she had yielded, allowing him to possess her mind and do with it as he pleased. He had violated her in a way that was worse than any physical rape, and even now, in the bright light of morning, she could still feel the ugly residue of the priest's shadow on her soul.

What worried her most was that he might also have left behind some strange seed, some form of psychological semen that attached itself to the fertile wall of her subconscious, where it would develop and grow until it overpowered her own ability to think clearly and make decisions. The old woman downstairs was an example. Nicole feared that if she stayed here, she would become as much a slave as Svetlana. What she thought of as a sanctuary had led her into a different kind of peril.

Yet where else could she go?

She could never return to the house from which she had fled the night before. That house had already claimed two lives, and she was convinced she had narrowly escaped becoming its third victim.

She couldn't go to the police, not with the body of a dead policeman no more than ten feet from where her husband had died.

She had no money with which to leave town, no clothing to wear except for her nightgown and the bathrobe she had been given last night.

In the past, when she was in trouble, she had always been able to turn to Vassily. He was her protector, the man who shielded her from the police, hired lawyers to keep her out of jail, punished any clients who mistreated her, maintained her in a more luxurious lifestyle than any of the other girls. She had always felt that, in his own way, he loved her. Yet last night, she had fled the house, convinced that for some unknown reason, Vassily had decided to kill her.

Lying in bed, with the warm morning sunlight on her face, she wondered if that were really true. Certainly the policeman was dead. And she knew Vassily was capable of killing him. He had done such things before. But she also knew that if Vassily had turned against her, he would never have allowed her to get out of the house alive.

Very well, she thought, if it wasn't Vassily, then who was it she had heard in the house? Someone had been there, even after the policeman was killed. She had heard the footsteps while she was in the basement. She had seen the beam of a flashlight when she was hiding in the backyard. That hadn't been her imagination. Someone had followed her outside.

She thought about Rhostok's warning. His theory about the murders of those old men, about the deaths of her husband and his father, and how the trail of death was leading to her. She realized he was right, that she was probably the next victim. She should have listened to Rhostok, cooperated with him, told him about Vassily instead of going through that shameful charade at the police station. Now it was too late to go to Rhostok. Her only hope now for getting out of here alive was to seek Vassily's protection once again, to do whatever he wanted in exchange for her safety.

And yet . . . and yet how could she be certain that Vassily wasn't the real threat? How could she be certain he wouldn't harm her?

She thought back to two nights before, when he had come to visit her after Paul's funeral. He was never a man to show much emotion, but she had sensed his excitement when she described the opening of the safe-deposit box. She still didn't know how he had learned about it, but the contents of the box were apparently very, very important to Vassily. Something about that gruesome human hand was apparently extremely valuable, although he carefully avoided explaining what could possibly be so precious about a piece of dead human flesh. He had made extravagant promises to her that night, boasting of the great wealth that awaited him, and his willingness to share his good fortune with her, if she would only help him recover the hand.

She hadn't taken his claims of wealth seriously then, dismissing them as idle dreams, the kind of self-deception so common to Russian immigrants. But the *Episkop* had also questioned her about the hand. That was the part she found so puzzling. The two men were so vastly different— one a man of God, the other a member of the Russian mafia—yet they both desired the same thing.

Maybe, she thought, just maybe that horrible object could be her ticket out of Middle Valley. If she could find a way to recover the hand, Vassily would welcome her back. After all, he had made promises to her. And although Vassily could be a very dangerous person, he usually kept his word.

Thirty-Seven

Two hours later, Rhostok was staring down at the corpse of Otto Bruckner.

The body had been found by one of the younger policemen, who had been following up on an animal cruelty complaint called in by Bogdan Spiterovich, who lived next door. The Spiterovich poodle had died the previous night, Officer Leonard Moskal explained. In the opinion of the veterinarian who had examined the dog in the morning, someone had broken the dog's spine with a single hard blow to the back.

Like any good cop, Moskal had decided to canvass the neighborhood in an effort to find witnesses to the incident. The front door of the Danilovitch house was open, and he could see what appeared to be bloodstains on the wooden floor. He called out three times, and when no one responded, he entered the house and followed the bloodstains to the top of the stairway, where he discovered the body.

Bruckner's massive corpse was lying face down in a puddle of blood. There were no visible wounds on the body, no obvious bruises on his bald head. The amount of blood suggested a gunshot or knife wound, but any clue to what killed him would require turning over the heavy body. That, Rhostok agreed, would have to await the arrival of the coroner.

"What do you think happened?" the young policeman asked.

Rhostok shrugged, not trusting his voice. His job had taken him into the presence of death before. But the discovery of Bruckner's corpse had a particularly unnerving effect on him. This was, after all, the man known as the Incredible Bulk, a physical specimen so huge, so muscular, that his appearance alone was enough to intimidate the most violent suspects. Rhostok felt a shiver of fear. Who could possibly have brought down a man so large and powerful?

"Somebody had to take him by surprise," the young policeman said, which was the same thing Rhostok was thinking. "It's the only way this could ever happen to Otto."

Rhostok nodded. Because of Bruckner's enormous size, he had always thought of the big cop as invincible. But obviously, that had just been an illusion.

"What was he doing here?" the young policeman asked.

"Guarding a woman," Rhostok said.

"There wasn't anybody else in the house when I got here. I searched the place. It was empty, except for Otto."

So she was gone, Rhostok thought.

Four men had died since she had shown up in town, including two in her own bedroom, and now she was gone.

But where? And exactly what was her role in all this?

Thirty-Eight

Nicole knew the *Episkop* wouldn't permit her to leave the rectory. Not after the way he had plundered her mind and found her vulnerable to his powers. Yet she was determined to escape, unwilling to be enslaved like the old woman shuffling about downstairs. She slipped into her robe and sat on the edge of the bed, wondering how she could possibly get past Sergius. The answer came in the mournful tolling of the church bells next door, the familiar sound of a funeral service in progress. The *Episkop* would be officiating at the service. Svetlana would be downstairs, but Nicole was sure she knew how to deal with her.

Her leg ached as she rose from the bed. A large ugly bruise had formed on the inside of her thigh where she had bumped herself when falling into the cellar pit. She limped across the room. She heard no sound in the hallway outside the bedroom door. But when she reached out for the doorknob, her hand froze in mid-air. The muscles in her forearm tightened and her fingers stiffened. Intense pain shot up her wrist, up through her arm and shoulder. It was impossible to grasp the doorknob.

Breathing heavily, she drew back from the door. Almost immediately, the stiffness disappeared from her hand. Puzzled, she reached for the doorknob again. Her hand reacted in the same strange way. The fingers tightened and the pain returned, worse than before. Something, some unseen force, was preventing her from touching the doorknob. Was it the *Episkop?* Was she already falling under the spell of his wizardry? Was it some hypnotic suggestion intended to keep her under his control?

The more she thought about it, the more determined she was to leave. But how? If she couldn't touch the doorknob, how could she possibly get away? She stood, immobilized by the fear of what was happening, unwilling to test the dark powers that seemed to be swirling about her.

The spell was broken when the door was suddenly thrown open.

Standing in the hallway was Svetlana, an angry scowl on her face.

"Whore!" she snarled. "You come here to seduce my *Episkop.*"

Nicole could only stare at her in disbelief.

"I know your kind," Svetlana said. "It was a woman like you who caused him to lose the power to heal."

"No, please . . ."

"He has been fighting against the *Diavol.* He has been struggling to regain his gifts. He thinks you were sent to bring about a miracle that will restore his powers. But you are really sent by the *Diavol* to destroy him."

From behind her back, the old woman produced a large carving knife.

"I will not let this happen. I will not allow you to succeed."

Nicole drew back as the old woman advanced. She held her hands out in front of her, hoping to ward off any sudden thrust.

"The *Episkop* once saved my life," Svetlana said. "Now I will save his."

"No, please," Nicole begged. "All I want to do is get out of here. Let me go and I'll never come back, I promise you."

The old woman hesitated. The knife, however, didn't waver. It remained poised in the air, at an angle ready to slash Nicole's throat.

"I heard the *Episkop* last night," the crone said.

"You were listening to us?"

"I was protecting him, as I always do. I heard him say the church will fall. It is all because of you. Whore!"

Nicole stumbled against the wash table, knocking the pitcher to the floor. Unable to back up any farther, she dropped to her knees and clasped her hands as if in prayer.

"Please, please, I beg of you, let me go. I'll never come back, I promise." And suddenly, more craftily, she added, "If you kill me, what will the *Episkop* say?"

"He will say what he always says: Without sin, there is no redemption, and without redemption, there is no salvation. This will be my sin, and therefore great will be my salvation." As she raised her hand for the final thrust, Svetlana added, "I do this also to save the church of Saint Sofia, for as long as you are alive, the church is in danger of destruction."

"No!" Nicole screamed as the knife descended.

Thirty-Nine

O'Malley arrived at the Danilovitch house a half-hour later, making his way through a small group of curious neighbors and those members of the press who regularly monitored the activities of his office. Rhostok noticed the blonde reporter from Channel One, standing apart from the crowd, as if she wanted to be sure he noticed her.

O'Malley looked tired and his face was troubled. The leg brace seemed to weigh him down more than usual.

"Before you go upstairs, let's talk," Rhostok said. He led O'Malley into the living room, a small area filled with the heavy leather furniture in which Vanya Danilovitch once relaxed. "You were supposed to do a blood test on Wendell Franklin."

"It's not your jurisdiction, Rhostok. The man died in Scranton."

"There might be a connection to the way Otto died."

"Here we go again." O'Malley let out a long, tired sigh. "Every time I see you, you're working on another conspiracy. You never change."

"Did you run the blood test or didn't you?"

"Yes, we did."

"And what did you find?"

"Nothing."

"Then why did Franklin die?"

"I don't know."

"Tell me the truth."

"Oh, for God's sake, Rhostok." O'Malley stiff-legged his way across the room, his heavy leg brace thumping against the bare wooden floor. "I'm telling you the truth. Right now, I don't know why Franklin died. I mean, I know he bled to death, but I don't know why." He hesitated before admitting, "In any event, we have his body and we've scheduled an autopsy. Maybe that'll give us the answer."

"Yesterday you said it was hemophilia."

"That's what it looked like," O'Malley said with a shrug. "It's the only condition I know that would explain such profuse bleeding from a small wound. But what we've got right now is, quite frankly, a medical mystery."

O'Malley put down his briefcase and sank into an old leather wing chair, lifting his withered leg onto the ottoman.

"In a way, I'm glad you asked for that blood test, Rhostok."

Insisted on a blood test would be a better way to put it, Rhostok thought, remembering how stubbornly O'Malley had argued against it.

"The initial test results were intriguing," O'Malley said, as he settled back into the cushions. "Really intriguing. You know, I might make a new discovery as a result. Maybe even get my name on a disease. That's how doctors get famous."

He chuckled at his little joke, but Rhostok didn't join in.

"You see, Rhostok, most people think we know everything there is to know about blood. After all, it seems like such a simple fluid. But medical science still doesn't fully understand all the physical mechanisms that cause natural hemostasis, which is the medical term for blood clotting."

Like most doctors, O'Malley seemed to enjoy displaying his technical expertise.

"There are fifteen different clotting factors that have been identified in human blood. Those clotting factors are all interactive to one degree or another, appearing at various stages of hemostasis. About eighty-five percent of the individuals who suffer from hemophilia have a deficiency of factor eight, which is therefore called the antihemophilic factor. The remaining fifteen percent have a deficiency of factor nine, which is also known as the Christmas factor. Why they call it that, I have no idea. But those are the two most critical of the clotting factors." He paused and lowered his voice, as if he didn't want anyone to overhear him. "The analysis of Wendell Franklin's blood sample revealed no deficiency in either of those two factors."

"So he wasn't a hemophiliac."

"That's right. Wendell Franklin may have bled to death from the cut on his fingertip, but he wasn't suffering from hemophilia. Or at least not from any form known to modern science."

"You're sure there was nothing wrong with the sample."

"Positive. I drew the blood myself. You watched me. And it was the only sample in the lab last night. Factor eight has a half-life of ten hours, and factor nine has a half-life of one to three days. I looked it up, to double-check my memory. Based on the time of death, we were able to determine that the concentrations of both factors existed in the sample at the proper levels."

"Then there has to be some other explanation."

"Of course there has to be," O'Malley said. "But exactly what, I don't yet know. We checked for von Willebrand's disease, which also causes excessive bleeding from small cuts. But the platelet count in the sample was normal. So was platelet aggregation and morphology. Those checks also ruled out afibrinogenemia as well as Glanzmann's disease."

"I don't get it," Rhostok frowned. "A man just doesn't bleed to death from a small wound like that. Not unless there's a reason."

"You were at the bank," O'Malley said. "Did you actually see him cut himself?"

"It happened before I got there. He said he cut it on the metal door of the safe-deposit box."

"The box where they found the amputated hand?"

"That's right," Rhostok said. "The one edge was sharp. Franklin warned me about it and showed me his bloody finger. It didn't look like anything to worry about."

"And he didn't seem upset about it? He didn't think it was serious?"

"He was a little irritated, that's all," Rhostok said. "If he had a bleeding problem of any kind that he knew about, he would've have gone to a doctor or hospital, wouldn't he?"

O'Malley shifted in his chair, using his hands to move his leg brace to a more comfortable position.

"You'd expect him to, if he had a previous condition. But I did a quick check of his body when it was brought in. There were no bruises, which would be symptomatic of a bleeding disorder. Bleeders always have bruises somewhere on their body, the result of subcutaneous bleeding from the little bumps of daily life. The body also had four scars, one on the scalp, one on the right knee, and two on the left forearm. None of them showed any sign of suturing or abnormal healing. If Franklin had any previous history of unusual bleeding episodes, those wounds would have been treated differently. We'd be able to tell if someone took special care of him."

"What about drugs? Could that be an explanation?"

"We're running tests now for heparin, dextran, and Coumadin, all of which thin the blood and can cause hemorrhaging. But those drugs would have to be ingested in massive quantities to cause the degree of hemostatic inhibition we saw. And they almost certainly would have affected platelet morphology, which means they would have shown up in the original blood test. So I don't think we'll find any drug-based explanation."

O'Malley closed his eyes for a moment, as if he were going to fall asleep, but he quickly recovered and struggled up out of the chair.

"So basically, I have no medical explanation for what happened to Wendell Franklin. Now I think I'd like to go upstairs and see your dead policeman."

O'Malley didn't seem disturbed by the amount of blood that surrounded Bruckner's body. The morgue attendants rolled the body onto its back, allowing O'Malley to open the dead man's shirt. His hands protected by latex gloves, O'Malley quickly examined the chest, armpits, and groin.

When he was finished, he stripped off the gloves, tossed them in the biobag, and, with Rhostok's help, laboriously returned to a standing position.

"Aneurysm," he grunted, as he leaned his weight into his leg brace. "He's been dead about twelve hours. I won't know for sure until the autopsy, but if you want my best guess right now, I'd say it was a rupture of the abdominal aortic artery, probably due to an aneurysm. He died of natural causes. No relation to the way Wendell Franklin died, if that's what you're wondering."

"You can tell that just by looking at him?" Rhostok was skeptical.

"Like I said, it's my best guess until we get him down to the morgue. But your man doesn't have any visible wounds, there's a huge amount of blood on the floor, and it all seems to have come from his mouth and nose. That suggests an internal hemorrhage, and given the magnitude of blood loss, it had to be arterial in nature. The blood trail downstairs shows where the bleeding started. He probably came up the stairs looking for help."

"Did you notice his fingertips?" Rhostok asked. "They're blackened, just like Franklin's."

"Necrosis," O'Malley said. "It's not all that unusual." He looked around, as if realizing for the first time where he was. "This is the same bedroom where the guy died a few nights ago, isn't it?"

"Paul Danilovitch," Rhostok reminded him. "You thought he died of a heart attack."

"In point of fact, he did. The only question is whether it was artificially induced."

"The potassium chloride."

"That's right."

"Which would mean he was murdered."

"That's not what I said, Rhostok. All I meant was that it might have been triggered by the presence of potassium chloride in his system. And I'm not even certain of that." O'Malley motioned for his assistants to remove Bruckner's body. "In any event, the potassium chloride could have come from the supplement the widow said he was taking. You find some strange things in those products. If you can ever locate the bottle, I'd be glad to run some tests for you. But even if that supplement contains too much potassium, that's a case for the Food and Drug Administration, not you."

"Come on, O'Malley, a man died in this bedroom five days ago. Now we've got another dead man, a policeman. Don't you find that suspicious?"

"Coincidental, perhaps. Not necessarily suspicious. As far as I'm concerned, your friend Bruckner died of natural causes." O'Malley opened up his briefcase and busied himself with his forms, checking his wristwatch, writing down the time. "I know it's your nature to be suspicious, Rhostok, but it's normal for people to die. If you saw as many dead bodies as I do, you'd stop thinking that every death is part of some grand conspiracy. By the way, you never explained what Bruckner was doing here."

"He was guarding the widow."

"Really? And where is she?"

"I don't know."

Rhostok watched the attendants struggle to roll Bruckner's corpse into an oversized body bag. It was a tight fit. They had to bend his knees to get him inside, and it took four men, rather than the customary two, to carry him to the waiting van. O'Malley closed his briefcase and was getting ready to follow them downstairs.

"I'm seeing too many dead bodies lately," Rhostok said.

"It comes with the job."

"But these are coming one after the other. The bank president died this morning."

"Cerebral hemorrhage. That's what his personal physician said. At least it was fast. It's not a bad way to go."

"You already know about that?" Rhostok was surprised.

"The people at the bank told me about it. I just came from there." He held up a hand to forestall any questions. "Now don't start getting suspicious again, Rhostok. I was there with a technician from the health department, who was cleaning out the vault where the mystery hand was discovered. It's standard procedure. Any time human remains are found, the area has to be sanitized. They'll do the same thing here."

Rhostok followed him downstairs. Before they reached the front door, O'Malley turned to him.

"Look, I'm sorry about your friend," O'Malley said. "But like it's written in the Bible, you don't know the hour or the day when death will come."

"Yeah," Rhostok grunted. "But don't you think there's something strange about these deaths? Wendell Franklin bleeds to death from a cut on his finger, Harold Zeeman dies from bleeding in the brain, and now here's Otto, who bleeds to death from what you call an aneurysm. Don't you think that's peculiar, all three of them bleeding to death?"

"They're totally unrelated, Rhostok." O'Malley didn't try to hide his impatience. "There's nothing unusual about a fifty-year-old banker having a cerebral hemorrhage. Or an enormous person like Bruckner suffering an aneurysm. I'll admit that Wendell Franklin's case is a puzzle, but we'll figure it out. In any event, they all died from natural causes. It just happens to be an unusual cluster. Don't try to turn it into something it isn't."

"That's what Otto used to tell me."

"What?"

"He was always telling me I'm too suspicious, that I shouldn't try to turn everything into a murder case."

"That was good advice."

"I'm not sure Otto would think so. Not anymore."

Forty

The waiting reporters, all of whom recognized O'Malley, shouted out their questions as soon as he walked out of the house. Smiling his best political smile, he greeted many of them by name and proceeded to hold an impromptu press conference on the sidewalk. When O'Malley informed the reporters that Bruckner had died of natural causes, they lost interest and drifted away.

All except for Robyn Cronin, who was waiting for Rhostok by his car.

She tilted her head and gave him that artificial little smile again. Today she was wearing an electric-blue suit, shoulder pads, no lapels, again a skirt that revealed most of her thighs. Another power suit, he thought. Once again, her makeup looked as if it had been professionally applied, her blonde hair as perfectly set as if she had just come from the beauty parlor. He tried to picture what she might look like when she got out of bed in the morning and decided she would still be an attractive creature. Give her another six inches of height, and she'd probably be a breathtaking beauty. But squeezed into a compact five-foot-one-inch figure, she would always be considered "cute."

"It's only twenty-four hours," he growled. "You were supposed to give me seventy-two hours before you came snooping around again."

"Our agreement was that I wasn't supposed to interview anybody about what happened at the bank. I kept that agreement. I was up here working on something else." She kept her painted-on smile aimed at him, as if it were somehow supposed to soften him up. Her bright red lipstick glistened in the sunlight. "Now a policeman is dead. That's a story I have to cover."

"There's no story here. Bruckner died of natural causes. You want to move so I can get into my car?"

She was leaning against his patrol car, her rear end covering the door handle. She didn't move.

"What was Bruckner doing here?" she asked.

"I've got to get back to the station," he said.

"You were supposed to keep me updated."

"And you were supposed to stay out of Middle Valley."

"There's a story developing here, I think a big story, and I want to be part of it."

"You're supposed to report the news, not be part of it."

"You know what I mean."

"I've got nothing to say right now." He took her by the arm and pulled her away from the car door. She didn't resist. But surprised by the firmness of her flesh, he held onto her arm for a second or two longer than he should have. The look in her eyes told him she noticed. "It's a really bad day for me," he said as he got into the car. "I'll call you tomorrow. Maybe we can talk then."

"I want to talk now," she insisted.

"I'm telling you, there's no story here. I don't know why you're still hanging around. All the other reporters are gone." He started rolling up the window, but she put her hands on the glass, preventing him from closing it all the way.

"Those other reporters don't know the history of this house," she argued. "They don't know about the woman who lived here, or the way her husband died, or what she found in the bank vault, or, for that matter, how her husband's father died. That's what makes your policeman's death a news story. Not necessarily *how* he died, as much as *where* he died."

Rhostok started up the car, figuring that was the best way to end the conversation, maybe get her to back away so he could pull out without hurting her.

"Your man was up here keeping an eye on the widow, wasn't he?"

Rhostok said nothing.

"I've been doing some investigating on my own," she said. "I have a printout of the widow's criminal record from Las Vegas, where she was arrested twice on prostitution charges and was known by her professional name, Champagne."

Rhostok tried to keep his face from revealing his surprise. That was NCIC information, which was supposed to be restricted to authorized law-enforcement agencies.

"I've also got the results of her husband's blood test," she went on.

So she had also managed to breach the security in the coroner's office.

"I have a copy of her husband's father's autopsy," she continued. "And I've got transcripts of all the old man's interviews at Lackawanna Mental Health Facility. The doctors were convinced he was a menace to others, which was why he was kept in a secure cell. He was suffering from the early stages of Alzheimer's. There were also indications of delayed post-traumatic stress syndrome, although the doctors suspected those symptoms might have been faked. But there was nothing in the psychiatric records to suggest he was suicidal. No death-wish fantasies. No major depressive episodes. My conclusion? Homicide, not suicide."

Rhostok stared straight ahead, but his mind was reeling. He had tried to get those interview records himself, but the psychiatrists at the mental health facility had stonewalled him, citing privacy laws. He couldn't believe that this young reporter, whom he had originally dismissed as "cute," could possibly have succeeded where he had failed.

"You want me to go on the air with what I've got?" she asked.

There it was again, the threat. But this time, she wasn't smiling.

"What are you going to do?" she asked. "Just sit there?"

"Yep."

He continued to stare straight ahead, trying to figure out what he should say.

"Well, I can sit here, too," she said.

She turned around and sat against the car. Pressed her buttocks right up against the window next to him and just sat there. He tried to ignore it, but couldn't. There it was, all that soft warm flesh pressing up against the PPG double-laminated glass and flattening itself out behind that short blue skirt. He had an irrational urge to put his hand against the inside of the window and feel how much warmth she generated. See how she'd react to that.

"You don't have to treat me like the enemy," she said.

He shifted uncomfortably in the car, not certain what to do. He wasn't sure if she was innocent of the sexual impact of her action, or if it was meant as some form of insult. Either way, he couldn't safely drive away, not with her weight resting against the vehicle.

"I thought we had an agreement to cooperate," she said.

She had a pushy nature, like most media people. She was a little arrogant, too, especially the way she flaunted her body. But he had to admit she was a very good reporter. She was bright, inquisitive, and persistent and seemed to have excellent sources of information. And so far, she had been true to her word, not doing a TV report on the discovery of the severed hand.

"There's no law that says the police can't work with the press," she said.

What he found most intriguing about her, however, was the way she looked at things. She seemed to have a talent for putting together seemingly unconnected facts and arriving at the same conclusions he did. Even Bruckner, God rest his soul, had ridiculed Rhostok's suspicious nature. Finding someone with thought processes so much like his own was a surprising discovery. And human nature being what it is, he was flattered that such a bright young reporter thought the same way he did.

"You're not the only one with information," she said. "I'd be willing to trade my information with you."

"You want to trade? Like it's some little game?"

"If you don't agree, I'll go on air with what I found out about Vanya Danilovitch. It's a hell of a story."

Trust no one, his grandfather's voice was whispering in his ear. *Trust no one*. His grandfather was right, of course. But this was a particularly difficult situation. Given the reporter's threat to go on air, he was wondering whether he had a choice. With her ability to get information, it might be better to have her as an ally rather than an enemy.

"I know that you already have information about two of Vanya Danilovitch's closest friends being murdered," she said.

"You talked to Roman Kerensky, down at the Legion Hall."

"I also ran a check on the telephone calls between Florian Ulyanov and Vanya Danilovitch."

"How could you do it that fast?" He was stunned. "A phone check usually takes time. You need a warrant."

"The police need a warrant," she corrected him. "There are other ways to get the information."

"I bet you did it through the TV station in Kingman," he said. "They probably have contacts at the local phone company."

"Florian actually made two calls to Vanya." She checked her notebook. "The first was a fourteen-minute call placed at 3:56 P.M. on the day after Boris Cherevenko was murdered in Ocala. I assume Cherevenko's death was the topic of discussion. The second call was longer, forty-two minutes, which interestingly enough, was placed just two days before Florian himself was murdered. Maybe he suspected someone was coming after him and wanted to alert Vanya."

"And a few days later Vanya ends up in a mental hospital . . ." Rhostok started to think aloud and then caught himself, remembering the tape recorder she kept in her bag.

"Roman's theory is that Vanya wasn't mentally unstable, except for the mild Alzheimer's," she said.

"I know about Roman's theory."

"Do you agree?" she asked.

He shrugged.

"So now you're going silent again," she said. "You're not going to solve the case that way."

"Which case?" he asked. "Vanya's death, or what we found at the bank?"

"I think they're both part of the same case. Maybe even the death of the policeman they just carried out of this house."

He didn't respond, not wanting to admit he agreed with her. What bothered him even more was how quickly she was connecting the dots. Three days on the case, and she already had more information on Vanya than he had collected in two months.

"The silent treatment isn't going to work this time," she said. "I've got enough for one hell of a story. Three old men murdered. And a human hand found in the safe-deposit box of the last one. I can go on the air with it tonight, unless you cooperate, give me a reason not to."

"Okay, okay," he relented. "Let's talk."

He watched her rear end peel itself away from the window, its shape returning to its fully rounded contours. She turned and bent down closer to the narrow opening.

"Does this mean we're going to be working together?"

She gave him that damned perky smile again, and he found that, in spite of himself, he was smiling back.

When she got into the car, he was rewarded with the delicate floral aroma of her perfume. Something else mixed in there. Pipe smoke, it smelled like. Must be a boyfriend, he thought, because she wasn't wearing any wedding ring. But a boyfriend this early in the morning?

"Let's start with that cop . . ." she said.

"Officer Bruckner."

"Sorry . . . Officer Bruckner. He was protecting the widow, wasn't he?"

"Yes."

"And where is she now?"

"I don't know."

"She's gone missing?"

"That's right. We found Otto's body in her bedroom, and she's nowhere to be found."

"Maybe she went back to Las Vegas. According to her criminal record, that's the last place she lived."

"But her car's still in the driveway. Three-quarters of a tank of gas, and it started right up, according to the policeman who found the body."

"You don't think . . ." the reporter hesitated. "You don't think maybe something happened to her? That maybe she's dead, too?"

"All I know is that we found a dead officer in her bedroom and she's gone."

"But the police officer died of natural causes. There's nothing suspicious about his death, is there?"

"Not if you believe the coroner."

He didn't mean to let it slip out like that, but she had a way of getting people to say more than they intended. She stared at him, her eyes narrowing, evaluating. He'd have to be more careful with her, he realized. She still might know more about this case than she was willing to admit.

Forty-One

Nicole barely managed to avoid the first thrust of the knife by sliding frantically into the corner.

Svetlana would not be denied. She screamed out in unintelligible Russian as she raised the knife again. Nicole was trapped in the corner, begging for her life, one hand raised to protect herself, the other reaching for something, anything to use as a weapon. In the very last moment before the knife descended, Nicole's fingers found the handle of the enamel pitcher. Without even pausing for thought, she swung it up to deflect the knife. The pitcher hit the blade, knocking it out of the crone's grasp. The knife clattered across the room. The old woman turned away to recover it. Nicole grabbed at her skirt. The fabric tore off in her hands. The old woman screamed out in anger. Nicole lunged at her, grabbing a bony ankle. Svetlana fell to the floor, her head striking the uncarpeted wood. And suddenly, everything was silent.

Svetlana lay motionless on the floor, the knife well beyond the reach of her outstretched arm. Nicole waited, watching for any sign of movement. The old woman was still alive, still breathing. In the quiet that filled the room, it was hard to believe this tiny figure could have been filled with such murderous rage. She seemed so insubstantial, little more than an emaciated shell of a human. Stripped of her skirt, her legs were modestly encased in old-fashioned ankle-length bloomers. Now that the danger was past, Nicole felt compassion for the woman. It seemed obvious that her rage was inspired by love, inflamed by jealousy.

Nicole rose slowly from the corner. She bent over the old woman, gently stroking her hair.

"It's all right," she said when Svetlana opened her eyes. "I want to leave here. Do you understand? I want to leave. Will you help me?"

Forty-Two

"I assume you taped your conversation with Kerensky," Rhostok said, as they drove through Middle Valley.

"Definitely," Robyn replied.

"I'd like to get a copy."

"Didn't you take notes?"

"It makes people nervous when a policeman writes down what they're saying."

"I find the same thing."

"Anyway, Roman's an old friend. I figured I could always do a follow-up interview."

"If his lungs don't give out first," she said.

"I'd also like a paper copy of that phone check you did."

"Done. What else?"

"You can tell me how you get your information," Rhostok said. "That stuff you found out about Vanya and Nicole. I mean, I know you probably have a source in the coroner's office, but the NCIC is supposed to be off-limits to everyone except authorized police agencies, and the psychologists at Lackawanna never release anything except in court."

"We're not supposed to reveal our sources."

"Bull. If you want to work with me, I want to know how you're getting your information."

"Is this a trick of some sort? Are you faking cooperation just to get me to reveal my sources?"

"Christ, you're as suspicious as I am," he said with a chuckle.

"I'll take that as a compliment."

"If it makes you feel better, okay. Now tell me where you're getting all your information."

"We've got someone at the station, a consultant named Hamilton Winfield, who's got unbelievable contacts. He seems to know everybody. And I do mean everybody."

"I can tell you one person he doesn't know, and that's me."

"He might not have met you, but he can find out everything about you, from your bank account to your old school records, your latest performance review, even your shoe size, the kind of cereal you eat, and the last movie you rented at Blockbuster."

"He could really do that?"

"It's not unusual in our business."

"Then how do I know he hasn't done it already?"

She seemed startled, as if the thought hadn't occurred to her.

"If he has," she said softly, "he hasn't shared it with me."

They reached the outskirts of Middle Valley, where it blended into an industrial flatland that marked the Scranton city limits.

"I don't think you have to worry about Winfield," she added after a pause. "He's an old guy, maybe in his seventies or eighties. He used to be a famous foreign correspondent, which is probably where he made his contacts. I can get you a copy of his resume if you want. Now where are we going?"

"You'll see when we get there. Give me your tape recorder."

Keeping his eyes on the road, he fumbled at the controls until the tiny tape popped out. He put the tape in his pocket and tossed the recorder into the back seat.

"Now your cell phone."

"Why?"

"I want to make sure you don't hit the auto-dial button and have somebody listen in on us."

She registered her disgust with a loud sigh and slapped the small Nokia phone into his hand. It followed the tape recorder into the back seat, bouncing once before ending up on the floor.

"Be careful," she complained.

"Now your bag."

"That's personal," she protested.

"It's your choice," he said. "Either I check the bag, or I pull over and let you out."

Reluctantly, she opened her bag and placed it on the seat between them. He put a hand inside and felt around in the contents as he drove.

"You've still got that little gun," he said.

"My work takes me into some bad neighborhoods."

He felt around among a packet of napkins, some keys, a perfume bottle, a small tin of what he assumed were breath mints, a notebook, two pens, some credit cards, and a small wallet. Satisfied there was no other electronic gear inside, he slid the bag back to her.

"Anything else you want to search?" She didn't try to hide her sarcasm.

"I don't know. Is there anything else I should worry about?"

"You never know. I might be wearing a body wire."

"I wouldn't put it past you."

"You're really a piece of work," she muttered.

"I'm taking a chance on you," he said. "Normally, I wouldn't let a civilian get involved in an investigation. I'm breaking that rule because I think you can help me. But I have to be able to trust you."

"Trust is a two-way street. You haven't even told me where we're going."

"We're going to see a man who doesn't like the press. He's not going to be happy when you show up with me. And you're going to have to promise him you won't tell anyone about this meeting."

She started to protest, but he cut her off.

"You're in my world now, Robyn. Everything you hear, everything you see when you're with me has to be strictly confidential. You don't repeat it to anyone until the investigation is over. Do you understand me?"

"What about anything I find out on my own?"

"If it concerns this investigation, you share it with me, and I'll tell you when you can go public with it."

"That's called prior restraint, Rhostok. It's a form of censorship. And it's illegal. You're a cop, but that badge doesn't give you the authority to dictate what I report."

"Once this is over, I don't care what you report. But until then, you have to keep everything secret, especially from your friend Winfield."

"He's my boss, not my friend."

"I don't care what he is. What you find out on this trip stays secret until I say otherwise. That means no tape recordings, no notes, no computer files that anyone can access."

"Give me one good reason why I should agree."

"Because seven men are dead already, and if that hand came from the man whose name was on the wrapping paper, those deaths are just the beginning."

"I only count three men murdered. The others all died of natural causes."

"If you believe O'Malley," Rhostok said.

Forty-Three

Svetlana now seemed relieved at Nicole's desire to leave and was eager to help her be on her way. With Svetlana holding her hand, Nicole was finally able to break through whatever strange spell had earlier prevented her from leaving the bedroom.

The old woman led her down to the kitchen, where she prepared boiled eggs, toast, and coffee for Nicole. She disappeared while Nicole ate and returned with a stack of faded black garments.

"Widow's wear," she called them, and explained they were from a collection of donated clothing that was stored in the rectory until it could be distributed to the needy.

Her thigh still aching from last night's bruise, Nicole limped into the downstairs bathroom to change. The odor of mothballs rose from the garments as she unfolded them: a cheap black button-front cotton dress, black shoes, and black undergarments. On any other woman, the donated clothing would have looked dreary and unflattering. The shoes were comfortable, although a bit loose. But the dress had come from a woman less well-endowed than Nicole. When she was finally able to struggle into the garment, her breasts and hips stretched the fabric to its limits. The form-flattering way it emphasized her figure brought a frown of disapproval from the crone.

"I'll need some money," Nicole said.

Svetlana stared at her, uncomprehending.

"If you want me to leave town, I'll need some money."

The old woman sighed and scurried down the hallway to the small room she occupied. She returned with a change purse, from which she extracted two twenty-dollar bills, a ten, and six singles.

"This is all I have," she said.

Nicole felt ashamed. "I can't take it all. I just need enough for cab fare to Scranton."

She took one of the twenty-dollar bills and three of the singles.

"I'll return it to you, I promise," she said.

"There is no need. I lead a simple life."

Nicole telephoned for a taxi. When it arrived outside, she turned to Svetlana, wrapped her arms around her, and kissed her on the cheek.

Startled, the old woman responded, "God bless you, my child."

To the cabdriver, Nicole said, "Take me to the Lackawanna County Coroner's Office. I think it's in Scranton."

Forty-Four

"You're overreacting with this secrecy stuff," Robyn said. "If you tell me where we're going, I promise I won't jump out of the car and find a phone booth to call the station."

They drove through the Green Ridge area, past the old mansions of the mining barons, now occupied by lawyers and doctors and real-estate developers. They drove through the heart of Scranton, past the old court-house and its statue of John Mitchell, an early leader of the United Mine Workers Union. Robyn was quiet until they reached a cluster of buildings on the hillside above the downtown area.

"The University of Scranton?" she asked. "That's where we're going?"

Ahead of them, a Scranton police car sat blocking the road, its roof lights strobing their red and blue warnings. Beyond the police car, a yellow Pennsylvania Power & Light service truck was parked. A tow truck was removing a parked car, while a yellow backhoe waited to maneuver into position.

A policeman waved them to a stop. Rhostok rolled down the window of his squad car.

"Sorry, road's closed," the cop said, as if it weren't obvious.

"What's the problem?"

"We've got a sinkhole up ahead. A section of road about eight feet wide collapsed. We've got one car that went in. The driver's okay. They're trying to pull the car out now."

"Another sinkhole? It hasn't rained for over a week."

"The city engineers think it was triggered by an old mine tunnel collapse. They think it cracked a water line and the water gradually ate away the ground until there was nothing left to support the road. They say it could have been months in the making."

Perilously close to the edge of the sinkhole was a utility pole heavily laden with electric wires. The wires were stretched tight, and that was when Rhostok realized the pole had sunk vertically about ten feet into the ground.

"Is the power out, too?" he asked.

"It went out a few hours ago. The electric company's trying to reroute the lines."

"What's that terrible smell?" Robyn asked.

"Smells like hell, doesn't it?" the policeman shook his head. "It's sulphur fumes, coming up the hole. The guy from the Environmental Protection Agency says it's probably coming from an underground fire. Some old coal seam burning in an abandoned mine."

"At least you're not getting any methane," Rhostok said.

"They're measuring for it, but they're not sure. The equipment doesn't always work the right way. They've shut down and sealed off the university, just to be on the safe side."

"That's where we're headed," Rhostok said. "We're on official police business."

"Well, you can't get through here. This road will be closed for a couple of days, until they can repair the pipe and backfill the hole with gravel. But before they can do that, they'll probably have to flood it with water to cool it off. That damn sinkhole's hot. You stand near it, you can feel the heat on your face."

"We have to go to the science building," Rhostok said. "It's that building there, the one with the glass facing."

The policeman followed his pointing finger. He shook his head.

"There's a lateral crack from the sinkhole heading in that direction. The ground is splitting. That building should already have been evacuated."

"I can still see some lights on the top floor," Rhostok said. "They're waiting for us."

"Must be an emergency power generator," the policeman said. He stared up at the top floor, a little unsure. He had his instructions, Rhostok knew. But he also knew it was traditional to bend the rules for a fellow police officer.

"Well, maybe they haven't been fully evacuated yet," the policeman said. "Tell you what. You go back down Capouse Avenue, back the way you came, make a left on Spruce, another left in the first alley you come to, which is one-way traffic. You'll be heading the wrong way, but it's only a half-block until you make the first right. That'll bring you around the back entrance of the science building. Just be careful. We don't know if the building is safe."

Forty-Five

The rear entrance to the science building was unlocked. A single battery-powered emergency light illuminated the hallway. The elevators were inoperative, so they climbed the back stairs to the fifth-floor laboratory classroom of Professor William Altschiller.

"We're on emergency power," the professor explained. He gave Robyn a withering glance as he led them into his laboratory. "There's some sort of problem outside, and the electricity was cut off," he said. "The emergency generator takes care of everything except the elevators and the air conditioning."

The laboratory was warm and stuffy. It smelled of disinfectants and chemicals. A little body odor, too, Rhostok thought, clearing his nose with a snort.

"You should open the windows," he said. "Get some fresh air in here."

"I wish I could," Professor Altschiller said. "But these new buildings, the windows are all sealed. We've been working here without ventilation all afternoon."

"Where's your assistant, the young genius you said was going to help you?"

"He worked with me through most of the night, but when he came in this morning, he wasn't feeling good, so I sent him home."

"This is all supposed to be confidential," Rhostok reminded the professor. "I hope you warned him not to say anything."

"If it's so confidential, why did you bring a reporter with you?" He turned to Robyn. "I've seen you on TV," he said to her. "And irrespective of anything Rhostok might have told you, I must insist that everything I say here is completely off the record. I want no quotes attributed to me. I don't even want to be identified in any news reports." He turned back to Rhostok. "Does she have a tape recorder?"

"I already took it. Her cell phone, too. I left them down in the car."

Robyn glanced from one of them to the other. "What is it with you two? You're paranoid, you know that?"

"I'm doing you a favor, bringing you here," Rhostok admonished her. "Now why don't you try being quiet for a while? You might learn something."

"Indeed you might," Professor Altschiller said, his mood suddenly changing. "What we have is an extremely unusual artifact. I've never seen anything like it."

He led them to a counter on the far side of the room, near the windows. The hand was resting there on a glass tray, covered with a bell jar. It was lying palm down, the fingertips touching the glass.

"So this is where you brought it," Robyn said. She bent over to examine the hand. Her eyes showed more interest than they did the first time she saw it, Rhostok thought.

"Shouldn't you be keeping it in the refrigerator?" he asked. "Or did the fridge go out with the main power line?"

"Actually, I'm keeping it out here on purpose," Altschiller said. "How long do you think it was in the vault? Unrefrigerated, that is?"

"You listen to the bank president, he'll try to tell you it was in there for fifty years. But that's obviously impossible, isn't it?"

Altschiller raised an eyebrow, but didn't respond directly. "Do you think he could have been trying to deceive you, commit some sort of fraud?"

"There's no way to tell. Not now. Harold Zeeman died this morning. His doctor said it was a cerebral hemorrhage." Rhostok noticed the startled look Robyn gave him. She must not have heard about Zeeman's death. "But the hand couldn't have been in that vault more than a few hours," Rhostok went on. "Otherwise it would start decomposing, wouldn't it?"

"Normally, it doesn't take very long for that to happen, especially at room temperature."

"That's why I'm surprised you don't keep it on ice. It's pretty hot in here without the air conditioning."

"Ninety-two degrees at the moment," Altschiller said. "I've been monitoring the temperature since you left yesterday. Last night we kept the lab at sixty-eight degrees. The temperature started to rise when the sun came up. We get the morning sun coming through the windows, which builds up the radiant heat. Then the power went out, the air conditioning stopped, and by noon, it had reached ninety-three degrees."

It sounded to Rhostok as if the professor were stalling, as if there were something on his mind, but he was hesitant to come right out and say it. Maybe because of the reporter's presence. Or maybe because of the way she seemed drawn to the hand. They both watched the way she circled the examination table, studying the hand from various angles, almost as if she were seeing it for the first time.

"It's okay, she's working with me on this," Rhostok said, and then, glancing at Altschiller, added, "You look like you've been working too hard. Your eyes are red and a little bloodshot."

"It's just eyestrain," the professor said. "Too much looking through microscopes. When I get involved in something as interesting as this, I don't know when to stop."

He flicked a toggle switch below a glass panel on the wall. The frosted-glass surface flickered once, twice before lighting up. Altschiller slid two eight-by-ten X-ray negatives into the clips that lined the top of the glass. Almost reluctantly, Robyn turned her attention from the hand to the black-and-white negatives.

"We took some X-rays of the hand, both anterior and posterior views." he said. "That enables us to get a precise measurement of the bones without destroying any tissue. As a further precaution, we used special low-radiation equipment so as not to affect any aspect of the cellular material." He pointed to the ghostly images on the glass panel. "As you can see, although the fingers of the hand appear to be quite massive, much of that is due to the fleshy covering. The bones of the phalanges are just a little bit longer than normal. And the metacarpal bones, which are a much better determinant of height, are quite average in length. I'd put our mystery man's height at about five feet ten inches, give or take an inch or two. We're dealing with a middle-aged man here. You see those ridges at the tops of the shafts on the fingers?"

He indicated the junction points of the knuckles on the X-rays.

"Those ridges are formed from separate bones that appear at around age five and unite with the shafts at around twenty years of age. From the further development and wear at the joints, I'd put the subject's age somewhere between forty and fifty years. You can see the early stages of rheumatoid arthritis, particularly along the junction of the first and second rows of the phalanges."

"You mean the middle knuckles?" Rhostok asked.

"Sorry about that," the professor said. "I always try to use the more common terms, but every once in a while I forget."

"What about the little finger?" Rhostok asked. "The way it's bent to the side?"

"Congenital deformity of the fifth digit," the professor said. "Our mystery man was born with it. At first, I thought it might be the result of a broken bone that healed badly. But you can see on the X-ray that there's no apparent damage to the bone. There'd be heavier calcification around that area if it had ever been broken. It's a good identification marker, the sort of thing we look for in our line of work."

"When you find somebody missing a hand, that should be enough of an identification marker," Robyn joked.

The professor glared at her, but kept his voice as calm and dispassionate as if he were lecturing to his students.

"Now look at the hand itself, at what's left of the wrist," he said, directing their attention back to the bell jar. "The skin just above the stump has evidence of severe abrasion. It appears to be the result of rope burns. We did find some traces of abaca fiber imbedded in the skin, which is very unusual, considering how carefully the hand was severed."

"You still think it was cut off on purpose?" Rhostok asked. "No chance it was an accident?"

"No way. In an accidental dismemberment, the trauma usually causes a dislocation of the carpal bones."

He pointed to a cluster of irregular shapes on the X-rays.

"The human wrist has eight carpal bones in two rows, irregular shapes that are put together like pieces of a jigsaw puzzle. They're strong bones, but they're easily dislocated. And you can see for yourself that none of those bones are out of place."

Rhostok nodded his agreement, although he knew he would never be able to tell whether the alignment was correct or not. He had to take Altschiller's word for it.

"Couldn't the same thing happen if our man accidentally cut himself with an electric saw?" Rhostok asked.

"Or a power mower blade?" Robyn added, a mocking reference to Rhostok's initial conversation with her. Yet despite her attempts at sarcasm, she seemed fascinated by the hand.

The professor swiveled a goosenecked halogen light over the hand, illuminating it with a harsh glare that seemed to magnify every pore.

"Take a close look at the end of the wrist," he said.

Robyn crowded in for a better view.

"Look at the whitish area in there. That's the anterior annular ligament. It's a thick fibrous band that encloses the muscles and the nerves and protects the carpal bones, similar to the way plastic insulation is used to protect braided electric wires. The only way to make a cut this clean without causing shredding is with a medical scalpel. And you can see how all the surrounding ligaments, tendons, and nerve endings have been cut away from the radius and ulna . . . sorry, I mean the bones of the forearm . . . where they connect with the wrist. Whoever performed the surgery—and that's what it was, surgery—was very careful not to damage any part of the wrist. They cut off all the connections very carefully. The amputation was done by someone who knew their anatomy."

"A surgeon?" Rhostok asked, afraid that he already knew the answer. Altschiller was fitting the pieces together, adding scientific support to what had up until now only seemed an impossibility.

"That's a fair assumption," Altschiller said. "It was obviously done by someone with medical training. But there's no medical indication for amputation, no injury or pathology that would require cutting off this hand. Except for some minor pockmarks from a childhood infection . . ."

"What sort of infection?" Robyn asked.

"I'm not sure, but it might have been from the *vaccinia* virus, more commonly known as cowpox. It was transmitted from cows to humans during the milking process. We don't see much of it anymore, not since farmers switched to automatic milking machines." He paused before adding, "Some people think that's unfortunate."

"Why 'unfortunate'?"

"Well, cowpox left some minor scarring, like you see here, but it also had a wonderful side benefit. It conferred immunity to smallpox. When medical experts realized that fact, they used the *vaccinia* virus to create the vaccine that eventually eradicated smallpox. As a matter of fact, that's where the word 'vaccine' comes from: the *vaccinia* virus." Altschiller turned to Robyn. "That might make an interesting story for your health reporters." He seemed to be warming up to her, perhaps because of the unusual degree of interest she was showing in his explanations.

"You're saying this hand belonged to a man who must have worked on a farm where he milked cows," she said. Robyn stared at the hand, her eyes narrowing, evaluating. Up to something, Rhostok thought. But what?

"Yes, definitely," Altschiller said. "He must have milked cows, probably at an early age from the way the scarring has faded."

"And he was immune to smallpox?"

"I assume so. And the hand looks perfectly healthy, even now, more than twenty-four hours after it was brought here. I have no idea why anyone would amputate a perfectly healthy hand."

"And leave it in a safe-deposit box," Robyn added.

"That's certainly a puzzle," the professor agreed. "But I find myself more fascinated by the hand itself than the identity of the person who performed the amputation. We scraped some minute soil samples from under the fingernails."

He inserted a glass slide under a huge microscope and turned on the viewing light, standing aside to let them take turns looking through the double eyepiece. The samples were unrecognizable, especially under the powerful lens: irregular shapes, some with sawtoothed edges, others smooth, all the same dull gray color. They made no sense to Rhostok, who continued to study them as the professor explained his findings.

"Those are extremely fine particles of dirt you're looking at. Silt, actually. The kind of silt found in riverbeds and their flood plains."

"Maybe he worked around a river," Robyn suggested. "The Susquehanna and the Delaware rivers aren't far away."

"And the Lackawanna runs right through Middle Valley," Rhostok added.

"We did an analysis of the silt," Altschiller said. "It doesn't match the characteristics of the soil samples generally found in any of the local watersheds. More important is the lack of chemical contamination from the various pollutants found in most American rivers these days. In addition, the hand doesn't show any evidence of manual labor. No calluses. The only scars on the skin are those pockmarks on the back of the hand. The scars are interesting, for the reason I mentioned earlier. But whatever our mystery man did for a living, it wasn't manual labor. And it definitely wasn't along any American river."

"How can you be sure of that?" Rhostok asked, worrying about where this was going.

"Every river in America has been studied, sampled, and analyzed for its water quality," Altschiller explained. "It's part of the compliance procedures of the Clean Waters legislation. The samples are updated every year at various locations along the rivers to determine changes in the water quality. The samples are like fingerprints, and they're kept on file for instant access by environmental groups. We tried a computer match-up and it came back negative. We can't match it to any American river."

"Was it possible that it could have been a river in Canada?" Robyn asked. "Or some upstream source where the water is still clean?"

"I didn't say the silt came from an unpolluted river," Altschiller pointed out. "The particles contain a high level of fecal matter and heavy metals. That means the river runs through a large populated area that doesn't treat its sewage or industrial wastes. But strangely, we found no evidence of modern chemical compounds such as heptachlor epoxide, PCBs, chlorinated hydrocarbon derivatives, or other sediment-borne toxins or in-place pollutants normally found in waterways near polluted areas today. This man was tied up and left to drown in a river that shouldn't exist."

"You didn't mention drowning before," Rhostok said.

"I can't tell for sure since I don't have access to the victim's lungs. But based on the blood gases, drowning would be a logical assumption to make. That's one of a series of really puzzling mysteries about this hand, the silt sample being the first."

"What's so mysterious about drowning?" Rhostok asked.

"It's not the drowning. The mystery is why all that cyanide didn't kill the guy before he drowned."

"What?"

"You're looking at the hand of a man who was drowned in a river that shouldn't exist, after a massive dose of cyanide failed to kill him."

The old man and the boy finished their lunch, throwing the crumbs off the ledge for the creatures of the forest below. While the boy drank his soda, the old man continued his story.

"Rasputin became the confessor and spiritual advisor to the Imperial Family. The Empress considered him a living saint. He became the single most important religious personage in Russia, a man who reorganized the hierarchy of the Orthodox Church and personally selected the Patriarch of Petrograd and the leader of the Holy Synod. Yet he was never formally ordained as a priest."

"But how can that be, if he was not a priest?" the boy asked.

"Not all holy men are priests, and not all priests are holy men," the old man replied. "One of the most revered religious figures in Russian history was the ascetic hermit Makari, who was also never ordained. After Rasputin's first vision of Our Lady of Kazan, it was Makari who sent him on a journey that would end up ten years later at the Imperial Palace."

"He became a stranniki, *one of the holy wanderers," the boy said, eager to show that he remembered his earlier lessons.*

"He was not an ordinary holy wanderer," the old man said. "There was never anything ordinary about Rasputin. His first journey took him two thousand miles on foot across the Ural Mountains, down through the steppes of the Ukraine, through Romania and Bulgaria, and into Greece. He traveled across vast unpopulated areas and went for days without seeing another human and eating nothing but grass and weeds. But the pilgrimage became a kind of seminary for Rasputin. He looked deeply inwards, meditating on the meaning of his visions of Our Lady and preaching the word of God to all he encountered.

"He discovered he had the ability to calm the fears and address the hopes of strangers and was able to offer advice that later would prove prophetic. His ability to cure the sick grew stronger, and he never hesitated to use it. By the time he returned from his pilgrimage, he had already gained fame as a healer and a prophet."

Forty-Six

The taxi deposited Nicole in front of the Lackawanna County Building, a red sandstone structure whose lawns were edged with yellow flowers and shaded by maple trees. After she passed through the metal detector, the security guard took her aside. Although no weapon could possibly be hidden in the tight dress she wore, he insisted on subjecting her to the scrutiny of his magnetic wand. She had long ago grown accustomed to security guards who wanted to examine her body more closely. This one was more thorough than most, examining her both front and back before directing her to the elevators.

The second-floor hallway of the old building was lined with government-gray filing cabinets. Occupying every available space atop the cabinets was a dusty collection of cardboard storage boxes, desktop projectors, three-ring binders, hole punchers, staplers, and other bureaucratic overflow from the offices behind the doors. The clutter gave the hallway the feeling of a seldom-visited storage facility.

Halfway down the corridor, gold lettering on a frosted glass door identified the Office of the Coroner, Thomas M. O'Malley, M.D., D.F.M. Nicole shuddered at the thought of what awaited her beyond that door, but she knew she had no choice. She straightened her skirt, took a deep breath, lifted her chin, and entered the office with as much dignity as she could muster.

The receptionist took her name and seemed surprised when O'Malley agreed to see Nicole immediately. She ushered her through a small alcove and held open the door for Nicole to enter a warmly decorated office. One wall of the office was covered with dozens of framed photos, many of them signed, showing O'Malley at various stages of his life with prominent political and religious figures, including a photo with Hillary Clinton, taken on one of her visits to the Rodham family in Scranton. A large gold-framed painting of the Irish countryside hung above a non-working white marble fireplace. The fireplace was flanked by two antique armoires. A long black leather couch occupied the far wall. In the middle of the room, silhouetted by the windows behind him, Thomas O'Malley waited for her at his desk.

He grinned and lifted himself to a standing position, his metal leg brace creaking with the movement.

Nicole held his hand a little longer than was necessary, letting him feel the softness of her fingers, until she saw his welcoming smile melt into a look of anticipation that was sadly familiar to her.

It was the typical male reaction, she thought. They were always ready, always watching. Always waiting for some little signal that a woman might be available for their pleasure. It didn't matter whether the woman was single, married, or, as in her case, recently widowed. They all wanted the same thing. This one with the metal brace on his leg was no different. Touch his skin just a moment longer than etiquette required, and he was ready. An easy man to manipulate, she thought.

If she played him right, she could get what she wanted from him with little more than a bit of flirting and some empty promises. She sat down and crossed her legs, allowing the skirt to rise just above her knees.

"What can I do for you?" he asked.

He was doing everything but licking his lips, she thought. He tried to keep his eyes on her face, but they kept drifting down to the open buttons that revealed the valley between her breasts.

"You were kind to me when my husband died," she said. "I came here because . . ." She tried to find the words, to construct the lie that would be most appealing to him. "Well, because you seem like a good person and I . . . I . . ." The hesitancy in her voice was real, and it surprised her. It used to be so easy to lie to men, but now the words seemed harder to phrase. "I . . . I think I can trust you."

"I'm glad you feel that way," he said, accepting the compliment with a wet-lipped smile. "But things have changed since then," he went on, his voice turning solemn. "The police are looking for you now."

"I didn't do anything wrong."

"Then you shouldn't have run away."

"I was frightened."

"Maybe so. All I know is that they found a dead cop in your house, and you were gone. What I should do right now is call the Middle Valley police and tell them you're here."

His hand reached for the telephone.

She knew exactly what O'Malley was up to. Threatening to turn her in to the police was his crude way of trying to establish control over her, to put her at his mercy, so that she'd submit more readily to his demands. It was an old game, one she had played with other men, usually those who felt unsure of their abilities with women. She knew he had no intention of making the call, but she had to play the role he expected of her. She gently placed her hand on top of his.

"Please don't," she said.

"I could get into serious trouble," he told her. "They find out you were here and I didn't turn you in, they might consider it harboring a fugitive, or obstruction of justice."

She kept her hand atop his while he went through the ritual of pretending to struggle with his conscience. She realized her hand was trembling.

"Of course, there aren't any arrest warrants out on you," he said. "And no charges pending, at least not yet."

He put his other hand on top of hers and squeezed it firmly.

"Oh, well, what the hell; as far as I'm concerned, you're just a frightened young woman looking for help." His tone of voice changed, turning friendly. "If you don't want me to call the police, I won't. At least not for the time being."

He stroked the back of her hand with two fingers, stroking so gently that despite her revulsion it sent tremors up her arm.

"Frankly, I don't blame you for not going back home. They probably haven't cleaned up all the blood yet."

"Was it . . . did someone . . . ?" She couldn't seem to make her throat function properly.

"Was it murder?" O'Malley supplied the word she couldn't bring herself to speak. "It doesn't appear to be a homicide, although we found a large unexplained abrasion on the back of his neck. But that wasn't what killed him."

"Then how . . . ?"

"The cause of death was a massive internal hemorrhage, primarily due to a rupture of the abdominal aorta. He bled to death in a matter of minutes."

Nicole pulled her hand back in horror, remembering the policeman's face and the blood gushing from his mouth.

"There wasn't anything you could have done," O'Malley assured her. "Even if he had made it to the hospital, no one could have saved him. Not when the circulatory system suffers so traumatic a collapse."

"How awful!" she said, and immediately realized how stupidly inadequate her words were.

"It happens," O'Malley said. "People die." He gave her a sly smile. "But that policeman was the second man to die in your bedroom in the last week."

"Is that an accusation?"

"Of course not. Both of those deaths were due to natural causes. So was the death of the president of the Middle Valley State Bank."

"Mr. Zeeman?" Her mouth went dry.

"I guess you didn't hear about that," O'Malley said in a voice that sounded a little too casual. "He died this morning. Cerebral hemorrhage. A vein popped in his head and bled into his brain. He was dead before his head hit the desk. You probably didn't hear about Wendell Franklin, either. I think you met him, didn't you?"

"He was with us at the bank," she murmured.

"Cut his finger on your safe-deposit box, that's the story I got," the coroner said. "Can you imagine, he bled to death from that little wound?"

Nicole was stunned at the news of the additional deaths. She remembered with a shudder how they had all been crowded together in the vault. Zeeman so polite to her, and Franklin so rude. She had been close enough to rub shoulders with both of them, close enough to smell their body odors. The big policeman had been there, too, waiting to take fingerprints. Now they were all dead. She clasped her hands together to keep them from trembling.

"That makes four deaths, if you include your husband," O'Malley said. "It seems to be a cluster, and your local police department thinks there's some grand conspiracy. But those deaths were all due to natural causes. The sort of things people die from all the time." He seemed to be enjoying the fear that was showing on her face. "Still, the interesting coincidence is that all these people have some kind of connection to you. You've had close contact with every one of them, haven't you?"

That was the most frightening part of it all, she thought.

Rhostok's warning that her life might be in danger no longer seemed like the improbable imaginings of a suspicious policeman. But these were deaths from natural causes, not murder. And that made it all far more sinister. Her thoughts flashed back to the Ukrainian psychic who had refused any more readings of her future. Maybe this was the reason why. Maybe the psychic had foreseen the shadow of death hovering about her. The death of a child, the death of a husband, the deaths that struck down so many around her . . . and yet to come were the awful events predicted by *Episkop* Sergius. Fate had cast her in the role of an unwitting harbinger of doom. Yet no matter what sins she had committed, she couldn't understand why others must die for her misdeeds.

"You look a little queasy," O'Malley said in a suddenly solicitous voice. "Maybe you should go over and sit down on the couch. Take a deep breath, maybe lie down for a while."

Lie down? Her feminine instincts flashed a warning. One minute he's talking about death and the next minute he wants her to lie down on his couch? Was all this talk of death a clever trick, a morbid manipulation of her emotions by a man who knew how to prey on the bereaved?

"No, I'll be fine right here," she said. "All I need is a minute or two." She needed to compose herself, she thought. She had to put everything else out of her mind and focus on the reason she came here.

"Take your time," O'Malley said, although he seemed disappointed that she didn't accept his offer of the couch. "You know, when you called earlier, I was glad to hear you were okay. I was kind of worried about you, being all alone in that old house."

She nodded.

"All those memories . . ." he said.

Her eyes filmed over.

"Nobody to talk to . . ."

She bit her lip.

"Nobody to comfort you . . ."

The words were almost hypnotic. He seemed to know exactly what she had been feeling.

She watched his eyes drift down from her face again. She could almost feel them on the soft inside curves of her bosom, as if his gaze had lips that were caressing her skin.

"A beautiful woman like you, I'm surprised you don't have more friends."

He was toying with her, she could tell. Waiting for her to make the first move.

"I'd like to think of you as a friend," she said, getting back to the reason for her mission. "You said if I ever needed help, I should call you."

He stiff-legged his way around the desk and motioned towards the leather couch.

"Why don't you come over here and tell me about it."

She hesitated. It wasn't very long ago that she would have moved smoothly through the rituals of flirtation and seduction, playing with a man's libido until he was willing to pay whatever price she demanded. But a month of marriage, a month of being faithful to one man had changed her in a way she had never thought possible. Now she felt awkward, even embarrassed at being forced to flirt with a man she barely knew.

"Don't be nervous," O'Malley said. He crossed the room to open one of the armoires, revealing a well-stocked bar inside. "Would you like a drink?"

Her first instinct was to refuse. Liquor was man's best friend when it came to lowering a woman's defenses. Yet a strong drink might be just what she needed to help her through the next few minutes.

"Maybe I could use one," she agreed, and then quickly regretted it when she saw the size of the glasses he was filling.

"Jameson's Irish whiskey," he said. "On the rocks."

The glass he handed her contained enough whiskey to render any woman unconscious. His own glass contained twice as much.

"I always pour large economy-size drinks," he explained, as he carefully extended his paralyzed leg and lowered himself onto the couch beside her. "That way I don't have to get up so often for refills." He took a quick, almost nervous drink and smiled. "Now how can I help you?"

"Maybe I just need someone to talk to," she said, stalling for time. "The people in that awful town—it's like they don't want to have anything to do with me."

Nicole's drinking experience was mostly white wine and champagne. She had never liked whiskey, and was reminded of the reason why when the undiluted alcohol burned the inside of her mouth before spreading its numbing effect. She could feel the heat as the liquid made its way down to her stomach.

"They don't like strangers up there, that's for sure," O'Malley said. He took a long drink and ran his tongue over his lips to be sure he didn't leave anything behind.

"That's the way they are, those Russians," he continued. "Second and third generation, and they act like they're still in the Old Country, expecting the Secret Police to come knocking on the door."

"But it was my husband's hometown," she complained. "They knew him, so why couldn't they accept me? I'm Russian, too, you know. At least on my mother's side."

"Maybe it's your background," he said. "That Las Vegas business."

"How did you know about that?"

Forty-Seven

"I . . . I must have heard it from one of the cops." O'Malley quickly took another drink. "As far as them not accepting you, it's just the nature of the people up there. They don't like outsiders, even their own kind." He took another drink, a longer one this time. His glass was already half empty.

"I expected something so different," she said. The alcohol was loosening her tongue. "When I first saw that town from the highway, it looked like a dream come true. I thought Paul and I were going to live in a lovely little community in a nice house with a white picket fence and flowers out the back. I can't have children, but I thought I could make friends and have a normal life." Her voice cracked, and she raised the glass to her lips again. The second drink didn't seem as harsh as the first. "I should have known better. Nothing ever works out for me."

"It's a deceptive kind of place," O'Malley said. He slid almost imperceptibly closer to her. "Sitting down in the valley between the mountains, it looks like a picture postcard when you first see it. But it's really a disaster area. The Environmental Protection Agency should buy up the town and move everybody out, like they did in Times Beach, Missouri, or that area around the Love Canal in upstate New York." He took another swallow of whiskey. "You probably heard about the methane gas that comes up from the abandoned coal mines. It doesn't have any odor, doesn't give off any warning of any kind until a spark or a flame ignites an explosion. Probably at your husband's funeral, you didn't see any candles in church, at least not real candles, did you?"

"No," she said, trying to remember. "I guess not."

"That's because they don't want to take any chances with the methane. They use those artificial electric candles instead. It's a hell of a place to live, where you're afraid to light a candle in church because the building might blow up."

"You're right about that," she agreed.

She was beginning to feel relaxed in his company. Somehow, whether it was the whiskey or their individual loneliness, they were slipping into an almost normal conversation. He seemed no longer the hunter, she no longer the wary prey. It was a pleasant feeling.

He continued with his criticisms. "They've got the methane, the mine cave-ins, and sinkholes. There're even some of those old veins of coal that catch fire underground; they say the temperature down there is over two thousand degrees. Closest thing to Hell you'll ever find. Sometimes the earth above the fires cracks open, and you can feel the heat and smell the sulphur. But do you think those crazy Russkies are willing to move? No, they're too stubborn. You ask me, they were born to suffer."

And then, apparently remembering her ancestry, he quickly apologized.

"Oh, Jesus, there I go again. I'm sorry if I offended you. I don't have anything against the Russians, really I don't. It's just the liquor talking."

"Don't apologize," she smiled. "My mother used to say the same thing, that we were born to suffer. And in my case, it certainly turned out to be true." She took another drink of whiskey, a longer one this time. "It's like there's some kind of curse on me."

"I don't believe that for a minute," O'Malley said. While she had been talking, he had managed to slide closer to her. "You're such an attractive woman. You ever do any modeling?"

"Please," she said. "Don't ask. You have no idea what my life has been like."

"It can't be any worse than mine." He unexpectedly turned serious. "I've been dragging this piece of steel around since I was eighteen." He adjusted his trouser leg over the brace.

"I'm sorry," she said, feeling a sudden rush of sympathy for him, and then just as quickly wondering if she was once again being manipulated, if the whiskey and the appeal for sympathy were simply his idea of foreplay. She hid her confusion with another quick drink.

"Look, I know you're feeling bad about your husband." O'Malley moved closer still. His good knee was almost touching hers. "But these things happen. In my line of work, I see it every day. People I knew, people I didn't know, all dead. I don't let it get me down." He looked at his empty glass and smiled sadly. "Except maybe I drink more than I should, but I can always blame that on being Irish, right?"

"The Russians drink a lot, too." She smiled sympathetically and offered to get him a refill, eager to get away from his encroaching body. She could feel his eyes on her as she walked, a little unsteadily, to the liquor cabinet.

She returned with his drink and curled her legs protectively beneath her. His eyes immediately went down to her black-stockinged knees beneath the too-short black skirt and then back up to her face.

"Why so sad?" he asked. "Thinking about your husband?"

"Not just him," she said. "The others that died, too."

She took another drink of Jameson's, a long slow drink, enjoying the way the alcohol dulled her senses and took the edge off her anxiety. She was beginning to think O'Malley was actually a pretty nice guy. He seemed so understanding.

"Come on, relax." O'Malley patted her shoulder. "Like I said, these things happen."

"But the men that died . . ." The glass trembled in her hand. "They all had a connection to me."

"I'm telling you, it's nothing to worry about. They died of natural causes. The timing was just a coincidence." O'Malley put his arm around her shoulders, as if to comfort her. "If I knew it was going to upset you so much, I wouldn't have said anything. So let's not talk about it anymore, okay? Now give me a smile, will you?"

He shook her playfully. It reminded her of the way Paul used to tease a smile out of her. She managed a weak grin.

"That's better," he said. His arm remained wrapped around her. "Now why don't you tell me what you want. I know you didn't come here just to talk."

She couldn't put it off any longer, she realized.

"I . . . I need your help," she said, trying to work up to it, without being too abrupt.

He pulled her closer.

"You just tell me what you want."

"I came here because I know I can trust you," she said, still unable to give voice to what she had come there to ask.

The whiskey smell was heavy on his breath. He seemed unaware of how tightly he was squeezing her shoulders. But the words he spoke were soft and compassionate.

"I understand," he said. "I know what it must be like for you, being a widow without anyone to turn to."

"It does get lonely," she whispered.

She wasn't surprised when he made a move to kiss her. He seemed almost shy about it, like a little boy afraid that his first move might be rejected. His kiss was amazingly gentle for a man his size. His lips barely touched hers, lingered for a moment as if to taste her, and then lightly brushed from one side of her mouth to the other. The incredibly delicate tenderness of his touch wasn't at all what she had expected. Nor was her reaction.

She didn't pull away. She had come here not wanting to offer herself to him, had hoped for a way to avoid being pawed by him, but he seemed warm and friendly, so considerate of her feelings, and now that the first physical contact was made, she wasn't resisting. Was it fatigue? Had the alcohol worked its chemical alchemy on her natural feminine resistance? Or was it fear that was driving her, as it had so many times in the past, to take comfort in the arms of any available man?

She relaxed and opened her lips to allow his heavy tongue to enter her mouth. She twisted her body in his arms until she found a comfortable position while he explored the inside of her mouth.

When he finally pulled back, he was breathing heavily.

"I better lock the door," he said.

She waited for him on the couch while he turned the key in the lock, slid the inner bolt, and for extra security, propped a chair against the doorknob. He closed the miniblinds, as if he were worried that somebody might be watching from the treetops outside the third-floor window.

When he started to unbutton her dress, she reached out to feel the metal that encased his leg. Her hand trembled as she ran it up to the ball joint at his hip and down to the swivel joint at his knee. The leg inside felt withered and weak. The metal felt cold and smooth and powerful.

She wondered about the loneliness the brace must have imposed on him. What was it like for him, she wanted to ask. Limping through life with a disability. Had he ever danced with a woman? Taken a girl for a walk? The thoughts stirred an odd feeling within her. She had felt many things for the men who had taken her in the past: disgust, contempt, bitterness. But never sympathy.

"Does it hurt you?" she asked.

"Nothing hurts right now," he said, just before he slipped his tongue hungrily back inside her mouth. "You're the most beautiful woman I've ever kissed," he said, and in her alcohol haze, she was convinced that she was performing an act of great charity by allowing him to take such liberties with her.

It felt good to be in a man's arms again. She was going further with O'Malley than she had planned. But she was certain she would be able to pull back if she merely allowed herself a little more pleasure.

A little comfort, that was all she wanted.

Something to make up for the nights of loneliness since Paul's death.

Something to make up for the tears and the sorrow and the fears that seemed at times to overwhelm her in the lonely darkness. Fears and sorrow that she knew would return as soon as she left O'Malley's office.

When his lips went down to her neck, down to the swelling mounds of her chest, she shivered and wrapped her arms tightly around his head. Smelling his pomade and the sweat of his scalp, she felt her body responding powerfully to him.

She had to regain control of her emotions, she thought. It was time to remember the reason she was here.

"I didn't mean for this to happen," she said, trying half-heartedly to pull away. "I came here to ask for your help."

"Anything," O'Malley said. "Anything you want."

His wet lips came up, kissing her on the cheeks, the mouth, the forehead, the eyes, his hands still fondling her breasts through the thin fabric of her bra.

"I want you to return the hand to me," she said.

"The what?"

"The hand . . . the one we found in the safe-deposit box. It belongs to me. I want it."

"Don't talk crazy."

He buried his face in the hollow between her breasts.

"Legally, whatever was in that safe-deposit box is my property," she said. "That hand was taken from my husband's box. It belongs to me, and I want it back. Now."

Forty-Eight

"Cyanide?" Robyn repeated the word. Rhostok noticed a strange sparkle in her eyes. "You just told us that the man drowned."

"As I said, it's a very unusual specimen."

It was all sounding ominously familiar to Rhostok. He had heard the story before, that long-ago afternoon up on the mountain ledge overlooking the valley. Poison that didn't kill. He once thought of it only as a myth, told by an old man trying to embellish history.

"The part about the cyanide," Rhostok said. "Are you sure about that? Is there a chance you could be mistaken?"

"Not a chance. Especially when you consider the magnitude of the concentration. We're not talking about a small amount of poison here. The level of cyanide in our mystery man's blood was enough to kill two or three mature elephants. And the equipment we use for this particular test is extremely reliable. It can detect quantities as minute as one part per billion."

Altschiller led them to a boxlike stainless-steel instrument in a far corner of the room, which he identified as a photospectrometer. It had a viewing hole, an eyepiece, and a slot in the bottom where a paper printout emerged. Everything today seemed to end up in the form of a printout, Rhostok thought. Now the machines not only solved your problems faster than you could yourself, they even took your notes for you and provided you with a neatly printed record.

The professor unfolded a four-foot section of printout. It looked to Rhostok like a continuous line graph. But penciled notations separated the graph into segments, some of which Altschiller apparently found more interesting than others.

"We can identify the chemistry of any sample by heating a small amount until it glows, then passing the resulting light through a prism and examining the resulting color spectrum. Every chemical produces its own individual color in the spectrum. This printout translates the results into a graph. Now look at this," he said, pointing to a section of the chart where the lines took a sharp jump upward. "That's the cyanide. It appears to be present at a very high level—unbelievably high. So high that we ran the test four different times, just to be sure we were getting an accurate reading. The results were the same each time."

Altschiller took off his glasses and rubbed his bloodshot eyes.

"You brought me an artifact that poses a series of profound mysteries," he said. "Mysteries for which I have no scientific explanation."

The rubbing seemed to make his eyes grow redder.

"Perhaps I'm just too tired," he sighed. "Maybe that's why I can't figure it out."

"What is it that's so hard to figure out?" Robyn asked.

"Well, for one thing, why our mystery man didn't die from the cyanide poisoning. I have no explanation. The ingestion of potassium cyanide always results in death—always. You've read about the famous cyanide capsule in spy novels and the history books. It's what Hermann Goering took to commit suicide during the Nuremburg trials. A single drop inside the capsule produces an agonizing and certain death. There is no antidote. Even if there were, it could never be administered in time, because death can occur in a matter of seconds. Yet the level of cyanide in the blood sample we examined indicates our man ingested the equivalent of about sixty or seventy of those capsules."

"Then what's the mystery?" Robyn asked. "The cyanide killed him."

"I don't think so," Professor Altschiller said in a voice filled with awe. "The cyanide seems to have had no effect on this fellow. Like I said, he died by drowning."

"How can you possibly think that?" Robyn asked.

Now she was in her argumentative mode, Rhostok thought. Not necessarily disbelieving, but testing and probing to see if Altschiller would change his story.

"If you found evidence of all that cyanide in the blood, and if cyanide is as lethal as you say, how can you possibly contend that the man died from drowning?" she persisted.

It certainly didn't seem possible to Rhostok. Not in this day and age, when modern science had discredited the ghosts and superstitions of past centuries. But Altschiller was a highly respected forensic scientist, a scholar with a reputation for careful, methodical work. He wasn't the sort of person to make a claim he couldn't support, no matter how astonishing it might be.

"All I had to do was measure the oxygen in the venous blood," the professor said. "Cyanide binds with cytochrome oxidase to prevent oxygen from being released to the tissues. It blocks the aerobic metabolism within the cells."

Rhostok half-listened as Altschiller launched into a technical explanation of his findings. The old memories were beginning to stir within him again, memories of his grandfather's voice dropping to a whisper as he repeated ancient stories of blood and religion, cures and curses.

"In layman's terms, the cyanide stops the cells from breathing," Altschiller went on. "The oxygen remains locked in the blood. Without oxygen transference to the tissues, the victim becomes hypoxic and suffers an agonizing death. The blood in the veins ends up with a high residual oxygen level, the same level found in arterial blood. It's a simple test. A good pathologist will suspect cyanide poisoning as soon as he sees a bright red color in the venous blood."

The professor paused after the long explanation, as if to emphasize the point he was making.

"Now there is a certain amount of oxygen depletion in this case," he continued. "But the level of depletion is nowhere near that which would be consistent with hypoxia due to cyanide poisoning. The venous blood I tested exhibits a level of oxygen depletion normally associated with asphyxiation or drowning, which, given the presence of river silt under the fingertips, was the probable cause of death. Also, there were no anomalies in oxygen distribution between the blood and the tissue samples. This fellow's metabolic system appeared to be immune to the cyanide, which makes him the first person in recorded medical history to exhibit this characteristic."

Altschiller stared at the hand under its protective glass shield, shaking his head at the specimen's refusal to reveal its mysteries.

"I just don't have the answer," he said. "Because I've never seen anything like it. It defies medical explanation."

"There's probably a very simple answer," Robyn suggested.

"If there is, I'd like to hear it," Altschiller said.

There was a simple answer, Rhostok thought. But not one that he wanted to voice, at least not yet. He had heard the stories about the cyanide from his grandfather. He used to think those stories were just the old man's way of reinventing his past, trying to glamorize his own history the way old men often do. Living in that half-world where reality and fantasy overlap. Trying to impress an admiring grandson.

And now, here it was, all these years later, his grandfather's strange story coming back to haunt him.

"What are you thinking, Rhostok?" Robyn interrupted his thoughts. "You haven't said anything. Do you know something about all this?"

Testing him now. He didn't want to sound like a fool. This was no place to repeat the old superstitions. He was in a scientific laboratory, flanked by two rational thinkers. He had to put aside primitive fears and deal with the facts as they were being laid out.

"Let's deal with what we know," Rhostok said, slipping into his police mode. "Your tests tell us the hand belonged to a middle-aged male, around forty-five years old, born on a farm, little finger deformed, about five-feet-ten inches tall, cyanide in the blood, but not the cause of death. Our man was tied up with old-fashioned natural-fiber abaca rope and thrown into a river. Not just any river, but a river with no trace of modern chemical pollutants. After he drowns, his body is recovered and somebody cuts off his right hand at the wrist. You say the amputation was performed by a doctor." He reached for an answer that he knew was almost certainly wrong, but probably fit the facts. "What that tells me is that maybe the hand came from a morgue. They've got doctors in the morgue, right? And a morgue is where a body would be taken after it was fished out of the water."

Rhostok realized he was sounding like Otto Bruckner, offering up simple answers to questions that even a scientist was unable to resolve.

"The part about the morgue sounds logical," Altschiller agreed. "But you still haven't explained why the cyanide didn't kill him."

"Or how the hand got into the safe-deposit box," Robyn pointed out.

"And if I remember correctly," the professor added in a sly voice. "You told me you've already been in contact with all the area hospitals and morgues."

"No one's reported any recent amputations of a hand, or the admission of any patient, living or dead, with a missing hand," Rhostok said. "At least not yet. But I'll keep trying."

"All right," Robyn turned back to Altschiller. "You said there were two mysteries you couldn't explain. The first big mystery is the cyanide. What's the other big mystery?"

"I would think it would be obvious to you by now," Altschiller said. "Just take a good look at the hand." He leaned in closer to the bell jar, his red eyes reflected in the glass. "Look closely. Don't you see something very unusual about it?"

Rhostok stared at the hand, trying to figure out what the professor was seeing that he didn't.

"I give up," he finally said.

Altschiller's face was almost touching the glass. He seemed mesmerized by the object inside.

"It looks as fresh as the moment it was amputated," he said in a voice filled with wonder. "The flesh doesn't appear to be susceptible to the normal process of decomposition."

"That's because I had it frozen," Rhostok quickly said, reaching for another easy answer. "I kept it frozen so it wouldn't decompose."

"That was very prudent of you, Rhostok. But the hand wasn't frozen during the time it was in the safe-deposit box. It was already thawed out when you brought it here, and it's been sitting out at room temperature ever since. And look at it. Compare the color with your own hand. It's so . . . so perfectly natural and healthy-looking, it's absolutely unbelievable."

"Couldn't the fact that it had been frozen earlier slow down the process of decay?" Robyn asked.

"In actual fact, the very process of freezing should have altered the cellular structure. But I couldn't find any evidence of those or any other changes. Everything about this hand, the blood chemistry, the tissue samples, the lymphatic fluid, everything is consistent with a hand that was removed from a body moments ago. Not hours ago. Not days ago. But moments ago."

Altschiller gently lifted the bell jar, exposing the hand. Again that dry, musty smell, like old wheat in a field, wafted up. He selected a probe and touched it to the bloody stump at the wrist. A drop of blood adhered to the tip of the probe, glistening under the halogen lights.

"Look at that," he whispered, the wonder in his voice turning to awe. "The blood has barely thickened. Normally the physical characteristics of blood start changing as soon as it is exposed to air. It should be dried out and crusted by now. But this blood has the same consistency as blood that was just drawn from a living body. Even when I smeared some samples on glass slides, it still didn't dry out. It seems to have a life of its own."

"Maybe it has something to do with all that cyanide," Rhostok said, still trying to find a rational explanation, still afraid to believe the hand was in any way connected with the old stories.

"The cyanide wouldn't account for such remarkable effects," Altschiller said. "Another peculiarity is the apparent absence of any molecular change in the fleshy tissue. I found no sign of the microbial activity that normally precedes putrefaction. Nor is there any apparent release of gases, which is also highly unusual, considering how warm it's been in my laboratory—not to mention the confines of the bank vault. None of the normal changes that occur in dead human flesh are evident here."

"Maybe whoever cut it off used some kind of preservation technique," Robyn said.

"Why would anybody do that?" Rhostok asked.

"Hey, I don't know," she said. "I'm just looking for other possible answers."

"There are only three techniques I know for preserving dead flesh," Altschiller said. "One is alcohol, and I looked for that, but found absolutely no evidence that the hand had been in contact with an alcohol-based preservative. The second is desiccation, or a drying-out process, which is what you often see in human remains in the high Andes, or in desert areas. But as you can see, the hand hasn't been exposed to that process, either. And then there's embalming, but it's fairly obvious this hand hasn't been embalmed."

"But it does have a funny smell," Rhostok said. "Like moldy wheat or grass."

"I noticed that, too," Altschiller said. "But it's not related to any preservative I know. I took some scrapings from the skin. There are some spores I can't identify, but they're not consistent with preservation techniques. In any event, the fluid nature of the blood indicates that the stump of the wrist was never treated or medicated after the amputation. And that's where any preservation technique would have to have been applied."

He pressed the skin with the probe, and they watched it give against the metal and then resume its shape when the probe was removed.

"You brought me a very rare find indeed, Rhostok."

"You mean weird, don't you?"

"I mean rare. Extremely rare," the professor said, the awe back in his voice. "I've read about such things, but I never thought I'd come in contact with one of them myself."

"It's just a hand," Rhostok said.

"Not just an ordinary hand. It's much more than that. Based on my testing, I'm convinced what we have here, as impossible as it may seem, is a classic example of an *incorruptible*."

"A what?"

"An *incorruptible*."

It was a word from another time, Rhostok thought. He stared at the hand, half-expecting to see it suddenly come alive, to curl its fingers into a fist and smash at the glass. He had heard of such things, of course, but as with all the old legends, was never sure how much he should believe.

"That's a fancy word," Robyn said. "Does it come with an explanation?"

"I can define what an incorruptible is," the professor said, "but I can't explain it. The term is applied to human flesh, usually entire corpses, but occasionally body parts or even specimens of blood, which appear to be impervious to the normal process of decay and decomposition that follows death."

"That's scientifically impossible," Robyn said.

"You're looking at the impossible right now," the professor said. "Although extremely rare, the history of such phenomena goes back two thousand years, to the beginning of the Christian era. Most such artifacts are kept under lock and key in churches or monasteries, where they are considered treasures of the faith and venerated as signs of divine intervention, as hints of immortality. The skeptics dismiss such beliefs as religious superstition, but no one has been able to dispute the case studies on incorruptibles, which are well documented, or the physical evidence, which is astounding. The apparent suspension of normal physical processes remains one of the great mysteries of forensic science."

Altschiller's face was flushed. He removed his glasses and rubbed at his eyes, which seemed to be growing redder with each moment.

"All of which leads me to believe," he said in a voice that suddenly turned solemn, "that what we have here is not just an ordinary severed hand. What we're dealing with is a relic of major religious significance."

"How did Rasputin work his cures, Grandfather?" the boy asked. "I mean, what exactly did he do?"

"The old people said he would kneel at the bedside of the sick, close his eyes, and begin to pray aloud. He would appear to be calling out to someone he saw in the distance, someone invisible to the others in the room. Soon his face would become pale and ashen, as if the blood had drained away. Sweat would break out on his forehead. He would raise his right hand and grow suddenly silent, straining with concentration. The cures were often instantaneous. Fevers would break. The comatose would open their eyes. The bedridden would rise. And Rasputin would be left shaken and drained of his strength, often on the verge of collapse."

"So he cured others, not just the little Tsarevich."

"Hundreds of others during his lifetime," the old man said. "Some cures were very public and easily verifiable, like that of Anya Virubova, whom the doctors abandoned as dead when her skull was crushed. Other cures were in private and obscure circumstances. After the Revolution, the Communists established the Murayev Commission in an attempt to discredit Rasputin and his miraculous abilities. But not one single individual of the hundreds whose cures were attributed to him ever came forward to speak against him."

Forty-Nine

"Don't look at me like I'm crazy," Nicole told O'Malley. "I just want what's rightfully mine." She was using the logic Vassily had supplied before her unsuccessful visit to the police station. "It's no different from claiming a body. Unless there's evidence that some kind of crime was committed, you're supposed to release the body to anyone who has a rightful claim to it. And according to Paul's will, I inherit everything he owned, including the contents of that box."

"You're definitely crazy," O'Malley laughed. "Beautiful, but crazy."

"I'm serious," she insisted. "I want the hand. I want you to return it to me."

She felt his fingers moving up between her legs. She closed her eyes and tried to squirm away, only to be held back by his other arm around her waist.

"I know what you really want," he said. "I know the kind of woman you are. All anybody has to do is look at you."

He pulled at the front of her bra, ripping open the elastic, and watched her breasts spill out. She tried to cover them with her hands.

"Please don't," she begged.

He pulled her arms aside, exposing her flesh to his hungry eyes.

"Stop it! Stop it or I'll scream!"

"No one will hear you. It's after one. Everybody's gone out to lunch."

"Please," she moaned, trying to pull away. "Don't do this to me. I only came here to ask your help."

"I know what kind of help you want." O'Malley was slurring his words. The alcohol was strong on his breath. "You're lonely. You miss your husband. You miss the loving, don't you?"

He pulled her half-naked body against his and tried to cover her mouth again with his wet lips.

"You said you'd do anything for me," she reminded him.

"I will, I will. I'll do anything for you."

"Then promise you'll return the hand to me."

"I don't have the damn hand," he responded angrily. "Rhostok never turned it over to me. I don't know where the hell it is, and right now, I really don't care."

If what he said was true, there was no longer any reason for her to submit to him. She knew she should have left right then. She should have somehow fought him off and buttoned up her dress and fled. But the alcohol had spread its pleasant glow through her body, diminishing her will to resist.

"You really don't have the hand?" she asked. "You're not lying to me?"

"Why the hell would I lie about that? Forget about the hand. Forget about your husband. Take off your dress."

She tried, although with less effort this time, to free herself from O'Malley's grasp. He forced her hands behind her back and continued his attack. She pleaded with him to let her go, but he laughed and continued to fondle her. His face was red and his breathing was growing faster. He was close enough that she could see the throbbing of a vein in his forehead.

"Forget about the damn hand," he said. "Forget about your husband and Zeeman and Franklin and whoever else is dead. Forget about everything."

He lowered his mouth to her breasts, kissing first one and then the other with amazing gentleness. She arched her neck back, trembling at the wetness of his tongue. This wasn't at all what she had intended. She had thought O'Malley would be an easy mark, just another horny man who could be easily manipulated into doing her bidding. But now the situation was reversed. It was O'Malley who was having his way. He had softened her with whiskey, offered her sympathy and understanding, played on her loneliness and fear, and now, half drunk, she no longer had the strength or even the desire to fight him off.

What she was doing was wrong, she knew. Terribly wrong. This was behavior she thought she had left behind. What would Paul think if he could see her now, she wondered: half naked before this man she had met only once before? After a month of marriage, a month of being faithful to a husband she loved, Nicole was overcome with shame at how she was responding.

"You're not the first widow to come to me," O'Malley said. "I know how to make you forget."

"If only you could," she said.

She wanted desperately to forget.

Forget about the hand.

Forget about Vassily.

Forget about the *Episkop* and her stepfather and all the others in between.

Forget about the deaths of all those men.

Even, if only for a few moments, forget about Paul.

She was tired, and weak, and emotionally drained.

What she wanted more than anything else was to put it all out of her mind. Drown her memories in this man's passion. Find a few blessed moments of forgetfulness in someone's embrace. Was this what widows did, she wondered? Use other men's arms to help them forget their sorrows? If so, it seemed to work, at least for the moment. She, who had been repelled by his clumsy advances immediately after her husband's death, now found herself responding to O'Malley. She wrapped her arms tightly around him, holding on with all her strength. She returned his kisses with growing passion of her own. Perhaps they were using each other for their own desperate needs. But none of that mattered to her any longer.

She slipped a hand free and used it to draw him closer, this man with the steel brace on his crippled leg, hoping he could make her forget everything, if only for a little while.

She was sure it couldn't be wrong.

What was it the *Episkop* had told her last night?

Without sin, there can be no redemption.

Without redemption, there can be no salvation.

Perhaps that was why she was here.

O'Malley's activity increased.

Perhaps, she thought, this was a step on the road to her salvation.

Fifty

An incorruptible?

Human flesh that doesn't decay?

A religious relic?

Rhostok could imagine the uproar such words would provoke among the fundamentalist Old Believers in Middle Valley. Up until that moment, until the professor uttered those astonishing words, Rhostok had been hanging onto a faint hope that there was some simpler, less sensational explanation for the origin of the hand.

Yet he knew, had known from the very beginning, but had been afraid to admit even to himself, that the professor's theory was the only possible explanation.

Robyn continued challenging Altschiller. "Are you *serious?* This business about incorruptibility—is that based on scientific theory or is it some sort of superstitious nonsense?"

"I can assure you, it's not nonsense," he responded. "As I said, I haven't seen any examples myself. At least not until now. But the literature is filled with cases, some of them quite extensively documented."

And some of them told in old stories handed down through the generations, Rhostok thought. He had just never expected to be told by a highly respected professor of forensic anthropology, here, at the University of Scranton, that such things actually existed.

"Bodies have been buried for ten, fifty, a hundred years, and more," the professor continued. "And when the graves were opened, the bodies were found to be uncorrupted, without any sign of physical decay. The flesh was pink, the joints flexible. Rather than dead, the individuals appeared to be merely asleep, as if they might awaken at any moment."

A wave of uneasiness washed over Rhostok as he listened. He seemed to be caught in some strange labyrinth, where the answers he sought kept changing; where every mystery, on closer examination, revealed another, more baffling mystery hidden inside. What had started out as a simple investigation into the suspicious death of an old man had grown into a complex web of murder, unexplained deaths, and now seemed to be leading into the realm of the supernatural.

"Those cases you're talking about, if they're authentic, must involve some special embalming technique," Robyn argued, "maybe the kind the Egyptians used."

"I'm not talking about mummification," Altschiller said. "That's a very simple technique, involving the removal of the intestines and the brain and the drying-out of the body, oftentimes using various resins to enhance the process. It's fairly easy for a skilled person to accomplish, especially in the hot, dry climate of the Middle East. But the remains, if you've ever seen a mummy, are stiff and shriveled and discolored. All the blood is long gone, and the skin breaks apart like old parchment when even a slight amount of pressure is applied. But an incorruptible is something else entirely. In most reported cases, the corpse was never embalmed or otherwise treated before burial. The skin remains flexible. The blood remains liquid. The eyes remain clear and fluid."

If what Altschiller said were true, if this hand, this piece of human flesh that refused to decay, were really blessed with the gift of immortality, that changed everything, Rhostok realized.

Despite the name on the paper in which the hand was wrapped, he had refused to believe this could actually be the hand of Rasputin. Until now, it seemed impossible that the hand could have been in the vault longer than a day, much less over half a century. Until now, he was certain the hand was part of some sort of macabre deception, intended perhaps to frighten the superstitious. But now, he would have to start over again, go back and review every detail of his investigation, reexamine every suspicion, rethink every assumption he had made.

"It still sounds impossible," Robyn insisted, although Rhostok detected a softening in her voice. "It defies logic."

"Oh, I agree," Altschiller said. "It not only defies logic, it defies the laws of physics and biology and everything we know about the process of death and decay. But it happens. And it's supported by testimony from medical authorities who have examined the exhumed corpses."

"Then it must be something about the way they're buried, don't you think?" Robyn countered. "Special conditions in the soil or burial vault might be responsible."

She was doing the same thing to the professor that she had done to

Rhostok during their first encounter, he realized. Questioning everything he said, challenging him to support every statement, as if she were searching, like a prosecutor, for some inconsistency or evasion that could be turned against him unless he agreed to cooperate. That was her job, and she was very good at it. But Rhostok knew she had met her match in Altschiller.

"Incorruptibility has nothing to do with the manner of burial," the professor said. "I could cite case after case in which human corpses were buried under the most dreadful conditions, yet they remained in a totally lifelike state."

"Name one," she challenged him.

Rhostok wondered whether it was just a game with her, something reporters were taught to do, or whether she was genuinely interested in the truth. For his part, he didn't need any further convincing. His mind was already working furiously, applying a policeman's logic to the professor's theory and discovering that it led to some stunning conclusions.

"I could cite the case of Andrew Bobola," the professor said. "He was a Jesuit priest who was beaten to death in Poland in 1627. His body was buried and reburied at least a dozen times in different locations over a period of three hundred years. For sixty of those years, the body rested in wet soil among decaying corpses. Yet, in 1922, the body was found to be in a lifelike state, and the blood that covered the fatal wounds was freshly congealed."

The words washed over Rhostok, each one a further confirmation that he was finally on the right track. He tried to keep his face calm, tried to hide the excitement that was building within him. The professor had provided the key that was helping Rhostok understand at least part of the strange series of events that had baffled him for weeks.

"The corpse of Charbel Markhouf, a Lebanese, was buried without a coffin," Altschiller went on. "It was found seventy years later, floating in the mud in a flooded grave. Yet the body looked as healthy and pink as if he had just died, with no putrefaction whatsoever. Then there's John of the Cross, whose body was actually buried in quicklime, which is a substance so caustic that it can burn away human flesh. The burial was in 1591. But when the corpse was exhumed in 1955, more than three and a half centuries later, it was still moist and flexible. The quicklime had had no effect. I've seen what happens to bodies that are in the ground for fifteen years, and there's not much left, believe me. But can you imagine, three and a half centuries in quicklime, and there's zero effect? Zero?"

If the hand was truly invulnerable to decay, Rhostok thought, that meant it could have been placed in the vault at almost any time. Not within hours of its discovery, as he had earlier assumed, but weeks, months, even years earlier. If it was incorruptible, it could easily have been sitting in the vault for half a century, ever since Vanya Danilovitch first rented the box in 1946.

Robyn shook her head, apparently unwilling to accept the professor's account.

"Interesting," she said. "But those stories sound more like religious fairy tales than scientific fact to me."

"It's easy to think that way, if you don't know the details," Professor Altschiller said. He sat down and took a deep breath before continuing. He suddenly sounded very fatigued. "But I've read the autopsy reports. We had a section on this when I studied at Fordham." He stopped to catch his breath again. "Another example was Catherine Laboure. Her body was exhumed seventy years after her death. The official autopsy revealed all her internal organs were still intact, and the last meal she had eaten was still in her stomach. Her eyeballs were still viscous and bluish-gray, as they had been in life. The autopsy was performed by a Dr. Didier. As for Charbel Markhouf, his corpse was examined by the French Medical Institute, and the facts were verified."

If the mystery hand was invulnerable to decay, how far back could its existence be traced, Rhostok wondered. Why stop at fifty years? Why not go back almost a century? According to Altschiller, that was certainly possible. And if that was so, then despite Rhostok's earlier doubts, this piece of human flesh in front of them could well be the right hand of the man whose name was inscribed on the brown wrapping paper: the legendary *starets* Grigorii Effimovich Rasputin.

"Perhaps one of the most famous and most carefully documented cases of incorruptibility was that of Francis Xavier," the professor continued from his sitting position. His face was flushed and his breathing was becoming more labored, but like any teacher, he seemed eager to share his knowledge. "Xavier was a missionary who died in China in 1552. In his case, a deliberate attempt was made to destroy the body by packing the coffin with quicklime. As with John of the Cross, the quicklime had absolutely no effect. Xavier's corpse was then buried in direct contact with the earth for six months. At the end of that period, the corpse was exhumed and found to be in exactly the same condition as it was at the time of death.

"When the skeptics demanded an independent investigation, the Viceroy of Goa called in his chief medical authority, a Dr. Saraiva. The doctor and his witnesses found the blood was still fluid and the body absolutely untainted. Dr. Saraiva's report, taken under oath in a court of law, stated that according to everything he knew about medicine, the body could not possibly have been preserved in such pristine condition by any natural or artificial means."

Rhostok knew the only man who could confirm whether this was Rasputin's hand would have been Vanya Danilovitch, who had placed it in the vault in 1946. But Vanya was dead, and so was his son, and probably anyone else Vanya would have told, including Florian Ulyanov and Boris Cherevenko.

"I wouldn't rely on a single doctor's statement," Robyn said. "Especially a statement that was made centuries ago, when people were more gullible and subject to religious pressures."

Altschiller managed a weak smile at her response.

"There were others who shared your skepticism, including a later commissioner of the East India Company. He had the body exhumed again, more than a hundred years later. The report at that time said Francis Xavier's eyes were still so clear and penetrating, he seemed to be almost alive. The flesh remained firm and pink and flexible. And as with this hand before us, the blood was as fluid as that of a living person. The preservation of Xavier's body was so obviously miraculous, the commissioner converted to the Catholic faith on the spot."

Rhostok wondered if he could find a sample of Vanya's handwriting. He realized he should have thought of that immediately. He should have asked Nicole or searched the house. If the inscription on the oilskin paper matched Vanya Danilovitch's handwriting, it would prove he was the one who had deposited the hand in the vault. But what would Vanya have been doing with Rasputin's hand? And why would he have kept it secret?

"You're talking about something that happened in Asia a long time ago," Robyn muttered. "As far as I'm concerned, it's ancient history, and not very reliable."

"Your friends in the press don't think so," said the professor with a sly smile. "As late as 1974, a carefully researched article in *Newsweek* reported that Xavier's body was still as fresh as though he were merely asleep."

Altschiller's eyes were getting darker, redder now. He let out a slight grunt and clutched his stomach.

"What's wrong?" Rhostok asked. He reached out to steady the professor, but Altschiller waved him off.

"Probably something I ate. I'll be okay."

"I didn't intend for you to spend the whole night working on this," Rhostok apologized.

"It's a fascinating artifact. I couldn't resist."

"You should get some rest. You don't look good."

"I can't sleep. Not now. I'm too excited. I've examined thousands of human remains, but this is the first time I've had the opportunity to examine what appears to be a true incorruptible. I find it absolutely fascinating."

"Isn't it possible there could be another explanation?" Robyn persisted. "One with a scientific basis?"

"Not for this phenomenon," Altschiller said. "Not yet, anyway. Incorruptibility defies every law of nature, which qualifies it as a miraculous event in the view of most of the world's religions."

"Miraculous?" Robyn murmured. "You think it's miraculous?"

"You may not believe in miracles," Altschiller said. "But this is as close as you'll ever be to one. If we can identify this hand, we'll find it probably came from a saint."

A saint?

Rhostok wondered what his grandfather would say about that. The old man had told him that Rasputin (if that's whose hand it truly was) had been called many things by his enemies: a rogue, a sorcerer, a satyr, an agent of the Devil. But the old man always believed that no one understood the source of Rasputin's powers.

"Of course, the Catholic Church doesn't accept incorruptibility of the flesh as a proof of candidacy for sainthood." Altschiller had to stop to catch his breath again before continuing. "Pope Benedict made that clear in *De Cadaverum Incorruptione*. But incorruptibles are the rarest of religious relics and are almost always associated with saints, and now that I've had a chance to see one for myself, I find the phenomenon to be nothing short of a miracle. I'm looking forward to conducting more intensive tests on the relic."

"You've already answered all my questions," Rhostok interrupted. "I appreciate everything you've done, Professor. I really do. But I'm afraid you're not going to be able to perform any more tests. I have to take the hand . . . the relic . . . with me."

The abrupt announcement caught Altschiller by surprise. It took a moment before he could respond.

"You can't do that. The most important work is yet to be done. This is an amazing specimen. Surely you realize the significance of what you brought me?"

"I do. But I also know we could both be facing legal problems if the coroner finds out I let you examine it before I turned it over to him. He's already threatened to file a complaint with the D.A."

"A religious relic doesn't belong in the county morgue," Altschiller said.

"I'm sorry, Professor. I don't think I can hold him off any longer."

Altschiller slumped back in his chair. He stared at the hand.

"I'd really like to continue my testing," he pleaded. "I could tell you more about the hand, including what saint it might have come from, than the coroner ever will. After all, the identification of human remains is my particular area of expertise."

"I don't have any choice," Rhostok said.

He removed the bell jar covering the hand, only to be stopped by Altschiller, who leapt from the chair and grabbed his arm.

"Don't!" the professor shouted. "Don't touch it without protective gloves! The cyanide level in that relic is still lethal. Anyone mishandling it could suffer an agonizing death."

When Rhostok replaced the glass cover, Altschiller slumped back again, exhausted by the effort. He lowered his head and began to rub at his eyes.

When the professor stopped rubbing his eyes, his knuckles were covered with blood. Rhostok stared at him, too shocked to say anything.

"Oh my God!" Robyn gasped.

What looked like thick red tears flowed down the professor's cheeks. They were seeping from his eyes, which were now obscured behind a hideous curtain of blood.

"I can't see," Altschiller whimpered.

He raised the palms of his hands to his eyes, rubbing them into the sticky liquid, trying to clear his vision.

"I can't see!"

"Take it easy, professor," Rhostok said. "You'd better lie down." He guided Altschiller to the floor, where he put a cushion under his head. "It's just a little bleeding. You'll be okay."

Robyn was already calling 911.

"Bleeding?" The professor sounded astonished. "A hemorrhage! How could I have made such a terrible mistake?"

He reached out for Rhostok's arm.

"You've got to call Detrick," he said.

"Who?" Rhostok asked.

Altschiller tried to explain, but he was choking on the pink froth that came bubbling up from his throat.

"Call . . . Sherman . . . Detrick," was all he managed to say.

By the time the paramedics arrived, he was dead.

Fifty-One

Although Altschiller was dead, his body continued to bleed. That fact puzzled the paramedics, but having decided there was nothing further they could do, they contacted the county morgue to arrange for the removal of the body. The sound of sirens indicated the Scranton police were already on the way. Rhostok volunteered to stay behind, releasing the paramedics for other duties. As soon as they left, he carefully wrapped the hand in plastic sheeting and placed it in the bottom of Robyn's oversized handbag.

"Remember, they can't search your bag without a warrant," he said.

The reporter, who seemed frozen with horror at the way Altschiller died, simply nodded.

By the time O'Malley showed up, the paramedics were gone, and the Scranton police were on the scene, although they didn't seem to know what to do.

"You keep showing up around dead people," O'Malley said. He was breathing heavily from the effort of having dragged his metal-braced leg up the five flights of the emergency stairway.

"I was going to say the same thing about you," Rhostok responded.

"That's my job." O'Malley slowly circled the corpse, careful to avoid stepping into the widening pool of blood that surrounded Altschiller's corpse. "I have to certify the cause of death."

"Don't you have assistants, deputy coroners to do that work?"

"This one happened to be close by. My office is just a few blocks away. And when I heard the Middle Valley police chief was here . . ."

"Acting police chief," Rhostok corrected him.

"Ah, yes, I keep forgetting." O'Malley bent his good leg to get a closer look at Altschiller's face. "Nothing unusual here," he said to the two Scranton policemen who were awaiting his verdict. "It's basically oral bleeding, no sign of any wound or other trauma. Pending an autopsy, I'd say death was due to massive hemorrhage from a bleeding ulcer."

"All that blood, from a bleeding ulcer?" one of the Scranton cops asked.

"He could have been bleeding internally for an hour or more, without even being aware of it," O'Malley said. "Quite a bit of blood can build up in the stomach cavity, and when the patient collapses, it all comes out."

"If it's a bleeding ulcer, then why was blood coming out of his eyes?" Rhostok asked. "I can understand the mouth, but why the eyes?"

O'Malley shrugged. "I've seen hundreds of cases of bleeding ulcers," he said. "None of them are exactly alike. In this case, there could have been some sort of backup in the nasal passages, forcing blood up into the lachrymal ducts . . . the tear ducts."

Having apparently said all he was planning to about Altschiller's death, O'Malley began to walk around the laboratory, examining the equipment.

"This is out of your jurisdiction, Rhostok," he said. "What were you doing down here?"

"Altschiller was a friend of mine."

"Professor of forensic anthropology, wasn't he?" O'Malley toyed with the printout of the photospectrometer.

Rhostok wished he had remembered to hide that, too. And suddenly he worried about written notes, any documentation the professor might have been making. That seemed to be what was on O'Malley's mind, too, as his eyes combed the room.

"In layman's language, he was an expert on human remains," O'Malley continued. "What was he working on?"

The question was casual enough and perfectly natural, but Rhostok immediately grew cautious.

"Some kind of research, I guess. I don't know much about that kind of stuff."

O'Malley gradually made his way around to the now-empty bell jar.

"Whatever object he was studying is gone now," O'Malley said. He replaced the glass cover on its wooden base. "You wouldn't have given him that severed hand you found in the bank, would you? Is that why you're here, in his laboratory?"

Rhostok shot a glance at Robyn, sending her a be-quiet signal with his eyes.

"I'm sure you know Robyn Cronin from Channel One," he said. "She wanted to meet the professor, to do a story on the work he does for local police departments. I brought her down here to meet him."

"Really?" O'Malley turned his attention to Robyn. "My understanding is that Altschiller didn't like publicity. I'm told he hated reporters. He wanted nothing to do with the press."

"Exactly," she responded, calmly picking up on the lie. "That's why getting an interview with the professor would be such a coup. I was hoping to be the first TV reporter to get his story, and I thought Rhostok might be able to convince him to talk to me."

"You two are friends now? Rhostok is doing favors for you?"

"It would have been a good story," she said, ignoring the sarcasm. "Unfortunately, we arrived too late."

"Too bad," O'Malley said. "All you've got now is the obituary of a man who died from a bleeding ulcer." He turned back to Rhostok. "As for you, I'm tired of waiting. You've got to learn to follow the rules. I want that hand."

"Like I told you, it's evidence. I've got an investigation going on."

"An investigation of what? How the hand got in the vault? Quit playing games with me, Rhostok. In cases like this, analysis and disposition of human remains are my responsibility, and I won't have you challenging me. I'll give you five hours to turn over that hand. If you don't, I'm filing misconduct charges with the District Attorney's office. Maybe they'll even upgrade the charge to obstruction of justice. Think about it, Rhostok. I know you Russians are stubborn, but if you don't change your mind and give me that hand, this will be the end of your career in law enforcement. Depending on the judge, you might even be looking at a prison term. And what for? When it's all over, the hand will end up in the morgue, where it belongs."

Rhostok had stopped paying attention to the coroner's words. Staring at the pool of blood on the floor, he thought back to what his grandfather had told him about Rasputin. The Russian mystic had the ability to stop the flow of blood. Could that ability now be acting in reverse? Was Rasputin reaching out from the dead to punish those who disturbed the sleep of his relic?

When the boy finished his soda and the old man was done with his beer, they lay back on the rock ledge to watch the clouds form their strange shapes in the sky.

"You said Rasputin was called a sinner, that he had many enemies," the boy said. "How could a holy man have enemies?"

"History is filled with the stories of holy people who were persecuted and killed because of their beliefs. The generals hated Rasputin because he was a pacifist who convinced the Tsar not to enter the Balkan War. The merchant class hated Rasputin because he took the side of the poor. The conservatives

hated Rasputin because he pushed for more rights for the Jews. The hierarchy of the Orthodox Church hated him because he was a threat to their power. The politicians hated him because of his influence over cabinet appointments. The nobility hated him because he was so close to the Imperial Family. And of course because he was a peasant."

"Did anybody like him?"

"He was beloved by the Imperial Family. And also by the muzhiks." After a pause, the old man added. "Their affection for Rasputin was probably the only thing the Imperial Family had in common with the muzhiks."

Fifty-Two

Nicole stared up at the young man. He wore some sort of green clothing, with what looked like a green shower cap on his head. Hanging loosely around his neck was a white gauze mask.

"Don't be frightened," he said in a gentle voice. "I'm Dr. Waverly."

A doctor? He seemed hardly old enough to shave, much less to have spent eight years in medical school.

"You probably don't even know what happened, do you?"

She tried to shake her head, but for some reason, it didn't want to move.

"You collapsed on the sidewalk in front of the county building," the young doctor said. "You were unconscious when the paramedics brought you to the hospital. We treated you for shock. That's what those IV bags are for."

Nicole glanced up at the clear plastic bags hanging above her bed. Long tubes connected them to the back of her left hand, where they disappeared beneath a patch of white adhesive tape.

"How long has your leg been bothering you?" he asked.

The mention of her leg reminded her of how she had limped out of the coroner's office, made her way outside, and, finally, unable to navigate the steps, stumbled and fell.

"It's been hurting since this morning."

She glanced down at the odd tent-like shape in which the bedsheet had been arranged.

"Don't get upset," he said, apparently sensing her concern. "Your leg is still there. We just want to keep anything from coming in contact with the exposed skin."

He gave her a reassuring smile.

"We've got you stabilized for the time being. We've given you a spinal block, so you're no longer in any pain. We've aspirated a rather large surface blister on the front of your thigh, which turned out to be filled with blood. What we're trying to deal with now is the swelling in your leg. Normally, this type of edema is the result of a buildup of serum fluid in the underlying tissue. The standard treatment is a Lasix drip, which helps the body eliminate excess fluid. With swelling this severe, we'd also insert a local drain to draw out the fluid more quickly to avoid tissue damage. But in your case . . . there's a complication."

The young doctor sat down beside Nicole.

"Most of the fluid buildup in your leg isn't serum. It's actually blood. A large amount of blood. We estimate almost a pint, which, when you add it to the amount of blood we drained from your blisters, is about twenty percent of the total blood volume of a woman your size. That amount of blood being diverted to your leg means less blood was available to your brain, which probably caused your fainting spell."

His voice sounded tired and clinical, as if he were dictating a postoperative report.

"We don't know where that blood buildup in the leg is coming from. It's certainly not coming from the femoral artery or any large vein. There doesn't seem to be any sign of the kind of trauma that would induce internal bleeding."

"I bruised my leg last night," she said.

Dr. Waverly shrugged off the comment.

"That type of injury would produce superficial damage at the most, particularly when you're dealing with the upper part of the thigh. The fatty tissue provides a lot of protection."

"Then . . . what could it be?"

"My first thought was hemophilia. The kind of internal bleeding we're seeing would certainly be consistent with hemophilia, where the blood can slowly seep from dozens of broken capillaries. We would have asked if you had any history of blood disorders, but you were unconscious. We ran a quick test for factor eight, and there was no evidence of hemophilia."

The young doctor stood up and stretched.

"Sorry," he said. "I'm not getting enough sleep." He ran his fingers through his close-cropped hair and let out a long sigh. "Anyway, we've got you stabilized for the moment. Lucky for you, we just happen to have one of the top hematologists in the country visiting with us this week. You ever hear of Dr. Paul Zarubin? He's been written up in *Time* magazine."

"I don't read *Time*," Nicole said.

"Well, Dr. Zarubin is the man who wrote the book on blood chemistry. We studied his work in medical school. Anyway, he's taken personal charge of your case. He's pumping you full of coagulants, thromboplastin, and fibrin and even some new experimental drugs. If anybody can get you through this, Dr. Zarubin is the man to do it."

Fifty-Three

Any other TV reporter would have already been on the phone, Rhostok thought. He wondered why Robyn wasn't calling in the story, asking the station to send a cameraman over to videotape her standing in front of the university science building, maybe with one of the police cars in the background, breathlessly explaining to the viewers how Professor William Altschiller collapsed and died after making one of the most important discoveries of his career.

Instead, she quietly followed Rhostok to his car. There she kept the handbag with its precious cargo on her lap, her arms wrapped protectively around it.

"I could use a drink after all that," she suddenly announced. "Not in a bar, though. My apartment's on the way back to Middle Valley. We could stop there, if you don't mind."

In their new spirit of cooperation, it seemed a reasonable request.

Robyn Cronin lived in the Green Ridge section of Scranton, an area of historic stone mansions built by the mine owners a century ago. A wave of condo conversions had turned many of the stately structures into elegant multiple-unit dwellings. The unit Robyn rented was on the ground floor, which had been divided into four two-room apartments, each with high ceilings, crown molding, leaded-glass windows, and a baroque fireplace. The rooms were sparsely decorated, in keeping with the transient lifestyle of a television personality. Bright red and yellow cushions and a few choice collectibles helped reduce the austerity of the place. Five Hummel figurines on the mantel caught Rhostok's attention. Four of the five porcelains were Irish leprechauns dancing a jig. The fifth was playing an exquisitely detailed violin, a tiny pipe in his mouth.

"These are collector's items, aren't they?" he asked, picking one up.

"Maybe. I know they're old. They belonged to my grandmother."

Robyn kicked off her shoes and quickly began neatening up the room, rearranging the pillows and closing the laptop computer at her home workstation.

"My grandfather left me an old set of *matryoshka* dolls," he said. "I keep them on the mantel, too."

"A tough cop like you plays with dolls?" She chuckled. "That's hard to believe."

"Well first of all, I'm not really tough. At least not when I'm out of uniform. And in the second place, *matryoshka* dolls aren't toys, even though children like to play with them," he explained. "*Matryoshkas* are a form of Russian folk art. They're sets of nesting hollow dolls, with a different face painted on each doll. When one doll is opened, it reveals another smaller, more intricate doll inside. Each set has a different theme, and all the figures are part of the same story. The final doll, maybe the twelfth or the twentieth, is sometimes no larger than a grain of rice, with a face so tiny, you need a magnifying glass to appreciate the artwork."

When Robyn seemed satisfied the room was presentable, she padded across the oak floor to a wooden cabinet, which opened up into a small bar.

"The reason I mention it . . ." He gently replaced the figurine on the mantel. ". . . is that this investigation reminds me of a *matryoshka* set."

"You see everything through Russian eyes, don't you?"

"It's who I am."

"I assume then, that you're a vodka drinker," she said. Without waiting for a response, she poured some Stolichnaya into two glasses.

"You think it's funny, don't you?" he bristled.

"Not at all." She took the drinks into the kitchen, where he heard her cracking open an ice cube tray. "It'll make for a more interesting story," she said when she returned and handed him his drink. "How you combine Russian folklore with modern police investigative techniques."

She sat down on the couch and curled her stockinged feet beneath her. She motioned for him to sit beside her and seemed disappointed when he chose the facing wing chair instead.

"This doesn't taste like Stolichnaya," he said after taking a sip.

"It must be the Scranton water in the ice cubes," she explained. "I ran out of bottled water yesterday, so I used tap water. I can go out and get some packaged ice, if you want."

"No, it's okay," he said, taking another, longer drink.

"You were talking about those Russian dolls," she said.

"Right. The *matryoshka*. Like I said, they're designed with faces on them, often famous people, but sometimes they're custom-made to resemble your relatives or friends. But the best *matryoshkas* aren't just a bunch of faces. They tell a story. It starts out seeming very simple, maybe the face of Tsar Nikolas for example, and you think the next face will be the Empress. But then the next face might turn out to be Lenin, and then Trotsky, and then Stalin, and maybe a starving peasant, and suddenly you realize that instead of individual faces, you're looking at Russian history. Or maybe it's just Communist propaganda. But you don't know for sure which story the *matryoshkas* are telling until you reach the final one. The best *matryoshkas* take you by surprise."

He took another sip of vodka before continuing.

"And that's exactly what's happening with this investigation. Everything seems to interlock. Every mystery seems to reveal another. And just when I think there's a pattern developing, like maybe a serial killer after some old men, everyone in the case starts dying of natural causes."

"Except us," Robyn said.

"Except us," Rhostok agreed. "So far, we've got three known murders, five deaths from what seem to be natural causes, and one perfectly preserved human hand which, on closer examination, turns out to be a religious relic. It's a classic *matryoshka* set. Solve one mystery, and you solve them all. The question is, how many more *matryoshkas* will there be in this series?"

"You mean how many deaths."

"Exactly. Every time I think I'm getting closer to the truth, it seems like the *matryoshkas* have another surprise waiting for me."

"But you know the answer to one mystery, don't you?" She gave him that cute smile again, the same one she gave him that first night at the police station.

"You already know whose hand it is," she said. "You knew it even before you took the hand to Altschiller."

"I was never really sure," he said.

"Weren't you?" Her voice had an edge to it. "I think all you wanted from Altschiller was a confirmation. I noticed you didn't tell him about the paper that was wrapped around the relic. Or the writing on that paper."

"Nothing gets past you, does it?"

"I'm a reporter. It's my job to remember things like that. What was written on the paper? Something in Russian, wasn't it?"

"Not Russian," Rhostok said. "It was Old Church Slavonic."

"Are you going to tell me what it said, or do I have to seduce you?"

She shifted to that playful smile again. He wasn't sure whether she was serious or just teasing him.

"At first, I thought the writing must have been some kind of mistake," he finally said. "Or maybe something purposely intended to mislead whoever found the hand."

"What did it say?" she pressed.

"Old Church Slavonic is a language that isn't used much anymore, except in Orthodox churches."

"Rhostok . . ."

"It was just a name. A man's name."

"The name was Rasputin, wasn't it? Grigorii Effimovich Rasputin."

The old man took the boy into the bushes to pick blueberries for dessert. He gave the boy most of the sweet berries he picked, smiling at the way they disappeared into the young mouth.

"What about the Bolsheviks?" the boy asked. "They must have hated him, too."

The old man didn't answer immediately. When the boy looked at him, he thought he made a mistake in mentioning his grandfather's old enemies. The pain of those faraway days still showed in the old man's face.

"The Bolsheviks certainly made a show of hating Rasputin," the old man said. "But they were happy to have him around. His influence over the Tsar and Empress offered them a convenient way to turn public opinion against the throne. Radicals have always been skilled at demonizing their opponents, and the Bolsheviks were masters of the art."

The old man shook his head sadly.

"Rasputin was an easy target. He didn't live the ascetic life of Makari or John of Kronstadt. Like many muzhiks, he loved wine, women, and song. And like many Russians, he often took these vices to extremes. Soon the Saint Petersburg newspapers were filled with stories of his 'debaucheries,' which were picked up and amplified by eager gossips. The fact that he was a married man seen in the company of prostitutes was reported in shocking detail by newspapers that ignored the same behavior by politicians, generals, and the nobility. Every night Rasputin spent on the town was reported as a 'drunken revel,' and his love of gypsy music was considered a sign of his degenerate ways. He was accused of being a

member of the Khlysty sect and engaging in its rituals of group sex. Vicious handbills were distributed in the streets. He was accused of the most obscene crimes.

"And the greatest scandal of all was the accusation that he shared the bed of the Empress Alexandra."

"Was any of it true?" the boy asked.

"Some of it was true, yes. Rasputin did have a dark side. He often drank to excess, but so do many Russians, then and now. He struggled with his lust for women, but so did many other holy men, including the great Saint Augustine. And he had friends among the Jews, the Gypsies, the homosexuals, and other groups considered degenerate by the intelligentsia of the day. But did that make him an evil person?"

The old man left the question unanswered.

Fifty-Four

"Don't take me for an idiot," Robyn said. "Everybody knows about Rasputin. The Mad Monk. The shadowy figure behind the Russian throne. You think you're the only one who knows anything about Russian history?"

"But to think this might actually be his hand . . ."

". . . the hand that worked all those miracles and cured all those people," she finished the sentence for him. She carefully removed the plastic-wrapped hand from her bag and placed it on the table, where they could study it. "Imagine, it survived all these years, and now it's here, right in front of us." She seemed to shiver, and her voice dropped to a whisper. "I almost feel like we should say a prayer or something."

"Assuming it's genuine," Rhostok said.

"How can there be any doubt? Everything we heard from Altschiller . . . a man's hand, the cowpox scars, the cyanide in the blood . . . I saw a movie about Rasputin, and I read a book about his life. That's how they tried to kill him. They invited him to a private party, and they poisoned him with cookies and wine laced with cyanide. But the poison didn't work. What was the doctor's name? The one who was in on the plot?"

"Lazovert. Dr. Stanislaus Lazovert. He filled little cream-and-chocolate cakes with powdered cyanide and poured liquid cyanide into the wine glasses that Prince Yussopov would later fill with Madeira and give to Rasputin."

"And it had no effect on Rasputin, did it? He ate all the cakes and drank all the wine and asked for more." Her eyes sparkled with excitement. "It must have been an amazing sight to see."

"According to Lazovert, there was enough cyanide in each little cake to kill twenty men, but Rasputin asked for more wine and started to sing."

"His powers were so great, they couldn't kill him."

"Not at first," Rhostok said. "So they used a gun. A Browning pistol. While Rasputin was praying before an icon in the parlor, Prince Yussopov crept up behind him and shot him in the chest."

Robyn's drink was forgotten.

"But once again, he didn't die," she said. "They thought he was dead, but he wasn't."

Surprised by the enthusiasm she showed for the story, he continued.

"That's right, Dr. Lazovert was unable to find a pulse. He pronounced Rasputin dead and left the room. Yussopov couldn't find a pulse either. But while he was bending over Rasputin, he saw his victim's eyes begin to twitch. First the left eye opened . . ."

"Yes . . . yes . . ."

"Then the right eye opened. Yussopov later was reported to say his blood ran cold in his veins, his muscles turned to stone, he wanted to run away, but his legs refused to obey him." Rhostok was telling the story exactly as his grandfather had told him. "Rasputin called out Yussopov's first name. *Felix, Felix* . . . He jumped to his feet and, with a loud roar, grabbed Yussopov by the neck. Rasputin's eyes bulged with fury, and blood trickled from his mouth."

"Twice they tried to kill the holy man," she said. "And twice he lived. That proves Rasputin had supernatural powers, doesn't it? Because even his assassins believed it."

And it sounded to Rhostok as if Robyn Cronin believed it, too.

Fifty-Five

Rhostok was puzzled by the transformation that seemed to come over her. The skeptical reporter, who had challenged Altschiller repeatedly and had seemed so unwilling to believe the hand might actually be an incorruptible relic, was now urging Rhostok on, wanting to hear him tell a tale that had been told and retold in the most isolated Russian villages and the halls of European royalty. It was a tale that would defy belief if it had not been verified by eyewitnesses, confirmed by an official autopsy, and subjected to the most scrupulous investigation by hostile Bolshevik commissions. And it seemed to be a tale with whose details the reporter was intimately familiar.

"The others were already celebrating his death, weren't they?" she said. "They were upstairs smoking cigars when they heard Yussopov's screams."

"Yes," Rhostok said. "The prince struggled free and called out for Vladimir Purishkevich, who was upstairs with Dr. Lazovert. 'Shoot! Shoot!' the prince screamed. 'He's alive! He's escaping!' By the time Purishkevich came downstairs, Rasputin was already outside, running through the snow in the courtyard."

"With a stomach full of cyanide and a bullet in his chest, he was still alive!" Robyn gleefully exclaimed. "Rasputin had power over death itself, didn't he?"

"It certainly seemed that way." Rhostok found himself caught up in her unusual excitement, describing the scene to her in the same words he remembered his grandfather using. "Purishkevich was an expert marksman. He took careful aim and fired, but the shot missed. He fired again, and apparently missed again. He wondered if it was his nerves, or whether Rasputin was as invulnerable to bullets as he was to cyanide. Just as Rasputin reached the gate, Purishkevich fired again. Rasputin crumpled into the snow. Coming closer, Purishkevich fired again. This time the bullet entered Rasputin's head. His body went into convulsions and then stopped. Purishkevich had no doubt. This time, Rasputin was dead. He kicked Rasputin's head, sending a spray of blood across the snow. Once again, more carefully this time, Dr. Lazovert felt for a pulse. Finding none, he again pronounced Rasputin dead."

". . . and Prince Yussopov began to smash at Rasputin's head with a heavy steel club," Robyn breathlessly picked up where Rhostok left off. "He was insane with hatred, smashing at Rasputin over and over again. Blood splattered everywhere. He struck again and again, not stopping until he fainted with nervous exhaustion and was dragged away by the soldiers."

"You already know this story," Rhostok said.

"They tied up his corpse, rolled him up in a carpet, and dumped him into a hole in the ice in the Neva River," she continued. "Rasputin was poisoned with massive amounts of cyanide in both liquid and powdered form, was twice pronounced dead from gunshot wounds to the chest and the head, his temple was kicked in, and he was beaten savagely with a heavy steel weight. And yet . . ." Her eyes sparkled. ". . . and yet, when his frozen corpse was pulled from the river two days later, it was determined that he had been alive under the ice. Twice he was pronounced dead, and twice he came back to life. It was a miracle."

"No one has ever been able to explain it," Rhostok agreed. "At the autopsy, they found water in his lungs, which proved that Rasputin's death was due to drowning."

"And what else . . ." she asked. "What about his right hand?"

"You already know the answer to that. They found that his right hand had worked its way loose and was frozen near his forehead, with the fingers raised, as if his last gesture had been an attempt to make the Sign of the Cross."

"Exactly!" she said in a triumphant tone. "And that's the hand we have here, right in front of us. Rasputin's right hand. The hand that worked the miracles. The hand he used to bless the sick, and cure the Tsarevich and so many others. The hand he raised in prayer at the moment of his own death."

"But none of the old stories say anything about Rasputin's hand being removed," Rhostok said. He was beginning to feel fatigued, his words coming more slowly. "We know Rasputin was buried beneath the center aisle of a church being built near Tsarkoe Seloe . . . we know the Empress placed an icon and a personal letter as remembrances in his coffin . . ." He found himself struggling to complete the story. ". . . and we know his body was dug up two months later by the Bolsheviks, doused with gasoline, and burned on a pile of logs . . . but there's no record . . . of his hand being removed."

"A group of émigrés in Paris claimed his penis was removed," she said. "They revered it as a relic at regular meetings of their group."

"I heard about that." Rhostok wondered if it was the vodka that was making it harder to speak. "But I'm not sure I believe it."

"If his sexual organ was removed, then why not the hand that performed miracles?"

Rhostok had no answer. He tried to form the words, but his lips wouldn't move. His tongue was growing numb.

"Can you imagine the power this hand represents?" Robyn stared at the relic in its protective plastic wrapping. "It once controlled the destiny of the Russian empire . . . it worked miracles, wrote prophecies, and cured illnesses that defied the medical science of the times. The fact that it survived in such perfect condition for almost a century is perhaps the greatest miracle of all. What miracles do you think it can still perform?"

He wanted to tell her that mortal flesh could not perform miracles by itself, but his mouth and throat felt paralyzed.

"Do you believe in miracles, Rhostok?"

She waited for him to respond, and when he couldn't, she smiled and answered for him.

"Of course you do," she said. "How could anyone not believe in miracles when they see something like this? A relic that defies the laws of nature. The professor said it's a sign from God, and I believe him. It's a sign that we can still rely on divine intervention to perform the impossible."

The glass dropped from Rhostok's hand. His fingers, however, remained frozen in an open position. Robyn smiled at him. He watched her get up from the couch and come towards him. She looked closely at his eyes. He felt her raising one eyelid. She shook him by the shoulder. He was unable to respond. He watched her go into the bedroom and return with a rectangular stainless-steel container. She carefully placed the Rasputin relic in the container and snapped it shut. He wanted to stop her, but couldn't move, couldn't talk. Slowly, his head sank against his shoulder. His eyes closed. The last thing he heard was her voice, growing muffled and distant before he lost consciousness.

"I'm sorry, Rhostok. You're a great guy, and I really like you. But this is something I have to do."

Fifty-Six

Whatever drug Robyn had given Rhostok allowed his mind to awaken before his body was ready to move. He listened for any sound in the apartment, but the rooms were silent. When he was finally able to open his eyes, the room was dark. Still sluggish, he struggled to rise from the couch. His legs felt heavy, but slowly, he was able to regain control of his muscles.

"Robyn?" he called out, uselessly.

No response.

She was gone.

And as the empty table before him confirmed, the Rasputin relic was gone with her.

With a click and a flash of light, the television set across the room flickered to life. A timer had apparently activated it. Below the TV, a VCR unit began automatically recording the lead-in promo for the six o'clock Action News.

Was that why she had taken the relic, he wondered? To do the story she had been so eager to get? He stared at the image on the screen, waiting to see how she had betrayed him.

The program started with the usual brief preview of the news to come, delivered by Lee Montgomery in his self-important baritone.

"Coming up on Action News, a devastating fire at the University of Scranton, an unemployed thirty-year-old mother of four wins ten million dollars in the Pennsylvania lottery, and a Scranton baseball team ties for second place in the State High School playoffs. All that plus an update on the local power outages when we come back with Action News at Six."

Rhostok stared at the screen as the image of Lee Montgomery faded into a commercial of an SUV bouncing its way through a rocky streambed. Three commercials later, the Action News logo returned. Rhostok watched the yellow logo fly through the animated sky and explode over northeastern Pennsylvania before dissolving through to Lee Montgomery, who looked up from his script as if the camera had surprised him in the middle of his work.

"Good evening, I'm Lee Montgomery, and *this* is Action News at Six. Sitting in with me tonight is Mary Pat Andrews."

"Good evening," Mary Pat said, flashing a bright smile that ended in cute dimples. She had a tiny cleft in her chin and crinkly laugh lines by her eyes. "Our lead story tonight is the devastating fire that brought three engine companies to the University of Scranton campus."

The video image cut to the kind of fire footage TV stations love to run, always more spectacular at night when the orange flames showed up more clearly than in the daylight, but still dramatic at this hour. The flames glowed behind the burned-out skeletons of window frames and burst through the roof to climb up into the early evening sky. The building looked frighteningly familiar to Rhostok.

"You're looking at live footage from the University of Scranton, where the fire has already consumed the upper floors of the science building." Lee Montgomery's voice had the false excitement of a man who had reported hundreds of other similar fires. "No injuries have been reported. The building was believed to be empty at the time of the fire.

Electricity had been cut off due to damage to nearby power lines." The video showed a fireman using one of the new automated ladder-mounted hoses to pump water onto the roof, while other firemen below directed their high-pressure hoses towards the windows.

"Fire Chief Thomas DeLucca told Action News the blaze apparently started in a fifth-floor laboratory area. There was some concern that methane gas might be seeping from a nearby mine subsidence, but that proved unfounded. Still no word on the cause of the blaze. Although fire-fighters at first feared the entire building might be consumed, the flames now appear to be contained in the upper floors."

Back to a live shot of Lee Montgomery. "And now, we have late word that the fire may have started in the laboratory of Professor William Altschiller, the noted forensic anthropologist." Cut to a photograph of a smiling Altschiller in his white lab coat, probably lifted from the university catalog. "In a sad coincidence, Professor Altschiller died earlier this afternoon. Altschiller was the recipient of a number of awards for his work with the United Nations in Bosnia, with the Department of Defense, and with local law-enforcement agencies. The loss of his laboratory so soon after his death is a sad footnote to a distinguished career."

Back to a shot of a solemn Lee Montgomery as he shuffled the papers before him. "We'll be following that story closely, Mary Pat, with a special Action News team at the scene. But it looks for now as if the fire is contained."

Now Mary Pat, smiling and chipper again, happy to get on with her part of the news, said, "Thanks, Lee. Now to the heartwarming story of Helen Jenkins, an unemployed single mother of four who won last night's Pennsylvania lottery drawing for ten million dollars . . . that's right, folks . . . ten million dollars."

Rhostok stayed with the news, watching Mary Pat babble on brightly about the lottery winner and the interplay between the two of them as they went through the rest of the night's stories, carefully modulating their delivery from cheerful to serious as the news required. The white-haired Don Weller did his weather segment, and the group traded jokes and chuckles with sports reporter Hank Jacobs. When the animated Action News logo disappeared after flying once again through the sky over north-eastern Pennsylvania, the timer automatically turned off the TV and VCR, storing the newscast for future review. There had been no mention of the Rasputin relic. Maybe Robyn was preparing her story for the next day.

Forty-five minutes later, Rhostok was at the Channel One news studio, demanding to see Robyn.

"I'm sorry, Officer," the night receptionist said. "But she's not here. She normally works days."

"Has she called in?"

"Not since I came on duty, but I'll check the logs for you." The receptionist was being pleasant and cooperative, obviously in deference to Rhostok's uniform. "I'm sorry," she said. "There's no record that she called in."

"I have to find her."

"If it's important, I could try calling her at home."

"She's not home," he said. "I just came from there."

"Excuse me, Officer," said a familiar baritone voice behind Rhostok. He turned to see Lee Montgomery. The newsman's face was heavily caked with makeup. Although it gave his skin a healthy glow on camera, in real life the makeup had a peculiar orange tint. "Did I hear you say you're looking for Robyn?"

He looked at Rhostok's shoulder patch and name badge.

"You're that policeman from Middle Valley, aren't you? The one who's involved in that hand-in-the-bank-vault story." He suddenly grew more interested. "Is that why you're looking for Robyn?"

"Do you know where she is?"

"We'd all like to know," Montgomery said. "She hasn't shown up for work since yesterday. She claimed she was following the story with you. That was unusual enough, but then she stopped answering her cell phone this morning. None of us have been able to contact her all day. It's very unprofessional."

He wiped at the makeup on his forehead.

"Can I see her office?" Rhostok asked.

"Of course, but you won't find anything there. It's just a cubicle she shares with one of our night reporters."

Montgomery led him down a narrow corridor to the back-office area. The African-American woman who shared Robyn's cubicle started to protest the search, but Lee Montgomery quickly calmed her down. She stepped aside and watched Rhostok go through the folders and drawers.

"What are you looking for?" she asked. "Maybe I could help."

"I don't know. Something that might tell me where Robyn is."

"Well, you won't find it here. When two people share the same desk, we don't keep anything personal around."

"What about the computer?"

"We share that, too. Actually, I use it more than she does. She works mostly with her own laptop. I'll be glad to run through her files for you, but it's all strictly business. We even use the same password."

"Nice kids," Rhostok said, indicating a picture of two little girls on the woman's desk. "Twins?"

"Identical," she smiled. "Grace and Chloe. They're six years old now."

"And who's that?" Rhostok pointed to a small photograph of a middle-aged white woman.

"That's Robyn's mother."

"Where does she live?"

"I'm not sure where her mother lives now. She used to live in Philadelphia, I know. But I thought she moved up here a while ago." She gave a sigh and shrugged. "Robyn never talked much about her personal life . . . even to Jason."

"Jason?"

The young woman suddenly stopped talking. Her eyes darted to Lee Montgomery, as if she were afraid she had let some secret slip.

"Jason is our news director . . . or perhaps I should say former news director," Lee explained. "The rumor is that Robyn had an affair with him."

"Maybe she's at his place," Rhostok said.

"I doubt it. They broke off their affair because he didn't support her in one of our internal meetings. She seemed very bitter about it. I don't think she'd ever go back to him."

"You seem to know everything that goes on around here," Rhostok said.

"I'm a newsman," Lee Montgomery smiled. Some of the orange makeup had smeared off onto his shirt collar. "But seriously, there's one person who might know where she is, and that's Hamilton Winfield, the man who sent her off on your hand-in-the-vault story in the first place. He seems to know more about everybody in this place than even I do."

"Winfield? She mentioned something about him," Rhostok said. "He's some kind of consultant, isn't he?"

Lee Montgomery motioned him back out into the hallway, out of hearing of any of the other staffers.

"He's a ratings consultant. An absolutely dreadful man, a really odd creature. Always seems to be freezing, and complaining about the lack of heat. Of course, it's against station policy to give out home addresses, but I might be willing to bend that rule in your case, if . . ."

"If what?"

"If you give me an exclusive when you find out whatever the hell's going on in Middle Valley."

"I already promised that exclusive to Robyn."

"Yes, but she's flown the coop, hasn't she? From an ethical standpoint, that moots any exclusivity agreement you may have had with her."

Fifty-Seven

If Hamilton Winfield had chosen his living quarters for security reasons rather than appearances, he couldn't have done better.

The address Lee Montgomery gave Rhostok led him to the top floor of a two-story building whose vacant bottom floor once housed a bakery. The building sat in the middle of a fenced-in parking lot, which made it impossible to approach from any direction without being seen. The ghastly yellow glow of sodium-vapor lights illuminated the empty lot. The building next door housed a police station, which offered additional protection. The entrance to the apartment was up a single flight of wooden stairs. A motion-sensing device activated large floodlights as soon as it detected Rhostok's approach. A security camera was mounted on the side of the building, to transmit the image of anyone climbing the stairs. A small intercom and an oversized peephole in the door served as the final checkpoints.

Rhostok pressed the doorbell and waited, wondering if Winfield was at home.

Hearing no sound from inside, he pressed the doorbell again, this time identifying himself on the intercom.

"I know who you are," came a tinny voice from a small speaker. "Hold your horses, will you?"

The voice was followed by a rustling of chains, the clicking of a lock, and the removal of what sounded like a metal bar. At last the door opened just wide enough for Rhostok to slip inside. It was like stepping into an oven. The room was dark, except for the red glow of a large electric heater in one corner, which sent out waves of stale, overheated air.

"You're here about the girl, aren't you?" The old voice moved in the darkness, and a shadow passed in front of the space heater. "I knew I shouldn't have trusted her."

"Do you know where she is?" Rhostok asked.

"All I know is we lost contact with her sometime last night. She claimed she was with you the last two days, and then she stopped calling. When was the last time you saw her?"

Rhostok fumbled his way along the wall, trying to keep a distance between Winfield and him. He wondered how any normal person could put up with the heat.

"Late this afternoon. She took a piece of evidence when she left."

"The relic?" the old man's voice quivered. "She took the Rasputin relic? Do you know where she went?"

"How did you know it was a relic?" Rhostok asked. As his eyes grew accustomed to the darkness, he was able to make out some of the old man's features. He seemed incredibly old, with heavy eyebrows, hollow cheeks, and a twisted nose. His eyes, reflecting the red glow of the heater, peered out from deep beneath the eyebrows. "You couldn't have heard that from Robyn, because she didn't find out it was Rasputin's hand until a few hours ago."

The old man sank into a chair near the heater.

"I think she suspected something like it right from the start," he said. "She's a smart one, she is. Smarter than all the rest of them put together. Maybe too smart for her own good."

"Is that a threat?"

"Not at all. Just a simple observation of fact. By taking the relic, she exposed herself to grave danger."

"Why? What makes the relic so dangerous?"

"Do you have a tape recorder on you?"

"No," Rhostok said, and after a pause added, "You can search me if you want."

"Goddamn tape recorders," the old man grumbled. "All the reporters use them now. You can't say anything in confidence any more."

"You can trust me," Rhostok said. "I won't repeat anything you tell me."

"I've heard that before," the old voice said. "From more important people than you. Anytime I hear those words, I know it's a lie. Why the hell should I trust you?"

"Because I never told anyone you're a phony."

He heard a sharp intake of breath in the darkness.

"Do you know who I am?" the old voice tried to sound important.

"Your name is Hamilton Winfield," Rhostok said. "You were an international correspondent a long time ago, but you're not a ratings consultant. I picked up a copy of your resume at Channel One, and I called the television stations in New York and Boston where you were supposed to have worked. They never heard of you."

For a moment, the only sound in the room was the contented humming of the space heater.

"Did you tell Jason?" the old voice asked.

"No."

"Did you tell Lee Montgomery?"

"No."

"Does anyone else at the station suspect?"

"I don't know," Rhostok said. "I think they just can't figure you out."

"Because the ratings are up," the old voice said. "As long as the ratings are up, they'll believe anything I tell them. Unlike you, it would never occur to them to check up on me. Especially since I was given complete control over their jobs by the owners of the station."

He gave a self-satisfied chuckle at the thought.

"It helps to have contacts in high places," he said. "Have a seat, young man, and we'll talk. You'll have to excuse the heat in here. I spent ten years in a Russian labor camp in northern Siberia, and my blood thinned out. I lost three toes to frostbite, and my body's temperature-regulation system was permanently damaged. I haven't felt warm since I was repatriated."

Hamilton Winfield lit his pipe. In the dim glow of the match, Rhostok thought he saw a grin on the old man's face. As if he were happy to at last have someone *willing* to listen to him, rather than being forced to because of his power over them. He reminded Rhostok of his grandfather, who enjoyed reliving the memories of his youth.

"Why don't you tell me what you know about the relic first," Winfield said. "It'll save me some time, avoid having to go over the same ground twice."

The old man puffed on his pipe, making little slurping sounds while Rhostok sat in the darkness and told him about the deaths of Vanya Danilovitch and his son Paul, about Nicole and the safe-deposit box and the discovery of the hand, and about Professor Altschiller's conclusion that it was indeed a relic. He told Winfield about the murders of Vanya's two old friends, and the deaths, by natural causes, of all those who came in contact with the relic except for Robyn and himself. And finally, he explained his own suspicions that the deaths were all linked somehow to Rasputin and his power over blood. That some sort of curse might be at work.

Hamilton Winfield listened in silence. He didn't speak until after Rhostok was finished.

"You've done well, as far as you've gotten," Winfield said. "But there are a few things you've missed."

"Such as?"

"Did you know that Robyn Cronin was a second-generation Russian-American? Her real family name was Kronstadt. Her grandparents came from Riga in 1918 and settled in Philadelphia. Her father is dead. Her mother is terminally ill with cancer of the spine, is confined to a wheelchair, with less than three months to live." He drew on his pipe, the embers growing red as the air passed through them. "Of course, I'm sure Robyn didn't tell you any of that, because she's managed to keep it hidden from everyone."

"Why would she keep such things secret? Being Russian isn't anything to be ashamed of."

"Not everyone who came over from Russia settled in communities like Middle Valley," Winfield said. "Some of them had things to hide, or people to fear. The Communists regularly sent agents over to spy on the immigrants, and in some cases even executed those they considered enemies of Russia, as they did with Trotsky in Mexico. People like Robyn's grandparents, who helped support the southern White Army in the battle against the Bolsheviks, quickly went underground when they arrived in America. They changed their name, moved around frequently until they spoke English, and then adopted a different ethnic heritage. Cronin sounded vaguely Irish, and they found, as many Russians do who wish to hide their true nationality, that adopting even a mild Irish brogue is the ideal way to camouflage a Russian accent. It all worked out well, because after all, everyone loves the Irish."

Rhostok thought back to the leprechauns on her mantle. Her grandmother's, she had claimed. *Trust no one.*

"She told you all this?"

"Of course not. It's a family secret. The skeleton in their closet."

"Then how did you find out?"

"I have access to all sorts of information." Winfield smiled as he let out a long stream of smoke. "I know all about you and your parents, for instance, how they died, and how your grandfather raised you. He was a great man, your grandfather. Many in Russia still remember him as the last of the Don Cossacks, the only leader who refused to allow his men to participate in the *pogroms.* He was very fortunate to survive the slaughter at Voronezh."

"You actually have a file on me?" Rhostok didn't know whether to be impressed or intimidated.

"There are files on everyone. It's just a question of knowing where to look."

"But this isn't like a credit check or a court record search. You've been looking into my family history. My grandfather warned me about men like you, men who secretly collect information on others."

"It didn't seem to bother you when we were discussing Robyn's family."

"She was an employee of yours. I could understand why you'd want to know about her background. But you never met me. Like you said, I'm just a small-town policeman."

"During my years in Russia, I learned never to trust the police."

"Still, why did you need a file on me?"

"It's not a file. Just a few facts. The important ones."

"But why?"

"Because I suspected that Vanya Danilovitch was killed by a policeman."

Fifty-Eight

"Access to patients in the high-security wards of state facilities is limited to a small number of specialized employees," Winfield explained. "But given the violent nature of some of the patients, there's a fairly porous policy when it comes to law-enforcement officers and others with similar official duties."

"I wasn't there the night Vanya was killed," Rhostok said. "You can check the sign-in sheets."

"In the confusion surrounding the discovery of Vanya's body, one of the sign-in sheets appears to have gone missing."

"And you think that points to me?"

"At first, I did. You were one who brought him to the hospital in the first place. You and that German policeman . . ."

"Otto."

"Yes, the late Otto Bruckner. Either one of you would have been permitted access that night. And either one of you would have been physically capable of throwing him off that roof." Winfield waved his pipe at Rhostok. "Now don't go getting excited on me, young man. I'm not accusing you of murder. I'm just letting you know what I was thinking when I heard what happened to Vanya."

"So you think it was murder, too."

"Of course. Knowing what I do about the poor man, there's no other possibility."

Winfield spoke with an arrogance that Rhostok found irritating. Here was a man who faked his resume, was skilled at conducting background checks, had powerful friends, and was apparently conducting his own independent investigation into the death of an old man in a small town. Why? What was in it for him? Was he some sort of con man? Who did he work for? Rhostok had a lot of questions, but the one he asked was the one he thought was the most important.

"Do you know who killed Vanya?"

"I have a pretty good idea."

"Give me a name."

"I'm afraid I can't. Not yet. Not until I confirm a few more facts. However, I do know *why* he was killed."

"Dammit, quit playing games with me," Rhostok said.

"Take it easy," Winfield soothed him. "I've been working on this for over a year. You think I haven't gotten impatient, you think I don't want the answer, too?"

"I'm sorry," Rhostok apologized. "I'm just feeling tired right now. It hasn't been a good day for me."

"You're lucky to be alive. You know that, don't you?"

"I'm beginning to get that impression. Now look, I've told you everything I know, so why don't you do your part? Tell me what this is all about."

"Very well, but as I told you, I still don't have all the answers."

"Just tell me what you know," Rhostok said, tiring of the verbal sparring. "Can I turn on a light?"

"I'd prefer you didn't. In the labor camps, I learned to see just fine in the darkness."

The room was getting hotter. Rhostok was sweating freely. His shirt was soaked. The air was filled with the smoke from Winfield's pipe. The fumes left a bitter but familiar taste in Rhostok's mouth.

"The tobacco you're smoking, it smells like the kind my grandfather used to smoke."

"It's Russian tobacco," Winfield said. "*Czerwony Snieg*. It's an acquired taste. I have it sent to me specially by some old friends."

"Are you Russian?" Rhostok asked.

"Does it matter?"

"It might help explain why you're interested in the Rasputin relic."

"The answer is no, I'm not Russian. Let's just say I represent certain interests. People who collect objects."

"This isn't an ordinary object," Rhostok said. "It's not the kind of thing normal people collect."

"You're quite perceptive, considering you're only a small-town police officer."

In the gloom, Rhostok watched the wrinkles on Winfield's face rearrange themselves into what resembled a grin.

"I don't mean that in any derogatory sense," Winfield said. "It's simply that this affair has moved from one continent to another, from one town to another, and you're the first police officer who seems to have grasped the issues involved."

"Who are you working for?" Rhostok asked. "Who are these other interests you claim to represent? Are they the people who put you in charge at Channel One? Was that part of the plan?"

"Do you want me to tell you what I know, or would you rather cross-examine me?"

"Sorry." Rhostok backed off.

He waited while Winfield cleared his throat with a raspy cough.

"About a year ago, one of our people had an opportunity to talk to a Patriarch of the Russian Orthodox Church in Kiev. You know what a Patriarch is, I assume?"

"Of course. It's like a Cardinal in the Catholic church."

"Actually, he was a retired Patriarch, the way I heard it. He claimed to be one hundred and thirty years old, although our contact said he was in his early nineties."

"A lot of the old-time Russian priests are like that," Rhostok said. "They want people to think they're immortal."

"This particular Patriarch wasn't immortal. He died a few hours after our man met with him. He was struck by a car as he was on his way to church. The police in Kiev determined it wasn't an accident."

"He was murdered?"

"Not by our people," Winfield said. "We would have preferred to keep him alive. The Patriarch was from Western Siberia, the village of Tyumen, not far from where Rasputin was born."

"He didn't claim to know Rasputin, did he?" Rhostok smiled.

"No, he didn't. As a matter of record, he didn't even begin his monastery studies until the year after Rasputin's death."

"That would be 1917," Rhostok said. "Rasputin was killed in 1916."

"The monastery where the Patriarch studied for the priesthood was at Ekaterinberg."

"That's where Tsar Nikolas and the Imperial Family were executed in 1918."

"Very good," Winfield said. "Apparently you know your Russian history very well. That's unusual among the second generation here in America."

"My grandfather told me all the old stories."

"I'm beginning to believe Robyn's grandparents gave her similar cultural instruction," Winfield said. "My not realizing that fact was a terrible oversight on my part." He puffed on his pipe and let out the smoke in a narrow stream.

"According to the Patriarch, the Bolshevik guards who executed the Imperial Family ransacked their quarters for jewelry and other valuables. One of the guards showed up at the monastery later that night. He had salvaged a crystal reliquary from a hiding place under the floorboards. Inside the reliquary was a severed human hand. The inscription on the reliquary identified it as the right hand of Grigorii Effimovich Rasputin."

Just like the inscription on the oilskin paper, Rhostok thought.

"It was almost two years after Rasputin's death," Winfield continued. "Yet the hand was still perfectly preserved, the flesh still pink, the blood still liquid. It must have been the extraordinary condition of the hand that frightened the guard into turning it over to the priests. As you probably know, in the Russian church, incorruptible flesh is considered to be one of the most important signs of sainthood."

Rhostok listened in silence. It was almost as if he were once again sitting at his grandfather's knee, hearing an old man telling tales that had been told and retold.

"The Imperial Family had enormous faith in Rasputin's powers," Winfield said. "To them, he was a holy man, a saint, their confessor, and their spiritual guide. But most important of all, the life of little Alexei, the heir to the Russian throne, depended on Rasputin's powers. Hemophilia was always fatal in those days, when medical science still had not come up with coagulants."

"I know all about that," Rhostok interrupted.

"You don't know all of it," Winfield snapped. "There's a part of the story that's always been obscured from public view. I wasn't able to piece it together myself until last year. If you'll stop interrupting me, I'll tell you about it."

Suitably chastened, Rhostok fell silent.

"On at least two documented occasions, the Saint Petersburg church bells were already ringing to announce Alexei's death when Rasputin was called in. By raising his hand in prayer, he was able to stop the boy's hemorrhages and return him to health. So you can imagine how devastating the news of Rasputin's death must have been to the Empress. She knew that her son was doomed to suffer further bleeding attacks. Without Rasputin's intercession, she knew the boy would die. That was why the Empress gave orders to have the right hand removed from Rasputin's body during the autopsy. Who could blame her? She had seen Rasputin raise that hand to save her son's life on a number of occasions.

"She commissioned a Viennese jeweler to create a gold and crystal reliquary for the hand and kept it at Alexei's bedside. She must have hoped the relic would continue to stop the bleeding attacks, even after Rasputin's death. And in fact, it did seem to work. There are no reports that little Alexei suffered any further life-threatening attacks of hemophilia during the two years the relic remained at his bedside."

It fit perfectly with everything Rhostok's grandfather used to tell him about the Empress and her devotion to Rasputin. But as his grandfather said, although many criticized Alexandra for allowing a self-ordained monk to control her life, what mother would not revere a miracle-worker who saved her child's life?

"Well, of course, it had to be kept secret," Winfield continued. "It would create a great scandal if the Empress's enemies learned what she had done. Yet even those enemies, the ones who hated Rasputin the most, believed he had supernatural powers. And the belief in the healing power of relics has been a constant in the Orthodox Church. Which explains why the Ekaterinberg monks were delighted to have such a precious object delivered to them. They hid the reliquary from the Bolshevik leaders. There was a bit of an inquiry later, when the reliquary couldn't be found among the Imperial possessions.

"A gold and crystal reliquary was listed on the inventory, you see, although the listing didn't identify the relic itself. And the soldiers who later dug up Rasputin's body and burned it in Petrograd reported that the right hand was missing. But the hand wasn't found, and after a few years, the entire affair disappeared into the many myths that surround Rasputin's life."

Winfield sounded relaxed now, Rhostok thought. He seemed to enjoy the telling of the story, relishing the small details much the way his grandfather had. But this was a part of the story Rhostok's grandfather either hadn't known or had declined to disclose.

"After a few more years, the relic was secretly transferred to the Ukraine, to a monastery in Starokonstantinov. The young priest who was in charge of the relic was becoming a prominent figure in the Orthodox Church. He went with the relic as its guardian. But they should have kept the relic in Ekaterinberg, because the Germans rolled through the Ukraine in 1943. They burned all the monasteries, claiming the Orthodox Church was cooperating with Stalin."

"That was partially true," Rhostok said, in defense of his grandfather's church. "The Orthodox leaders cooperated with Stalin, but it was the only way they knew to protect the faithful from further persecution."

"You and I know that, and perhaps the Germans did, too. But the invaders used it as an excuse. The monastery at Starokonstantinov was looted and burned in 1943 by the Nazis. It was the last the Patriarch saw of the crystal reliquary and the Rasputin relic."

"What I don't understand is how the relic got from the monastery to Middle Valley," Rhostok said.

Winfield took a deep draught on his pipe, as if he needed the smoke to recharge his strength. The embers glowed brightly in the bowl, casting a red glow on his face as he continued.

"The German Army had a highly organized system of looting. In every country the Nazis invaded, special *Einsatzstab Reichsleiter Rosenberg* units of art and antiquity experts followed soon after the combat troops. Those *ERR* units took control of national museums and private collections. Every item of value was carefully catalogued, crated, and sent back to the Fatherland, where the loot was divided up by Hitler, Goering, Goebbels, and others. Everything of value was stripped; there were no exceptions.

"By the end of the war, the finest art treasures of France, Holland, Belgium, Poland, and Russia were stored in hidden warehouses throughout Germany and Austria. By the end of the war, there were fourteen hundred repositories containing over fifteen million looted items. Initially though, no one was sure the Germans actually had the Rasputin relic. There were some Russians who thought it might have been hidden by one of the monks. All that was known at the time was that the relic disappeared. Just like that!" Winfield snapped his bony fingers for emphasis. "The single most valuable religious treasure of Russia simply vanished."

"But the Germans had it."

"Well, of course they did, although it appears they didn't understand what it was. They were scooping up everything that looked valuable. I imagine they were impressed by the magnificent crystal reliquary that housed the relic. You've got to remember, no one knew the significance of the relic except the monks at Starokonstantinov. They certainly wouldn't tell the Germans what it was. The Patriarch said he was lucky to escape with his life."

"Wouldn't Rasputin's name have been inscribed on the reliquary?" Rhostok asked. "The Germans must have had interpreters who could read Russian."

"I'm sure there was an inscription," Winfield said. "But we're talking about a reliquary in a monastery. Not a major work of art. Somehow it slipped through and ended up with golden chalices and a couple of thousand other unidentified Russian religious antiques."

The top of the bowl glowed again as Winfield took another long draw on his pipe. It made a hollow sound, and sparks danced up into the darkness.

"After we heard the Patriarch's story, we started trying to trace the path of the relic," Winfield continued. "Through records kept by the Germans, we were able to trace the looted contents of the monastery to a sealed mine tunnel in Unterberg, a small town near Berchtesgaden in Austria. That was where Hermann Goering hid his portion of the treasures looted by the German Army. The sealed tunnel was discovered in May of 1945, and its contents were liberated by the advancing American troops."

"So you found where the reliquary had been hidden."

"Yes and no. We determined where we thought it had been hidden, but that's where we lost it again. We checked the records of the Monuments, Fine Art, and Archives section of the U.S. Army's Office of Military Government, which was responsible for the recovery of looted artwork. There was no entry for a crystal reliquary.

"Of course, a small reliquary was easy to overlook," Winfield continued. "There were thousands of items in that tunnel, enough to fill about thirty railroad cars. The military authorities estimated the treasures in the Unterberg tunnel were valued at over five hundred million dollars. I'm talking 1945 dollars. And remember, that was before the enormous escalation of art prices that has taken place over the past fifty years. With the prices being paid for fine art and antiques today, what some of those works would sell for, even the most conservative estimate, would place the current value of the treasures in that tunnel at five billion dollars."

Rhostok shook his head in disbelief.

"Don't shake your head," Winfield said. "The artwork found in that tunnel included Van Gogh's famous *Sunflowers* and his *Bridge at Arles,* some of the Monet *Haystack* and *Rouen Cathedral* series, various Renoirs and Rembrandts, and—well, you name it. It must have been like walking into the storage rooms beneath the Louvre. There were hundreds and hundreds of paintings, manuscripts, and sculptures in crates and boxes and neatly arranged on shelves. An absolutely amazing collection, unmatched by any museum today. And of course, given all that volume, so many thousands of other items, there was apparently a lot of souvenir-hunting by the American soldiers."

"I could see taking a Luger pistol or a Leica camera for a souvenir," Rhostok said. "Maybe even a small painting. But are you trying to tell me someone took a human hand for a souvenir? The guy would have to be very strange."

"Or very religious," Winfield countered. "A perfectly preserved hand in a crystal reliquary—any soldier with a religious background would recognize it as a valuable relic. And we have to assume it had some sort of inscription. The Patriarch didn't say so, but a relic of that stature would certainly include some sort of engraved prayer or other identification."

"Any inscription would be in Russian," Rhostok said. "The Cyrillic alphabet." He suddenly remembered the penciled lettering on the brown wrapping paper. "But maybe in Old Church Slavonic. Of course! That's how it got past the German curators! Their translators could read standard Russian, but not Old Church Slavonic. The average American GI wouldn't be able to read it, either."

"You're very good at these things, figuring out the details," Winfield said. "Very, very good. Our people came to the same conclusion, but it took them a little longer than you. Anyway, there was a considerable amount of confusion and excitement when the Goering treasure was discovered. I was a correspondent in those days, reporting on the story, so I have some firsthand knowledge of events, although I knew nothing of the relic at the time. The American Military Command made a decision to transport the artwork from the Unterberg tunnel to the village of Unterstein, where it was put on display."

"An art display? In a war zone?" Rhostok was astonished. "Why would they do such a thing?"

"Propaganda, the ego of the local commander, I don't know. Strange things happen in wartime. There were a lot of visiting dignitaries and politicians touring the conquered areas, kind of strutting around, looking for a way to get their pictures in the newspapers back home. Part of the Goering treasure was put on display at a local inn, and it was run just like a tourist attraction. The soldiers even put up a sign: 'The Hermann Goering Art Collection—through the courtesy of the 101st Airborne Division.' Unfortunately, the reliquary never reached Unterstein. Of course, with thousands of other pieces in the collection, it was easy to overlook a single item. There was so much gold and jewelry, who cared about an unknown Russian artifact?"

Rhostok didn't hear the last half of what Winfield said. His attention was focused on a number that sounded familiar.

"Did you say the 101st Airborne?" he asked. "They were at Unterstein?"

Fifty-Nine

"Didn't I mention that before?" Even in the darkness, Rhostok could see a playful smile on Winfield's lips. "It was the men of the 506th Parachute Infantry Regiment of the 101st Airborne Division who liberated Goering's treasure. A fascinating story, that outfit. They landed behind enemy lines at Normandy on the night before D-Day, they fought in Holland, held off the German counteroffensive at Bastogne, and finally fought their way to Hitler's mountain hideaway in Berchtesgaden, where they found the sealed tunnel, among other things. They were true heroes, those men."

"And one of those heroes stole the Rasputin relic," Rhostok said. He knew where the story was going now; he knew how the relic had ended up in a bank vault in Middle Valley, Pennsylvania.

"A lot of looting went on at the end of the war," Winfield said. "When we started searching for the relic last year, our problem was to identify and locate the soldier who had taken it. Imagine trying to find a thief more than fifty years after the crime was committed. Of course, we had plenty of suspects. Between the time of the Normandy invasion and the discovery of the treasure, casualties had reduced the 506th to half its normal strength. But the roster in May 1945 still listed seventy-eight officers and fourteen hundred twenty-two enlisted men. It would have taken us years to locate the survivors among them and interview each of them."

"But you didn't have to find them all," Rhostok said. "All you needed to find was someone who could read Old Church Slavonic."

"Unfortunately, that's not a language normally listed on military records. We settled for a computer check of all Russian-sounding names among the men attached to the regiment when it was stationed at Berchtesgaden. It turns out there were twenty-three men with Russian-sounding names in the unit at that time. Fourteen of them were in Charlie Company, six of them in the Special Reconnaissance Platoon."

"Special Reconnaissance," Rhostok repeated in an awed whisper. "Vanya Danilovitch was in the Special Reconnaissance Platoon. So that's how you found him."

"I wish it was that easy," Winfield said. "Like I said, we found twenty-three Russian-sounding names in the personnel records of the 506th. Unfortunately, the name of Vanya Danilovitch wasn't listed."

"But he was in the Special Reconnaissance Platoon. I saw the photographs and the newspaper articles."

"Oh, Vanya Danilovitch was in the platoon, all right. But his name wasn't listed that way. Apparently in those days, he went by the name of Vincent Daniels."

"He Americanized it," Rhostok said, remembering the conversation with Roman Kerensky at the American Legion. "He changed it when he was in high school and changed it back after the service."

"That's what made him so hard to find," Winfield said. "We tracked down the location of every one of the men with Russian-sounding names and hit a blank wall. All twenty-three of them were dead. Eight of them had died of natural causes or in accidents."

"And the other fourteen?" Rhostok already knew the answer, but he wanted to hear it from Winfield, wanted to hear whatever details the old man could add.

"Murdered," Winfield said in a low voice. "Murdered before we could talk to any of them. That's when we knew someone else was searching for the relic. Someone who managed to stay one step ahead of us. Sometimes by only a matter of days."

"You're positive those men were killed because of the relic? There's no other explanation?"

"The Patriarch was killed just hours after our contact spoke with him. We assumed someone else spoke to him after we did, and that person wanted to be sure the Patriarch didn't reveal his identity. Then, while we were searching the computer records at the St. Louis Military Records Center for the Russian-sounding names, we found someone else had already initiated an identical search. We know someone got the names, because the St. Louis computers are programmed to record and report every request for data."

The heater reflected an excited glitter in Winfield's eyes. His voice was growing stronger. He reminded Rhostok of an old hunting dog. The years had stiffened his joints and thinned his blood. But someone who knew his skills had set him on the trail of an ancient quarry. And like the old hunting dog he was, Hamilton Winfield was very good at following cold trails.

"Whoever it was, he got the names of those veterans and started tracking them down and interrogating them. Torturing them, actually. And when they couldn't produce the relic, he killed them, to be sure they didn't reveal what he was after. He was very skilled at what he did. He didn't leave a fingerprint, a clue of any kind. He just went down the list alphabetically, from Arbatchev to Ulyanov, tracking them all to their current addresses. He even interviewed the widows and children of the eight veterans who died of natural causes."

"How did he find out about Vanya?"

"Maybe a photograph, maybe from one of his friends, maybe from Florian Ulyanov's telephone records, which is where we made the connection between Vincent Daniels and Vanya Danilovitch. The killer added Vanya's name to the bottom of his list, which is why he was the last veteran to be killed. By that time, of course, the killer knew Vanya must be the soldier who stole the relic."

"You keep referring to the killer as 'he,'" Rhostok pointed out. "The killer didn't have to be a man, it could have been a woman, couldn't it?"

"You're thinking maybe it was Robyn Cronin? I've already ruled her out. The Patriarch was murdered in Russia. The others were killed in locations all around the country. I checked Robyn's work records. She was in Scranton when most of the murders occurred. Also, there were elements in the murders that suggest a man did the killing. The mutilation of each victim's right hand is evidence of torture; when someone denied having the relic, the killer wanted to be sure they were telling the truth. In addition, it was a symbolic calling card, probably inspired by the relic being a right hand. Female killers don't usually go in for that sort of brutality."

"You think Vanya knew about the deaths of his friends?"

"According to the telephone records, yes. The veterans had a 'phone tree' going, alerting the others to any new deaths. They knew someone was after them, killing them one by one, going down the list in alphabetical order. The irony is that Vanya would gladly have turned over the relic to save the lives of his friends, but he was suffering from the early stages of Alzheimer's. He had partial memory loss and couldn't remember where he had hidden the relic."

"My God!" Rhostok blurted out. "That explains why his house was ransacked, the holes that were dug in the cellar. It wasn't an intruder! It was Vanya, searching his own house for the relic. He couldn't remember that he put it in the vault."

"Exactly!" Winfield said.

"And the rent on the vault was free for senior citizens, so he didn't even get billed for it. If they had sent him a bill for the safe-deposit box, he would have recalled where he had hidden the relic. But why did he bring it back and then keep it locked up all those years?"

"My theory is that he planned to have it buried with him when he died. That's a Russian tradition, isn't it, putting relics or other mementos in the coffin?"

Rhostok nodded, remembering how he had placed a photograph of himself beneath his mother's dead hands before they had closed her coffin.

"Time was running out for Vanya," Winfield said. "When the last of his friends was killed, he still hadn't found the relic. So one morning, he woke up, went outside, and shot holes in a parked car with his deer rifle."

"Scared the hell out of the neighbors," Rhostok said. "They thought he was going crazy."

"Crazy like a fox," Winfield said. "He did it on purpose, to get locked up in the violent ward. Except for that memory loss, his mind was still okay. He knew the killer would be coming after him, so he was looking for a place to hide. He thought he'd be safe locked up in a cell, with twenty-four-hour guards watching over him."

"Strategic retreat, that's what another old veteran called it," Rhostok said. "But it didn't save him."

"Unfortunately, no. Whoever killed him managed to get in and out without a trace. The pertinent sign-in sheet is missing. And no one remembers any visitors out of the ordinary that day. This killer is very good at what he does. He just melts into the surroundings."

"Maybe he has help," Rhostok said. "One person does the killing, the other person does the setup, makes the initial contact."

"And handles any necessary cover-up," Winfield said. "I like the way you think, Rhostok. Maybe we could work together in the future."

"I doubt it."

"Why not? You're a good investigator, and I'm limited in my ability to move around. I could use someone like you. There's good money in what I do."

"That's the problem," Rhostok said. "I don't know what it is that you really do."

"I told you. I collect objects."

"How did you get the job at Channel One? Who do you work for? I don't think it's the people who own the TV station."

Winfield let out a low chuckle.

"Hardly," he said. "That would be too obvious, wouldn't it? Even a fool like Jason would have found me out."

"But there must be a connection, you showing up at the TV station at this particular time."

"Expediency. That's the connection. Vanya Danilovitch was the last Russian from the 506th. The killer got to him before I did, as he did with the others. But what convinced me he had the relic were the extraordinary measures he took to protect himself, and the condition in which you found his house."

"You had access to my police reports?" Rhostok couldn't hide his surprise.

"I told you, I have access to all sorts of information. When I learned the Danilovitch house was ransacked and holes were dug on the property, I knew someone was searching for the relic."

"You didn't realize it was Vanya doing the searching?"

"When I found out about the Alzheimer's, I assumed that was the case. But I also was working on the assumption that he never found the relic."

"You were guessing."

"It was the only lead I had left. It seemed likely that the relic was still hidden somewhere in Middle Valley. That meant the killer was here looking for it, too. I had to find a way to come here and fit in, just as my adversary had done before me."

"A small town like Middle Valley, a stranger would stand out," Rhostok said. "Particularly someone who wasn't Russian. So you picked Scranton, instead."

"The people I work for made all the arrangements. The television news job was the perfect cover. It gave me the opportunity to send people into Middle Valley to investigate without arousing suspicion. And with the news crew under my command, I had a ready-made staff to do my bidding. You didn't suspect a thing when Robyn came to see you, did you?"

"Those anonymous news tips she told me about. They were as phony as you were."

"The tips were legitimate," Winfield protested. "It's simply that I provided them myself. It was a way to test the employees. See which ones I could depend on."

"You didn't trust them, did you?"

"In my line of work, I trust no one. There's too much competition in the collecting field." Winfield set aside his pipe, the embers in its bowl dying out. His voice was growing tired. "I don't even know if I can trust you, Rhostok. But I do know you're intelligent, and you've already demonstrated you can keep a secret. Will you help me? I can make it well worth your while."

"It's not money I'm interested in," Rhostok said. "I just want to end the killing and the dying, and try to understand why it happened."

"Do you know the value of the Rasputin relic? Do you have any idea, any idea at all, of how much that piece of dead flesh is worth to the right people?"

"It's not worth all the lives it cost."

"Very noble. But unless you help me recover it, the deaths will continue."

"You haven't proved you have a legitimate claim to the relic," Rhostok said. "Until someone with a better claim comes forward, right now it probably belongs to the widow of Paul Danilovitch."

"Perhaps, and perhaps not," Winfield said. "But before we discuss ownership, we have to find the relic. And in the process, you just might learn the identity of my competitor. That would make you very famous, indeed, capturing a murderer who left a trail of death across two continents."

"How do I know I'm not sitting in the room with the murderer right now? How do I know it isn't you?"

"You don't. But you already know I don't have possession of the relic. If I had recovered it, I would have left by now."

Rhostok stared at the old man. He had explained, truthfully, Rhostok thought, how an important religious relic had traveled from a monastery in Russia to a safe-deposit box in Middle Valley. He had given a motive for the murders of at least fourteen old veterans of Normandy and Bastogne. And he had even explained why he himself was here. But he still hadn't mentioned one factor that troubled Rhostok even more than the rest.

"You know so much about the relic," Rhostok said. "Tell me why everyone who's been involved with it so far is dying. I'm not talking about the murders. I'm talking about the people who've been dying natural deaths. It seems everyone who's been near it so far is dead. Except for Robyn, the widow, and me."

"You're assuming that Robyn is still alive," Winfield said.

Sixty

"Others have been killed for the relic," Winfield said. "My competitors would have no problem killing a woman."

"Unless she's working with them," Rhostok observed, and then, realizing that Winfield had skillfully changed the subject, said, "But you haven't answered my question. You explained why those old men were murdered for the relic. But why are all the others dying?"

"As you said, they all died natural deaths."

Winfield's voice sounded suspiciously casual.

"But each of those deaths was related to a form of bleeding," Rhostok said. "And if there was one thing Rasputin was known for, it was his power over blood."

"Rasputin died a long time ago. Do you seriously think his spirit or ghost or whatever you want to call it somehow caused those deaths?"

"My grandfather would say so, yes. He'd say it was some sort of curse that afflicts anyone who disturbs the relic."

"And what do you think?"

"I don't know," Rhostok said. "I honestly don't know what to think."

"Well, it's possible your grandfather would be right," Winfield said. "Certainly there've been a number of deaths, murders as well as natural deaths. It might not be a curse in the traditional meaning of the term, but there does appear to be something sinister going on."

Winfield seemed to playing with the idea, as if it were a joke. But for Rhostok, it was a deadly serious matter. If it were some sort of curse, the retribution of a mystic figure who was murdered more than eighty years ago in a distant country, then surely Rhostok himself was doomed to die, just like everyone else who had anything to do with the relic.

He fell silent as he considered that possibility.

That Rasputin had a vengeful streak was no secret. He had destroyed many political and personal enemies in his lifetime. And in the famous letter predicting his death, he also promised, with amazing specificity, the awesome consequences that would follow his murder.

But the revenge for his death had already been exacted on the Imperial Family, the Russian nobility, even the Russian nation itself.

So why seek further revenge?

And why seek it here, in Middle Valley?

Why punish people who had nothing to do with events surrounding a death that took place so long ago?

Wendell Franklin had no Russian ancestors, nor had he even touched the relic. He didn't deserve to be punished by any curse. Nor did Zeeman or Bruckner. And especially not Altschiller. The professor had less reason to be punished than anyone. Of them all, Altschiller was the one person who treated the Rasputin relic with the respect it deserved. Not just respect, but awe. Rasputin certainly had no reason to punish Altschiller.

"What is it?" Winfield asked. "Why are you suddenly so quiet?"

"I was thinking about Professor Altschiller."

"A good man. I was sorry to hear about his death."

"I just remembered," Rhostok said. "He wanted me to contact someone."

Winfield's voice turned wary. "Do you remember who?"

"It was a German name," Rhostok said. "He said it just before he died. He wanted me to contact someone called Detrick."

The name brought an instant reaction from Winfield. He froze and his eyes narrowed.

"Never heard of him," he said.

Winfield was well practiced at hiding his emotions. But for the first time that night, Rhostok was certain the man was lying.

"There was another name he mentioned," Rhostok recalled. "I think it was . . . Sherman. Yes, that was it. Sherman. Detrick and Sherman. Those were the names. Maybe it was one person named Sherman Detrick. Maybe it was two different people."

Winfield turned his pipe bowl upside down and knocked the coals into an ashtray. It was the signal to Rhostok that the conversation was over. After that, he refused to say anything more. He rose from his leather recliner and led Rhostok to the door. Although he tried to hide it, the old man was visibly upset.

Who was this mysterious Detrick, Rhostok wondered. And why did the mere mention of his name cause so dramatic a change in Winfield's behavior?

Sixty-One

Thinking he might have overlooked something on his earlier search, Rhostok went back to Robyn's apartment. He let himself in with the duplicate set of keys he had taken from the apartment earlier that evening. The place was just as he had left it. A delicate hint of perfume lingered in the air. The two vodka glasses were still on the table. There was no sign of any telltale sediment in the bottom of his glass, which suggested that she had used a liquid drug. Something more exotic than sleeping pills. Not the sort of thing that would normally be available to an otherwise healthy young woman. Maybe some powerful medication she had stolen from her mother's painkillers, which meant his drugging had been preplanned.

The closets were full of clothing; none of the dresser drawers had been emptied. Her jewelry, what little there was of it, was in a small lacquered box, and a matching suitcase and carry-on bag remained behind. Wherever she had gone, he thought, she was traveling light. Even her laptop computer was left behind.

Rhostok remembered what the night reporter had said about Robyn not using the company computer. She did all her work on her laptop. He turned on the computer and booted up, hoping to find some clue to where she might have gone. As he anticipated, her files were protected by a security password. He made a quick phone call to his liaison officer at the Pennsylvania State Police. Every local state police unit had the necessary software to bypass security passwords. Technically, use of the software required a court order. The reality, however, was quite different. A short drive later, Rhostok was settled into a back room at State Police Headquarters in Dunmore, where the software instantly bypassed Robyn's password and allowed him to start scrolling through her files.

It was a tedious process. Fortunately, Robyn tended to affix fairly descriptive names to her files, which allowed Rhostok to pass up the routine news stories she had been working on. Although he was sensitive to the invasive nature of his search, he checked her old e-mail files as well. Fortunately, again, the subject lines were descriptive enough for him to avoid any that might have sounded too personal. In any event, there weren't many of those. Only a few e-mails of a casual nature to friends or relatives. Either she was living a very lonely life, or she was being extremely careful about her communications, clearing her e-mail files regularly.

His eyes began to ache as he scrolled through routine files about fires, police corruption, traffic accidents, weather forecasts, election returns, health-related stories. Each of those had dozens of other subcategories, many of which were easy to skip past. The health-related stories, for example, included reports from the National Cancer Institute, Sloan-Kettering Memorial Hospital, the National Institutes of Health, and web page after web page of stories about the latest medical breakthroughs, alternative therapies, cancer specialists, and even care of the terminally ill.

His index finger was growing numb as he scrolled through similar subcategories on Pennsylvania politics, Lackawanna County history, the latest census data, and dozens of other subjects. Some files read like final edited on-air copy, and others were nothing more than notes of interviews and thumbnail descriptions of people she had talked to. She seemed to have stored everything on her computer except personal information. It wasn't until the files dealing with Middle Valley that he found anything interesting. He smiled at her description of him: "Typical stubborn Russian. Rugged features, sandy hair, nice smile, but a one-track mind."

She recapped their first encounter, making some side notes for possible future stories about mine canaries and the methane gas seepage that followed mine cave-ins. She had page after page of research on the Old Believers, which didn't surprise him. She had shown a lot of interest in that subject when they first met, even talking about doing a story on Russian mysticism. That explained why she had the results of a Google search on *Episkop* Sergius, which had turned up a single old magazine story that mentioned the "cures" he once performed. After a file on hospice care, a file on rabid squirrels, and a file on lead contamination at a former battery manufacturing site, the subject matter took a surprising turn.

Rhostok found himself scrolling through file after file on Rasputin: excerpts from books, magazine articles, photographs. He read through the first few, but they contained nothing he didn't already know. One file was a listing of Rasputin's cures. Another was a compilation of his prophecies. Apparently she was giving herself a background briefing on Rasputin, the way a good reporter should. The only unusual thing about it was that her Rasputin files started two days before their visit to Altschiller, two days before Rhostok told her about finding Rasputin's name on the wrapping paper.

He sat back, stunned. She knew it was Rasputin's hand even before he took her to see Altschiller! What he took for skepticism, the way she challenged the professor, must have been her effort to validate what she already suspected.

As if to confirm his fears, the next series of files dealt with religious relics. She had listings of almost every known relic, whether authentic or questionable. She had copied web pages that dealt with pieces of the True Cross, the Crown of Thorns, the foreskin of Christ, the milk of the Virgin Mary, Veronica's Veil. One extended file told the stories of the blood of Saint Januarius, which liquefies every year on his feast day; the tongue of Saint James; the hand of Saint Stephen of Hungary. There were files devoted to the miracle cures attributed to various relics, to the miraculous spring at Lourdes, to the image of Our Lady of Guadalupe, to Padre Pio in Italy. Robyn had copied that portion of the Catholic Encyclopedia dealing with the three miracles required for the canonization of saints. And finally, there was one last file.

An entry from the memoirs of Maurice Paleologue, the last French Ambassador to the Russian Court. It described a meeting with a Madame T, who reported that shortly before his death, Rasputin said:

I KNOW I SHALL DIE AMIDST HORRIBLE SUFFERINGS. MY CORPSE WILL BE TORN TO PIECES. BUT EVEN IF MY ASHES ARE SCATTERED TO THE FOUR WINDS, I SHALL GO ON PERFORMING MIRACLES. THROUGH MY PRAYERS FROM ABOVE, THE SICK WILL RECOVER AND BARREN WOMEN WILL CONCEIVE.

The date on that final computer file was the evening before they went to see Altschiller.

Rhostok let out a long sigh. While he was distracted by the deaths of Vanya and Paul Danilovitch, Robyn had concentrated on what to her was the bigger prize. And now she was gone, with what was arguably the most valuable religious relic in modern Russian history. A relic for which more than a dozen old heroes of the 101st Airborne had been murdered, and which might have a curse on it that had caused four other deaths so far. And in a tribute to her cleverness, she left no trail by which he could follow her.

Still, he wasn't ready to give up just yet. He had one lead left—the name Altschiller had gasped out with his dying breath.

Rhostok turned to the state police computer, clicked on a search engine, and with fingertips that were growing increasingly numb entered the words "Sherman+Detrick."

What came up on the screen surprised him even more than the files Robyn had kept on Rasputin.

Sixty-Two

A little more work on the state police computer produced proof that Altschiller once worked for Detrick. When Rhostok went to a search engine and entered "Altschiller+Detrick," he found the *Scranton Times* article the professor had found so annoying. The Detrick reference was buried in a story about one of the professor's trips to Southeast Asia, the one that caused his political problems with fellow faculty members at the University of Scranton.

A few more clicks on the search engine produced a road map that would lead Rhostok directly to Detrick. According to the map, it was a straight shot down Route 81 through Harrisburg, then over the Maryland border, pick up Route 70 just south of Hagerstown, and coast down into the first valley of the Catoctin Mountains. The driving information indicated it would be a four-hour trip at a speed of sixty-five miles per hour.

It was after midnight when Rhostok left the State Police District Headquarters. He felt exhausted and stiff, but assumed it was due to the aftereffects of the drugging. He gassed up the car in Scranton, had a flame-broiled burger and two cups of black coffee, and set off into the night. Two hours later, somewhere in Lancaster County, he pulled over into a rest stop and slept until dawn. Fortified with some more coffee and an egg on a muffin, he continued south, planning to reach Detrick at the beginning of the workday.

The weather grew warmer as he headed south. A humid haze hung over the countryside in Maryland. A string of three U.S. Marine helicopters appeared from over one of the ridges, their rotors filling the valley with heavy thudding vibrations. According to the map, he was only forty-five minutes from the presidential retreat at Camp David. Rhostok turned off Route 70 at Frederick, headed north on 15, and within a short time, he pulled to a stop.

He had reached Detrick.

The Detrick the professor wanted him to contact.

The mistake Rhostok had made, a mistake he realized when he read the information displayed on the computer screen, was thinking that Detrick was a person.

In fact, as the search engine revealed, Detrick was a military installation.

Fort Detrick, Maryland.

The site of the U.S. Army Medical Research Institute of Infectious Diseases.

As that long-ago afternoon drifted into evening, the old man told the boy of the long lines of the sick and the poor who had mingled with influence-seekers and fixers outside Rasputin's modest rented house in Saint Petersburg. How large sums of money given to the mystic as bribes were turned over to the very next group of peasants who came pleading for help.

But the boy was less interested in Rasputin's altruism than in his mysticism.

"The prophecies, Grandfather. You promised to tell me about the prophecies."

"Ah, yes, the prophecies," the old man said. "Everyone wants to know about the prophecies now, when it is too late to do anything about them . . . or at least too late to do anything about most of them."

"Tell me about them, Grandfather."

"From his earliest childhood, Rasputin had the ability to see the future," the old man said. "He could see events before they happened, sometimes very clearly, as if it were a series of photographs. Sometimes very dimly, visions in which he could not make out the faces of the players."

"How far into the future could he see?"

"Sometimes he saw the near future, sometimes he saw distant events. He saw an image of Prime Minister Stolypin's assassination, and twenty-

four hours later, Stoylypin was shot. He predicted a great famine in Russia, and four years later, a million people starved to death. He predicted the Imperial rule would not last more than three months after his death, and just one day short of the three month prophecy, the Tsar signed the Articles of Abdication. He predicted not only his own assassination but even the timing of it. And he predicted that his body would be burned and the bones scattered, a prediction that seemed in error when he was given a proper burial on the Imperial Estate. But two months later his body was dug up and burned with gasoline by the Bolsheviks, and his bones were scattered to the winds in exactly the way he foresaw."

"But if he could see the future, why couldn't he prevent his own death?" the boy asked. "If he could see the future, couldn't he see the assassins were planning to kill him that night? Why didn't he escape?"

"Those are the same questions they asked about our dear Lord Khristos *when He was being nailed to the cross," the old man said in a sad voice. "Why didn't our Lord flee from the Garden of Gethsemane when He knew the Romans were coming? And why didn't John the Baptist go into hiding before he could be arrested and beheaded by Herod's soldiers? The same questions are asked of all men who claim to be prophets and are persecuted by those who don't understand their message. The true martyrs are those who go willingly to their deaths. And so, too, with Rasputin. He knew his death was ordained. That he must die to fulfill his role on Earth. But before he died, he left a series of final prophecies."*

The old man knocked the ashes out of his pipe by striking it against the rock.

"Knowing he would be killed by an assassin, Rasputin sent a letter to the Tsar. In that letter he warned that if it were one of the Tsar's relatives who brought about his death, then none of the Tsar's family would remain alive for more than two years. In fact, two of the three assassins were related to the Tsar, and Rasputin's prophecy was fulfilled eighteen months later, when the Imperial Family was slaughtered by the Bolsheviks."

In a reflex from the days when he was being hunted by the Bolsheviks, the old man brushed away the pipe ashes so as not to leave any trace that he had passed this way.

Sixty-Three

Security at Fort Detrick had apparently been tightened after September 11, 2001. Three members of the military police guarded the front gate. Mounted on the roof of the guard booth were two closed-circuit TV cameras. Vehicles were being stopped, photo IDs checked, some waved through, and others turned away. The MP who blocked Rhostok's car refused to acknowledge there was anyone named Sherman on the base. But inside the guard booth, Rhostok could see another guard making a phone call. After a short conversation, the second guard opened the security window.

"Do you have an appointment with General Sherman?"

General? This was getting interesting, Rhostok thought.

"Tell him that Altschiller is dead," he said.

"Who?"

"Professor William Altschiller, from the University of Scranton. Tell him the cause of death was a hemorrhage."

After relaying the information and listening to the response from the general's office, the MP issued two passes, one for the car windshield, and a second one that would gain him entrance to Building 625. Following his directions, Rhostok drove slowly onto the post, observing the fifteen-mile-an-hour speed limit. His route took him past the imposing white concrete structure of the National Cancer Institute and past the boxlike structure that housed the headquarters of the Army Medical Research Institute, or USAMRIID, as it was identified on its exterior signage.

The MP's directions took Rhostok to the far end of Fort Detrick, out of sight of other office buildings and behind the military barracks. The two-lane road led over a low rise and down through a dense grove of Norfolk pines. At the end of the road, shielded from the sun and from outsiders, a one-story dark-brick building waited menacingly among the evergreens. A double barrier of tall cyclone fences surrounded the building. Strung along their tops were coils of sharp metal concertina wire. Red diamond-shaped signs warned that the fences were further protected with high-voltage electricity. There were no bushes, shrubs, or other areas of concealment between the outer fence and the building itself. A small sign identified the site as Building 625. There was no sign to explain what went on inside the building.

The MP at the outer perimeter gate compared the security pass with Rhostok's photo ID, took his gun, and waved him through to the second gate, where the ID procedure was repeated.

A third MP waited at a desk just inside the building entrance, where the glass doors afforded him an unobstructed view of the approaches to his post. Behind him, guarding what looked like two heavy stainless-steel elevator doors, were two more MPs armed with well-worn AK-47 assault rifles. They watched impassively from their posts as the MP at the desk performed the third ID check.

He motioned Rhostok to a green Naugahyde couch in the waiting area while he punched some numbers into the telephone keypad.

There had been no attempt to make the lobby attractive. An octagonal red and white sign identified the area as a Level 4 Biological Hazard Zone. Emergency evacuation procedures were spelled out in large red lettering on two other signs. Hanging on the wall beside the signs were breathing packs equipped with white hoods, transparent face plates, and full-body biohazard coveralls. On each side of the steel doors, within easy reach of the guards, were emergency alarms: large red bar-type handles recessed into the wall.

After the MP hung up the phone, he stared at Rhostok. Rhostok stared back until the MP lost interest and turned away.

Rhostok wasn't sure what to expect. He wasn't even sure coming down here was a good idea. After all, he didn't have much to go on except for a dying man's gasp and an old newspaper article. But it was the only lead he had, and he was determined to pursue it, no matter how obscure it might be. He rubbed his eyes and tried to fight off his unusual fatigue.

The steel doors between the two MPs slid apart. In the open space stood a slender woman in a white lab coat. She wore no makeup, and her hair was almost entirely hidden beneath a protective hair cover. A small red caste mark in the center of her forehead identified her as Hindu. Her skin was flawless and pale, the color of a cameo, which didn't fit Rhostok's image of India, a nation whose inhabitants he had always imagined as dark-skinned.

She seemed oddly out of place in this high-security environment, a fragile creature flanked by armed MPs in full combat uniform. She appeared to be serenely unaffected by the proximity of the MPs, who immediately shouldered their weapons and snapped to attention. The guard at the desk jumped to his feet and saluted. Whoever she was, Rhostok thought, she seemed to command a lot of respect.

The woman smiled as she came towards Rhostok, the steel doors closing behind her.

"I am Dr. Veda Chandhuri. General Sherman will join us shortly," she said, reaching out to shake his hand. "We're both glad you came to see us."

Her grip was delicate, her fingers smooth and cool. By contrast, his own hand felt rough and clumsy in her grasp.

"How are you feeling?" she asked. "Are you fatigued?"

"It was a long drive," he admitted.

She studied his face.

"Your eyes are a little red," she said.

"I just need some sleep."

"I am told you knew Professor Altschiller. I was very sorry to hear about his passing." She spoke with a British accent that, perhaps because of the distant land where she had learned her English, was both more musical and more elegant than the clipped language spoken by the British. "Perhaps we should go inside."

She motioned to the guards with a nod of her head. The steel doors hissed open again, revealing a brilliantly lit corridor of stainless-steel walls inset with double-paned glass windows. What took place behind the windows was shielded from view by heavy blinds. The hallway floor and ceiling were both coated with a highly reflective white enamel paint on which not the slightest blemish or scuff mark was visible. A steady stream of cool air flowed through the corridor. As they passed one of the rooms, a carelessly adjusted window blind gave Rhostok a partial view of a figure in a bulky white decontamination suit bending over a cage that contained what looked like a small monkey.

Dr. Chandhuri led Rhostok to an unoccupied laboratory. Entry was gained with a plastic security card. Once inside, she quickly closed the hallway window blinds. The steel door, Rhostok noted, was self-locking. A slot on the inside suggested the key card was required to exit as well as enter.

"Do you know what we do here?" she asked in a pleasant voice.

"Something to do with biological warfare, according to the Internet."

The doctor's lovely smile faltered, as if she were trying to decide whether to express her displeasure at his choice of words.

"A rather crude way of putting it," she said. "But then, it seems to be a common form of verbal shorthand used by those who don't know any better."

She checked to make certain the door was locked.

"Actually," she continued, her British accent stretching out the word to four syllables. "Actually, we don't deal with germs, and we don't conduct warfare. Our mission is to study microorganisms, most of which occur very commonly in nature. We study bacteria, protozoa, fungi, and various growths. They all have many useful applications, such as pesticides and fertilizers. That's all we do here. We study them. Nothing more."

"You make it all sound very normal," Rhostok said. "Is that why you have all that barbed wire and those MPs outside?"

"Well, we *are* a government agency, doing government research. A certain amount of security is necessary these days." She paused. "But I'm not at liberty to go any further into the details of our work. Tell me about Professor Altschiller's death. The guard at the gate said you mentioned something about a hemorrhage."

She was sounding very casual about it, but Rhostok had the feeling she knew more about Altschiller's death than she was letting on.

"According to the coroner, he died from a bleeding ulcer," Rhostok said.

"Did you actually witness his death? What were the symptoms?"

"It wasn't pretty. Blood was pouring out of his mouth and his nose. It was even coming out of his eyes." Rhostok looked around impatiently. "Where is Sherman? That's who the professor wanted me to see."

"He'll be here soon. Did Altschiller complain of any stomach pains?"

"Some, but he didn't seem to be in much pain when I saw him the day before."

"Then it probably wasn't a bleeding ulcer." Her voice was calm and soothing. "How did you happen to be there at the time he died?"

"He was examining . . ." Rhostok hesitated, wondering how much he should reveal. "He was examining a piece of evidence I brought him."

"What sort of evidence?" Dr. Chandhuri asked.

"What is it with all these questions?" Rhostok asked. "I came here to see Sherman, not to be interrogated."

"General Sherman will be joining us soon," she said. "But Professor Altschiller was a friend of mine, also, and you may find our interests overlap. So if I may ask you again, what sort of evidence was he examining?"

"It was a human hand . . . a severed human hand that was found in a bank vault."

He would have expected the doctor to show some surprise. Her face remained impassive. She didn't even lift an eyebrow. Did she already know about the hand?

"Normally such . . . um, objects . . . would come under the purview of the local medical examiner's office, not a college professor," she said. "Did you think there was anything unusual about this hand? Was there any particular reason you took it to Professor Altschiller?"

"Yes," Rhostok said. "The safe-deposit box where we found the hand hadn't been opened in more than fifty years. That seemed unusual."

At last, Rhostok got a reaction from the doctor: a smile.

"And what was the condition of the . . . the hand?" she asked.

"It looked perfectly normal. It was still oozing blood, as if it were a fresh wound."

"Ah, just as the legends describe it," Dr. Chandhuri said.

Sixty-Four

"There were rumors that such an object existed," Dr. Chandhuri explained. She was trying hard to sound casual, but the pencil in her hand was trembling. "We were never sure the rumors were true."

"You already knew about the hand?"

"We knew there were people searching for it. But that didn't necessarily mean it existed. Some of us thought it was a chimera, a fantasy that existed only in the minds of the seekers. After all, human flesh that doesn't decay violates the laws of physics."

"It's real," Rhostok said. "And it doesn't show any sign of decomposition."

The doctor opened a folder, which she attached to the top of her clipboard.

"I have no doubt that what you found was a real hand," she said. "The question is whether it truly was the legendary artifact, or a clever imposture designed to deceive any searchers. Was any documentation found with the hand? Anything that would provide a provenance?"

"No." Rhostok decided not to tell her about the name on the wrapping paper. His police training had taught him to always hold back at least one vital piece of information which might later come in handy.

"Well, at least you took the hand to the right person," Chandhuri said. "If anybody could analyze it properly, it would be Altschiller."

"That's what I thought," Rhostok said.

"And what was his opinion? After his testing?"

"He said he couldn't find any sign of decomposition. He had the hand overnight, exposed it to ninety-degree temperatures, and didn't find any of the physical changes that should have taken place. He seemed really amazed. He said it was incorruptible."

"That was the word he used?" Chandhuri asked. "Incorruptible?"

"He said he had heard about such things, but this was the first time he had ever seen one himself."

For a moment, the only sound in the room was the cool hiss of the ventilation system.

"Did he determine whose hand it might have been?"

"No." Rhostok turned cautious again.

"Oh, come on," Chandhuri smiled. "Altschiller was a forensics expert. You said he ran a number of tests. He must have had some idea, otherwise why would he tell you to call Sherman?"

Rhostok wondered about that himself. An army biological research center was an odd place to be discussing a religious relic.

"How about you first?" he said. "Why don't you tell me why you're so interested in the hand?"

"From a purely scientific aspect, it's a fascinating object," Chandhuri smiled.

"But this isn't a normal scientific laboratory," Rhostok persisted. "It's a military research facility."

"As I told you, we study microorganisms here. Although some microbes can be quite deadly, many others have beneficial aspects which are useful for medical and other civilian purposes. Any interest we might have in examining the artifact would be to determine what sort of chemical or biological reactions might be at work, preventing decomposition and preserving it in such pristine condition."

"The professor said it was a miracle."

"We don't believe in miracles here," Chandhuri said. "It's a matter of policy," she added. "Now, please, let's get back to Altschiller's examination of the hand. What did his testing reveal?"

"He said it was the hand of a middle-aged man, about five-feet-ten, with cowpox scars that suggested a farming background."

She wrote something in the folder.

"Anything peculiar about the blood analysis?" she asked.

"He said there was a high content of cyanide in the blood. Enough to kill twenty men."

Another quick note in her folder.

"Was that the cause of death?"

Rhostok had the feeling she already knew the answer.

"No," Rhostok said. "According to the professor, the blood gases indicated the man died by drowning."

"Amazing!" Chandhuri said, as she wrote. "Absolutely amazing that even the blood gases would be intact after all this time. What else?"

"He found some hemp fibers imbedded in the flesh."

"Rope fibers?" Chandhuri said, without looking up from her writing. "The victim's hands were tied before he was drowned?"

"That's what the professor said."

"What else?"

"That's about it, except for a few specks of silt the professor found under one of the fingernails. He said the silt came from a river that doesn't exist in North America."

Chandhuri made one last notation and finally looked up.

"Well, that settles it," she said. "It all fits. I think there's no need for us to play any further guessing games. We both know where the silt came from, don't we?" Without waiting for his reply, she answered her own question. "It was the Neva River, which flows through Saint Petersburg in Russia."

Rhostok nodded.

"And the hand belonged to Grigorii Rasputin, the famous Mad Monk," Chandhuri continued. "It was removed from his corpse by order of the Empress Alexandra, in the hope that the hand that had performed so many miracles would continue to protect her son. What you found in the vault was a priceless relic, Officer Rhostok. Truly priceless."

"A priceless Russian relic that I had never heard about," Rhostok said. "I thought I knew all the stories about Rasputin. My grandfather even told me about a group of Russian exiles in Paris who used to revere a dried-up object that was supposed to be Rasputin's penis. But he never mentioned anything about Rasputin's hand."

"Only a small circle of people ever knew about the relic," Chandhuri explained. "And they all had important reasons to keep it secret. The Empress kept it secret, because it would create a scandal if the public found out she was venerating the relic of a man so many people despised. After her death, the Russian Orthodox Church kept the secret, because incorruptibility is one of the proofs of sainthood, and they didn't want to glorify a man they considered a debaucher. The Communist government never had control of it, but they maintained the secret as part of their war against religion. For almost a century, the existence of the relic was a closely guarded secret, while it passed from owner to owner, always accompanied by death, often violent death."

The part about death was certainly true, Rhostok thought.

"There's a curse on it, isn't there?" he said.

"A curse? Yes, you could call it a curse." The doctor's thin lips parted in a smile. "But not the supernatural kind."

"Try telling that to all the people it killed. Starting with the Empress

Alexandra and ending up with four people who bled to death in the last three days."

"You actually think those deaths are the work of a man who died almost a century ago?" Chandhuri smiled at the idea.

"I think it's a possibility. I think Rasputin might be punishing those who disturb his relic."

Chandhuri's smile grew broader. "You realize most people would laugh at you for making such a claim."

"That wouldn't mean I was wrong."

"But you'd be investigating a ghost. Even if you proved those deaths were the result of some supernatural curse, who would you arrest? Rasputin is dead. Would you lock up his hand?"

"I don't know what I'd do. Burn it, maybe."

"You'd burn a priceless relic?"

"If that's what it took to prevent other deaths."

"Well, first you'd have to find it, wouldn't you?" Chandhuri said. "I understand that after having the relic in your custody, you were careless enough to lose it."

There was only one way she could have known the relic was missing.

"Hamilton Winfield told you about that, I guess."

"He's one of our consultants in this matter," she confirmed. "He's been helping us search for the hand. He told us the relic was stolen, by someone you both trusted."

"She worked for Winfield, a reporter named Robyn Cronin."

"An unfortunate choice of employee on his part."

"Unfortunate for her, too," Rhostok said. "He told me she'd probably be found dead, with the relic at her side."

"He should never have said that."

"It sounds like I'm not the only one who thinks there's a curse on the relic. Maybe Winfield thinks so, too."

"There may be a tragic history associated with the relic, but the idea that any of those deaths can be attributed to a man who died almost a century ago defies logic."

"So does the condition of his hand," Rhostok reminded her. "We're talking about flesh that doesn't decay. A relic that has the power to defy the laws of nature might possess other powers, too."

"I think you're getting carried away. Before long you'll be claiming that the Revolution, the tragedies and famines that befell the Russian people in the thirties, even the German invasion of Russia, were all part of Rasputin's revenge."

"He predicted those events would happen."

"You're a real believer, aren't you?" Chandhuri said. "But if you look a little more closely at the deaths, including the ones in your little town, the idea that Rasputin might be exerting some sort of supernatural revenge through the relic falls apart."

"The first owner of the relic was the Empress Alexandra," Rhostok countered. "And it was in her possession when she and the entire Imperial Family were slaughtered by the Bolsheviks."

"But why would Rasputin ever wish to inflict such a horrible death on the one person who used all of her powers to defend him against his enemies? If he didn't reach out from the grave to punish his assassins, why would he reach out from the grave to destroy his most faithful admirer?"

"Rasputin was devoted to the Imperial Family," Rhostok said. "But he warned them what would happen if one of their relatives killed him. He could see the future, but like other prophets, he couldn't control it."

"That proves my point," Chandhuri argued. "If he could not control the future, then I don't see how these deaths could be any sort of revenge on his part. They are simply the workings of destiny. In my country we call it karma, the Wheel of Life."

"If it is destiny, then it's working through the last remains of Rasputin," Rhostok insisted. To him, the condition of the hand was proof enough that strange powers were attached to the relic. With such physical evidence to support his belief, none of the arguments the doctor offered could alter his view.

"You're a stubborn man," Chandhuri said. "I know you're fascinated, as Altschiller probably was, by the incorruptible nature of the relic. But that peculiarity of nature doesn't automatically confer any unusual powers on Rasputin's hand. Most Western religions take the position that religious relics possess no mystical powers of their own. Their incorruptibility is considered a sign from God, and they are venerated as such. For a Christian to think that their benevolent God would create a relic and then kill anyone who disturbed it is nothing less than blasphemy."

"Then maybe it's . . ."

"What? The Devil?" Chandhuri smiled again. "I doubt it, even though there are many people who think Rasputin was a servant of the Devil. Look at it rationally. If Rasputin or the Devil or any other supernatural power was really out to punish anyone who disturbed the relic, why did he wait fifty years to punish Vanya Danilovitch for stealing it from that German tunnel? Why not strike him down immediately, as you think happened to Professor Altschiller?"

"I don't know."

"I thought not," she said, a little too smugly. "You don't know anything at all about the real source of the relic's power."

"Do you?" Rhostok asked.

Sixty-Five

"I need a little more information about Professor Altschiller's death," Chandhuri said, raising her pencil again. "How long was it from the time he first saw the relic until his death?"

"Why?"

"I'm trying to establish a time line," she said. "Please, how much time elapsed?"

"I gave him the relic two days ago about mid-morning, and went back there after lunch yesterday."

"So that was a little more than twenty-four hours." She made a notation in the folder. "Now if you don't mind, let's go back to the very beginning. When was the relic discovered?"

"Three days ago."

"That would be Tuesday. Do you remember the approximate time?"

"Why is that important?"

"Part of any medical investigative procedure is to construct a chronology of events. Now please, exactly when was the relic discovered?"

Rhostok rubbed his left arm. She checked her watch, and made a notation in her folder.

She seemed to be recording his movements, as if that were part of her chronology.

"The safe-deposit box was opened at about five-thirty in the afternoon," he said. "I got there about fifteen minutes later."

She consulted her watch again. "That would put the discovery about sixty-four hours ago."

Watching her write down the timing, Rhostok wondered why she was being so precise. He knew there was something she wasn't telling him, but couldn't figure out what it might be.

"When did the first death occur?" she asked, pencil poised.

"I thought Winfield told you what happened."

"Only in general terms, and his information was all secondhand. He didn't actually see the victims. And he was never in the bank. You can provide details no one else can."

"I came here to see Sherman."

"Don't you want to know why those people died?"

"The coroner already determined that."

"But you don't believe him. You think some supernatural power is at work. And I think there's a simpler explanation."

Rhostok settled back in his seat. He stared out the window at the concertina wire glistening in the sunlight.

"The first death," she repeated. "Tell me about it."

"That would be the tax agent, Wendell Franklin. He cut his finger at the bank, and bled to death from that tiny cut."

"Did you see how he sustained the injury?"

"You mean the cut? No, but he told me he cut himself on the safe-deposit box. The one with the relic. It wasn't bleeding that badly when he left the bank, but I guess it just didn't stop."

"How soon after that did he die?"

"His body was discovered the next morning. If you want the exact time of death, you'd have to check with the coroner." Rhostok shifted uncomfortably in his chair. He flexed his toes, which seemed to be stiffening up. "Why don't you just get this information from the coroner's office?"

"He doesn't seem to be releasing much information about this particular death. Even Winfield hasn't been able to tell us much about it. I think you know more about these deaths than anyone. For the time being, let's assume Franklin died in the middle of the night. That would put his death about eight or nine hours after the initial contact." She made another notation. "Was Mr. Franklin tested for hemophilia?"

"The coroner said the results were negative. He ran some other tests, too, but he still doesn't know what caused the bleeding."

"I'm not surprised," Dr. Chandhuri said. "Did you see the body?"

"Yes." Rhostok rubbed his arm again. It felt as if the skin were drying out.

"Did you notice any odd . . . discolorations on his body?"

"Just his fingertips. They looked kind of dark, almost black. At first I thought maybe it was from the newspaper. You know how the ink from the newspaper gets on your fingers? But by the time I left, the blackening seemed to be under his fingernails, too. It seemed to be spreading, even after he was dead."

"A common symptom in cases like this. Who was next?"

"Well, the next reported death was the bank president, Harold Zeeman. He died at his desk yesterday morning at 10:42."

"That would be . . ." The doctor made a note. ". . . forty-one hours and twelve minutes from the time the vault was opened."

"Zeeman's doctor said it was cerebral hemorrhage," Rhostok said. "I never saw the body."

She noted that, too.

"But Zeeman wasn't the second death. That would have been Otto Bruckner, one of my police officers. His body was found after Zeeman's, but he died sometime during the night. The coroner said it was due to a ruptured abdominal aorta. There was blood all over the place."

"You saw Bruckner's body."

"Yes," Rhostok nodded. "And his fingers were turning black, too, like Franklin's. The coroner said it was because the body was there overnight."

"The policeman's body was discovered . . ." She turned a page in her folder. ". . . in the Danilovitch house. What was he doing there?"

"Guarding Nicole . . . Mrs. Danilovitch."

"Why?"

"Well, because of the earlier deaths. I knew Vanya and two of his friends were murdered, and Nicole's husband died under suspicious circumstances. I was worried she might be next, especially after what we found in Vanya's safe-deposit box."

"You were right to be concerned about her, but for the wrong reason." Chandhuri said. "Do you know where she is now?"

"I wish I did," Rhostok said. "She disappeared the night Bruckner died."

He could imagine how frightened she must have been, seeing a giant like Bruckner bleed to death in front of her eyes. No wonder she ran. She was a lonely widow in a strange town, with no one willing to show the tenderness and sympathy she needed at the time. Maybe if he had been kinder, shown more compassion, instead of always playing the role of the suspicious cop, she might have come to him instead of taking off into the night.

"You're not aware that Nicole Danilovitch was rushed to Scranton Memorial Medical Center yesterday afternoon?"

Rhostok's mind had been drifting, barely listening to the doctor. It took a moment for the words to register. When they did, he snapped alert.

"Nicole? What . . . what happened . . . ?"

"She was found feverish and unconscious on a sidewalk in Scranton.

She was transported to the hospital, where doctors discovered an extremely large hematoma on her right thigh . . ." Apparently seeing the confusion in his face, she explained, "A hematoma is a large subcutaneous swelling filled with effused blood. When doctors aspirated the hematoma, two and a half pints of blood were drained. The loss of that amount of blood from the circulatory system would explain why she fainted. She was given plasma, but unfortunately, our contact at the hospital informed us last night that the hematoma was swelling again."

Rhostok tried hard to hide his reaction. He wasn't sure about this doctor and the mysterious General Sherman. For all he knew, this might be a case of mistaken identity, or some manipulative lie, concocted for reasons yet unknown to him.

"You heard this from Winfield?" he asked. "You're sure it wasn't a mistake?"

"No mistake. It was Nicole Danilovitch. One of our people is at the hospital. He reported that she was given plasma and a series of hemostatic drugs, but the hematoma was swelling again last night."

Rhostok still didn't want to believe it. It was hard to reconcile the cold medical terms he was hearing with his memory of Nicole's warm, firm body when she pressed it against him on her front porch that night. Almost pleading for him to wrap his arms around her. How many times had he run the image through his mind, fantasizing about what he could have done, how easily he could have taken advantage of her loneliness that night. Or the next day, when she showed up in that pink dress at the police station, almost willing to trade her body for the contents of the safe-deposit box. And how wrong it would have been both times, so soon after her husband's funeral. Twice he did the honorable thing. But the memory of how sweet she smelled and how comfortably she seemed to melt into his arms had kept him company ever since.

"How bad is she?" Rhostok asked.

"She wasn't expected to survive the night," Chandhuri said.

"That was last night?" he asked, barely able to get the words out. "How is she now . . . this morning?"

"I don't know. We haven't heard anything since last night."

"Dear God, no!" Rhostok said. "Not her, too." He buried his face in his hands, trying to shut out the image of Nicole lying alone and frightened in a hospital bed, her body attached by tubes and wires to the same kind of monitoring equipment and IV bags that sustained his grandfather during his final hours. He could remember the constant beeping of the heart monitor, the humming of the blood-oxygen indicator, and the frightening shriek they made when the body they monitored failed to perform according to their programs.

"I should have been there," he moaned. "I should have been there for her."

"I'm sorry," the doctor said. "I didn't realize . . ."

She left the rest unsaid, but Rhostok knew what she meant.

She had seen the depth of his feelings for Nicole, even before he had been willing to admit them to himself.

Sixty-Six

At Dr. Zarubin's request, Nicole had been moved to a private room after her initial treatment. She dozed fitfully through the evening, the drugs not quite strong enough to keep her fully unconscious.

Sometime during the silent hours of the night, when the normal hospital rhythms had slowed and the lights dimmed for sleeping, a shadowy figure slipped into her room. In the dimness, she couldn't make out exactly who the silent visitor was. Medical personnel had been coming and going for hours, so this particular late-night caller didn't alarm her. She assumed it was the nurse, coming to give her more of those bitter red pills she found so difficult to swallow. They were supposed to thicken the blood, she had been told, although she overheard one of the doctors say the pills didn't appear to be helping.

She couldn't tell who the black form approaching her bed was.

If it wasn't the nurse, it was probably one of the doctors, maybe Zarubin, the blood specialist who seemed so interested in her life history, asking all those questions about her mother and trying to find out about her biological father. Strange questions, she had thought, and wondered what his interest in her father had to do with the bleeding in her leg.

The figure paused beside her. She felt the bedsheet being slowly removed from her body. Shivering, she braced for the pain of yet another examination.

"It is what I feared," a cavernous voice proclaimed.

She was frightened by the immensity of the dark shadow hovering over her bed. Instinctively, she tried to close her legs, to protect herself from further pain.

"Be quiet, *malyutchka*. I have come to deliver you from your pain."

Through the vague haze of medication and fatigue, she finally recognized the voice.

It was *Episkop* Sergius.

He had hunted her down.

She was too weak to resist, too weak even to turn away from him. All she could do was lie there and allow him to enjoy whatever perverse pleasure he had in mind.

She heard the rustling of his cassock. What was he doing now? She could hear his breathing, heavy and deep, the familiar sound she had heard so many times before when men approached her in darkened rooms. She waited for his next move, waited with dread for the feeling of him climbing on top of her. But from the sound of his breathing, she realized he had something else in mind.

He was kneeling, that's what he was doing, she realized. He was kneeling beside her bed in the darkness.

"You have the bleeding, *malyutchka*. I have seen this same bleeding many times before. In Russia we called it the *krovoizliyanie,* and it killed many people."

"What do you want?" she murmured.

"I am here to help you."

"You can't help me. The doctors are doing everything they can, and it doesn't help. What can you do for me?"

"I can stop the bleeding."

"How?"

"Through prayer."

"That's ridiculous."

"You must have faith."

But Nicole had little faith in this strange-smelling priest with his old-country ways. She didn't want to admit he might have powers she didn't understand. He was a fraud or a con man or both, she thought. She had seen men like him perform on stage in Las Vegas, men who pretended to read your thoughts and predict the future. But it was all trickery and deceit. This one was no different. She was convinced that what he had done to her the night before was some form of hypnosis. Not the dark power that her mother had warned her some priests possessed. Just a trick. And those bizarre theories about testing his will by confronting temptation? Just an excuse to use women to satisfy his desires.

What in the world did a strange creature like him have to offer her?

"Salvation," he answered in response to her unvoiced question. "I can offer you salvation."

He was doing it again, she realized with a shock, exactly what he had done before—answering questions she hadn't yet asked.

"There is no need to speak," he said. "I know what you are thinking before your mouth forms the words."

It was positively weird, Nicole thought. Maybe she was hallucinating. Maybe it was the drugs. Maybe it was a dream.

"It is no dream," he said in a soft, almost intimate voice. "I am here to help you."

Maybe this wasn't a trick, she began to think. Maybe there was more to him than she realized.

"You cannot understand my powers," he said. "They are not of this Earth."

All right, she thought, if you can read my mind, tell me what you want me to do.

"You must first tell me your sins, and I will forgive you."

If he could read her mind, then he should already know her sins.

"It is not enough that I know your sins. You must be willing to admit them openly, and show a desire to repent. Only then can I stop the bleeding."

Could he really cure her, she wondered. Was it possible?

"With God, all things are possible. Now confess to me your sins."

She didn't know how to make a confession. She wasn't a religious person.

"It matters not. All that matters is that I am a *starets*. The Living God speaks through men like me. We are the way He makes His wishes known to the world. God sends His consolation to His people in the form of righteous and pious messengers like me, who enable others to become one with the Incarnate Spirit."

What did he want her to do, she wondered.

"First, you must accept the Lord *Khristos* with your whole heart, with your whole being, with all of the life that is within you, and you must do this without expecting anything in return."

All right, she thought. Why not? She had nothing to lose by humoring him.

"What you have to lose is only your evil past," he said.

"All right," she said aloud, finally finding her voice. "I'll do it."

"Do you accept the Lord *Khristos*, expecting nothing in return?"

"Yes, I do," she murmured.

"Are you willing to follow the Lord *Khristos* and His representatives on Earth, in retribution for the sins of your soul and the sins of your flesh?"

"I am willing to follow," she said.

"Then I will enlighten you."

Nicole felt a curious luminosity seep into her eyes. The room was still dark, but she was soon able to discern every detail of the *Episkop* quite clearly. She watched him rise up from his kneeling position and extend his arms over her body.

His eyes were closed, his brow wrinkled in intense concentration. He raised his hands upward in prayer, the index finger of each hand touching its thumb.

"In the name of the Lord *Khristos,* through the intercession of our beloved Lady, the Virgin of Kazan, the martyrs Cyril and Methodius, the Living God Danila Phillipov, and all the holy men and saints who have gone before me, I forgive you your sins and welcome you into the congregation of the true believers and upholders of the faith of the original faith of our fathers, the Old Ritual Holy Russian Church."

He made the sign of the cross on her forehead and began to pray over her in an unintelligible tongue she assumed was Russian. He blessed her three times and began to pass his hands slowly over her body, the open palms hovering less than an inch from her body. Waves of heat seemed to radiate from his hands. She felt her body go limp, her muscles relaxing, her flesh hungrily absorbing the pleasant warmth. It was far more soothing than any medication the doctors had given her.

"And now, *malyutchka,* confess to me your sins."

He resumed his kneeling position beside the bed. She began in a wavering, awkward voice, ashamed at first to tell the full story of the unmarried stepfather who seduced her, at the age of eleven, in her own mother's bed. Sergius himself, with his strange way of looking into her thoughts, had described the act to her last night, but this was a time for full confession, he told her. She must give voice to all the details of her sins if she expected full salvation.

Obediently, she confessed to the pain, the shame, and the secret anger she had carried through her teenage years. She told Sergius how she hated the man who violated her. At times, she wanted to kill him for denying her the normal teenage thoughts and dreams her friends enjoyed. At other times, she loved him desperately, physically, and overwhelmingly and hated herself for those moments of weakness. And finally, she came to hate her mother, too. If her mother had been a better lover, more willing to fulfill the man's sexual desires, he wouldn't have had the need to seek out Nicole.

At least, that was what her stepfather told her, while he tutored Nicole in the art of pleasing him. He turned her into his young courtesan, teaching her to do the things her mother refused to do: all the things that he said were so very important to men, no matter how much they repelled Nicole's mother. Assuring her all the while that when she was grown up, she would thank him for what he taught her.

Sometimes it was easy. Just a few grunts in the night and it was over.

Other times it was more difficult. Even bloody. But it was always impossible to deny him. Until, finally, without even realizing she was pregnant, she hemorrhaged and was rushed to the hospital, where the doctors told her she had had a miscarriage. The scarring of her uterus, they said, meant she would never be able to have children. But worse than the scarring of her uterus was the scarring of her soul that followed. Her mother accused her of being a seductress and blamed Nicole for what had happened. It served her right, her mother said. It was God's punishment for her evil behavior. Her stepfather simply laughed and said it was a blessing, that at least she wouldn't have to take the pill.

Without the strength or the courage to fight back, she ran away from home two months later—and was quickly trapped in worse evils than the one she had tried to escape.

All she ever wanted was a chance at a normal life, she told the *Episkop*. Instead, she was forced to perform unspeakable perversions to enrich a series of men who traded her among themselves, taking her from Brooklyn to Miami and finally to Las Vegas, where her protector was Vassily. There were times, she told the *Episkop*, when she almost took a razor to her face, convinced that her beauty was the cause of her enslavement, and only by destroying that beauty could she free herself from the hell her life had become.

She explained how Fate intervened in a way that she never expected. Just when she had given up hope, Vassily introduced her one evening to Paul Danilovitch. Vassily took them both out for a night of partying. She had no memory of what happened after the second drink, but when she awoke in the morning, there was a wedding ring on her finger, a marriage certificate on the motel dresser, and Paul Danilovitch was telling her how proud he was to be her husband.

The *Episkop*, who had been listening intently, broke his silence.

"This Vassily, he is from Russia?"

"From Moscow, at least that's what he says."

"Do you fear him?"

"He protected me."

"Why do you think he wanted you to marry Paul Danilovitch?"

"I didn't say he wanted me to marry Paul."

"But it is true, isn't it?"

Thinking about it now, reflecting on the sequence of events, she realized with a shock, that it might well be true. For a man who had been so violently possessive of her, so eager to take all the money she earned, Vassily seemed surprisingly pleased when Paul showed him the marriage certificate. Had it all been arranged beforehand? And if so, how could the *Episkop* know that, when Nicole had refused for so long to admit it to herself?

"Perhaps you should tell me more about your friendship with this Vassily."

There was no point in keeping any secrets from him, Nicole realized. She told him how she had been "bought" by Vassily from her former employer. The "purchase," she was told, had been arranged by the *Organizatsya,* the Russian version of the Mafia. She knew resistance was futile, if not fatal, so she did as she was told. Vassily dressed her better than her previous managers and apparently charged his customers more.

"And he is here now, in Middle Valley, this Vassily," the priest said.

"Yes."

"You came to my house in great fear last night. I offered you refuge. And in the morning, because of your fear of this Vassily, you left my house in hopes of appeasing him. You were weak and lonely. You sinned with the great spy, the one who calls himself O'Malley."

"How did you . . . ?" But of course, she thought, he could read her mind. "I'm sorry," she said. "I didn't mean to, not at first."

"You exchanged your body for nothing. You thought you could make peace with this Vassily by giving him what he so desperately wants, but you failed in your efforts."

"The coroner told me he didn't have the hand," she said. "Was he lying?"

"No, *malyutchka.* He told you the truth. He never had the sacred object."

"Sacred?"

"You are a true innocent in all of this, *malyutchka.* You have sinned in the flesh, as so many of us have. But your sins were committed out of fear. And it is your sin that makes redemption possible. Now you will find the comfort of God. You will have no need for men like Vassily and the others. The Lord *Khristos* will be your protector."

Sergius gave her his blessing, making the Sign of the Cross and praying over her. The words were again incomprehensible to her, but oddly comforting and hypnotic in the way his voice rose and fell. And finally, he spoke to her again in English.

"As you have welcomed the Lord *Khristos,* He now welcomes you back into His open and loving embrace. Through the power He has invested in me, you will enter His holy church cleansed in spirit and cleansed in body. In His name I forgive you your sins. In His name I release you from the ugliness, corruption, and guilt the world has visited upon your soul. And in His name, I will now remove from your flesh this foul work of the *Diavol.*"

She followed the *Episkop*'s gaze down to the monstrosity her leg had become. It was swollen to twice its normal size. The network of veins beneath the skin bulged and throbbed with their heavy load of blood and fluids. The first huge blister had collapsed when her leg was aspirated, but another was forming again. Whatever painkillers they had given her seemed to have suddenly worn off. She could almost feel the blood pushing its way to the surface; her heart pumping it from deep within her body to the swollen red area of her thigh; the skin stretching from the force of the blood being fed to it.

"This bleeding is the last attempt of the *Diavol* to possess your body. If you will pray with me now, I will rid your body of the *krovoizliyanie* which he has visited upon you, in the same way I have cured others in Russia."

The *Episkop* extended his hands above her leg. His voice boomed out in a powerful tone that sent a thrill down Nicole's spine.

"I exorcise you, unclean and evil bleeding, symbol and manifestation of the *Diavol,* the visitation on Earth of the enemy from Hell! Begone, evil spirit and diabolic nether creature! I exorcise you in the name of the Lord *Khristos!* Be gone and be uprooted from the body of this holy innocent who was entrusted by her own words into the protection of the Lord!"

Nicole watched as he lowered his hands to her leg. She was willing to endure whatever pain he would inflict, if it would only help cure her. She could feel his hands on her flesh, but the expected pain didn't materialize. His touch felt cold. The contact with her thigh was wonderfully soothing, almost frosty. She let out a soft murmur of relief.

"Leave, therefore, now and forever, leave this temple of the servant of the Lord," he called out to the otherwise empty room. "Leave, therefore, now, seducer of this woman, molester of all that is good within her. Humiliation is yours. You shall not be victorious. The mark of your evil will disappear from this woman. The Lord *Khristos* and His legions and armies of angels will trample you and send you back to the serpent that is your dwelling place on Earth. Leave now, I command you in the name of God!"

The door was suddenly thrown open, startling Nicole with a flood of light from the hallway. Someone stood framed in the doorway. The *Episkop* didn't seem to notice. He continued with his recitation.

"May the holy temple of God's servant, Nikoleta Baronovich Danilovitch . . ."

He made the Sign of the Cross between her breasts.

". . . become a symbol of the *Diavol*'s failure for all to see. May her very flesh . . ."

He repeated the Sign of the Cross on her forehead.

". . . become in its purity a source of fear and terror for all things foul."

He repeated the Sign of the Cross over her leg.

"God the Father commands you!"

Another Sign of the Cross.

"God the Son commands you!"

Another Sign of the Cross.

"God the Holy Spirit commands you!"

Another Sign of the Cross.

"The Holy Russian martyrs command you!"

The Sign of the Cross was frantically repeated with every phrase he shouted.

"The healing power of the mysteries of the Holy Russian Church commands you! The unwavering faith of Saints Cyril and Methodius commands you! Get out!"

He grabbed her leg, squeezed it, and screamed out his words of exorcism.

"By all the power that flows from the blood shed by the followers of the True Faith during their time in the wilderness, in the name of the twenty thousand martyred Old Believers, I myself command you, get out! Give way, evil one, fountain of lust, source of all temptation, prince of deception and pride, give way, I command you by the power that destroyed your kingdom before and will destroy it again. I order you in the name of God to depart from this person whom He Himself created. I command you in the name of the Living God Danila Phillipov; in the name of Grigorii Rasputin, who performed this same holy act and evicted you through the power of God so many times before, get out! Begone!"

His energy spent, Sergius collapsed across Nicole's bare legs. Instinctively, she reached out to touch him. Beads of sweat covered his face and soaked his beard. She wiped his cheeks with her fingertips, caressing him gently as she did so.

The spell was broken when the supervising nurse, who had been standing transfixed in the doorway, turned on the room lights.

"What's going on in here?"

Nicole shielded her eyes from the light.

"What was he doing to you?" the nurse demanded.

Nicole stared lovingly into the face of the *Episkop*. She touched his cheek with exquisite tenderness.

"He was praying," she said in a gentle voice. "He was praying to save me from the *Diavol*."

Without thinking, she had used the Russian word.

"And now the *Diavol* is gone," she said, still stroking the *Episkop*'s face.

"Get him off her," the nurse commanded two orderlies, who had entered the room behind her. "What kind of priest is he, lifting up her nightgown and fondling her? Get him off her and call security."

Nicole tried to fight them, holding tight to Sergius's shoulders. His eyes were still half-closed. He let out a deep groan, as if being aroused from sleep.

The orderlies managed to pry the *Episkop*'s limp body from Nicole's grasp and dragged him to a nearby chair. The nurse broke an ampule of ammonia and waved it in front of his nose in an attempt to revive him.

Dr. Zarubin had been summoned by one of the other floor nurses. He quickly checked Sergius, saw that he was okay, and asked the nurse what the priest was doing there.

"He was shouting and moaning," she said. "I heard him all the way out at the nurse's station. I looked in the door and he was yelling and waving his hands in the air and feeling her legs. It looked like he was going to rape her."

"He was praying for me," Nicole said softly.

"It wasn't like any kind of praying I ever saw," the nurse insisted.

"He was casting out the *Diavol*," Nicole explained.

Dr. Zarubin turned to her.

"Are you all right?" he asked. "Did he hurt you?"

"Look for yourself," Nicole said.

She held up her nightgown and there, down below the fluffy mound of her pubic hair, was the smooth white skin of her legs. Incredibly, no blister was visible where it had been on her right leg. No swelling reddened her skin. No blood was collecting beneath the surface. No ugly spidery tracings marked the location of hemorrhaging veins.

All traces of the bloody affliction were gone.

Her leg looked perfectly normal.

Sixty-Seven

Dr. Zarubin's face registered shock. He took a slow step forward, staring in disbelief. Hesitantly, he reached out to touch her thigh. The supervising nurse watched in stunned silence. Zarubin ran his hand from the top of Nicole's knee to her groin, as if he didn't believe what his eyes were seeing. He poked at her flesh with his thumb, testing the firmness, probing to determine if she felt any pain.

"What did he . . . what did he do?" Zarubin asked in an awe-struck whisper.

"He prayed for me," Nicole said again, smiling now at the confusion on the assembled faces.

Zarubin shook his head, refusing to accept the explanation.

"You don't pray away massive hemorrhagic blistering," he said. "It must have been the drugs."

"It was the *Episkop*," Nicole insisted. "The *Episkop* and his prayers."

"We gave her painkillers, as you instructed," the supervising nurse said. "Also some factor eight coag, but only the dosage you prescribed."

Zarubin looked at Nicole's chart to see what other type of treatment might have been given her.

"Nothing," he murmured. "There's nothing here that would have stopped the bleeding, much less drain away the subdermal fluid buildup." He turned to Sergius, who was still slumped in the chair, breathing heavily with his eyes closed. "He must have given her something. It's the only explanation."

Zarubin bent over Sergius.

"Wake up," he whispered harshly. "I want to know what you did to my patient."

When Sergius didn't respond, the doctor shook him roughly.

"Wake up. Tell me what you did."

"Maybe there's something on his hands," the nurse suggested. "Some kind of salve or ointment. He was holding her leg when I came in."

Zarubin examined the *Episkop*'s limp hands.

"Nothing," he said. "Just a little perspiration, but that's normal for a man who's passed out."

The nurse cracked another ampule of ammonia and waved it under the *Episkop*'s nose. This time he responded by muttering something in Russian and tried to move his head away from the fumes.

"Wake up, damn you!" Zarubin shook him again. "Can you hear me?"

Sergius rolled his head and, with a long groan, finally opened his eyes. He ignored Zarubin. His gray eyes slowly focused on Nicole.

"We must leave now," he told her.

Sergius attempted to get up from the chair but slumped back on his first try. He closed his eyes and took a deep breath, as if summoning some inner strength. On the second try, he succeeded. Standing erect, his massive bearded figure towered over the doctor, the nurse, the orderlies.

"Put on a robe," he ordered Nicole.

"My clothes are in the closet," she said.

"Put on a robe," he insisted. "The clothing you were given was worn in your sinful action this afternoon. You will not wear the clothing of sin again."

"She can't leave the hospital," Dr. Zarubin said. "For her own sake, she has to stay here. At least overnight."

"She is cured," Sergius said.

"I don't believe it."

"You saw it yourself. The mark of the demon has left her, cast out with the evil serpents that infested her soul and made her unclean."

Nicole swung her feet out of bed. The supervising nurse tried to block her way.

"You can't leave until the doctor authorizes your release," she said.

"Her place is with me," the *Episkop* responded. "She has given herself to the Lord and the Lord has accepted her. That is why she is cured."

"You can't cure hemorrhagic bleeding simply by praying," Dr. Zarubin insisted.

"Others have done it before me. This is the way of the *starechestvo*."

"Russian superstition," the doctor argued.

"You fool!" Sergius said. "You saw for yourself. Do you not believe your own eyes?"

"He cured me," Nicole said in a defiant voice. "You couldn't help me, but he did. My leg is healed." She raised her nightgown. "Touch it again if you don't believe me."

"It's simply the superficial appearance of remission." Zarubin seemed unwilling to accept any other explanation. "It doesn't mean a lasting cure has been effected. I've seen hundreds of cases of hemorrhagic disorders, and none of them has recovered this quickly."

"Then perhaps you should begin praying," Sergius said. His voice turned low and menacing. "This woman belongs to the Lord *Khristos* now."

"I want to run some tests before I release her."

"No! You will perform no more tests. You will not question the workings of the Lord. She is cured, and she will come with me."

He held out his hand for Nicole. When Dr. Zarubin attempted to block the way, the *Episkop* struck him to the floor. Two security guards came through the door, but froze in their tracks when Sergius turned the full glare of his anger on them.

"Get back!" he commanded.

They retreated to the far side of the bed. The supervising nurse bent over Zarubin, cradling his head on the cushion of one of her fat legs.

"I don't know who the hell you think you are," she said. "But you've got no right to come in here and assault people. I'm going to call the police."

"I am the Protector of the Faith. I am the rebirth of the Holy Russian Church. My powers come from the Lord. No one in this room can stand before me."

Nicole was at his side, feeling her body resonate with the sound of his voice. She felt sorry for the others in the room. She could see the fear and confusion on their faces, their unwillingness to accept the miracle the *Episkop* had performed. But the fear Nicole had once felt in his presence was gone. He had cured her. Her body provided all the proof she needed of his saintliness. She was the vessel of his good works, the beneficiary of his prayer. She would follow him wherever he led, convinced she had finally found the one man who had the power to protect her from all earthly harm.

"I am going with him," she said.

"He must have hypnotized her," the nurse said. "She sounds like she's in a trance."

Dr. Zarubin raised himself in one last attempt to stop them.

"Please don't take her," he pleaded.

"She is not of your world any longer," Sergius said. "We must now be about the work of rebuilding the Holy Russian Church, to reclaim it from the heretics and resurrect it in a glorious rebirth."

"You don't understand," Zarubin said. "There are people all around the world dying from similar hemorrhagic disorders. Bleeding to death for reasons no one understands. At least tell me how you stopped the bleeding. This is the first cure I've ever seen for this type of condition."

"I was merely the instrument, the means by which the power was transferred," Sergius said.

Nicole wrapped herself in a robe from the closet and, head bowed, waited behind her *Episkop* for his signal to leave.

"If you go now, you'll be condemning others to death," Zarubin pleaded. "If you won't tell me how you cured her, please let me run some tests. It's vital that I get some answers."

Sergius nodded to Nicole, and she started for the door.

"In Mother Russia, the bleeding comes as a punishment," he said. "It comes out of the night and strikes down all whom it touches. Many, many thousands have died through the centuries. Only a few, a very few, have survived the flowing of the blood."

"He's crazy," the nurse said.

Zarubin ignored her.

"How have those few survived?" he asked.

Nicole was already in the hallway.

"Tell me how they survived," Zarubin shouted.

Sergius turned. He stood framed in the doorway.

"There is only one way," Sergius said. "Through the intercession of the one man who showed his mastery over the bleeding, the man who was martyred for the miracles he performed, the man whose bones were burned and scattered by the Bolsheviks and the Antichrists who took over the Holy Russian Church."

He paused, his eyes sparkling with an energy that overpowered the people in the room.

"That man is the Great Saint and Intercessor, the reincarnation of the Holy *Khristos,* Grigorii Effimovich Rasputin!"

At the mention of the name, Zarubin's face went pale.

Sixty-Eight

The room in which Rhostok was being questioned had many of the features of a maximum-security holding cell. Heavy iron screens protected the windows. The window glass itself was edged with metallic alarm tape. The room door was metal, with a self-locking mechanism. Beyond that were the steel lobby doors and the heavily armed MPs guarding the building entry and access through the double barrier of electrified fencing. The protection against outside intruders worked just as effectively in reverse, turning the building into what seemed an escape-proof prison. And Dr. Chandhuri's questioning seemed as relentless as any investigating officer's.

Yet he was beginning to feel more comfortable with her. He liked her approach, the careful way she asked questions, building a time frame, looking for similarities or for what Altschiller called anomalies. Maybe it was her scientific background, he thought. Or maybe this was the way all federal investigators were trained. Either way, it was helping Rhostok see things differently, drawing his attention to facts he had previously ignored.

"Who else was in the bank when the vault was opened?" she asked. "Not necessarily in the vault, but physically present in the bank?"

Now see, he thought, that was something he hadn't considered. Maybe it was important, maybe not. But a good question.

"Well, the bank secretary was there," he recalled. "Her name is Sonya Yarosh. She's at least ninety years old, so you'd think if anybody was going to die, she would have been the first because of her age. But I saw her watering her flowers yesterday morning, and she looked perfectly healthy."

"Ninety years old? How long ago did her ancestors come over?"

"Oh, it wasn't just her ancestors who immigrated. She did, too. She was born in Petrograd, I think."

"Petrograd?" Dr. Chandhuri looked up from her file. "You're sure of that?" she asked. "You're sure this woman was born in Russia?"

"According to Sonya, she came over in the 1930s, during one of the purges."

"And she's still alive! Very good! Exceptional! We'll be contacting her."

"And there was the bank guard, a fellow by the name of Eddie Bielaski. He went into the vault later, when Otto was there dusting for fingerprints. But I think Eddie's okay. He showed up for work the next day. I saw him after Zeeman had his stroke, and he looked perfectly healthy to me. As far as I know, Eddie's still alive."

"What do you know about his background? Was he an immigrant, too?"

"He came over some time after the war."

"Wonderful. We'll look him up as well. What about the next day? Did anybody enter the vault the next day?"

"Well, you'd have to ask the bank people about that. I do know that the vault was closed in the morning for cleaning. The health department came in and cleaned everything with bleach."

"The health department did that? And they used bleach? Is that normal in your jurisdiction?"

"I guess so. I know there's always a cleanup crew whenever there's a messy death."

Dr. Chandhuri took a pair of latex gloves from the pocket of her lab coat.

"While we're waiting for Sherman, I'd like to do a workup on you," Chandhuri said.

"A workup?"

"A medical workup. You know, take a health history, a blood test, that sort of thing."

Rhostok watched her slip the latex gloves over her delicate fingers.

"Why do you need all that?" he asked.

"Well, I would think that would be obvious," she said. "Of all the people who were actually inside the vault, you seem to be the only one who's still alive. I'd like to find out why, and how much longer you have to live."

Sixty-Nine

The idea that his own life might be at risk wasn't exactly a surprise to Rhostok. He had seen others who came into contact with the relic die soon after, and the possibility of his own vulnerability had occurred to him. It was a thought he had tried to suppress while he carried on his investigation. But Chandhuri's statement, delivered in her matter-of-fact style, made it seem inevitable. He rubbed his right arm, which was feeling heavy. When he saw her making a note of his action, he stopped.

"I assume you're of Russian ancestry," she said.

"Doesn't it show?"

"I'll take that as a 'yes.'" Chandhuri said. She checked a box on a preprinted form attached to her clipboard.

"Our information is that you're second-generation American, is that correct?"

Winfield again, Rhostok thought.

"My grandparents all came over around 1919, 1920, after the Revolution."

"You're second generation then," she said. "That was on both sides, your mother's and father's?"

"All my grandparents were Russian. They grew up in the Old Country, but my parents were born here. Does that make a difference, me being Russian?"

"Russian American," she corrected him. "The distinction might be very important. I understand both your parents are dead."

Rhostok nodded, wondering exactly when Winfield supplied her with this information.

"Is it true your father died in a mine explosion?"

"If you already know the answers, why do you need to ask me these questions?"

"I'm sorry, but I have to confirm certain basic facts, and there are other questions which only you can answer."

After providing the details of his parents' deaths, Rhostok answered a series of questions about his childhood diseases, a checklist of specific foods served in the Rhostok household while he was growing up, and changes in his diet since then. Every time he made a movement, every time he scratched his arm or coughed or flexed his fingers, he noticed the doctor made a notation.

"Did your parents or grandparents ever talk about friends or relatives who died from bleeding disorders?"

"Only about Tsarevich Alexei's hemophilia."

"What about outbreaks of a larger magnitude? Hemorrhagic episodes that affected dozens, maybe hundreds of people?"

"Not that I remember."

Chandhuri thumbed through the file, looking for a specific page.

"The reason I ask is because hemorrhagic diseases were far more common in Russia than in any other country. Usually there were a variety of symptoms, not just bleeding." She found the sheet she was looking for and read from it. "There was a major outbreak in 1891 in eastern Siberia, in the Ussuri district. Your grandparents might have been aware of it. There were dozens of other outbreaks during the following decades, but nobody paid much attention. The outbreaks were localized, and the Russian people were preoccupied with the war with Germany, the Revolution, the murder of the Imperial Family . . ."

". . . and the death of Rasputin," Rhostok added.

Chandhuri looked up from the folder and smiled.

"Just a few more questions," she said. She inserted a digital thermometer into his mouth, took a reading, and noted the temperature on the form.

"How are you feeling?" she asked. "Are you experiencing any unusual aches or pains?"

"I feel fine," Rhostok said.

"You look exhausted."

"That's because I've only had four hours sleep."

"Your eyes are bloodshot."

"I was rubbing them on the way down. Trying to stay awake."

"How about your hands? You've been rubbing your arms and scratching a lot. Are you feeling any numbness in the fingertips?"

Rhostok rubbed his fingers together. The numbness he had noticed in his right index finger the night before seemed to have spread to the tips of all the fingers on that hand. The other hand felt perfectly normal.

Without waiting for an answer, Chandhuri made a notation on her clipboard.

"What about your feet?" she asked.

"My feet are fine."

"Except for your toes?"

Rhostok nodded. "They feel a little . . . I don't know, stiff, I guess."

Another notation by Chandhuri.

"Now, I noticed you've been scratching your arms. There, you're doing it again."

"It's just a little itchiness," Rhostok admitted. "That's not unusual, is it?"

"Not by itself. However, in combination with fatigue, bloodshot eyes, numbness in the extremities, you're displaying a specific pattern of symptoms."

Rhostok flexed his fingers, hoping the numbness would disappear, that the loss of feeling was some sort of normal reaction to not getting enough sleep.

"It won't go away," Chandhuri said, watching his activity. "I'm afraid it'll only get worse."

She placed her clipboard on the table and reached out towards Rhostok's neck. Rhostok pulled back.

"Calm down," Chandhuri said. "I just want to see if there's any swelling under your chin."

Rhostok allowed the latex-covered fingers to probe gently beneath his jawbone, down both sides of his neck, and along the inner edges of his collarbone. When she was finished, Chandhuri made another notation on Rhostok's chart.

"What is it?" Rhostok asked. "I'm okay, right?"

"Let me draw some blood first, and then we'll talk," she said. She wrapped a rubber strip around his arm, instructed him to make a fist, and expertly, almost painlessly, inserted a needle into a vein in his forearm. The procedure was a routine part of every physical exam, but this time there seemed something ominous about the dark red liquid that moved from his vein into the clear plastic tube. And instead of the customary piece of cotton and a Band-Aid over the needle wound, she applied a quick-drying sticky substance, which she described as medical glue, and a pressure bandage that she wrapped tightly around his arm.

"We don't want to take any chances," she explained ominously. "In your condition, even a tiny puncture could be dangerous."

After labeling the sample, she stripped off the latex gloves and wrote some additional comments on her clipboard. When she had finished writing, she looked up at Rhostok and said, "There appears to be some minor swelling of the glands in your neck and around your thyroid. I'm afraid you're already in the initial stage."

"Initial stage of what?"

She hesitated, as if trying to reach for the right words to explain her diagnosis.

"The symptoms you have are the precursors of a particularly virulent bleeding disorder. I won't have confirmation until the blood testing is completed, but it appears the disorder has already taken root in your circulatory system. That's why you feel numbness in your extremities. The redness in your eyes is the result of microscopic hemorrhagic activity."

"A bleeding disorder . . ." Rhostok tried to think it through. "You mean like hemophilia?"

"Much worse."

"Then it has to be a curse on the relic, no matter what you say," Rhostok insisted.

"You're back to that again," Chandhuri sighed. "I told you before, it's pure superstition."

"But the relic is the key," Rhostok argued. "Rasputin had the power over blood. He cured bleeders when he was alive, and now that he's dead, his relic seems to be working in reverse. Everyone who was in that vault, except perhaps Eddie, is dying from a bleeding disorder. We're all ending up like the Tsarevich."

"The Tsarevich suffered from hemophilia," Chandhuri said. "It's totally unrelated to this particular disorder. Hemophilia is an inherited blood defect. Alexei inherited it through his mother, the Empress, who came from a long line of German bleeders."

"Alexei's uncle died of a stroke," Rhostok argued. "Just like the bank president."

"That's a common occurrence with bleeding disorders. They strike first at the body's weakest points, which vary from person to person."

"But Rasputin had the power to control bleeding. He cured the little Tsarevich."

"Not a permanent cure," the doctor said. "He merely stopped specific attacks."

"He stopped the bleeding and saved Alexei's life," Rhostok stubbornly argued. "That's what Rasputin did. He stopped the bleeding when all the best doctors in Russia failed."

She looked at Rhostok with a sympathetic smile on her thin lips.

"You may believe Rasputin had some sort of supernatural powers. And it may surprise you to know that I think so, too. But there is a perfectly natural explanation for the bleeding deaths that occurred in Middle Valley. What we're dealing with are fairly typical cases of alimentary toxic aleukia, or ATA as it is commonly described in the literature. Initially, it can cause headache, vertigo, burning of the eyes and throat, itching skin, swollen neck glands, even laryngitis. The symptoms can vary from person to person and can quickly advance to internal hemorrhaging. Initially, the bleeding attacks weak points in the circulatory system, causing symptoms that can be easily misdiagnosed as stroke or bleeding ulcer or other common disorders."

"ATA? The coroner never mentioned anything about that," Rhostok said.

"I'm not surprised. As I said, the symptoms can easily be misdiagnosed. Your coroner might be an excellent doctor, but like most American doctors, his experience is limited to conditions that are prevalent on the East Coast of the United States. A highly civilized region, with relatively civilized illnesses. As a result, he's unequipped to recognize disorders of this nature."

"I'm not following you," Rhostok said.

"Do you remember what happened with the anthrax cases?" Chandhuri asked. "Initially, the patients were diagnosed as suffering from symptoms of flu or pneumonia. Only after the first victims died did the American medical community learn to recognize the symptoms of anthrax infection." She shook her head in apparent disgust. "Most American doctors would be unable to recognize a case of the Black Plague, a disease that wiped out one-third of the population of Europe in the fourteenth century. Up until a few years ago, Lassa fever cases were almost always misdiagnosed in the United States, which resulted in the needless death of every single person who contracted the disease. Both of those are hemorrhagic disorders—bleeding diseases, if you will—which still thrive in certain parts of the world.

"There are dozens of similar diseases, all of which can cause death within days. Yet like the diseases of my native India, they are unstudied in American medical schools—except perhaps as footnotes in textbooks. I'm not surprised your coroner couldn't come up with a proper diagnosis."

Chandhuri was warming to a subject that apparently troubled her.

"American doctors tend to look down on 'foreign' doctors like me. They are so very careful about allowing us to be licensed. They think doctors from the Third World are somehow inferior. And yet there are provincial doctors in Bangladesh, Dakar, and New Guinea who are diagnosing and treating diseases the names of which most American doctors don't even know. It is one of the great failings of American medical professionals, thinking they know everything. If it isn't an American disease, it isn't part of the curriculum. Given the pressures of time and money in American medical schools, diseases that are out of date are out of fashion and are often ignored or covered in an extremely superficial manner."

Rhostok listened patiently to her outburst before trying to get her back on track. "This bleeding disease—you learned about it in India?"

Chandhuri shook her head apologetically.

"Oh, no," she admitted. "I learned about ATA through my work here, at the Biological Defense Laboratory."

"So you know how to cure it?"

"Unfortunately, there is no cure."

Seventy

It was a death sentence, delivered in a calm feminine voice.

"Oh, come on," Rhostok said. "There has to be a cure."

Chandhuri slowly shook her head.

"But you're a doctor," Rhostok insisted. "You seem to know all about this disorder or disease or whatever it is. There has to be a cure. This is a medical research facility. Isn't there something you at least could test on me?"

"I'm sorry. I'm very sorry for you, but there is no cure for what you have. Or at least no cure that we know of." She closed the folder in which she had been taking notes. "You see, this particular disorder has never before appeared in the general American population. It occurs most commonly in Russia, with some sources dating early outbreaks back to the Middle Ages. The disease was discovered and named by Russian scientists, and the Russian military has been studying it intensively since the 1930s. Our information on ATA is rather limited, but we do know that death usually occurs within forty-eight hours after initial exposure."

"That's why you were so interested in the time frame."

"Exactly," she said. "You've already survived much longer than the others."

"You said the Russians have been studying it. Maybe they know of a cure."

"If they do, they're not sharing it with anyone."

"But you could call them, couldn't you? Aren't doctors supposed to share information?

"Unfortunately, the only Russian doctors who are familiar with your disorder are in the Russian military. And they're under orders not to share that information with anyone."

Seventy-One

Before Chandhuri could say anything further, the card-activated lock on the laboratory door clicked open, and the man Rhostok had traveled all this way to see entered the room.

He wore the olive-green uniform of an army officer. A single silver star decorated each shoulder. He was younger than Rhostok expected, a handsome young man with plump, boyish cheeks, clear blue eyes, and pouty lips. He brusquely introduced himself as Nathaniel Sherman, declined to shake hands, walked around Rhostok slowly, studying him closely, and then turned his attention to Chandhuri.

"How far have you got?"

She surrendered her clipboard to him with a sigh. After glancing through the pages in the attached folder, he turned back to Rhostok. "We're glad to have you here," he said, a remark that Rhostok found puzzling, given the death sentence Chandhuri had just delivered. "Do you have any questions for me?"

"Am I really dying?" Rhostok asked. It wasn't one of the questions he originally came here to ask, but it was more important to him than any other at the moment.

Sherman frowned. "I'm sorry about that, but the answer is yes."

"And there really is no cure?"

"Not yet. There's no known antidote for your condition. At least not in the Western world. But we hope to find one. By tracking this outbreak, we may get some answers. Where is the clothing you wore when you were in the vault?"

"It's already been washed."

"That's unfortunate."

"Unfortunate? Why?"

"We would have liked to screen it for samples."

"What kind of samples?"

"You were telling Chandhuri the bank vault was cleaned with bleach."

"Yes."

"That's too bad. And I understand a fire destroyed Altschiller's laboratory."

"I didn't tell her anything about that."

"We do have access to information from other sources," Sherman said. They were almost the same words Winfield had used.

Rhostok had taken an instant dislike to Sherman and thought he detected a similar feeling in Chandhuri.

"You're not really a general, are you?" Rhostok asked.

"I'm wearing the stars," Sherman said.

"He's not a military man," Chandhuri said in a sour voice. "He's a molecular biologist, like the rest of us."

"I never went to military school, and I certainly didn't come up through the ranks," Sherman muttered. "Nevertheless, I *am* a general, and I'm the commanding officer here."

He handed the clipboard back to the frowning Chandhuri. Her friendly attitude had vanished since the younger man's arrival. She seemed uncomfortable in Sherman's presence, although she obviously deferred to him.

"This is a military installation," she explained to Rhostok. "The Pentagon requires an officer above the rank of colonel to be in charge of our operations. There were no officers available with the scientific credentials required for the position, so they made him a general and put him in charge."

"You could call it a laboratory commission," Sherman said. "It's just as valid as a battlefield commission."

Rhostok didn't trust the young general. He didn't like the way he happened to arrive at the particular moment when Chandhuri was talking about the Russian military's research on bleeding disorders.

"You were listening in on us," Rhostok said.

Sherman didn't bother to deny it. "All the rooms here are constantly monitored, especially when we have visitors. It's not a violation of your privacy rights, if that's what you're worried about. Not as long as you're in a high-security area. If you looked closely, you'd have seen a notice to that effect in the waiting room."

"You don't talk like a scientist," Rhostok said. "You sound more like a security expert."

Sherman gave him one of those wide-open, you-can-trust-me grins that always put Rhostok on his guard.

"Around here, we're all security experts. Aren't we, Veda?"

She agreed with a nod, disliking her superior's use of her first name.

"Of course I was listening," Sherman admitted when he turned back to Rhostok. "You seem to be asking a lot of questions."

"And I think I deserve better answers from you," Rhostok said.

"You mean about the hand? The Rasputin relic? You found that, not us. What more could we tell you?"

"I think there's something more here than you're admitting. I may not be as smart as the two of you . . . but I think you're hiding something."

"Hiding something?" The phony smile seemed frozen on Sherman's face. "There's nothing for us to hide. According to your own story, that hand has been in the vault for more than fifty years. Veda has been very open with you. Some of what she told you is confidential, but . . . considering your condition, maybe she was justified. My feeling is that whatever infected you and the others probably grew on that hand. Maybe that same biological reaction is what kept the hand intact. By killing the bacteria, it prevented the normal process of decomposition."

It sounded logical to Rhostok, but yet . . . "That's not what Professor Altschiller thought," he said.

"Ah, yes, Altschiller. He always had strange theories."

"But he worked for you in the past."

"Altschiller wasn't a biological scientist. He was a forensic anthropologist, a bone collector. He worked for my predecessors. But that was a long time ago."

"They had him looking for samples of biological warfare agents when he went to Cambodia and Laos, didn't they?"

The young man's cockiness faded.

"Would it do me any good to deny it?"

"What did they call it in Cambodia? Yellow Rain, wasn't it?"

"You know about that?" Chandhuri interrupted. "You know about his work?"

"Yes."

"Altschiller would never say anything about his assignment," Sherman said. "And it was never fully reported in those newspaper articles. How did you find out about that project?"

"Like you, I have my sources," Rhostok said with a smile.

The source was the *Scranton Times* reporter who had interviewed Altschiller after the Yellow Rain expedition and agreed to keep the real purpose of the trip secret. That is, until Rhostok telephoned in the middle of the night and convinced him that, since Altschiller was dead, there was no reason to keep the secret any longer.

"Fucking media," Sherman swore. "Some reporter must have been your source. But he must have also told you Altschiller didn't find anything significant. A few leaf samples and some twigs with yellow residue. There was a difference of opinion about what the residue was. Some highly respected scientists theorized it was bee droppings, or some sort of pollen."

"But that's not what your predecessors thought, was it?"

Sherman shrugged. "A lot of that has already been published in scientific journals, so I guess there's no harm in telling you. The field reports said it was residue from an aerial spray attack on Hmong tribesmen. Samples were tested here and at the biomedical laboratory in Edgewood. It wasn't pollen, but we also couldn't find any of the chemical agents we were familiar with at the time."

"But you had the yellow residue, didn't you?"

"The only substance our people could identify was lauryl sulfonate. It's a chemical surfactant used in household soaps and detergents. The only rational explanation for the presence of an artificial surfactant deep in the jungle would be that it was sprayed there to wash away any traces of biological or chemical agents."

"Why would anyone do that?" Rhostok asked. This was information the reporter hadn't mentioned. "Were they afraid of leaving evidence behind?"

"Not necessarily. The process is also used to neutralize deadly residues before troops move in. One of the major problems of biochemical warfare is the longevity of the agents. They interfere with the occupation of the affected territory. You saw how difficult it was to clean out the Senate Office Building in Washington. And that was just a minor discharge of anthrax spores, compared to the huge volumes that would normally be used in battlefield conditions. It's amazing how long some of these agents retain their deadly capabilities."

"Like the mustard gas at Ypres," Dr. Chandhuri said.

"That would be a good example," Sherman agreed. "The Germans used mustard gas at Ypres in 1915 during the First World War. Almost fifty years later, a farmer in the region was cutting down an old tree. He sat on the stump to eat his lunch. By evening, his backside and hands were covered with enormous blisters, which are the classic symptoms of mustard gas. An examination of the tree revealed that mustard gas residues had been trapped in tiny crevices in the bark in 1915. New layers of bark and tree growth covered it over the years, but the mustard gas was still lethal a half-century after it was first released."

"Fifty years?" Rhostok asked. "It lasted that long?"

"There are only two ways to eliminate biochemical residue," Sherman said. "The most effective way is to burn it."

"Altschiller's laboratory was burned," Rhostok recalled. "It was completely destroyed, just a few hours after he died."

"The other way to eliminate the residue is to neutralize it with some type of surfactant or bleach," Dr. Chandhuri said. "That's what the Russians did in Afghanistan, and the Vietnamese did in Laos."

"The bank vault was cleaned by someone from the health department," Rhostok said, "which means it's probably safe."

"That explains why we couldn't get any samples . . ." Chandhuri started to say, and then stopped when Sherman glared at her. The two quickly looked away from each other, then back. One embarrassed. One angry. Rhostok had seen such expressions before. In interrogation rooms, when one suspect let something incriminating slip out.

"What was that you just said?" Rhostok stepped between the two to break their eye contact with each other. "What samples? When did you try to get samples?

Chandhuri tried to look around Rhostok, trying to get a signal from her superior.

"She was talking about the samples Altschiller tried to get from Cambodia," Sherman said. "When we heard about his death, we were reminiscing about the work he did in Cambodia."

Chandhuri smiled with relief and nodded her head in rapid agreement. "That's right," she said. "We were talking about the professor this morning, discussing the samples he brought back. They turned out to be useless."

She wasn't as good a liar as Sherman.

"Let me get this straight," Rhostok said. "We're talking about biological weapons here. You had Professor Altschiller looking for evidence of biological warfare in Laos, right?"

The two doctors stared at him with blank faces.

"That's why you asked about my clothing. You're looking for samples of those same biological agents in Middle Valley, aren't you?"

Rhostok was searching their faces, waiting for confirmation, when a buzzer sounded in the outer hall. He heard the distant whoosh of the metal lobby doors, followed by the sound of running feet. Military boots, he thought, from the sound of the heavy heels.

Probably the MPs.

Probably summoned by Sherman with some unseen alarm.

Sure enough, a young MP stuck his head in the door.

"Are you needing any help in here, sir?" he asked Sherman. Behind the MP's helmeted head, Rhostok could see the barrel of his comrade's weapon.

Sherman stepped forward and put on his artificial smile again.

"What do you think?" he asked Rhostok. "Are we going to have a problem with you?"

Rhostok shook his head. "No," he muttered. "No problem."

At a nod from Sherman, the MP closed the door.

There was a brief hushed conversation outside. Only one set of footsteps walked down the corridor. That left one MP to guard the door, Rhostok thought.

"I'm afraid we're going to have to keep you here," Sherman said. "There's no point in attempting to get away. If you try to escape, the guard outside the door has instructions to shoot you."

Seventy-Two

"What the hell are you talking about?" Rhostok stared at him in disbelief. "You can't keep me here."

"It's just temporary," Sherman said. "Consider it protective incarceration. That would be the legal term, wouldn't it?"

"I'm a police officer," Rhostok reminded him. "I'm conducting a legitimate investigation."

"And this is a high-security military installation. I'm the commanding officer. If I say you stay here, then stay you will."

"Who the hell do you think you are?" Rhostok said. He kept his voice low, so as not to alarm the guard waiting outside the door. "You're impeding an investigation, you're violating my rights, you're interfering with the actions of a police officer, you're guilty of unlawful imprisonment, you're . . ."

"Calm down," Sherman said. "It's all for your own good. You're in no condition to go anywhere right now. The more effort you expend, the faster you're going to deteriorate."

"But I have to go back . . ." Rhostok said.

"Don't worry, we'll find the relic. Probably beside the body of that TV reporter. Robyn, what's her name, Cronin? Or should I say Kronstadt."

"You know her real name."

"Of course we know about her. Who do you think advised Winfield to use someone of Russian ancestry to get us the relic?"

"You bastard . . . but why?"

Sherman looked at him with a pitying smile.

"If it wasn't for your meddling, that reporter would have delivered the relic to Winfield, and this would have all been over."

"All those people who died . . ."

"Unfortunately, that would have happened in any event. Exposure to the relic doomed all of you."

Rhostok felt his eyes growing hot. His throat was tightening, just as Chandhuri said it would. The numbness was spreading to his other fingertips.

"You had Vanya killed . . . and the others . . . you bastard . . . you're behind it all . . ."

Heedless of the guard outside, Rhostok started towards Sherman. But the general sidestepped him easily.

"You see what I mean?" Sherman sighed. "You're already slowing down. You're in no condition to leave."

"We had nothing to do with those murders," Chandhuri suddenly said.

"That's enough," Sherman said.

"No," Chandhuri insisted. "I think he has a right to know."

"That's confidential information."

"He won't be able to tell anyone," Chandhuri said. "He's already dying. I think he has the right to know."

Sherman hesitated, as if trying to gauge Rhostok's condition.

"Well, what the hell," he relented. "Tell him. He's not going anywhere. And then we'll move him to an unoccupied lab where we can keep an eye on him."

"We had nothing to do with the murders of those old men," Chandhuri said in a gentle voice. "They were heroes. We would never be party to such a thing."

Maybe Chandhuri wouldn't, Rhostok thought. But Sherman? The young general's smile was beginning to look more like a smirk.

"Our people heard rumors about the relic from a Russian defector in the late 1960s," Chandhuri continued. "We weren't sure it even existed, that the stories might be Russian disinformation, part of an effort to confuse us. We've had people trying to track down the truth ever since."

"Winfield said the search started just last year," Rhostok pointed out.

"Mr. Winfield doesn't always tell the entire truth," Chandhuri said. "Did he warn you of the deadly nature of the relic?"

"We talked about the murders, but not about the people who bled to death."

"He should have warned you," she said. "He should have warned you of the dangers, even before the relic was found. It would have saved lives."

"And created panic," Sherman butted in.

"You are dying because you disturbed the relic," Chandhuri continued. "But not because of any superstitious curse. The relic was infected with a rare, antique strain of toxic mold that once grew on spoiled Russian wheat. Inhalation or contact with the mold spores produces a particularly virulent form of ATA in the victims. That's what triggered the bleeding in those who came in contact with the relic—a deadly toxin produced by a form of Russian mold."

That explained the wheaty odor of the relic, Rhostok thought. But it only led to another question.

"If it's so deadly, then why didn't Vanya die?" he asked. "Vanya carried the relic all the way back from Austria over fifty years ago. Why didn't the mold kill him?"

"Because he was born in Russia."

"You're in dangerous territory here, Chandhuri," Sherman warned her. "This is highly, highly confidential information."

Seventy-Three

"I don't care," Chandhuri said. "You can report me if you want to, but I will not have this man die with the belief that we are murderers. It would be very bad karma for him to take that belief into his next life, and bad karma for me to allow it."

She turned back to Rhostok, ignoring Sherman's anger.

"The man known as Vanya wasn't affected by the mold because he was born in Russia. He was naturally immune to this specific strain of toxin."

"How could that be?" Rhostok asked. "I thought you said the toxin was always fatal."

"It has to do with his being Russian," she said. "Not just having Russian ancestors, as you do, but with his actually being born *in* Russia, and having lived there as a child."

"I'm warning you, Chandhuri," Sherman said.

"Have you ever heard of fusaria?" she asked.

"No."

"This is national security information," Sherman said.

"He could learn this from any biology textbook," Chandhuri argued. Turning back to Rhostok, she explained, "Fusaria are fungal growths. There are thousands of types of fungi. Molds and mushrooms are two of the most common forms. Sometime during the 1930s, Russian scientists identified two types of fusaria with very unique properties. These particular fusaria had the ability to produce deadly microtoxins known as tricothecenes. Today they're more commonly known as the T2 toxins."

"From this point on, you're revealing classified information," Sherman cautioned her.

She seemed oblivious to his warning. "The T2 series are among the most potent natural toxins known to science. Exposure to these toxins triggers an exceptionally severe form of ATA, which produces symptoms such as those you observed in the Middle Valley victims, as well as a number of other side effects. All of which lead to an agonizing and certain death.

Perhaps you might not want to hear about it, considering your own exposure to this toxin."

"Go ahead," Rhostok said in a soft voice.

"You know about the bleeding, of course. But you don't know the extent of the hemorrhagic damage inflicted by these toxins. The internal bleeding affects every organ of the body, including the gonads in men, the uterus in women. The lungs fill with blood. Blood vessels burst in the brain. Severe destruction of bone marrow occurs. Excess blood can flow from any bodily orifice, including the mouth, the nose, the eyes, the ears, the anus. If the victim survives long enough, the extremities turn black and often burst open as gangrene and necrosis set in. And finally, the fingers, the testicles, the toes simply begin to drop off."

She paused and shrugged, as if trying to shake off an unpleasant memory.

"Of course, that only happens to those lucky enough to survive longer than forty-eight hours. Most victims don't."

Rhostok felt his breath catch in his throat. What she described was a lot different from the peaceful death of Wendell Franklin, or the sudden deaths of the others. He tried to hide the fear in his voice. Tried to keep his words calm and unemotional, even though the numbness in his fingertips warned of the impending horror.

"So the longer I live, the worse it's going to be?" he asked.

"I'm sorry," she said. "I don't mean to imply all those symptoms will apply to you, specifically. I was talking about the general run of T2 cases."

"But that's pretty much what I can expect, isn't it?"

She nodded her head sadly.

"If this T2 is so deadly, how come we've never heard about it?" Rhostok asked. "Every other disease seems to get a lot of publicity. Why not this one?"

"Because it hasn't been seen in the United States until now. Almost all of the human deaths from T2 toxins, and there have been hundreds of thousands in the last century alone, have occurred in Russia."

"Russia?" Rhostok was puzzled. "Why Russia?"

"The outbreaks were due primarily to the peculiarities of the Russian system of agriculture. You're aware, I'm sure, of how primitive Russian harvesting and storage procedures have always been. The fusaria that produce the T2 toxins grow mostly in grains such as wheat, millet, and rye. With their poor harvests, the Russians have always used every last bit of grain they grow. Infected grains are often mixed in with the good, contaminating the entire lot. And the primitive storage facilities are the ideal breeding ground for these particular fusaria.

"As a result, the world's most potent strains of T2 toxins are those found in Russia, where they have been thriving and infecting the population for centuries. There are probably a number of strains to which the average Russian has already acquired a certain amount of immunity, but there are many others that can still cause widespread death. There've been major outbreaks in 1916, 1920, in the 1930s, during the Second World War, and even as late as 1970. This is the first time we've seen an outbreak in America."

"Fortunately, we know the source of this particular outbreak," Sherman said.

"You're certain it's the relic?" Rhostok asked. "How can you be sure?"

"That should be obvious even to you," Sherman said. "By your own testimony, everyone who bled to death had contact with the hand you found in the vault. Therefore, the hand must be the carrier."

"But how did it get infected in the first place?"

"There's nothing complicated about it. These toxins all start with simple fungal growths."

"The hand was in the vault for almost half a century."

"The T2 toxins are very stable," Sherman said. "They've been stored for years without losing their killing power."

"They've been stored?" Rhostok asked in a shocked voice. "Why would anyone store such a deadly thing?"

Sherman smiled, as if enjoying a private joke.

"If you bothered to read that entire article about Yellow Rain, you'd know that T2 toxins were weaponized toxins to be used in biological warfare. The major powers have stores of T2, in addition to nerve gases, phosgene, adamsite, tularemia, and anthrax viruses, along with dozens of other chemical and biological poisons."

"I thought those were outlawed. Aren't there treaties prohibiting their use?"

"As weapons, yes. But in research laboratories, no. And of course there are rogue nations such as North Korea and Iran that ignore the treaties. It's public knowledge that the Russians actually increased production of biological weapons after the treaties were signed. And as long as even a single nation possesses such weapons, other nations must learn how to defend against them. There's a tremendous amount of research in this field going on all over the world. Most of it is devoted to finding vaccines and antidotes, which isn't banned by existing treaties."

"So that's why the professor wanted me to call you." Rhostok finally understood.

"Altschiller must have seen the mold spores on the relic," Sherman said. "But like I said, he was primarily a bone collector, not a biologist. He was so fascinated with the spiritual aspects of apparently incorruptible flesh, he never considered the spores might be toxic fusaria. Not until he recognized his own symptoms."

"You still haven't told me why the toxin didn't kill Vanya." Rhostok repeated his earlier question. "He was exposed to the relic more than anyone else. If the toxin is as deadly as you claim, he should have died fifty years ago in Austria."

"It's a case of classic Darwinian theory," Chandhuri explained. "Over the centuries, hundreds of thousands of Russians have died from the various strains of fusaria and the toxins they produce. But eventually, immunities build up in the population. People who are susceptible to a particular fusarium die, while the ones who are immune survive, until finally an entire population consists of people with an immunity to a particular strain of fusarium. In the 1880 outbreak, for example, the mortality rate of those exposed was estimated at seventy percent. In the 1920 outbreak, the mortality rate of those infected with an identical strain dropped to ten percent. So we are assuming the immunity to individual strains is growing in Russia. The same thing happens in other species, where insects build up immunity to pesticides, and where bacteria build up immunity to penicillin."

Sherman interrupted her, speaking rapidly, apparently deciding that if any secrets were to be revealed, he would be the one to reveal the most important.

"The story is that the monks at Starokonstantinov knew of a unique strain of the fusarium, one to which the Russian people had developed a natural immunity. Apparently they learned of it from a fourteenth-century treatise on wheat in the monastery's collection of ancient books. It was useless information until the Rasputin relic turned up and the monks were searching for a way to protect what would become the monastery's greatest treasure.

"Well, this long-forgotten fusarium turned out to be the ideal solution. The monks realized the fusarium would trigger a fatal hemorrhage in foreigners, but would have no effect on the native Russians who came in contact with it. The monks dusted the Rasputin relic with that fusarium, confident that it would protect their treasure from being stolen by foreigners while allowing it to be safely venerated by the Russian faithful. Ironic, wasn't it? They were using a bleeding disease to protect the relic of a man who was supposed to have the power over blood.

"The Germans who looted the monastery and actually handled the relic probably *did* bleed to death. But in wartime, who noticed? Especially considering the horrors of the Russian front. So there's your 'curse' of Rasputin." Sherman laughed. "It's known today as the Rasputin toxin. There's nothing mystical about it."

"Vanya Danilovitch was born in Russia," Chandhuri said. "He inherited and grew up with a natural immunity to the Rasputin toxin. Therefore, the toxin on the relic had no effect on him. But the others, the bank president, the tax agent, your policeman, poor Professor Altschiller—they were of other nationalities. They had no immunity. That's why they died. You have Russian ancestors. That's the only reason you've lasted this long."

As she explained how the immunity diminished through the generations, Rhostok seemed to remember there was someone else who should be dead, too. Someone else who had been in the vault. Everyone else who entered the vault, including Nicole, was infected and dead or dying . . . except for . . . who? Someone he couldn't quite remember. He winced as a sharp pain shot through his skull.

"Do you have a headache now?" Sherman asked.

"Another symptom?" Rhostok asked.

"Perhaps you should lie down," Chandhuri said.

"No, I'm . . . sort of okay," Rhostok lied.

"I'd like to be getting his symptoms on tape," Sherman said. "We should be clearing a room with a video monitor."

"Why? Why should we do that?" Chandhuri asked.

"So that we have a record. Proof."

"Is death not enough proof? He's a human, not a laboratory animal to be studied."

"How much longer do I have?" Rhostok asked. It was getting harder to speak.

"A few hours, tops," Sherman said.

In a gentler voice, Chandhuri elaborated. "Perhaps five hours," she said gently. "Perhaps six. I'll bring you some morphine when the pain gets more intense."

"But why . . . why am I dying?" Rhostok asked. "My ancestors were Russian. I should be immune . . . shouldn't I?"

"Your grandparents grew up in Russia," Chandhuri explained. "So they were immune. But environmental factors weaken the immunity. Your parents were born in the United States and grew up with American diets. You're the second generation in your family to be born in America. Like your parents, you had no exposure to any fusarium in the American food chain to help maintain your immunity. The only reason you've survived this long is due to whatever immunity you inherited from your grandparents. It's your Russian genes that have kept you alive."

"But those genes have weakened," Sherman said. "They've been able to fight off the toxin for a while, but they aren't strong enough to save you."

The little fingertip on Rhostok's left hand was turning numb now, the first of the fingers on that hand to go. He stubbornly tried to will the feeling back, to use the power of his mind to force the numbness to retreat. It didn't work. Yet some inner voice told him not to give up, no matter how hopeless the situation might be. It was the voice of his grandfather, describing how he escaped across the frozen steppes after the slaughter at Voronezh. It was the voice that comforted a little boy when his parents died, urged him to keep going, keep breathing, keep thinking. With the stubbornness his grandfather had instilled in him, Rhostok rallied his spirit and returned to the question that still remained unanswered.

"If you didn't kill Vanya and the others . . . then . . . who?"

"We don't know exactly," Sherman equivocated.

"In a general sense, we know that Russian nationals are involved," Chandhuri quickly explained. "At least one, perhaps two, according to Winfield."

"But if the relic is infected with this deadly toxin, why would anyone be willing to murder people to recover it?"

"You still don't get it, do you?" Sherman said. "It's not the relic we want. None of us give a damn about the relic."

Seventy-Four

"It's not the relic that everyone is after. It's the toxin on the relic," Chandhuri explained. "Whoever killed those old men wanted to recover the toxin spores and take them back to Russia. We want to stop that from happening and recover the spores ourselves if possible."

"But . . . why?"

"For Christ's sake, man, haven't you been listening?" Sherman nearly shouted at him. "The Rasputin toxin is the silver bullet that everybody in biochemical warfare has been searching for. Forget about Star Wars and smart bombs and the nuclear arsenal, or any of the latest technological marvels. From the Russian point of view, the Rasputin toxin is the single most important weapon in the modern world. A tiny spore from a monastery in the Ukraine could make Russia impregnable."

As usual, it was up to Chandhuri to explain things in a calmer manner.

"The problem with biochemical weaponry is that by nature it is nondiscriminatory. Such weapons are deadly to soldiers on both sides. Wind shifts and weather factors make them impossible to control on any battlefield. That's the real reason Iraq didn't use biochemical weapons during the Gulf War and why no other country has used them since the First World War. Not because of any sense of morality. They were afraid of killing their own troops. And troops advancing after a biochemical attack have to cope with soil contamination and other long-lasting residual effects. That's why such weapons have become the dinosaurs of modern warfare."

"Unless . . ." Sherman said. "Unless you come up with a toxin that kills everyone except your own people. And that's exactly what the Rasputin toxin does. The Russians can release it on a battlefield without worrying about the safety of their own troops. They wouldn't even have to wear protective gear. The Rasputin toxin could be used to defend Russian cities or other areas with large civilian populations, because the whole damn country is immune. It's the perfect defensive weapon, which fits the Russian bunker mentality. Think what it would have meant when Hitler attacked in 1941. If the Russian military had known about the Rasputin toxin then, they could have wiped out the invading German armies to the last man, without harming a single Russian citizen or destroying a single building."

Rhostok was finally beginning to understand.

"Our countries are friendly today," Sherman continued. "But that could change in the future, and then we'd face a real problem. The Rasputin toxin would make biological warfare practical on the most massive scale, while insulating the Russians from its effects. No one would dare attack a nation that possessed such a weapon. It therefore becomes the ultimate implement of war."

"And remarkably economical, too," Chandhuri added. "It's the one weapons system even a bankrupt nation could afford to produce."

Certainly worth killing a few old men for, Rhostok thought.

"The Rasputin relic contains the only known spores of this fusarium," Chandhuri continued. "The others were all destroyed when the monastery was burned. We simply have to recover the relic before they do. Either that, or destroy it."

"Now it's gone missing," Sherman said. "We were so damn close, and now it's gone."

Before the young general left the room, he instructed Chandhuri to find an unoccupied lab with a working closed-circuit TV camera, where they could keep Rhostok under observation.

"Rivers of blood . . ." Chandhuri mused after Sherman left. "Wasn't that part of Rasputin's final prophecy? And now, a single spore from Rasputin's hand, grown in a culture, multiplied a millionfold, and then released on the world . . . that would truly fulfill his terrible prophecy. What an awful prospect." She shook her head in dismay.

"Perhaps you were right," she told Rhostok. "Perhaps this is the curse of Rasputin. This is his revenge on the world that rejected him."

Maybe that was true, Rhostok thought. But it wasn't Rasputin who killed Vanya and the other veterans.

And as he sat there, he finally remembered who else had been in the vault.

Too late, perhaps.

But now he was certain he knew at least one of Vanya's killers.

Seventy-Five

As the morning sunlight poured through the window, Nicole stood naked before *Episkop* Sergius.

Once again he stared at her with iron gray eyes that seemed able to penetrate into the depths of her mind, stripping away any resistance, any false modesty. He had cured her instantly, miraculously, and spirited her away from the stunned Dr. Zarubin. The *Episkop* was her savior and, for that reason, she felt no shame in exposing herself to him.

She waited patiently for him to decide what to do.

Sergius watched her from a chair barely two feet away from her. Close enough to reach out and touch her heavy breasts. Close enough to caress the nipples that were stiffening in the cool air. She waited while he slowly stroked his beard, while his eyes examined her naked skin.

How many times had she exposed herself to men before? But that was always with the seductive camouflage of darkness and cosmetics. She had never allowed herself to be exposed like this, stripped of makeup, her hair a tangled mess, without the erotic masquerade of carefully chosen under-garments. But none of that mattered now. The *Episkop* had forgiven her sins, cured her of her evil impulses, and she was now his to do with as he willed.

"Turn slowly," Sergius said.

She obeyed without question, pausing slightly when her body was in profile. It was the view of her that most men enjoyed. It was a movement she had practiced in front of mirrors. Inhale a little, so that her chest expanded, soft mounds of flesh protruding above the hard contours of her ribs. Stomach flat, the result of daily aerobics. Navel swelling a bit until it disappeared into the thicket between the tops of her thighs.

He still made no move to touch her.

Maybe he was just a watcher, she thought. She had her share of those. Men who preferred to look. Passive men.

"Do not confuse me with those other men," he said, reading her thoughts.

Perhaps he was testing himself again, she thought. She recalled the strange ritual he had performed that first night, claiming that he was pit-ting himself against temptation, building his discipline. Well, in the past she had tempted men who had tried to resist her, men who treated her much worse than this priest did. If anyone deserved what pleasures she could offer, it was him, this holy man who had delivered her from pain.

"You must rid yourself of such thoughts," he said with impatience. "They interfere with my concentration."

In spite of his admonition, she felt herself responding to him. Her body cried out for his touch. She wanted to feel the roughness of his hands on her flesh again. To feel his fingertips caressing her navel. To tremble at the mysterious energy that flowed from him.

But Sergius didn't move.

He closed his eyes and blessed himself.

"Lord *Khristos,* I pray for the soul of this woman you sent to me," he murmured. "Deliver her from the evil thoughts that infest her mind, which befoul her entire being and create a home for the putrid manifestations of an ancient evil, the loathsome abomination that still inhabits her flesh."

Nicole was a woman accustomed to compliments, words of praise for her lovely figure. This was a time for tenderness, the sensitive moment when she was ready to submit to him. Why did he have to destroy it by unleashing such vile language at her? The way he mixed his epithets with prayer, with appeals to God, seemed to give them an added, almost sacrilegious force. It stripped away any erotic feelings she had, making her suddenly conscious of her nudity, of the unreality of the situation, of the barren room in which in the *Episkop* sat contemplating her naked body with what looked like distaste.

For the first time since childhood, Nicole blushed in front of a man. She could feel the redness spread from her face to her neck to her chest.

"It is good that you have once again rediscovered the feeling of shame," Sergius said. "It is a sign that you are regaining your innocence." His voice was powerful and resonant again, full of the strength that had overwhelmed her in the hospital. "But it is not you whom I denounce. I denounce the *Diavol* that still infects your blood. He lies silent now, but he is still there within you. My powers are not yet strong enough to banish both him and the evil he has visited upon you. But that will soon change. For you are indeed the anointed one, selected from among all women to help me fulfill the prophecy."

His hands came forward. She expected them to embrace her, to explore the delights of her naked body. Instead, he raised his hands to her head, pressing them tightly against her temples. She felt dizzy. Her knees grew weak. All that prevented her from falling was the firm grip of his hands on her head. He brought his forehead closer to hers, until they were almost touching. The pupils of his eyes grew larger and brighter, until she was unaware of the rest of him.

"I see within your soul my salvation," he said.

The whole substance of his being seemed to concentrate itself in his eyes. It was a hard gray gaze that seemed to penetrate into the deepest and most hidden places of her mind.

"You were once a sinner," Sergius said. "I too have sinned. And, like you, my sins were those of the flesh. But my sins were far greater because I was a man of God, a holy *starets* who once had the power to cure the sick. By taking advantage of the women who came to me seeking help, I lost that power. Now you, another sinner, have come to help restore that power to me."

She resisted at first, but his mental powers were too strong. Slowly, her thoughts began to cloud. She glimpsed dozens of images: her brutal deflowering, the horrors her "stepfather" had inflicted upon her, and the faceless men who followed him. And then, joyfully, the images that had haunted her life were gone. Wiped out forever, she hoped, by the mystical power of Sergius's gaze. It was a moment of sheer ecstasy. She gladly surrendered her mind to him, allowing his thoughts to merge with hers, overpowering her will, making it part of his own. There couldn't be anything wrong with this, she thought, as she felt a lifetime of fear and shame evaporate. She wanted to shout with joy, to cry out in celebration of her deliverance. But locked in his gaze, all she could do was stand mute and stiff before him, submitting to his extraordinary display of mental power until, finally, he was satisfied.

Slowly, the *Episkop* withdrew his pupils from inside her head.

His eyes grew smaller.

They shrank back into their sockets, back behind the protective skin of their lids.

Nicole's mind was limp, exhausted from the strange mental coupling. She felt a thin line of sweat trickling down the valley between her breasts. She wanted to lie down somewhere. Lie down and sleep. Sleep until she could recover from the unusual encounter.

"You are once again a true innocent," Sergius said. "I have taken your sins upon myself."

His voice echoed and reverberated deep inside her skull, which felt now like a hollowed and empty shell ready to be filled with whatever Sergius decided to place there.

A loud knock on the door interrupted them.

"*Vayditye!*" Sergius called out.

At his command, the door opened to reveal Svetlana wearing a black dress with a high white collar. A white lace handkerchief, folded to form a triangle, lay neatly on her gray hair, with the center tip of the fabric touching the top of her forehead. Tiny hands held an enormous tray.

Sergius appeared too exhausted to help the old woman. She placed the tray on the floor between his chair and Nicole's feet. On the tray was a white ceramic pitcher of water, a white ceramic bowl, a folded white towel, and a large block of yellow soap. From the soap came the powerful chemical odor of naphtha.

Keeping her head lowered, Svetlana slowly withdrew from the room.

"Now you must cleanse yourself," Sergius said. "Before we can proceed, you must perform the rite of purification."

His words restored motion to Nicole's limbs. Obediently, she knelt before him to begin the rite. Sergius bowed his head and began rhythmically chanting a series of prayers, his words picking up speed until they were running together breathlessly. From time to time, he struck his chest with a closed fist.

Late morning sunlight streamed through the window as she bathed. The water was cold and refreshing on her skin. She shivered with pleasure at the rivulets that raced down her legs to the floor. The harsh chemical soap foamed quickly and filled the room with its pungent fumes. She washed slowly in the golden sunbeams, stroking her body, stretching her arms, arching her back, and caressing her breasts with the cleansing water. Sergius seemed to have little interest in her naked body, except to be certain she performed a thorough cleansing.

"Wash away the sins of the flesh, *malyutchka,*" he interrupted his prayers to say. "Remove the fingerprints of a thousand men who ravished your body."

The fumes from the soap made her feel lightheaded. The naphtha burned her eyes and felt harsh on the sensitive area under her arms, around her breasts, and especially between her legs. The powerful cleansing chemicals penetrated her pores until the underlying flesh tingled in response.

Each breath she took drew more of the powerful fumes into her body. They burned her throat and nasal passages as they made their way deep into her lungs, where she felt a sharp pain as the fumes seemed to eat away at the very lining of the air sacs.

"Purify your inner self, *malyutchka,*" the priest murmured. "Remove the inhaled residue of evil acts performed in rented rooms."

No sauna, no massage, no whirlpool had ever been able to produce the purifiying sensation induced by the harsh soap. When she was finished washing, her flesh tingled in a way she hadn't felt since childhood. The invisible residue of age was washed from her skin, exposing a freshness and smoothness she hadn't seen since her teenage years. Her breathing felt clear and strong. A rush of sweet air flowed through her lungs, bringing with it a powerful burst of energy. Even the colors in the room seemed more vibrant to her eyes. She felt young again, strong and fearless, and, yes, even virginal.

As the *Episkop* had promised, she was purified in both flesh and spirit.

"You will pray with me now," he said. "And this evening, when we perform the ceremony that fully restores the power of healing to me, I will banish the bleeding from your body forever, *malyutchka.*"

With an almost fatherly tenderness, he carefully arranged her hair, brushing it back over her ears until he was content with her appearance. She felt childlike again.

"Together this evening, we will both be redeemed."

Seventy-Six

When Dr. Chandhuri repeated her promise to bring him morphine, Rhostok realized the finality of his situation. Death, probably painful, was only hours away. Chandhuri was searching for a room in which Rhostok could be observed while he died. His last moments would be videotaped and time-coded, just like those of the monkey he had seen earlier, so that unknown scientists could study his death throes.

Would death come quietly, he wondered? He didn't want to go like Altschiller or Bruckner, in some violent hemorrhage that left him struggling for his last breath in a pool of his own blood. It would be simpler if he took the morphine Chandhuri supplied, made a small incision in his fingertip, no larger than Wendell Franklin's wound, lay down on the floor, closed his eyes, and drifted off into final sleep. The coroner said it wasn't a bad way to go. Let the bleeding start, let the blood drain slowly from his heart until all the systems shut down and his brain stopped functioning. Dying in that manner would be the easiest way to go, Rhostok thought.

But he was too angry to die.

He was angry at the scientists who locked him in here like some laboratory animal.

He was angry at Vanya's killers who even now roamed free in Middle Valley.

He was angry because all this time he had overlooked an important detail that positively identified at least one of the killers. Now, too late, he knew who it was. And with that knowledge, he was more certain than ever that the death of Nicole's husband was a carefully concealed murder, too.

In explaining the frightening ability of the relic to cause hemorrhagic death, Chandhuri and Sherman had supplied the motive. Unknowingly, they had also supplied the key to a killer's identity. The proof was in the list of people who were exposed to the toxin.

Altschiller was right when he said, "It is in the deviations from the normal that identity can be proven."

If Rhostok had only seen the deviation earlier, he could have unmasked a killer, someone who had been comfortably hiding behind a false identity. Probably one of the *shpala* his grandfather warned him about: the "sleepers" trained and sent here as teenagers to blend into American society and, when the time came, perform whatever tasks their masters in Russia required. He thought of his grandfather's admonition: *Trust no one. Expect betrayal.* The old man was always wary of the *shpala*, but Rhostok had assumed that with the end of the Cold War, such infiltrations had also ended. The knowledge of how skillfully he had been duped infuriated Rhostok. And as the fury built, he felt some of his strength returning. He had to get back to Middle Valley before he died.

But escape seemed impossible. He considered the barriers he'd have to overcome: windows barred, door locked, armed MPs patrolling, no weapon for him to use. Even if he overpowered Chandhuri when she came back with the promised morphine, even if somehow he took away the door guard's weapon, there were still the steel doors, the lobby guards, the double electrified fence to stop him. One signal from any guard, and there'd be dozens, maybe hundreds of others converging on the laboratory. This was, after all, a military installation, with guards all the way back to the main gate. It was hopeless, he thought. There was no way out.

"How are you feeling now?" Chandhuri asked when she returned.

"Angry," Rhostok said.

"I understand. This is not a good way to die."

"How much longer do I have?"

"Five hours, perhaps six."

"That's the same thing you said a half-hour ago."

Chandhuri offered him a sad smile. "I wish I could say it was longer. But even the five hours is guesswork, based on your current symptoms. We simply don't know enough about this particular toxin. That's why Sherman wants to observe you."

"Five hours would be enough time for me to get back home, to die in my own bed."

"Better than dying here," Chandhuri agreed. "Better than having your dying moments videotaped and observed by scientists."

"Like they're doing with the monkey across the hall?"

"And with the rabbits and the mice and the dogs and the goats . . ." She shook her head sadly. "That is the most difficult part of the work we do. At least it is for me. Some of the others . . . they get used to it. But never me. In my country, we revere all living creatures."

"Then why do you do it?"

Chandhuri let out a long sigh. Her eyes focused on some distant point beyond the walls of the room. "When I was a child, I lived in Bhopal, a large city in central India. The main source of employment in the town was a Union Carbide plant that produced pesticides. On the night of December 3, 1984, a valve was accidentally opened, a safety disc burst, and a cloud of methyl isocyanate gas was released. The gas killed two thousand people within the first few hours. The official death toll was later put at five thousand, although unofficial reports claim that more than twenty thousand people died. I was away at college in Madras at the time. But my entire family, my mother, my father, five brothers, and three sisters died from that invisible gas."

"I'm sorry for you," Rhostok said.

"A dying man feels sorry for me," Chandhuri smiled sadly. "How miserable my life has become. But such is the working of karma. I knew this great tragedy was inflicted on me because of some terrible deeds I must have performed in a previous existence. To change my karma, I decided to devote my life to finding ways to protect people from future mass poisonings. And that is how a peace-loving Hindu came to work at an American army biochemical research laboratory."

"Surrounded by people working with poison gases and chemicals," Rhostok said.

"Some of them chemically similar to the one that killed my family," Chandhuri responded. "Perhaps that is how I will die, too. A broken vial, an undetected leak in one of these rooms, a failure of the monitoring systems. Don't think we don't work with fear as our companion."

She pointed to the emergency biohazard suit on the wall. It hung at the ready, folded up inside a plastic tube. The white hood, large enough to cover the head and shoulders, had a small glass eyepiece. A flexible rubber hose connected the hood to an air tank. "In case of any leak, that unit would be the only way out. The difference between life and death. The only problem is that nerve gases and toxins are invisible and odorless. We have a joke here that the best way to tell that a leak has occurred is when you see people start dropping dead."

"Maybe you should get yourself some canaries," Rhostok said. "That's what my grandfather used in the coal mines to detect methane gas. The canaries would die first, because they were more sensitive."

"Perhaps your canaries are more accurate indicators than any we have here," Chandhuri said. "However, I have no fear of death. I hope only that when it comes, it arrives quickly and without too much pain."

"That shot of morphine should take care of any pain for me," Rhostok said.

Chandhuri stared at him. She seemed to be studying Rhostok, as if trying to make up her mind about something.

"The morphine?" Rhostok asked again.

"You will get no morphine," Chandhuri said.

"You said I'd need morphine for the pain."

"I'm sorry," Chandhuri said. "I tried to convince General Sherman, but he will not allow it. Morphine will mask the symptoms. For scientific reasons, he wants the symptoms to progress naturally, as they would in the field."

"He wants to watch me suffer." Rhostok was stunned.

"It is purely for research purposes, he says, so that we can better understand the effects of the toxin. Unlike the Russians, we have no experience with T2 poisoning."

"You bastards," Rhostok said. "You want to watch me die, like the monkeys in the next room."

Seventy-Seven

"At least your family died in the privacy of their own home," Rhostok told her. "They didn't have men in white coats watching them squirm and scream out in pain."

"Please keep your voice down," Chandhuri said.

"You give me all that phony sensitive stuff about how you revere all living things, but you're going to be looking at a TV monitor like the others, taking notes while you watch me die."

"I will not watch you die," Chandhuri said. She was looking past Rhostok to the shelves of chemical jars that lined the far wall.

"Why not?" Rhostok asked. "Too many bad memories about the way your own family died?"

"That could be a reason." She rose and walked across the room, where she studied the labels on a row of jars containing various liquids.

"Or is it something to do with your damn karma?"

"That, also," Chandhuri said. She selected a jar containing a dense blue liquid from the top shelf, and another, almost identical jar with a similar liquid from the bottom shelf.

"So you're going to let the others watch, let someone else do your dirty work."

Chandhuri tested the cover on the jar to be certain it was secure. "No one will watch you die," she said. "I am here to help you."

"Help me?" Rhostok asked. "Do you have a cure?"

"There is no cure. Not yet. But I will help you escape, so that you may die with dignity."

Trust no one. Rhostok could hear his grandfather's voice. *Expect betrayal.*

"What's in it for you?" he asked.

"A better life when I am reborn." Chandhuri carefully placed the jar on the laboratory table. "Ever since Bhopal, I have spent my life trying to do good works in an effort to change my karma. To rob you of your dignity in your dying moments would be very bad karma for me. It will destroy any chance for happiness I might have in my next life."

"You really believe that?" Rhostok said.

"That is how I was raised." Chandhuri opened a drawer, searched around until she found a package of labels and a black felt marker. "Now please do not speak too loudly. I have turned off the audio monitor, but there is still a guard outside the door."

"You could lose your job for helping me," Rhostok said.

"A small risk, compared to the consequences I might face in my next incarnation."

"How do I get past the guard? Sherman gave him orders to shoot me if I try to escape."

"The guard will be no problem."

"What about the other guards? The steel doors? The electrified fence? How do I get past them?"

"You will walk past them all. No one will stop you." Chandhuri held up the first jar she had selected. "This blue liquid is methylene chloride. When it is heated to a temperature of five hundred six degrees, it produces carbonyl chloride, more commonly known as phosgene gas, which was the deadliest poison gas used by the German Army in World War I. Much worse than mustard gas. It is instantly fatal. It was responsible for eighty percent of the poison gas deaths in that war."

"Wait a minute, hold on there," Rhostok said. "You're not going to release poison gas just to get me out of here."

"Of course not," Chandhuri smiled. She rubbed the black magic marker across the label, obliterating the chemical name. "In its present state and in atmospheric concentrations of less than two hundred parts per million, methylene chloride is a relatively harmless chemical. It's used in a huge number of products, everything from paint thinner to aerosol sprays; you'll even find residues of it in the decaffeinated coffee you drink. At concentrations of eight hundred parts per million, it produces irritation to the eyes and throat, but not to worry, because it degrades quickly in the air."

"If it's so damn harmless, what's the point?"

"This is a very dangerous work environment," Chandhuri said. "We all worry about the chemicals and gases we work with. That's why you see all that equipment on the ceiling. Those electronic monitors constantly test the air quality in every laboratory. Specialized galvanic electrochemical sensors are used to detect gases such as phosgene. And since methylene chloride is a precursor to phosgene, the sensors will detect its dispersal."

A slow smile spread over Rhostok's face as he watched Chandhuri work on the second bottle and explained exactly how to penetrate the laboratory's multiple levels of security. The simplicity of her two-jar deception plan convinced Rhostok it could work.

Chandhuri went over the procedures carefully, warning Rhostok that any mistake could be fatal. He slipped the two jars under his belt, inside his shirt, and followed her out the door. The guard fell into step behind them, rifle at the ready, as Chandhuri led the way to the other laboratory.

He could feel the liquid sloshing in the two jars as he walked. Heating a teaspoonful of liquid from one jar over an open flame could kill everyone in the building. Was it only mildly noxious in this form, he wondered? Or was it a deadly killer, with Chandhuri using him as an instrument of revenge for the death of her family? Killing dozens of biochemists could be her retribution for the deadly cloud the chemists allowed to settle over Bhopal. For all Rhostok knew, Chandhuri would be outside the building perimeter, safe from harm, when he smashed the first bottle.

Rhostok was having second thoughts. After all, he had little to gain. At most, a few hours more of life before dying on the laboratory floor. *Trust no one.* And yet Chandhuri, who had been through a tragedy as great in some ways as the one his grandfather had endured, had placed her own trust in karma. "It's the way I was raised," she had said.

Now Rhostok had to decide whether he was willing to place his trust in another person's spiritual beliefs.

Seventy-Eight

Chandhuri stood in the darkened viewing room behind General Sherman, who had commandeered the chief security officer's upholstered swivel chair. Flanking the general were two security officers and Sherman's male secretary. Before them a bank of twelve-inch monitors relayed black-and-white images from the closed-circuit cameras in various laboratories.

On one of the TV screens, they could observe Rhostok's activities in the laboratory to which he had been taken. A videorecorder in extended-play mode was taping the images. One of the security people had just assured Sherman that the tape would provide six hours of recording time, at least one hour longer than the general expected Rhostok to survive.

The room to which Chandhuri had taken Rhostok was one of the surplus laboratories, stripped of its more elaborate scientific equipment. Only the most basic items, such as a Bunsen burner, a battered scale, and a few glass retorts had been left behind. Bulk chemicals, salts, and phosphates were stored out of sight in the floor cabinets.

Chandhuri watched the black-and-white image of Rhostok moving about the room, testing the windows and the doors, staring angrily up at the camera, which was mounted in a corner of the ceiling.

"Restless, isn't he?" Sherman said.

"Like a caged tiger," she responded with a grim smile.

They watched the image of Rhostok open a storage cabinet. He paused to study the contents, removing one container after another.

"He thinks he's going to find some way to escape," Sherman chuckled. "At least it'll give us something interesting to watch until he collapses."

The figure on the screen examined a jar of dark liquid, which Chandhuri recognized as one of the two jars she had slipped to him. She was surprised at how carefully he had concealed them up to that point, how adroitly he made it appear that he had just found the first jar in the cabinet.

"What's that he's got?" Sherman asked.

Neither Chandhuri nor any of the security people responded.

Rhostok threw the jar against a wall. The jar shattered, covering the floor with shards of glass and a pool of liquid. The point of impact was directly below one of the electrochemical sensors that constantly monitored the air.

"He's really angry," Sherman smiled.

"Can you blame him?"

"Make a note of his behavior," Sherman told the secretary. "It might suggest a neurological effect in addition to the physical ones."

No one except Chandhuri appeared to notice the barely visible fumes that rose from the remains of the shattered jar. They watched the screen as Rhostok's tiny image examined another jar, one which contained a similar dark liquid.

"Now what?" Sherman asked.

The tiny figure on the screen looked around the room, its gaze finally settling on a Bunsen burner. Still holding the jar, the figure turned a small knob on the side of the burner. A bright flame came to life.

"We should have disconnected the damn burner," Sherman muttered. "But what the hell, he can't do that much damage."

They watched, fascinated, as Rhostok's image placed a metal stand directly over the flame. Glancing up at the camera, the image smiled. He crossed the room, took a chair, and held the jar with the dark liquid up to the camera. It was close enough for the auto-focus lens to read the label.

"Methylene chloride," Chandhuri said, just in case anybody wasn't paying attention.

"What's he up to?" An edginess crept into Sherman's voice.

From the cheap speakers connected to the closed-circuit cameras came Rhostok's tinny-sounding voice.

"Since I'm going to die anyway," Rhostok said. "I might as well go fast."

When Rhostok's image returned to the Bunsen burner and poured some of the liquid onto the metal stand, Sherman jumped up. "Methylene chloride!" he shouted. "The bastard's heating it up! He's making phosgene gas! JesusChristAlmightyGod, he's committing suicide!"

They watched the tiny figure on the screen suddenly stiffen, clutch its throat, and collapse. After a single twitch of its legs, Rhostok's image was still.

"The bastard killed himself," Sherman said. "Damn him to hell!"

Chandhuri wondered how long it would take for the invisible vapor from the first jar to be detected by the sensors.

"If it gets into the ventilation system . . ." she said.

Before she could finish, a central alarm went off in the hallway. The red alarm light intended to alert any hearing-impaired employees started its frantic flashing. From outside the building, another siren began to wail, warning others to clear the area.

For what was probably less than a fraction of a second, no one moved. They stared at Rhostok's motionless image on the screen, as if their brains still weren't connecting what they had witnessed with the clamoring of the sirens.

It was a security officer who broke the silence. "He's dead. Let's get the hell out of here."

In the mad rush for the exit, Sherman shoved his secretary aside as he tore an emergency breathing unit from the wall.

"Phosgene!" he shouted beneath breaths from the mask. "Evacuate! Evacuate!"

Chandhuri was the last one out of the room. She walked slowly into the hallway, where she was jostled and almost knocked over by panicked employees rushing for the exit.

Her thin lips spread into a smile that suggested she was pleased with what she had accomplished.

Seventy-Nine

The air in the room smelled sweet and mildly anesthetic.

Rhostok knew he was dying, but it wasn't from the jars of blue liquid Chandhuri had supplied. Only one of those two jars, the one he had thrown against the wall, contained methylene chloride. As Chandhuri assured him, it was only mildly noxious as long as it remained at room temperature. But since it was a precursor to phosgene, when he smashed the jar, the vapors would be detected by the sensors, and the appropriate alarms sounded. The second jar, the one with the phony label, contained an inert blue liquid. When he heated it over the burner flame the inert liquid produced nothing worse than an odor much like maple syrup. But those watching from the viewing room would be convinced he had cooked up a fatal gas.

Following Chandhuri's instructions, he remained motionless on the floor, feigning death. It seemed like morbid practice for what would happen to him soon enough. He was careful not to move, not to give off any signal he was still alive even while the main alarm went off. He listened to the whooping, undulating siren that blasted through speakers in every room and echoed down the hallways. He could see the red alarm light flashing.

An automated voice interrupted the siren: "Biohazard alert! Evacuate the building! This is not a drill! Evacuate the building!"

Still following Chandhuri's instructions, Rhostok waited fifteen seconds after the first announcement, while the building erupted in panic.

From the hallway outside, he heard doors opening, feet thumping, fists pounding on doors.

The automated computer voice interrupted the siren again: "Biohazard alert! Evacuate the building! This is not a drill! Evacuate the building!"

The MP guarding the laboratory threw open the door, shouted for Rhostok, and then apparently seeing the protruding legs, didn't shout a second time. By then, Rhostok was certain no one was any longer watching on the closed-circuit TV.

He slowly lifted himself from the floor. The Rasputin toxin was spreading through his system, making even that simple act a difficult procedure. Following Chandhuri's instructions, he opened the glass case housing the wall-mounted biohazard suit. He unzipped the plastic protective sleeve and stepped into the bulky white plastic coveralls. The breathing unit was heavier than he thought. But the possibility of escape restored some of his energy. He lifted the bulky air tank over his shoulders, adjusted the straps, and pulled the white rubberized hood over his head. He checked the face mask to ensure there were no air leaks. Following the directions on the wall, he pulled the restraining pin from the air tank. A cold, metallic-tasting rush of oxygen automatically flowed through the tube and into his mouth. He felt like an astronaut, ready to walk out into space in his white self-breathing suit.

Building 625 had regular drills for emergency situations, Chandhuri had explained. But like anyplace else, during a real disaster people would panic, forget what to do, and try to save their own lives first, particularly when the enemy could be any of the dozens of deadly invisible gases or toxins that were stored on the premises. That was what had happened at Union Carbide in Bhopal, Chandhuri had told him, and she was correct when she predicted the same reaction would occur here. Her two-jar deception had worked.

Rhostok quickly joined the panicked crowd rushing down the hallway. There were at least a dozen other evacuees wearing white biohazard suits exactly like his. Anonymous behind the respirator hood, he headed towards the double steel doors, which were kept open and unguarded during evacuations. The automated recording continued its alert message. Everyone hurried in eerie silence towards the exit.

There were no guards to bar the way. The electrified gates were wide open. It was obvious the staff was drilled to get as far away from the building as possible in case of a leak. They all seemed to remember that part of the drill with no problem. They surged past the empty sentry boxes and kept going. An MP wearing a gas mask was directing them to an assembly point in what Rhostok assumed was an upwind position. Security people were hastily assembling portable decontamination showers nearby.

Rhostok stayed with the crowd until it reached the parking lot. After checking to be sure Sherman was nowhere in sight, he headed for his car, where he stripped off the bulky suit and dumped it in the back seat. Two other cars pulled out of the parking lot ahead of him. An MP in the road jumped out of the way, making no attempt to stop Rhostok.

The guards at the main gate had been alerted and were busy stopping all traffic from entering Fort Detrick. Everyone leaving was waved through without any identity check.

By the time Rhostok reached the outskirts of Frederick, a general alarm had been sounded. Local emergency units were responding, according to some prearranged disaster plan. A steady stream of ambulances, biohazard vehicles, fire engines, and police cars filled the lanes headed back to Detrick, sirens blaring, the drivers' faces grim. It would take some time before testing equipment would prove the "biohazard alert" was a false alarm. By the time they discovered his body was missing, he'd be out of Maryland and on 81 in Pennsylvania.

Rhostok flicked on the police scanner and listened to dispatchers in each of the towns he passed requesting all available crews to proceed to Fort Detrick, where the Regional Disaster Plan was now in effect. Maryland State Police units were being ordered to report to the Army Provost Marshal, who was coordinating security activities.

Rhostok relaxed a little when he crossed the border into Pennsylvania, slowing down to the legal speed limit. The adrenaline rush was easing off, and with it, so was his alertness. He stopped at a roadside Burger King for two large coffees to go and was alarmed to discover his fingers couldn't feel the heat of the containers. He tried flexing his hands and feet as he drove, but it didn't seem to help much. The symptoms were spreading. His eyes hurt from the methylene chloride, but the lingering irritation had the side benefit of helping keep his eyes open, helping him stay awake. If he didn't pass out and smash the car into a tree somewhere along the way, he'd reach Middle Valley in three more hours.

And then, if he had any life left within him, maybe, maybe he could unmask one of Vanya's killers.

But just in case he didn't make it that far, he had to get out a warning about the toxin that infected the relic.

He pulled into a rest stop and fumbled with his cell phone until he managed to key in the numbers to the Middle Valley police station. The effects of the toxin on his speech made it difficult for the duty officer to understand him. Although he recognized Rhostok's voice, he assumed the slow, slurred speech was a sign of drunkenness and advised Rhostok to go home and sleep it off. Rhostok got the same reaction when he called the Channel One Action News hotline number. He tried Nicole's cell phone number. As he expected, there was no answer. He tried to call Winfield. No answer there, either. He finished the second container of coffee and headed north again.

An hour outside of Scranton, he coughed up the first specks of blood. The loss of sensation had moved up his fingers to the palms of his hands. He could no longer feel his foot on the gas pedal. Why was he still driving, he wondered? What was the point? Even if he made it to Middle Valley, he'd be nothing more than a walking corpse, a zombie. There was nothing left for him to do but die. He thought of pulling off the road into the next rest stop, where he could let the toxin do its work without endangering other drivers. With any luck, he would go quickly, like Altschiller and Zeeman. He rolled down the car windows to let the mountain breeze blow through.

This wasn't how he had expected his life to end, but he was ready to accept it. The Orthodox faith promised life after death. He wondered if that promise also extended to those, like himself, who had abandoned the faith. And if so, what was waiting for him on the other side? If he believed the old stories, his grandfather would be there to greet him. He would once again be with his father and his mother, both showing no sign of the suffering they had endured in their final moments. That reunion alone would make dying worthwhile, Rhostok thought.

It was his mother who had suffered most. Now, as he faced his own death, he remembered those final moments before the coffin lid was closed on her. He was an eight-year-old boy, small for his age, his mother not yet thirty, her face so pale in the coffin, but at least blessedly free of the terrible pain that had ravaged her body for so many months. He could almost feel his grandfather's hand on his shoulder. He remembered thinking how he would have done anything, given anything, endured anything, if she would only open her eyes at that last moment.

For weeks afterward, he prayed as he never prayed before. He did childish penances, kneeling on stones until his flesh bled, giving up candy and bicycle-riding as sacrifices to offer up to heaven in the hope that the *Khristos* or the Holy Mother would look down in pity and restore his mother to life. Every night for weeks he went to sleep praying that she would somehow, by some miracle, be restored to life and come walking into the house and pick him up and kiss him once again. But it never happened. His prayers were never answered. That was when eight-year-old Viktor Rhostok, despite his grandfather's efforts, turned his back on God. He hadn't received the sacraments of the Orthodox Church since then.

With the numbness of death deadening his arms, all he could think of was his mother's suffering and his childish efforts to save her. It was only natural, he thought. He was brought into the world by his mother, and his final thoughts on leaving the world should be of her. What son or daughter could do otherwise?

And as tears rolled down his cheeks, a thought began to form in his mind.

It came slowly, not as a sudden flash of insight, and at first he wasn't even sure it made any sense. It had to do with a child's love for a mother. With the sacrifice a loving child was willing to make.

As the thought unfolded, he knew an act of utter audacity had been committed. One that fooled everyone.

His tears stopped, his jaw tightened, and he pressed his numbed foot down on the gas pedal, watching the speedometer increase to seventy, seventy-five, eighty miles per hour.

Death, at least for the moment, was no longer an option.

Not just yet. Not while he finally knew where the Rasputin relic was being taken.

Eighty

There were moments on the long drive back from Fort Detrick when Rhostok felt he was detached from his body. He seemed to be floating above the car, looking down on himself as he drove, thinking how useless it was for him to be attempting to hold off death to pursue some earthly goal. He had heard that such out-of-body experiences often precede death. It was a pleasant sensation, a kind of floating feeling in which the barriers of time and space disappeared. But he was unwilling to surrender so easily. Each time it happened, each time he felt himself drifting upwards, he willed himself back into his body and tried to concentrate on the dark road ahead.

Those moments of detachment, however, were also times of illumination. Floating above himself, he had the sensation that he could see things that were obscured while he occupied his earthbound body. What he saw might have been simply fatigue-induced illusions, or the whisperings of his subconscious making connections that were far too subtle for his conscious mind to discern. But each time he drifted away, he came back with another piece of the puzzle that had previously eluded him.

When at last he reached Middle Valley, his eyesight was failing, his throat ached, his arms and legs were completely numb, but his mind was surprisingly clear. He was finally able to see through the deceptions and lies that had been purposely laid in his path. He finally understood Nicole's role in the entire ugly sequence of events.

Carefully, forcing himself to stay conscious, he drove up the hill at the far end of town. By the time he stopped the car, his numb fingers were unable to remove the key from the ignition. He couldn't feel the door handles. Yet somehow, he managed to stumble out of the car and make his way up the stone steps. He looped his wrist through the handle of the heavy wooden door and, with what seemed to be the last of his strength, pulled the door open and slipped inside the Old Ritual Russian Orthodox Church of Saint Sofia.

The interior was dimly lit by the electric candles arranged on the side walls. A dozen parishioners, mostly old and bent, knelt in their pews, waiting for the *Episkop* to emerge from the Holy Door by the *iconostasis* to begin the service. They were the last faithful members of Sergius's once-thriving parish, chanting their litanies aloud as they had done all their lives, beating their chests each time they spoke the name of *Khristos*. The acoustics of the near-empty church gave a hollow ring to their voices. Rhostok leaned against a pillar in the back of the church, growing weaker by the moment.

Someone opened the door behind him. Rhostok felt a draft of air. He heard a whispered exchange between two men. A few stragglers, he thought, come to join the evening service. He heard them come up behind him.

"You are causing much trouble for me," whispered a voice with a heavy Russian accent.

Before Rhostok could turn, a sharp blow struck him on the back of the neck, driving him to the floor. It happened quietly enough not to interrupt the rhythmic chanting of prayers. When Rhostok tried to lift himself, a foot kicked out at him, catching him just above the kidney. He felt something pop inside and fell back, gasping with pain. The foot jammed itself against the back of his neck, pinning his cheek to the cold marble floor. He could feel something moving inside him, something flowing, a warm liquid oozing up into his throat. He tasted his own blood as it filled his mouth and seeped out between his lips, forming a dark pool that slowly spread across the worn marble.

Hemorrhage, he thought. The final symptom. He would die right here, appropriately enough, in the church he once rejected.

"He will not trouble us," the Russian voice said to its unseen companion. "It is the end for him now. You wait here."

The foot stayed planted against Rhostok's neck. He could see a slender figure moving towards the front of the church, entering a pew behind the worshippers. That would be the man with the Russian voice. Somehow Rhostok knew it was Vassily.

Slowly, as if testing to be sure Rhostok wouldn't jump up, the foot against his neck released its pressure. His assailant remained unseen, retreating back into the shadows. The peculiar sound of his footsteps confirmed his identity. Rhostok lay motionless, waiting to see what would happen next.

After a few minutes, the chanting of prayers stopped. The worshippers rose and began to sing an old Russian hymn about the coming of God. From a door on the side of the *iconostasis,* Sergius entered. He was wearing ornate golden vestments, the color reserved for auspicious occasions. On his head was the traditional *Episkop*'s crown. In a normal parish, there would be acolytes to attend him, to assist in the offering of the Mass. The dying parish, however, was unable to supply any young boys to carry the Bible and the Cross. On this occasion, Sergius was followed by a young woman in a white floor-length robe, tied at her waist with a white cord. Her head was covered with a traditional white *babushka,* knotted beneath her chin.

Rhostok blinked and tried to focus his aching eyes. The woman walked slowly, as if she might stumble and fall. At one point, in an unusual breach of the liturgic ritual, Sergius reached out to steady her. The *babushka* obscured part of the woman's face. Yet her lovely features were unmistakable.

It was Nicole, Rhostok realized. She was pale, her skin almost as white as the robe she wore. She was clearly on the verge of collapse. Dr. Chandhuri had said that Nicole was hospitalized yesterday afternoon, that the Rasputin toxin was working its way through her blood, that she wouldn't survive the night. Yet here she was, wan and frail, but assisting the *Episkop* in this service. Sergius must have somehow spirited her out of the hospital. Perhaps, like Rasputin with Alexei, he had somehow managed to staunch the hemorrhage, yet also like Rasputin, had not been able to effect a permanent cure. Or perhaps it was simply a question of heredity.

Like Rhostok, she was a second-generation Russian-American. She had been exposed to the Rasputin toxin at about the same time as he was, and she had the same partial immunity. Enough immunity to allow her to survive the night. But, like him, not enough immunity to survive much longer. With terrifying synchronism, the toxin had spared her life as long as it had spared his. Now they would die together. Here in this church. In front of a priest who once claimed he had the power to heal.

He listened as Sergius's cavernous voice filled the church with its presence. The language he used at first was Old Church Slavonic, but he soon switched to English. Lying on the floor, not quite helpless, but conserving what little strength he had, Rhostok let the words wash over him.

"We are gathered here this evening to witness the new resurrection," Sergius was saying.

From the floor, Rhostok watched Vassily standing patiently in his pew, awaiting . . . what? There was still no sign of the second assailant, no sound from the shadows to indicate his continued presence. Up at the altar, Nicole turned to gaze out into the church. From where she knelt, she could probably see Vassily, but she seemed to be searching the darkness for someone else.

"We are at the threshold of the restoration of the faith," Sergius continued.

Rhostok breathed deeply, hoarding the last of his strength for what he knew was coming.

"We will once again enter an age of miracles and wonders."

The flow of blood in front of Rhostok's face continued to grow, although more slowly than it seemed at first. Perhaps, he hoped, he would have a few moments more before death, time enough for one last desperate act.

"The Church of Saint Sofia will become a place of pilgrimage for the faithful from all over the world," came the words from the altar.

Nicole's shoulders shook as she coughed into a small cloth she carried. She glanced again at the back of the church, a worried frown on her face.

"The sick will be cured," the *Episkop* proclaimed. "The lame will walk. The dead will rise again."

The words seemed to strengthen Nicole, who lifted her chin and looked up at Sergius as if waiting for him to work one of those miracles on her.

"The instrument of their delivery, the sacred instrument of our own spiritual resurrection, will be the most precious relic of a prophet rejected in his own country, the great Russian healer and miracle worker, the man whose sainthood we are gathered here tonight to proclaim . . . Grigorii Effimovich Rasputin."

The thin puddle of Rhostok's blood began to tremble. The marble floor started to shake. In the last two weeks, there had been more than a dozen mine subsidences in Middle Valley. That one should strike at the exact moment Rasputin's name was mentioned seemed an uncanny coincidence. The rumbling lasted only a few seconds, ending with a sharp cracking sound. As dust floated down from inside the dome, the *Episkop* smiled and raised his arms.

"You see?" he said to the stunned parishioners. "The great saint announces his presence and looks down on us all with approval."

Rhostok watched Vassily, who had covered his head with his arms until the rumbling stopped.

"To those who question why a man reviled as a sinner and a debaucher merits sainthood, I say that many saints have been reviled during their lifetimes, rejected by the powerful, abandoned by their own church, and martyred for their faith. Is this not the story of our beloved Lord *Khristos?* The Scriptures say he was called a glutton and a drunkard who consorted with sinners. He was rejected by the elders, abandoned by his followers, and crucified for us."

Sergius knelt and blessed himself in the traditional Old Believer manner. When he arose, his booming voice dropped to a lower tone.

"Look closer to home, my children. We have seen that same process in our motherland, where the twenty thousand Old Believers were cast out of their homes and slain for professing their beliefs. We know of hundreds of thousands of our countrymen of all faiths who were condemned to death by the followers of Lenin and Stalin. Some of them were our relatives. Now at last, the Church in Russia has begun to venerate these martyrs as saints. Eight hundred fifty martyrs and confessors were recently canonized."

He gripped the edge of the altar and his voice rose to a thunderous volume. "But where, my brothers and sisters . . . where was the name of Grigorii Effimovich Rasputin in that litany of saints? The Church in Russia, following the lead of the Church in America, proclaimed sainthood for our beloved Tsar Nikolas and Empress Alexandra and the entire Imperial Family. That act alone makes Rasputin not only the Confessor of Saints, but the man to whom those saints turned in their darkest hours. He was the holy man, the miracle worker who saved the life of the youngest of that family of saints. How can the Imperial Family be considered saints while their confessor and spiritual guide is rejected?"

In his agony, Rhostok remembered his grandfather once asking the same question.

"We must wait no longer to reexamine the life of Rasputin. We have all heard the tales of his drinking and womanizing, but did not Saint Augustine admit to similar vices? Was not Saint Paul once guilty of slaughtering Christians? And do we not revere them now as great leaders of the early Church? Their good outweighed the bad. And so, too, we must consider the good that Rasputin did. A man will be known by his deeds.

"Yes, my brothers and sisters, he had weaknesses, as we all do. But he was never accused of molesting children, never lived in a luxurious mansion, never acquired wealth. Yes, those seeking favors and cures gave him large amounts of money, but he gave it all away to the poor, often on the same day he received it. He died penniless, his only asset the wooden house in Siberia where he raised his children. Should not such a man be exalted?"

The marble floor was cold against Rhostok's cheek. Listening to the *Episkop*'s eulogy, he kept watching Vassily, waiting for him to make his move.

"Many truths have been kept from us by those opposed to Rasputin.

"His enemies tell us of his drunken revels. They choose not to tell us he was a peace-loving man who saved untold thousands of lives by using his influence on the Emperor to keep our motherland out of the Balkan War. Blessed are the peacemakers, for they shall be called the sons of God.

"His enemies tell us that he seduced women. They wish us to forget that he sponsored Russia's first organized relief efforts to feed millions of starving peasants. Blessed are the merciful, for theirs is the kingdom of heaven.

"His enemies tell us he was an evil influence behind the throne. They wish us to forget that he pushed through Russia's first laws granting full rights to Jews and fought to give more freedom to the *muzhiks*. Blessed are those who hunger for righteousness, for they shall be fulfilled.

"His enemies tell us he caused the downfall of the Tsar. They forget that he warned the Tsar what would happen if he ignored the peasants. And it came to pass just as scripture said: 'Whoever shall exalt himself shall be humbled, and whoever shall humble himself shall be exalted.'"

A rush of air flowed over Rhostok, signaling that his assailant had opened the church door. Did that mean he left?

"Rasputin's enemies speak of dark deeds and evil acts. But I tell you, my brothers and sisters, his enemies are the true sinners. Like Satans, they have defiled a holy man's image with their tricks and lies. For the spirit of the Lord was truly upon Rasputin.

"How else can anyone explain his miraculous healing powers? Even his enemies admit that Rasputin did indeed stop the bleeding of the little Tsarevich. Yet he used this gift from God to cure many more people. His cures defied medical science at the time and confused his enemies. Rasputin cured children of diphtheria, scarlet fever, and even grave problems of the central nervous system. He cured adults of pneumonia, asthma, and arthritis, and even restored life to those given up for dead. He cured the rich and the poor alike. But most of those people this holy man cured were his beloved *muzhiks,* whose descendants still mourn his death.

"Truly this was a man of God. Truly a prophet without honor in his own country."

Nicole seemed to be faltering at the altar. Her head was hanging low, chin against her chest, shoulders slumped. Occasionally coughing spasms shook her body.

"As prophet, he had the ability to see the future. We all know how he predicted the deaths of the Imperial Family, the flight of the nobles, the rivers of blood that would flow. But there was one little-known prophecy that has escaped the attention of those who wrote about him. It was reported by the last French ambassador to the Imperial Court, and it is worth repeating here and now, at this auspicious moment. Here is what the great holy man Rasputin said of his death and his life beyond death."

Through fading vision, Rhostok could see Sergius raise a piece of paper, apparently to be certain he got the quotation right.

"'I know I shall die amidst horrible sufferings. My corpse will be torn to pieces. But even if my ashes are scattered to the winds, I shall go on performing miracles. Through my prayers from above, the sick will recover, and barren women will conceive.' Those are the words of Rasputin." Sergius waved the paper in the air for all to see. "And tonight, we will call upon Rasputin to fulfill that prophecy."

The prophecy was the same one Rhostok had read on Robyn's computer.

"We all know good works and good intentions are not enough to proclaim sainthood," Sergius continued. "The church has always demanded one final test. One final demonstration of God's favor. And we are privileged to announce that the final test has been met. We have in our possession a sacred relic, perhaps the most important religious relic to make its way out of Russia.

"The relic was hidden from the Communists at Starokonstantinov and lost during the German invasion," Sergius proclaimed, undeterred by the continued rumbling beneath the foundations of the building. "By what can only be considered divine intervention, the relic was liberated from the Nazis by one of our own parishioners, Vanya Danilovitch, who brought it back to Middle Valley and protected it until his death. Now it will take its rightful home, here among the last of the Old Believers."

Sergius shook a small silver bell. Nicole rose and made her way unsteadily to the "Royal Gate" in the middle of the *iconostasis,* which led to an area so sacred, only priests were permitted access. She stopped for a moment, looked back, her eyes searching the darkness once again. Apparently failing to find whatever she sought, she turned back to the gate, opened it, and stood aside. Rhostok watched a wheelchair slowly emerge through the Royal Gate. In it was an emaciated woman, her hair gray, her color sallow. On her lap was a stainless-steel box, which Rhostok knew contained the Rasputin relic. Because pushing the wheelchair was the duplicitous TV reporter, Robyn Cronin, aka Kronstadt.

The *Episkop* blessed them both, before gently removing the box from the older woman's lap.

The woman in the wheelchair must be Robyn's mother, Rhostok thought. Her mother who was dying from terminal cancer. It was for her that Robyn had stolen the relic in a last, desperate attempt to find a cure, and brought it to Sergius. She was seeking a miracle for her mother.

Who could blame her? Rhostok knew he would have done the same himself, as an eight-year-old boy or as a grown man sworn to uphold the law. From his own experience, he knew that no law was higher, no bond stronger than that which joined a child to its mother.

Still prostrate, he watched the *Episkop* open the container and carefully remove the relic from its plastic shield. Exposing the fatal toxins that protected the relic from its enemies . . . and killed the innocent. The *Episkop* was immune, having been born in Russia. The old parishioners also carried the immunity in their blood. But there were others who would come to worship here. How many more would come seeking healing and solace, only to die for their efforts?

The faithful believe that relics can cure, but Rhostok knew that this relic could kill.

"Prepare to witness a miracle!" Sergius proclaimed. "Flesh that defies nature! A sign of God's approval! Look! Look upon the Rasputin relic and then bow down your heads in prayer. This is the right hand of the great saint, perfectly preserved, in the same condition as the day he died, almost one hundred years ago. According to our faith, the incorruptibility of the flesh is proof of divinity. It is proof that the great healer and prophet Grigorii Effimovich Rasputin is truly a saint.

"And this hand, the right hand of our saint, the hand that cured so many Russians in the name of God, will now heal and cure once more." He held the relic before him, his eyes focused on the painted image of heaven on the ceiling. "O great healer above, let your powers come alive again to convince an unbelieving world of the powers of God."

A sudden crack sounded from somewhere beneath the floor, as if a bolt of lightning had struck deep underground.

"O great Saint Rasputin, I call upon you now to fulfill your prophecy." Sergius raised the relic over his head. "You promised us that after your death, you would go on performing miracles, that through your prayers from above, the sick would recover and barren women would conceive."

The thunderous crack was followed by a massive underground rumble, as another of the abandoned mine tunnels below Middle Valley gave way. The floor of the church quivered in protest. The ground beneath was moving, settling, huge plates of rock and coal tearing against each other. It was the Earth grinding its teeth, his grandfather would say.

The *Episkop* and, it seemed, everyone else in the church took it as an omen of assent from the man to whom they prayed. Rhostok himself was beginning to wonder if this were some strange paranormal phenomenon, a message from a powerful figure on the Other Side. Relics had been given credit for stopping floods, ending plagues, leading armies to victory. Why not send a signal of approval to the small group of believers? If approval it was.

"O great Saint Rasputin, as your faithful representative here on Earth, I call upon you to ask our Lord to restore in me the gift of healing! Not for my sake, but for the sake of those in need. Allow me to continue your mystical mission to help both the poor and the powerful conquer their illnesses here on Earth and find the redemption they desire."

Particles of dirt came floating down, shaken loose from the ceiling of the church. They fell like blackened snow against Rhostok's cheek. Nearby, a bird hit the floor with a soft thud, its fall cushioned by its feathers. It was one of the belfry sparrows, who had been chattering with excitement moments ago. The sparrow's neck might have been broken by the fall, but it seemed to be dead before it hit the floor. Soon another one dropped, a little farther away. Like the first, its wings didn't flutter when it fell.

Rhostok stared at the dead sparrows.

A warning sign, he thought.

He looked up to see Vassily beginning to make his move. The slender man slipped out of his pew and started for the altar. None of the worshippers paid any attention. They were focused on the *Episkop,* who was holding the Rasputin relic above the head of the woman in the wheelchair.

"By the power invested in me through this relic . . ."

He placed one hand on her head and touched the Rasputin relic to her cheek.

". . . and with the blessing of this hand which has cured so many others . . ."

If Robyn was expecting her mother to be cured, this was the moment she had been waiting for, Rhostok thought. It was the moment for which she had drugged him, stolen the relic, abandoned her job, turned her back on any possible future in broadcasting, and placed her trust in a discredited faith healer who believed Rasputin was a saint. Rhostok didn't think her sacrifice would be worth it. After all, whatever healing gifts the *Episkop* may have once had, they had vanished long ago.

". . . let this woman now be healed!"

The woman seemed to jump, although Rhostok couldn't tell whether Sergius had intentionally shaken her chair.

After using the relic to make the Sign of the Cross over the woman, Sergius turned and held it high overhead, waving it slowly back and forth for all to see, proclaiming loudly, ". . . and through the intercession of the great Saint Rasputin, let the grace of the Almighty *Khristos* be visited upon all who are with us tonight, curing them of whatever infirmities beset them."

If only it were so simple, Rhostok thought. Instead of a cure, he felt a sudden stab of pain, a spasm that shook his body. At the same time, Nicole let out a loud gasp and clutched her chest. The woman in the wheelchair threw her head back, as if suffering a sudden jolt of pain. Even Robyn, with a puzzled look on her face, seemed to experience an unpleasant twinge.

Vassily, unnoticed so far, stepped through the *iconostasis*, grabbed the *Episkop*'s arm, and wrenched the relic from his grasp.

"No!" Robyn screamed. "Stop him!"

The *Episkop* grappled with Vassily.

The woman in the wheelchair, perhaps seeing her last possibility of a cure being snatched away, began to cry.

Vassily pulled a gun from his pocket.

In the back of the church, Rhostok watched in horror as Vassily aimed the pistol at the *Episkop*.

He thought of the underground rumblings, the cracking foundation, and the dead sparrows that now littered the floor around him. The little birds were cousins to the mine canaries he kept in his office to warn of the presence of methane. Their deaths could only mean the explosive gas was seeping up from the mines below, making its way through the cracks that were appearing in the church floor. A single spark was all it would take to set off the kind of explosion that continued to take the lives of miners around the world.

"Noooooo!" Rhostok screamed, and with a strength that seemed to be suddenly and inexplicably flowing back into his body, he drew himself up from the floor.

Vassily turned towards the sound of his voice. With the practiced skill of an assassin, he took a quick, almost casual aim at Rhostok and pulled the trigger.

The tiny flash from the gun's muzzle ignited the methane.

Like a giant flashbulb, a sudden burst of brilliant white flame illuminated the scene at the altar, freezing the action for a millisecond. Vassily stared at his gun, a look of puzzlement on his face. The *Episkop* lost his grasp on the relic. Robyn's mouth opened in a scream that could no longer be heard. The woman in the wheelchair covered her face with her hands. And Nicole, for some strange reason, moved towards the woman.

The bullet hit Rhostok in his left shoulder. He could feel a bone snapping. But the pain was overwhelmed by the heat and force of the explosion, which knocked him off his feet. Flat on his back on the floor again, he watched the sheet of flame expand outward, exploding through the stained-glass windows, shaking the ancient side pillars, and pushing at the ceiling with primitive force. Having seen the results of dozens of buildings blown apart by methane or natural gas explosions, he knew what was coming next.

The methane, being lighter than air, was concentrated at the ceiling, which is where the force of the blast would be most powerful. The thick ceiling beams strained to contain the force of the explosion, but the pressure against them was too great. A giant hole burst through the far end of the roof, spraying debris into the night air. Its moorings shaken, the central beam shuddered slowly as it ripped itself free from the others. Rhostok watched helplessly as the giant beam crashed drunkenly to the floor, smashing a dozen oak pews and shattering the twin statues of Saint Cyril and Saint Methodius.

Rhostok crawled under the beam for protection against what he knew was coming next.

With its main support gone, the roof groaned slowly, trying to hold on. But it found the weight of its slate shingles too much to bear and finally caved inward. It came down slowly at first, bending and creaking until there was one last powerful crack and the golden dome of Saint Sofia Church collapsed.

Eighty-One

Before the violence erupted, Nicole had been praying silently, listening to the *Episkop*'s oration. Like the woman in the wheelchair, and perhaps others in the church, she was waiting patiently for the miraculous healing Sergius had promised. The power, he said, would flow back into him during this special evening service. There was a moment, when he proclaimed the sainthood of Rasputin and asked for his healing intercession, that she thought she felt a mild jolt hit her body. She dismissed it as another of the rumblings that had struck the church. Oddly, though, when Sergius pressed the relic to the cheek of the woman in the wheelchair, a similar jolt seemed to shake the woman's body.

And suddenly, Vassily was there, grabbing for the relic, struggling with the startled *Episkop*. She watched Vassily pull the gun and aim it at Sergius. She knew he was capable of murder, but this was incredible. To kill a priest, here in a church, right in front of an altar, in full view of people who had gathered in the hope of witnessing a miracle . . . it was the most incredibly evil act she could imagine. She couldn't let it happen. She started forward, stumbling over the hem of her long white robe, hoping to somehow stop him.

From the back of the church came an agonized scream. She turned at the same time Vassily did. Turned to see someone rising from a pool of dark liquid . . . was it blood? As her eyes adjusted to the far shadows, she realized it was Rhostok, rising from the floor.

"*The policeman will rise . . .*" She remembered Sergius's strange prophecy.

Vassily swore softly and pointed the gun at Rhostok.

She saw Vassily's finger close on the trigger, the gun lurch in his hand, and the flame, so small when it first shot from the end of the muzzle, immediately exploding into an immense sheet of white fire that illuminated the entire church. The strange fire flashed over the pews and rolled up the walls, where it seemed to gather force and explode against the roof.

"*The policeman will rise, and the church will fall . . .*" Sergius's words ran through her mind.

Vassily and the others were thrown to the floor by the blast. The old woman in the wheelchair sat exposed, an odd smile on her face as all hell was breaking loose around her. The worshippers, long accustomed to the dangers of mine disasters, quickly took refuge under their pews. A chandelier crashed next to the wheelchair. Overhead, the roof was groaning. The enormous fresco that covered the ceiling started to sag. Huge slabs of painted plaster began to break loose.

One section fell near Nicole, shattering into dozens of smaller pieces. Another crashed into the altar. The entire ceiling was caving in on them. The only refuge was the enormous marble altar.

Without thinking of her own safety, Nicole shoved the stunned TV reporter under the altar. The *Episkop* followed, squeezing into the small space.

Far above, an enormous groan signaled that the golden dome was breaking free from its last mooring and preparing to fall. The woman in the wheelchair was directly underneath. Heedless of the danger, Nicole hurried to save her. The ceiling was caving in.

"The holy place will be destroyed." The *Episkop*'s words were coming true!

A small chunk of debris struck Nicole's shoulder. A larger piece slammed into her back, knocking her to the floor. The woman in the wheelchair seemed oblivious of the destruction around her. Pieces of slate roofing, sharp enough to dismember anyone they struck, came whistling down to shatter on the floor. In the midst of it all, the woman in the wheelchair smiled blissfully. The falling debris somehow managed to avoid her. But a violent crack overhead drew Nicole's attention. The last beam supporting the golden dome was breaking. The dome was directly above the woman in the wheelchair. Nothing could stop it from crushing her.

The woman began to rise from her wheelchair. She wobbled unsteadily on legs that were atrophied from years in the chair, but she was rising. Nicole had been told the reporter's mother was suffering from cancer of the spine, yet she watched as the woman drew herself erect, seemingly without any pain. From beneath the altar came the screams of the woman's daughter. The *Episkop* was holding the reporter, restraining her from the certain death she'd face if she tried to rescue her mother.

But Nicole was closer. She stumbled to her feet and threw herself at the old woman, hoping to knock her out of the path of the dome. The woman was frail, her body eaten away by cancer, her muscles atrophied from months of being confined to the wheelchair. Yet when Nicole tried to pull her out of the way, the woman could not be moved. She remained where she stood, her body as rigid as statuary. Nicole struggled helplessly and finally sank to her knees, clutching the woman and awaiting her death. Nicole felt rather than heard the enormous crash. The concussion sucked the air from her lungs. . . .

They told her later that the cables that supplied electricity to the dome's lights must have tugged at the plummeting dome, providing just enough leverage to divert it slightly from its seemingly inevitable target. It crashed inches away from the two women.

When Nicole opened her eyes, it was all over. The holy place was destroyed. Only part of the walls remained standing.

Flames ate away at the *iconstasis,* blackening its sacred images.
"The saints will burn in the fires of Hell . . ."

Yet inexplicably, although they were surrounded by destruction, the two women had escaped injury. All around them was wreckage from the roof: slate, wood, beams, tarpaper, and glistening gold-painted remnants of the dome. Nicole couldn't move without her feet touching debris, many pieces of which were large enough to crush a car. The wheelchair was flattened under an enormous wooden beam. Yet they were both untouched, as if protected by some invisible hand. How close they had come to dying left Nicole frozen with shock. Her arms remained wrapped around the legs of the old woman, whose hands were raised in supplication to some unseen image in the sky above. Plaster dust coated her in a gray mantle.

"Praise God," the old woman said.

She reached down and, with a strength that seemed impossible for so frail a woman, pulled Nicole to her feet.

Eighty-Two

The explosion left dozens of small fires burning among the prayer books and pews. The fires, filtered by smoke and settling dust, cast a ghastly light over the scene. Rhostok could hear the first screams of parishioners, trapped in the rubble, hiding under broken pews. He could feel the pain in his left shoulder, where Vassily's bullet had struck him. Though not immediately fatal, it was a remarkably accurate shot under those conditions. Only a trained marksman could have spun around and, without aim, hit a target at that distance. A trained marksman, or a trained assassin, Rhostok thought. Vassily was part of the team that had been tracking down the relic, killing one old veteran after another, until they found the man who changed his name, Americanizing it before the war.

But Vassily's partner was nowhere to be seen. Two of them had entered the church. What had happened to the other one? Carefully, painfully, Rhostok crawled out from under the broken ceiling beam that protected him. His shoulder ached. His shirt sleeve was bloodied, but he didn't seem to notice that his bleeding had stopped. He stumbled through the debris, through the shattered boards and overturned pews, making his way towards the altar. Incredibly, the woman who had been in the wheel-chair was standing erect, staring up at the open sky through the hole that had once been the roof. Rhostok thought instantly of the *Dyriniki* who worshipped in that manner. And kneeling at the woman's feet, in what almost resembled a religious tableau, was Nicole. He silently thanked God for sparing her.

He could see no other signs of life, no movement, no indication that anyone else in that exposed area was still alive. What looked like Vassily's legs protruded from a tangle of plaster and lath boards. Behind him, the *iconostasis* burned furiously, its dry wood fed by methane gas still seeping from the fissures in the floor. The images of saints painted on its surface bubbled and blackened before flaring up. Loosened debris continued to fall from what was left of the ceiling. The golden rooftop dome, once the most visible landmark in Middle Valley, had come to rest atop what was left of the altar. With all the rubble, it was hard to tell whether the altar itself had survived.

A cool draft flowed against Rhostok's face. He knew it must be methane, but his lungs, starving for relief from the smoke and soot, wel-comed the cool taste of the contaminated air.

Like a drug, it seemed to soothe his tortured throat. It calmed his anx-iety. Gave him a sense of well-being. He remembered what his grandfather said about the effects of the odorless gas: a moment of euphoria before death. Was that why he felt his strength returning? It didn't matter, he thought, since he was dying anyway.

Between the golden dome and Vassily's legs, a lump on the floor caught Rhostok's attention. Covered with dust, but still recognizable. Rhostok walked over to it.

The Rasputin relic.

From it came a hissing sound, as if it were simmering in some invis-ible flame. The blood that had been trapped within its veins for almost a century was now beginning to ooze out, forming a wet pool in the dust. The top of the relic was swelling grotesquely, the fingers growing fat and finally splitting open at the knuckles. A yellowish fluid welled up in ugly fissures which were opening in the flesh.

The methane explosion had somehow jarred Rasputin's hand from its ancient slumber.

The period of incorruptibility was ended. For some unexplained reason, the long-overdue process of putrefaction had been triggered. It now advanced at an accelerated rate.

Maybe it was simply a by-product of the deterioration of muscle and tendon, but Rhostok was certain the fingers of Rasputin's hand were beginning to move, to flex themselves. Almost as if it were coming alive.

He thought of the deaths it had already caused.

He started to kick the relic towards the fire. It was lodged against the remnants of a ceiling beam. As he stepped forward to dispose of the toxin-infested relic, he heard his name being called.

"Rhostok!" It was Nicole's voice. "Behind you, Rhostok! Watch out!"

He spun around to see Vassily staring at him, gun in hand. The Russian was a bit unsteady on his feet, covered in plaster dust, but somehow he had survived.

"This time, I do not miss," Vassily said.

He raised his pistol and pointed it directly at the center of Rhostok's forehead.

He came closer until he was barely two arm lengths away. At this distance, it was impossible to miss. It was a Russian pistol, of a make Rhostok didn't recognize. From what he could see of the end of the barrel in the flickering firelight, the weapon was probably about a nine millimeter. That little round hole, not much larger than the size of a pencil eraser, was waiting for the command to spit out a piece of soft lead across a distance of no more than five feet into Rhostok's head. Having witnessed the effects of such close-distance shootings before, Rhostok knew that burnt gunpowder would be sprayed into his face with such force, it would penetrate the skin in a dirty circle around the impact hole.

But at least it would be over quickly. Better than bleeding to death. Clutching his useless left arm, Rhostok closed his eyes and began to pray aloud in Old Church Slavonic.

He heard the sound of the gun when it fired.

Felt the blast of gunpowder on his face.

Smelled the greasy odor of spent powder.

And waited. . . .

Eighty-Three

Rhostok waited for the impact, waited to be knocked off his feet by the slug, the way he remembered it happening in the old films of Russian civilians being executed by the Communists. How many times had he seen those films? A man standing at the edge of a mass grave, hands tied behind his back. A Red Army officer in full dress uniform walking up, raising a pistol. A puff of white smoke emerges from the gun. The prisoner seems to lose his balance and immediately collapses. The Red Army officer walks up to the next man and repeats the process.

Rhostok heard another gunshot, identical to the first.

How could Vassily have missed from such close range?

He heard someone screaming, cursing at Vassily. It was the voice of Robyn Cronin, coming from right over his shoulder.

Opening his eyes, he saw Vassily staggering backwards.

Another shot. It struck Vassily in the chest. Staggered him again. His gun dropped, but still he didn't fall. It wasn't like the old films at all. This time, someone was shooting at the executioner. A fourth shot rang out. Again, it appeared to hit Vassily in the chest. He let out a grunt, but like Rasputin when he was being chased through the courtyard of the Yussupov palace, he didn't fall.

Robyn stepped forward, took careful aim, and fired again. She was using that little .25 caliber automatic she kept in her purse—not a very powerful weapon. She fired again. Again the bullet seemed to strike Vassily's chest, but all it did was stagger him. There was no sign that the bullet had penetrated his body. But no miracle, either. Rhostok assumed the assassin was wearing a Kevlar vest. The protective fabric would stop bullets from far more powerful guns than a little .25.

Seeing her clip was empty, Vassily attempted to recover his own weapon. The gun was closer to Rhostok, who managed to kick it out of reach. Vassily swung at him, missing with a side-armed openhanded chop that was more like *kung fu* than a roundhouse punch. Rhostok almost stumbled over the Rasputin relic. Vassily swung again. This time, he hit Rhostok on the side of the neck.

The blow was struck with such force, it drove Rhostok to his knees. Vassily found a long piece of wrought iron that had come loose from the chandelier. He raised it above Rhostok's head, prepared to strike the final blow. His left shoulder shattered, Rhostok was defenseless.

And yet, Vassily hesitated. Why? What distracted him? Rhostok followed the assassin's eyes to the floor. To the Rasputin relic. Of course! That was why the Russian was here in the first place. That was the reason for his murderously methodical mission. How many men had he killed to find that piece of human flesh? Rhostok stared at Rasputin's hand. It seemed to be beckoning to him. Methane euphoria, Rhostok thought. The same euphoria that was responsible for his sudden burst of energy must be triggering hallucinations. The hand appeared to be reaching out to him. *Come, take me,* it seemed to be saying. *I will save your life as I have saved others.* Hallucination or not, Rhostok realized, Rasputin's hand, even its current state, was his only defense against Vassily.

Rhostok picked up the putrid relic and backed away from Vassily. He held the relic in front of him, relying on it to protect him from the iron bar Vassily was swinging slowly back and forth. In a way that those who believe in the protective power of relics never could have contemplated, the hand of Rasputin conferred a special protection on Rhostok. Rather than a supernatural power, however, the explanation was more mundane.

He knew Vassily would do nothing to damage the precious object further. The two men circled each other, Vassily looking for an opening, and Rhostok trying to think of a way to escape. He could throw the relic in the fire. Burning was the best way to dispose of the toxin, according to Dr. Chandhuri. It would distract Vassily. But probably ignite a murderous rampage. They continued to circle, parrying like swordsmen, Vassily with the rod of iron, Rhostok warding him off with Rasputin's hand.

It was the first time he had held the relic without wearing latex gloves. He recalled Altschiller's warning about the dangers of contact with the hand. But Altschiller wasn't talking about the toxin. He was warning about something else. Remembering Altschiller's warning, and remembering the stories about Rasputin's death, Rhostok held the hand carefully. He kept the stump end pointed towards Vassily, to avoid contact with any of Rasputin's cyanide-laced blood.

Vassily made a sudden jab, caught Rhostok off-balance, and grabbed for the relic.

Rhostok held on with his right hand. His left arm swinging uselessly at his side, he refused to give up the relic. Vassily dropped the iron bar and clutched the relic with both hands, pulling as hard as he could. Rhostok was afraid the relic would break apart. Drops of Rasputin's blood, still liquid after almost a century, splattered the floor. A spurt of blood hit Vassily's face. A few drops landed on his jaw. One drop landed on his cheek. And one drop landed in Vassily's angry, open mouth.

In the heat of the struggle, Vassily didn't seem to notice. It was, after all, just a single drop of liquid, probably at room temperature. But there was something different about this liquid, Rhostok knew. It was the blood of Grigorii Effimovich Rasputin. The miracle worker whose mystic powers defied those who tried to poison him.

Realizing what had just occurred, Rhostok let go of the relic. Backlit by the burning *iconostasis,* Vassily greedily clutched his treasure. The

Rasputin relic was finally his. He started to smile. The smile stiffened on his lips. He opened his mouth as if to say something, but no words came out. His face grew strained and distorted. The pupils of his eyes rolled up under their lids, leaving two white orbs staring at Rhostok.

A violent shudder shook the assassin's body. His jaw dropped and his tongue hung out uselessly. His chest started to heave. He gasped for air in wheezing, agonized gasps that didn't seem to help. His face turned blue. He was suffocating to death.

Vassily took two stiff-legged steps toward Rhostok, stopped, and then collapsed backwards into the flames of the *iconostasis*. There, among the burning images of the Russian saints, the fire began to consume Vassily's dead body. His hands held the Rasputin relic near his throat.

Sergius crawled out from beneath the altar. To him, a man who believed in miracles, it apparently looked as if the relic had come to life and strangled Vassily. He made the Sign of the Cross over the dead man and turned to Rhostok.

"The hand of Rasputin saved you," he said in an awed whisper. "He reached out from the grave to protect you."

That was not exactly true, Rhostok thought. He was saved by the hand of Rasputin, but not in the way the *Episkop* believed. It was a single drop of blood from Rasputin's hand that saved him. As Altschiller had warned, the eighty-year-old residue of cyanide that filled the veins of the relic was still deadly. As a native Russian, Vassily might be immune to the toxin, but he wasn't immune to the cyanide in Rasputin's blood.

Nicole came up behind them.

"The dead will kill the living," she murmured.

"What?"

"The *Episkop* saw what would happen," she said. "He told me the church would fall, the dead would kill the living, and the saints would burn in the fires of Hell." He could feel her body shuddering as she leaned against him. "These are the fires of Hell, aren't they?"

The rest of the *iconostasis* crashed into the flames, obscuring Vassily's body.

They found Robyn near a pile of debris. At first they thought she was dead. Her skin was a dull gray color. The blood had drained from her cheeks. Rhostok felt for the artery on the side of her neck. There was a pulse. A faint and erratic pulse, but a pulse nevertheless.

Sergius knelt down beside her. He removed a few particles of plaster from her forehead, a piece of tarpaper from her lips. Gently, he smoothed the hair from her face, arranging it neatly against her cheeks. The action revealed a head wound above her left eye, where falling debris must have knocked her unconscious during Rhostok's battle with Vassily. The eye was swollen.

"Come back to us, *malyutchka*," he said, taking her limp hands in his. "You showed your love for your mother. Come back to live with her again."

He tugged gently on her hands. Her head rolled to the side at an awkward angle. Her left cheek came to rest against her shoulder. Her mouth fell open. Sergius gave her a violent shake.

"Wake up, *malyutchka*," he shouted. "Come back."

Slowly, Robyn's right eye opened. She seemed to be struggling to open her left eye, but the swelling made it impossible. Her eyeball moved, searching their faces. She raised her head, her eyes scanning the devastation, the fire, the wreckage strewn everywhere.

"Vassily?" she asked.

"Dead," said Rhostok.

"The relic?"

"Consigned to the flames," the *Episkop* murmured. "Like the rest of Rasputin's body."

"The relic was my mother's last hope," she moaned. "She put all her faith in the relic."

"Relics do not cure, *malyutchka*," the *Episkop* said as he cradled her head in his lap.

"But you promised . . . you said . . ."

"I said the relic represented Rasputin's divinity," the *Episkop* explained. "But that divinity comes from a higher power. A human hand so perfectly preserved for almost a century is a direct message to us from God. That is why we revere such relics, because they bring us closer to God. It is not the relic that cures. What cures is God's grace, bestowed on those who have faith in what the relic represents."

"No one was cured," Rhostok said.

"No one?" the *Episkop* said with a smile. He raised Robyn's head so that she could see over his shoulder. "I think perhaps you are wrong."

Robyn lifted her head and let out a scream.

Rhostok could only stare in complete disbelief.

There, poking through the debris, searching for something, was Robyn's mother. The old woman moved unsteadily, still testing the fragile legs beneath her. As she searched, she was brushing the dust from her sleeves. They watched her bend over and, without the slightest indication that she was in any pain, tug at the handle of what she was looking for. It was the twisted wreckage of her wheelchair, smashed beneath the remnants of the golden dome.

"Mother!" Robyn cried. "Mother!"

Hearing her daughter's voice, the old woman turned and smiled. She abandoned the wrecked wheelchair and, walking with careful steps, her cloth slippers picking their way through the rubble, came to her daughter's side. She wrapped her skeletal arms around Robyn and squeezed with all the strength her emaciated body could summon.

Rhostok watched the sobbing women turn to enfold the *Episkop* in a three-way embrace.

"Thank you . . . thank you, *Episkop* Sergius . . . thank you . . ."

"It is not me you should thank," he heard Sergius murmuring. "Give thanks to the Lord God, and to the great Saint Rasputin, who interceded in your behalf."

"The pain is gone . . ." the old woman said.

"Is she . . ." Robyn asked. "Will she . . . ?"

"She will live," the *Episkop* said. "She is cured."

Robyn kissed the priest's palms.

"This was truly a night of miracles," the *Episkop* said.

Rhostok was happy for them, but his happiness was tempered with the thought that time was running out for him. It was already six hours since he had left Fort Detrick. The final hemorrhage, the fatal surge of bleeding, must strike at any moment.

"All were cured tonight," Sergius said. "Even you, Rhostok. Even an unbeliever such as you, a man who believes in the power of curses, but not the power of miracles. Did you not notice the bleeding has stopped?"

Rhostok raised a hand to his shoulder. It should have been hemorrhaging, he realized. But the blood seemed to have clotted. The bleeding in his mouth had stopped, too.

"Did you not notice the feeling has returned to your fingers?"

It was true. Hundreds of tiny needles were stabbing at his fingers and toes as numbed nerve endings returned to life. His vision was clearing. His breathing was less labored.

"Did you not feel your strength return as you approached the altar?" the *Episkop* asked. "How do you think you found the energy to win your battle?"

The blare of sirens announced the arrival of fire engines and paramedics, State Police, and emergency units from as far away as Scranton. The EMTs went to work on the injured parishioners. Two State Police officers came up to see if Rhostok was okay.

"I'm not sure," Rhostok said.

But when they tried to take him to an ambulance, he refused. "I've still got to arrest Vanya's murderer."

Eighty-Four

With fire companies responding from five different towns, the flames were quickly extinguished. Two representatives from the Environmental Protection Agency were on the scene, monitoring the methane emissions with special instruments. The injured parishioners were transported to area hospitals, which were operating under their Regional Disaster Plan. The paramedics wanted to take Nicole to the hospital, but she refused.

O'Malley soon appeared, picking his way through the wreckage until he reached what remained of the altar space. The *iconostasis* embers were still too hot for him to do anything more than stare at what remained of Vassily's corpse.

"None of this had to happen," O'Malley shook his head sadly. "All this destruction . . . this death . . . all because you were so damn stubborn, Rhostok."

He took over from the paramedic who was attending Rhostok's wound.

"I'm surprised you didn't bleed to death," he said. When Rhostok gave him a quizzical look, he quickly explained. "The bullet went through just above the clavicle. It missed an artery by less than an inch."

O'Malley examined the wound for what seemed an unusually long time.

"There's no bleeding now," he said, applying some antiseptic. "But you'll need to have it cleaned out and get a few stitches to close it. Minor stuff, compared with what the hospitals are going to be dealing with tonight."

Five parishioners had already been removed from the wreckage. A dozen more were being treated before being evacuated. Rhostok looked around for Nicole. He saw her hiding behind a column. She was watching O'Malley. The situation was still dangerous, Rhostok thought. Vassily might be dead, but his accomplice was still very much alive.

"The hospitals will be doing triage tonight," O'Malley said. "They'll be taking care of the serious cases first. A non-life-threatening wound like yours, you'll probably have to wait a few hours before they get around to you."

O'Malley rose, grunting as he pulled his metal-braced leg upright.

Behind him, Robyn was on her cell phone. From the unnatural sense of drama in her voice, Rhostok assumed she was phoning in an eyewitness account, probably getting her call patched through to a live on-air audio feed. Business as usual, he thought with a touch of bitterness.

For Rhostok, business as usual meant confronting Vassily's accomplice. He felt sure he knew who it was. Yet an arrest at this stage was impractical. He was dealing with someone so skilled in deception that he still couldn't connect his suspect to the murders of Vanya and Paul. In fact, he couldn't prove in court that Vanya and Paul had actually been murdered. Not unless he could find a way to get his suspect to confess. But how?

"Instead of wasting your time at the hospital, I could sew you up as good as new," O'Malley offered. "It's up to you, Rhostok. I can't do it here, with all the dust and dirt in the air. Too much possibility of infection. I could do it at your place, maybe take fifteen or twenty minutes, and then you're already home in your own bed, where you can get a good night's sleep. But like I say, it's up to you."

"Sounds good to me," Rhostok agreed. With his gun left behind at Fort Detrick, he felt defenseless here. At home, he had a shotgun to defend himself if the accomplice attacked. Before leaving, he looked around again for Nicole. She was no longer behind the column, but he knew she was watching and listening. He could only hope she wouldn't follow them.

Outside, O'Malley's car was hemmed in by two fire engines. He swore loudly before motioning Rhostok into the car. Rather than wait for the emergency vehicles to be moved, O'Malley drove his car up over the curb, skidded his tires on the grass, and wove his way impatiently around three ambulances before getting back onto the road.

"If you gave me that hand when you were supposed to, none of this would have happened," he lectured Rhostok as they drove. "Now, we've got all those people injured, a church is destroyed, and you're lucky to be alive."

"It must be my karma," Rhostok said.

"Your what?"

"My karma," Rhostok said. "My destiny. A doctor I met, a doctor from India, she said we're all controlled by our karma."

"You believe in that Indian mysticism stuff?" O'Malley asked.

"I'm beginning to believe a lot of things I didn't believe before."

Rhostok's house was less than five blocks away. If not for O'Malley's crippled leg, they could easily have walked there. Rhostok got out of the car first and watched O'Malley move the hand controls out of his way and extricate himself from the vehicle. The coroner used two hands to swing his stiff leg out and then lifted himself erect by holding onto the car door.

"Must be hard for you," Rhostok said.

"You get used to it."

"How old were you when the polio hit?"

"Why?"

"Just curious. It must have been one of the last cases in Lackawanna County. Didn't you get the vaccine?"

"It's none of your business," O'Malley said.

Rhostok opened the front door to allow the coroner to enter the house first.

"Christ, it's hot in here," O'Malley immediately complained. "You always keep the furnace on in the summertime?"

Rhostok smiled at the waves of heat that greeted him. At least he wouldn't be alone when he faced Vassily's accomplice.

"It must be a problem with the thermostat," he said. "I'll fix it." While he pretended to adjust the thermostat, he heard O'Malley close and lock the front door. "It doesn't seem to respond," Rhostok said. "Do you want me to open some windows?"

"That's okay. I won't be here long. Have a seat and let me take a look at that wound."

"How about here?" Rhostok asked, indicating a chair near the kitchen doorway. Out of sight down the hallway was the back door, which Rhostok assumed was unlocked. "Will this be okay? I'll move the light so you can see better."

O'Malley took off his jacket and opened up his tie. His face was already covered with sweat.

"Sorry about the heat," Rhostok said.

"Don't worry about it. Now let me see that wound again."

Dutifully, Rhostok opened his shirt. O'Malley removed the bandage and bent over to examine the wound more closely.

"How does it feel?" he asked.

"It aches a little. But I guess that's to be expected."

O'Malley placed his hand over Rhostok's shoulder. His thumb covered the entry wound. The rest of his fingers covering the larger exit wound.

"How about now?" O'Malley asked.

He gave the wounds a sudden, vicious squeeze.

Rhostok almost fainted from the pain. It shot through his left side, momentarily paralyzing his arm. His eyes filled with tears. His breath came in short gasps. His jaw began to ache. He stretched his head back in agony. Just when Rhostok felt he was going to lose consciousness, when the room seemed to be going dark, O'Malley released his grip. He seemed to know exactly when his victim had reached his limit.

"How did that feel?" O'Malley asked with a smile.

It took a moment before Rhostok had strength enough to respond.

"What do you want?"

"I think you know."

"The relic is gone. Burned. You saw what happened in the church."

O'Malley squeezed the wound again. Once more, the stunning pain shot through Rhostok's body, sending his body into a spasm. And once again, he released his grip just before Rhostok passed out.

"It can get worse," O'Malley said.

"Why are you doing this?" Rhostok gasped. "The Rasputin toxin burned with the relic."

Although O'Malley had released his grip, he kept his hand on Rhostok's shoulder, ready to squeeze again.

"You know about the toxin?" he asked.

"I'm not the only one."

"Who else knows?"

"Fort Detrick," Rhostok said.

"So that's where you disappeared to last night."

"It's all over. They know who you are."

"I think not. I think you're lying, Rhostok." He applied pressure to the wound again. "Are you lying to me?" This time, he didn't release his grip until he seemed satisfied with the answer.

"Now, before we proceed," O'Malley continued, "there are a few things I must know. For my own protection, of course. It's very important that I know who else might suspect me. You'll be honest with me, won't you?" He touched the bullet wound lightly, producing just enough pain to remind Rhostok of the consequences of lying. "Who else knows of my involvement?"

"That you were working with Vassily? I don't think anybody does. At least, they don't know your identity."

O'Malley pinched the bullet wounds. "Explain that."

"They think it's fairly obvious that a man like Vassily wouldn't be working alone."

"But he was," O'Malley insisted. "At least at first. I had nothing to do with those earlier murders."

"Maybe not with the out-of-state killings. Those were probably very simple for a man like him. It would be easy to strike up a conversation with an old veteran, get him talking about the old days. His Russian accent would help, because his targets were all from Russia. They'd invite him home, and that's where he'd strike." Rhostok had figured most of it out on the drive back from Fort Detrick. "But with Vanya, it was different. He was locked up in that mental ward. He was hard to get at."

"It was the name change that ruined everything," O'Malley said. "If Vanya had enlisted under his Russian name, Vassily would have found him a lot earlier, before the Alzheimer's wiped out that part of the old man's memory. Vassily said the name change cost him a year."

"And cost him the relic," Rhostok said. "The sad part of it is, Vanya probably would have surrendered the relic if he had remembered where it was. But the Alzheimer's was getting worse, so he faked his mental breakdown, knowing he'd be locked up behind bars in the high-security area of a state mental hospital. He thought he'd be safe there, and he was. Security was tight. There was no way Vassily could get to him, at least not without help. And that's when he called on you."

"I didn't want to get involved," O'Malley said. "Believe me, I had no idea he had already killed all those other old veterans. And I definitely didn't know he intended to kill Vanya."

"I'm sure you didn't. But you took him to the hospital. You go there all the time, whenever one of the inmates dies. You know all the staff and guards. It was easy to get Vassily inside, dressed as one of your morgue technicians. All you had to do was wait for one of the patients on the security floor to die. The rest was up to Vassily. But you're as guilty of Vanya's murder as Vassily was."

In fact, O'Malley's actions bothered Rhostok even more than those of the Russian assassin. Vassily was simply a throwback to the murderous old days in Russia, one of those *apparatchiks* who tortured and killed anyone declared an enemy of the state. It was easy to dismiss him as a product of the Communist regime. But O'Malley's crime was far more devious. He had lived among the people of Lackawanna County all these years, pretending to be Irish, joking and laughing and even getting elected to office. And now, after having won everybody's trust, he secretly brought an assassin into their midst, assisting him in his mission.

Trust no one. Expect betrayal.

"I assumed it must have been Vassily who broke Vanya's fingers trying to get him to talk," Rhostok said. "I thought you would have used sodium pentothal or some other drug. But now, I'm beginning to wonder even about that."

"Pentothal doesn't work on people with Alzheimer's," O'Malley said. "We were in Vanya's cell. He admitted he stole the relic. He said he wanted it buried with him to protect him in the afterlife. But he couldn't remember what he did with it. The guards would be coming back soon. I thought the pain might shock his memory. It didn't." He squeezed the bullet wound again, sending another jab of pain through Rhostok. "But pain works perfectly well on a healthy man like you," he said.

There was no point in trying to escape. O'Malley could paralyze him instantly with the pressure of a few fingers.

"Did they teach you that in Russia?" Rhostok asked.

"I'm Irish," O'Malley said.

"That's an old trick, hiding a Russian accent behind an Irish brogue. My grandfather warned me about people like you. You're one of the *shpala,* the sleepers. Beria sent over the first of your kind in the 1930s to spy on immigrants and wait for special assignments. After he died, the practice continued. You probably came over as a teenager during the Cold War, didn't you?"

"I'm Irish," O'Malley repeated. "Born in Boston."

"I think if I went to Boston, I'd find the real Thomas O'Malley died as an infant. You were given his identity, a Social Security number was issued in his name, and they sent you to the University of Scranton as an undergraduate."

"You're smarter than I thought," O'Malley said.

"Not smart enough. I fell for the polio story just like everybody else. All that heartwarming publicity about how you continued your studies from your sickbed. How they wheeled you onto the stage to accept your degree. How you went on to finish medical school on a full scholarship. It's a great story. It gets you the sympathy vote every time you run for office."

"The story is true. Every word of it. I'm damn proud of what I accomplished."

"Except you never should have contracted polio in the first place. Professor Altschiller always said the truth lies in the anomalies, the variations from the norm. Polio was wiped out a few years before you contracted it. Every child in America was vaccinated against it. And every grade school required proof of vaccination. If you went to grade school in America, you would have been immunized."

"Vaccinations don't always provide immunity," O'Malley said.

"But the Soviet Union was late with its immunization program. They sent you over here without a polio vaccination, didn't they? You must have felt betrayed when they abandoned you."

"I overcame my handicap," O'Malley insisted. "And I did it all on my own."

"They cut you loose is what you mean. All that training, the false identities—they figured it was all wasted when you became paralyzed."

"What makes you so sure I'm a Russian sleeper? Maybe I'm just someone with a false identity. That doesn't make me a foreign agent. People use false identities for a lot of reasons."

He was very good, Rhostok thought. Even now, even after admitting his role in Vanya's murder, the man was still unwilling to admit his past.

"Come off it already," Rhostok said. "If you really were Irish, if you were born in America, you'd be dead by now. You told me yourself that you were in the bank vault the morning after we found the hand. You told me you were there with someone from the health department to clean the vault. That was probably Vassily, wasn't it?"

When O'Malley didn't respond, he continued. "The residual toxin in the confined space of that vault would have killed anyone who didn't have natural immunity. You weren't immune to polio, but you were immune to the Rasputin toxin. That meant you had to have been born in Russia. And if you were born in Russia, then everything else made sense."

"You figured this out all by yourself? No one helped you?"

"It's a long drive from Fort Detrick," Rhostok said. "That gave me a lot of time to think."

"In that case, you know why I'm here."

"You didn't get enough spore samples from the vault. You came for the paper that was wrapped around the hand."

"Where is it?"

When Rhostok didn't answer, O'Malley sent another jolt of pain through his shoulder.

"I can keep this up all night," O'Malley said. "You won't die. Not right away. But you'll wish you did." He squeezed again and this time held his grip until Rhostok's face turned white.

"Where is the paper?"

"What good will it do you now?" Rhostok asked. "Vassily's dead, the relic's gone. You can tell the Russians Vassily screwed up and go back to your normal life."

"You don't realize how much those spores are worth to the Russians," O'Malley said. "With what they'll pay me, I can get the hell out of this valley, maybe move to the south of France, buy a villa, and live very nicely. No more worrying about your stupid elections. Now where is the wrapping paper?"

He squeezed again. O'Malley was so intent on getting the answer to his question that he didn't see the movement in the hallway behind him. Rhostok started speaking faster and louder to cover up the sound of the approaching footsteps.

"You were the perfect partner for Vassily," he said. "After helping kill

Vanya, you announced that he committed suicide. And everybody believed you, because you're the coroner."

"And when I tell them you died from that gunshot wound, they'll believe me again."

"You covered up the toxin deaths by saying they were all from natural causes," Rhostok continued. "But your worst crime was killing Paul Danilovitch."

As Rhostok expected, the mention of the dead man's name caused the figure in the hallway to stop.

"I didn't kill Paul."

"He inherited everything his father owned," Rhostok said. "Without knowing it, he became the new owner of the Rasputin relic. That made him Vassily's new target."

"Vassily didn't kill him, either."

"Not right away," Rhostok said. "The two of you were smarter than that. Besides, Paul didn't know anything about the relic. But he was a lonely man, and Vassily was running that escort service. One of you came up with the idea to arrange a marriage, so that when you got rid of Paul, his wife would inherit everything. That way, you could take your time looking for the relic."

"I didn't kill Paul. He died in bed with his wife."

"But you came up with the idea of the potassium pills."

The figure in the hallway remained out of O'Malley's sight, listening.

"I did the guy a favor," O'Malley finally admitted. "Vassily's original plan was to arrange an accident. At least with the potassium pills, the guy died in bed with a woman. His last moments were pure pleasure."

All that time he was talking, O'Malley didn't have any idea someone other than Rhostok was listening.

"It was the perfect way to kill a healthy man," Rhostok said. "Overstimulate his heart with a medication that the body normally produces. You explained it all to me, but at the time I didn't realize you were the one who supplied the pills."

"Vassily gave them to him in Las Vegas after the wedding," O'Malley said. "He told Paul the pills would prevent Alzheimer's. He told him to take two a day. From what was left in the bottle when I found it that night, I think the jerk doubled the dose." He laughed at the memory. "Talk about stupid."

"Did you hear all that?" Rhostok asked the visitor in the hallway.

Her face was covered with a ghostly coating of plaster dust. Her white gown was torn on one side. Her hair was a mess. She looked like a creature who had emerged from the grave. Her right hand was hidden behind her back.

O'Malley turned, and it was a moment before he recognized her. Then he shouted, "What the hell do you want?"

She took a step towards him.

"This doesn't involve you," O'Malley said.

"Yes, it does," Nicole said.

"If this is about the way your husband died, all I did was supply the pills."

"I heard."

Slowly, her hand came out from behind her back. In it was the wrought-iron bar Vassily had used in the struggle at the church.

"Stupid bitch," O'Malley muttered. He was a foot taller than her and over fifty pounds heavier. Even with the slender iron bar, Nicole would probably be no match for him.

"Not as stupid as you think," she said. "I saw you from the rectory window before the service, when you were getting out of your car."

O'Malley kept his right hand on Rhostok's wound, turning slightly on his leg brace to face Nicole. He lifted his left arm to defend himself. He was strong enough to absorb any blow, grab the iron bar, and turn it back on her.

"Vassily was with you," she said. "That's when I knew you must have been working with him. That's why I followed you here."

Nicole came forward slowly. She raised the iron bar above her head. As she telegraphed her move, O'Malley raised his left arm higher. His other hand squeezed Rhostok's wound. Nicole kept her eyes on O'Malley's. She started to swing the iron bar forward. The weight seemed too heavy for her to handle. For a moment, as the iron bar wavered in the air and seemed ready to fall of its own weight, Nicole looked terribly vulnerable. The bigger, heavier man smiled and moved to disarm her.

But projecting an appearance of vulnerability was a skill that Nicole had apparently perfected during years of dealing with men who enjoyed the illusion of control. It worked well enough for O'Malley to take her threat less seriously. He reached out too casually, Rhostok could see. And in an instant, the facade of feminine vulnerability disappeared from Nicole's face. Moving with the speed of a woman accustomed to dealing with abusive men, she tightened her grip on the bar, reached out with her left arm to block O'Malley's hand, and swung the bar down low. Unexpectedly low. The downward swing gave her extra leverage. The bar picked up momentum until it crashed against the exposed side of O'Malley's good leg. It struck on the side of his kneecap, the force of it caving the knee inward. The leg seemed at first to bend with the blow. Then it snapped at the knee. Her follow-through sent the good leg crashing against the metal brace.

O'Malley screamed and let go of Rhostok's shoulder. The policeman quickly spun out of the way. The coroner reached wildly for something, anything, to hold onto. He swayed back and forth on the metal brace. He tried reaching for the table. The tablecloth came off in his hands. With his good leg useless, O'Malley tottered on his brace before falling, like some diseased tree crashing to the forest floor.

As he lay there whimpering and clutching his shattered knee, Nicole quickly checked his pockets for any weapons. There were none.

Rhostok struggled to his feet, tried to stand, grew dizzy, and fell back on the chair.

"I think we need an ambulance," he said.

"Let him suffer," Nicole said. "I was always ashamed of what men did to me, but what he did, arranging for my husband to die in my arms, was unspeakable."

"That wasn't my idea," O'Malley moaned. "I only supplied the potassium pills. It was Vassily who gave them to Paul. It was Vassily who wanted him to die in bed, not me."

"No!" she screamed. "You were Vassily's partner in all this. I heard you confess!"

She slammed the iron bar against his shoulder.

"And you were his whore!" O'Malley shouted. In spite of his pain, he couldn't resist lashing back at her. "That's all you were to him, just another whore."

She raised the iron bar to strike him again.

"You made me kill my husband. Now I'll kill you, too."

"Stop!" Rhostok shouted. "In God's name, stop!" He grabbed her wrist before she could strike O'Malley again. "You weren't responsible for Paul's death. But this is murder."

He pulled her wrist down. She dropped the iron bar. Her anger spent, she leaned back against him. This time, unlike that evening on her front porch, he wrapped his arms around her and held on tight. It was a strange creature who nestled in his arms, he thought. Instead of facial powder, her face was caked with plaster dust. Instead of perfume, she exuded an odor of anointing oil and naphtha soap. Her hair was decorated with fragments of wood and flakes of masonry. Yet she had never looked more beautiful to him than she did at that moment, and he was determined this time never to let her go.

But at the sound of footsteps in the hallway, she spun out of his arms, grabbed the iron bar, and prepared once again to defend him.

Eighty-Five

Standing in the doorway, wearing a heavy tweed jacket over a woolen sweater, and with a scarf offering further protection to his throat, was Hamilton Winfield. Nicole quickly stepped between the visitor and Rhostok, waving the heavy iron bar as if ready to strike again.

The old man raised his open hand.

"Tell her I'm a friend," he said.

Nicole glanced back at Rhostok for confirmation.

"If you were a friend, you wouldn't have let me go through all that pain," Rhostok said.

"I wanted to hear his story," Winfield said. "You did an excellent job drawing him out."

"You were after the same thing he was," Rhostok said. "You want the wrapper, too. What were you going to do, shoot him when he found it?"

"If necessary, yes. I would have gladly shot him. Although I'm not sure that what the young lady did to him wasn't the greater punishment. He'll probably never walk again."

"What are you doing here?"

"Securing the house. You don't think I'd actually attempt to handle the wrapper myself."

Nicole, confused by the conversation, lowered the iron bar.

"So what happens now?" Rhostok asked.

"Nothing much. There'll be representatives of five government agencies here tomorrow.

"An FBI/CIA team will take O'Malley here into custody and debrief him. They'll probably cut some kind of deal in exchange for his cooperation. But whatever deal they cut, he'll spend the rest of his life in a wheelchair."

Nicole retreated to Rhostok's side. She kept the iron bar at the ready, still not completely trusting this strange man who wore winter clothing in the middle of summer.

"Pathologists from the Defense Research Institute will show up," Winfield continued. "They'll perform autopsies on Franklin, Zeeman, Bruckner,

Altschiller, and a young associate of Altschiller's, one Michael Chao, who helped in the analysis of the relic. Scientists from the Biological Defense Institute will conduct sweeps of your house, the police station, Robyn Cronin's apartment, and the debris of the church. They'll be looking for any traces of the toxin. From what we've seen so far, however, the spores are probably too large for any but the most limited airborne distribution."

"People are going to panic when they find out about the toxin," Rhostok said. "It'll be worse than the anthrax scare."

"We'll find a way to keep a lid on it. O'Malley will be shipped off to a safe house in Maryland. The autopsies will be done out of state. And we'll come up with some sort of cover story for the teams doing the toxin sweeps." He stopped to suck on his pipe. "Maybe we could say they were looking for evidence to support the claim that Rasputin was a saint."

"You'd need the *Episkop*'s cooperation," Rhostok said. "And he's not easily fooled."

"He's a priest without a church. He might go along with us, if we finance the construction of a new church for him."

"You'd actually do that?" Rhostok was dumbfounded. "Do you realize what that would cost?"

"Five, ten million dollars?" Winfield waved his pipe in the air. "That's small change in the Homeland Security budget. It's not much more than the cost of a few airport bomb-detecting machines. That kind of money would be easy to hide."

"What about the press? You've got a reporter who's already calling in the story."

"You mean Robyn? She doesn't know anything about the toxin. As far as she's concerned, the big news is the discovery of the Rasputin relic. I listened to her calling in the story. She thinks the relic cured her mother's cancer. By tomorrow, you'll have hundreds of pilgrims flooding into town looking for miracle cures. A month from now, if anybody starts talking about the toxin, those pilgrims will want samples of it to take home to cure their arthritis."

That was probably true, Rhostok thought. Winfield seemed to have figured everything out. No wonder they had brought him out of retirement. He had everything under control. Except for one thing.

"What about me?" Rhostok asked. "I know all about the toxin, and O'Malley, and Vassily."

"Ah, yes. You *are* a problem. We can't have you running around on the loose, not with all you know about the Rasputin toxin." Winfield's eyes hardened. "I could kill you. Right here and now."

"You'd have to kill me, too," Nicole said, speaking up for the first time.

"Easily arranged," Winfield said. He took a second pipe from his pocket, pointed the stem at a photograph on the wall, and squeezed his fingers around the bowl. A small flame burst from the end of the stem with loud report. The photograph shattered.

"I could kill you both and blame it on O'Malley. Then he wouldn't get off as easily." Winfield pointed the stem of the pipe at Rhostok.

"You'd really do that?" Rhostok asked.

"I'm afraid I'll have to," Winfield said. He moved the pipe to point directly at Rhostok's heart. "It's a national security issue. As far as I can see, there's only one other alternative."

"What's that?"

"You could come work for me."

"Do I have a choice?"

"I'm afraid not."

Epilogue

Rhostok knelt before the magnificent reliquary containing the remains of the Rasputin relic.

The bones, bleached and purified by the fire, had been lovingly collected from the ashes by *Episkop* Sergius. They were displayed in a gold and silver reliquary commissioned by an exiled Russian oligarch and constructed to Sergius's specifications under the supervision of an eighty-year-old Viennese artisan, whose father had been commissioned by the Empress Alexandra in 1917 to design the original version. A golden door covered the front of the reliquary. The gleaming bas-relief on the door portrayed Grigorii Rasputin, his left hand over his heart, his right hand raised in blessing. When the door was opened, it revealed a crystal window. Behind the window were the bones of the mystic's hand, arranged in the position of the Old Ritual form of blessing: the bones of two fingers upraised, and the thumb bone folded across the others.

On a stand beside the altar, the brown wrapping paper, purged of its spores but with Rasputin's name still visible, was pressed behind glass and treated as a secondary relic.

A new *iconostasis,* grander and more glorious than the original, filled the nave of the newly constructed church. A portrait of Rasputin, golden halo around his head, had been added to those of the other saints. The new church, a grand structure of gray sandstone, was built with a donation of fourteen million dollars, delivered by one Hamilton Winfield on behalf of "an anonymous admirer of Rasputin." Sergius had chosen to name his new house of worship the Cathedral of Our Lady of Kazan, in honor of Rasputin's protectress. It was topped with not one, but three golden domes, representing the three members of the Holy Trinity, and from its hillside position was visible throughout the Lackawanna River Valley.

Rhostok waited alone at the altar, as he had been instructed to do.

He watched an acolyte come out to light the hundred candles. It was an act that would have been impossible if Winfield's "anonymous donation" had not included enough funds to provide a special concrete foundation with a flexible plastic barrier to guard against any future infiltration of explosive methane gases.

Rhostok was surprised at how calm he felt. He had been warned by some that he was making a mistake, that it wouldn't work, that he should wait until he was absolutely sure. Others had cautioned him of the doubts that would attack him at the last moment. Certainly the crowds that came here to witness what he was about to do were enough to make any man nervous. In spite of it all, in spite of the fact that what was about to take place would change his life forever, Rhostok felt a sense of calm, an inner peace that he had once thought he would never achieve.

From high in the back of the church rose the powerful voices of the newly assembled Russian choir, singing without musical accompaniment as their ancestors had done before them. The singers were volunteers, drawn from the choirs of local churches. Some of them were here in defiance of their own priests, who still resisted the idea that a man they considered a debaucher should be proclaimed a saint.

The hierarchy of the Russian Orthodox Church, the same men who celebrated the sainthood of Nikolas and Alexandra and all their children, warned their followers against what they called "false prophets." As the head of an autocephalic church, however, the *Episkop* was not governed by their edicts. Despite the opposition of their superiors, a number of Orthodox priests, some bearded like Sergius, and others clean-shaven, came to the cathedral. Whether drawn by the power of faith or simply a desire to see for themselves what had become a major pilgrimage site in northeastern Pennsylvania, they were here, their black miters serving as markers of their special status.

It was not much different from the situation in the Russian Church almost a century before, Rhostok thought. The conflict then, according to his grandfather, had been between those who were offended by Rasputin's rough peasant ways and those who were amazed by the religious fervor he inspired.

The fervor was still evident today. Although the new cathedral was twice as large as the church that had formerly stood on the site, it still wasn't large enough to contain the crowd attracted by today's ceremony. Rhostok recognized many of those present as local citizens, either members of the rejuvenated parish or those who normally attended nearby churches and were considering switching their allegiances. Others were day-tripping tourists or curiosity-seekers. Most of those present, however, appeared to be the sick and the sorrowful, their anguished faces suggesting they were here seeking miracles for themselves or their loved ones.

As Winfield had predicted, the first of these pilgrims showed up the morning after Robyn Cronin's live report from the ashes of the church. They were locals, drawn to the site by her breathless account of the discovery of the Rasputin relic and the miracle cures attributed to it. Their numbers grew larger as Robyn and the Channel One marketing staff capitalized on the story. Publicity photographs showed her in a torn and dirty dress, hair askew, delivering her first live report from the burning wreckage. That report won her a promotion to co-anchor of Action News at Ten and local press recognition as a "hot new media personality."

Two weeks later, she did a report on the relic, tracing its journey from Rasputin's autopsy to Starokonstantinov Monastery to Unterberg, Austria, and finally to its eventual destruction in the fire at Saint Sofia Church. She followed that report a week later with another on Rasputin, detailing the many miracles and prophecies that had made him a saint to the *muzhiks*. Neither report mentioned anything about how she drugged Rhostok and stole the relic for her own purposes.

Now Rhostok watched her as she moved with her cameraman to the front of the church, self-importantly pushing her way through the crowd. As usual, she was immaculately groomed, blonde hair teased to make her appear taller, wearing one of her bright-red power suits.

Her reporting on the relic had gained national attention because of the recent flurry of interest in recovered Nazi loot. Tom Brokaw gave the story fifteen seconds on *NBC Nightly News*, dwelling on a brooding photograph of Rasputin while reporting that a specialist in religious art from Christie's auction house estimated the relic would have been worth ten million dollars to a private buyer. The *New York Times*, which originally broke the story of the similar theft of the Quedlenberg treasure by an American soldier, wrapped the Rasputin relic into a major feature on the continuing efforts to recover Nazi loot from museums and private collections. It mentioned the miraculous healings only in passing.

Rhostok smiled when he saw an obviously irritated usher insisting that Robyn wasn't permitted behind the iconostasis.

What Robyn still didn't know, what Tom Brokaw didn't report, what the *New York Times* article didn't describe, was the real story of the Rasputin relic and the deadly toxin it carried. Robyn didn't even know how close she herself had come to dying from it.

Even if the facts did somehow leak out, Rhostok knew it would make little difference to the crowds who came to Middle Valley every day, drawn by the hope of miracle cures. They came by car, by chartered bus, and lately even by air, making complicated flight connections to the small airport at nearby Avoca. It seemed not to matter whether they were Orthodox, Catholic, or even Christian at all. Like the Muslims who bring their palsied children to Lourdes, the Jews who bow their heads in prayer at Fatima, the Japanese Buddhists traveling to Padua to see Christ's lique-fied blood, they came here because of their belief in miracles, a belief rein-forced by the presence of so many others who shared the same faith in the supernatural.

So many visitors came while the cathedral was under construction that *Episkop* Sergius conducted special Sunday morning "healing masses" in a tent behind the rectory. Those most seriously ill were permitted to kiss one of the Rasputin bone fragments. Channel One, whose news programming was now the highest-rated in northeastern Pennsylvania, televised these services. The program was also syndicated to a growing list of cable and commercial TV stations. A highlight of each program was the testimony of individuals who claimed to have been miraculously cured at these services.

The medical community ridiculed the idea that serious illnesses could be cured by praying to the bones of a man the history books dismissed as a charlatan. Oncologists claimed the recovery of cancer patients, including Robyn Cronin's mother, were merely cases of temporary remission, not uncommon even in terminal cases. Fertility doctors claimed the seven sup-posedly barren women who became pregnant had never been truly sterile. The blind woman whose sight was restored must have been suffering from a psychological rather than a physical disorder, according to her ophthal-mologist. The story of the man restored to life after Sergius visited his hos-pital bed was dismissed because no death certificate had yet been signed. For every cure there was an explanation. And following every explanation, there were reports of still more cures. Which drew more visitors.

As he glanced up at the magnificent frescos on the high ceiling, Rhostok remembered what Professor Altschiller said about the mystical power that religious relics exert over the faithful. Wars had been fought, kingdoms destroyed, and cities made famous because of the presence of these reputedly divine artifacts. That was certainly what was happening to this small town in the middle of the Lackawanna Valley, he thought.

As the faithful poured in, old houses were converted into bed-and-breakfasts, restaurants opened, and souvenir and gift shops appeared. Soon a visitor could find lodging for the night in a Russian home, eat in a restaurant that served Rasputin's favorite sweets, drink in a bar that served the Madeira wine he preferred, buy a record of the Gypsy music he loved, pick up a set of nesting *matryoshka* dolls painted with the likenesses of Rasputin and the entire Imperial Family, stock up on Rasputin bookmarks and key chains, and even buy plastic Rasputin beards for the children. Old people who once were sensitive about their immigrant status now flaunted their Russianness.

Even those skeptics who rejected the deification of the mystic, who didn't believe in the miracle cures, couldn't deny the wonderful alchemy the relic was working on Middle Valley. The *Scranton Times* called it "an economic miracle," the transformation of a depressed mining town into a prosperous religious tourism site. A town that once barely subsisted on Social Security and welfare checks now thrived on tourist dollars. There was talk of a Days Inn opening up, and perhaps even the long-rumored reopening of passenger service on the old Delaware and Hudson railroad tracks. Caught up in the fervor, the Middle Valley Board of Trustees defied the ACLU's threat of a church-state lawsuit by officially proclaiming Grigorii Rasputin the patron saint of Middle Valley.

Winfield was right, Rhostok thought. If anyone ever found out about the toxin, the visitors would want it bottled to take home as a talisman. They were already giving ten-dollar donations for tiny vials of ash from the church fire, treasuring them in the belief that, mixed in with the ashes of the *iconostasis,* and perhaps even those of Vassily, were a few treasured grains of Rasputin's incinerated flesh. They were no different from the *Rasputniki* of Imperial Russia, who collected the mystic's fingernails and beard trimmings.

And how different from any of this was he himself, Rhostok wondered.

Here he was, kneeling in homage before the bones of a man who died almost a century ago, giving thanks for what was about to take place.

It was the most glorious moment of Rhostok's life. A moment that would never have happened if Rasputin's incorruptible hand had not almost miraculously made its way from an autopsy table in Moscow to a safe-deposit box in Middle Valley.

The choir started up again, the male voices dominating, powerful and resonant, and then withdrawing to allow the female voices to soar above them, announcing the beginning of the ceremony.

The *Episkop* Sergius appeared in the opening of the *iconostasis*. He was flanked by two acolytes releasing clouds of pungent incense from golden censors. His robe was woven of gold and silver thread. Atop his head was the golden crown announcing his ecclesiastical authority. He motioned for Rhostok to rise.

A single soprano voice soared through the air, clear and pure and silvery. The church bells joined in, all four of different sizes ringing in joyous unison. Outside the church, a cheer went up. Those gathered inside rose to their feet and jostled each other for a better view of what was happening in the back of the church.

The morning sunlight silhouetted the woman who stood in the open doorway. The accident of lighting, if that's what it was, seemed to produce an unearthly glow around her. She stood motionless for a moment, surveying the crowded church. Those attending would later say it was a mystical moment in which time seemed suspended, in which their own thoughts were subsumed by the beauty of the creature who stood before them. If this was a Marian apparition, it could not have produced a more powerful response.

Knowing she had arrived, Rhostok turned slowly. He was almost afraid to look for fear that she might disappear and be lost to him forever. She wore a long white gown embellished with lace that had been lovingly hand-embroidered in traditional Russian design by the women of the Sodality of Our Lady of Kazan. The veil that shielded her face was of so delicate a nature that it appeared almost completely transparent.

When her eyes finally settled on Viktor Rhostok, she smiled. It was unbelievable, absolutely unbelievable that a creature of such ethereal loveliness was smiling at him.

This was the moment everyone had warned him about.

When even the strongest of men have self-doubt. When his knees were supposed to weaken and his hands begin to tremble and he was supposed to look anxiously for a way out.

But Viktor Rhostok felt none of that.

He was transfixed.

Her beauty, as it had from the first moment he saw her, took his breath away. And when she began to move towards him, the cathedral seemed to grow still. The voices of the choir grew distant and disappeared. The ringing of the bells faded. He wasn't sure if she was walking towards him or floating, wasn't sure if this was a dream or some strange waking fantasy.

Cameras flashed throughout the cathedral, snapping him back to awareness. He again heard the bells ringing, the choir singing, the audience murmuring approval. The center aisle, where the woman walked, was covered with pink and white rose petals. She moved with the grace and poise of someone supremely confident in what she was doing. She kept her eyes fixed on Rhostok.

Resplendent in her white gown, she looked purer than any virgin, more angelic than the heavenly creatures whose images adorned the cathedral ceiling.

When at last she stopped, her veil was lifted by Hamilton Winfield. She handed her bouquet to Dr. Veda Chandhuri. Rhostok took her hand, and together they turned to *Episkop* Sergius, who began the wedding ceremony by welcoming them both back into the embrace of the Orthodox Church. The ceremony followed the old tradition, starting with the blessing and exchange of rings. In a break with tradition, Nicole and Rhostok had written part of their wedding vows themselves.

She, who told him she once thought of her beauty as a curse, said she saw it now as a treasured gift from God, to bestow upon the man she loved.

And he, who said he had been taught from childhood to trust no one, told her he gladly placed his future in her hands.

To seal their wedding vows, the *Episkop* placed the traditional silver crowns on their heads. Then he stepped aside and allowed both of them to enter the Royal Gate and kiss the reliquary containing the bones of Rasputin's right hand.

For if not for the contents of the reliquary, they would never have found each other.

And that, they both believed, was the true miracle of the Rasputin relic.

Author's Note

Although a work of fiction, this book is based on facts uncovered by the author during years of extensive research into the life of Rasputin, Russian religions and mysticism, the Imperial Family, the history of bleeding diseases in Russia, the Soviet military's use of agricultural molds to create deadly T2 toxin weapons for biological warfare, the history of the 101st Airborne in World War II, the records of Nazi looting of occupied countries, the postwar disposition of those looted treasures, the Russian immigrant communities in the Lackawanna River Valley, and the lingering environmental impact of the coal mining industry that employed those immigrants.

The legendary Rasputin relic has not yet been found.

Bone fragments of the Imperial Family have been recovered from the shaft where their bodies were thrown after the slaughter at Ekaterinberg, however. Some of those relics can be seen at Saint John the Baptist Russian Orthodox Cathedral in Mayfield, Pennsylvania, in the Lackawanna River Valley. The golden domes of dozens of Orthodox churches that can be seen in the small towns of the valley are a testament to the faith of the Russian immigrants and their descendants who live there. Middle Valley is intended as a fictional composite of those towns. The coal mines in which these Russians worked along with the Polish, Irish, and other immigrant groups have long been abandoned. Many are filled with methane gas and represent a continuing threat of cave-ins, surface subsidence, and pollution of local streams.

The particular fusarium to which the Russian people became immune remains to be rediscovered.

The more commonly known strains of the wheat fusarium have produced vast quantities of deadly T2 toxins which were weaponized, used against civilians in Laos, Afghanistan, and Yemen, and are still stored in certain of the world's biological warfare arsenals. The hemorrhagic effects of these toxins, including the various natural outbreaks of the resulting "bleeding disease" in Russia, are a matter of record.

As for Rasputin himself, a reevaluation of his spiritual legacy appears to be under way in Russia today. A growing number of religious and secular leaders are challenging the truth of the more notorious portrayals of the Siberian mystic.

Despite initial controversy, a movement for the canonization of Rasputin has been gaining strength. Among the most outspoken proponents of sainthood are Orthodox officials in Vladivostok, Verkhoturye, and regions of Siberia where Rasputin's memory is still revered.

The most likely possible date for canonization centers on December 16, 2016, the hundredth anniversary of Rasputin's assassination.

About the Author

William M. Valtos has been writing since childhood, when his plays were performed by fellow students in grade school. As an advertising executive, Valtos won the coveted *Clio* award. His novel *Resurrection* was the subject of the HBO film *Almost Dead*.

HAMPTON ROADS PUBLISHING COMPANY

. . . for the evolving human spirit

Hampton Roads Publishing Company
publishes books on a variety of subjects including
metaphysics, health, visionary fiction,
and other related topics.

For a copy of our latest catalog,
call toll-free, 800-766-8009,
or send your name and address to:

Hampton Roads Publishing Company, Inc.
1125 Stoney Ridge Road
Charlottesville, VA 22902
e-mail: hrpc@hrpub.com
www.hrpub.com